RIPPLES

SPIRITS OF THE BELLEVIEW BILTMORE

RIPPLES

SPIRITS OF THE BELLEVIEW BILTMORE

BONSUE BRANDVIK

Published by: BonSue Brandvik

Cover Design by: Cathy Casteleiro
Interior Layout by: Maureen Cutajar
Internal map of hotel, courtesy of Richard Heisenbottle

First edition: November, 2015

Library of Congress Control Number: TXu1-907-071

ISBN-13: 978-0-9896462-1-5 (print)
ISBN-13: 978-0-9896462-3-9 (e-book)

Belleview Biltmore Hotel

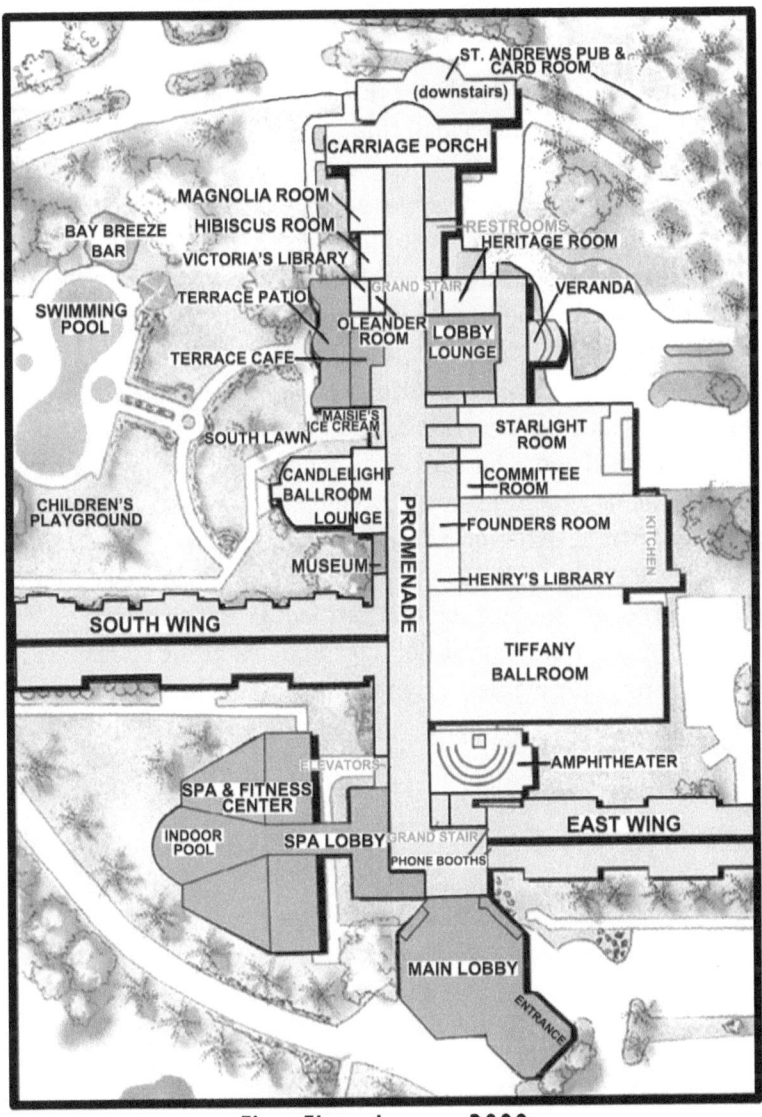

First Floor Layout, 2009

DEDICATION: To my husband, John Brandvik, whose love and unwavering support makes all things possible. I love you with all my heart.

And to my grandmother, Bertha Agnes Marie Johnson Ellis – an auburn-haired spitfire, who loved fishing, Southern Comfort, Camel cigarettes, and bright red fingernail polish, and who was the inspiration for the 'Bobbi' character in this book. She wasn't married to a bootlegger, but many incidents in this story are based in fact. She risked beatings from her zealous tyrannical father to go dancing. A horrific car accident destroyed her beautiful face and crushed one of her legs, but not her spirit. She spent a year in the hospital, separated from her young children, and later worked with a blacksmith, to design a brace that would allow her to strengthen her leg and eventually, do the impossible...walk again. During the Great Depression, she worked in a garment factory, learning to "sew almost anything from almost nothing." She taught me to respect my elders and fight for women's rights. She lived an amazing life, with few regrets. She was my idol.

THANKS TO: Thanks to the Clearwater Writer's Meet-up for their support, encouragement and valuable critiques throughout this process. I'm a better writer because of you. Thanks also to my editor, Cara Lockwood (www.EditMyNovel.com), my key Beta readers, Mary Buehrig and Christine James, and to Cathy Casteleiro, the genius graphic artist responsible for the beautiful cover design.

Additional thanks to Dan Shires and others at Life Link, Tampa Bay, for their everyday heroism and for agreeing to answer my endless questions about the organ/tissue donation process... and for understanding this is a work of fiction, and therefore, is not intended to depict reality. I do hope my readers will consider signing up to be an organ donor. Learn more at www.LifeLinkFoundation.org.

Thanks to the staff of Hubble Funeral Home, for giving me a tour of their facility and walking me through the process of cremation and ash scattering ceremonies. You were most kind and helpful.

Finally, thank you to everyone who fought so hard to save the historic Belleview Biltmore Hotel, and especially to Doris Hanson, for helping document the hotel in photographs. I'm heartbroken about the loss of this grand hotel, but happy that at least a small portion of the "White Queen of the Gulf" will survive, largely because of your efforts.

RIPPLES

SPIRITS OF THE BELLEVIEW BILTMORE

Chapter One

"Is she dying?" Lilyanna Thorne asked, a sense of dread tightening around her heart. "Can you at least tell me that much?"

"I'm sorry," the woman caller replied, "but I'm not a doctor, so I can't provide that kind of information. All I can tell you is that Lois Bloom was admitted to the Neuro ICU earlier today and her condition is listed as critical."

It was odd to hear *Grams* called by her real name. "Wait a minute," Lily said. "Neuro – that means she had a stroke, right?"

"Possibly," the hospital administrator hedged. "She's under Dr. Weston's care. He or someone on his staff should be available in the morning to answer your questions. You're listed as Mrs. Bloom's primary emergency contact, but if there's someone else you would rather I call..."

Lily sucked in a breath. Her mother, Veronica Bloom, had been Grams' and Gramps' only child, and she had died in New York – shortly after ditching Lily in Florida just before her fifth birthday. Growing up, Lily had often been told she was the "spitting image" of her tall, auburn-haired mother – beautiful, with blue eyes, light skin, and a brilliant smile. But that's where their similarities ended. Lily always suspected she inherited her father's disposition – whoever he was. Her mother had dreamed of Broadway fame, but Lily preferred a quiet life, and since her car accident three years ago, she had become almost reclusive.

"Ms. Thorne?" The woman cleared her throat.

"There's only Grams and me," Lily mumbled, pulling herself together. She snatched up a pen and notepad. "I'll catch the next flight down from St. Louis. What's the address of Morton Plant Hospital? "

After hanging up, Lily closed the blog post she had been composing, *"The Netherlands – a Good Place to Die."* After finalizing her travel arrangements, she struggled to her feet. "Damn leg," she muttered under her breath. The ache in her injured leg increased with each drop in barometric pressure, and the rainy spring season was just getting underway. She dragged two suitcases from underneath her bed, the thick layer of dust on them reminding her how much she hated to travel.

She knew she should call Scott, but hesitated. Her estranged husband would want to accompany her to Florida and being with him in a hospital would dredge up bad memories. Nevertheless, she steeled herself and placed the call.

"It's Grams," she began. She recounted the earlier phone call, which didn't take long.

"Poor Grams. I know she can't live forever, but this sucks," Scott said. "I'll arrange to take time off work."

"No!" she barked. "I mean, let me fly down and assess the situation first. I might need to be there for a few weeks. Maybe longer."

He reluctantly agreed. "How are you going to manage your blog without a laptop?"

Lily sighed. "I'll just post a notice that I'm away and let the site go dark until I return."

"Ironic," Scott said.

Lily ignored the sarcasm. Her blog, *Way to Go*, provided useful information to people with terminal illnesses, to help them prepare to meet the end on their own terms.

"I have to pack."

"Okay. What time is your flight?" Scott asked. "I'll drive you to the airport."

"I can call a cab," she protested.

"Knock it off, Lilyanna. You're going to need help with your suitcases."

He was right. Pulling luggage while sporting a leg brace and leaning on a crutch was nearly impossible, Lily conceded.

"See you soon," he said. "I love you."

"Love you, too," she replied out of habit.

The nonstop flight to Tampa was uneventful, and with help of airport personnel, she and her luggage were soon loaded into the Belleview Biltmore Resort's shuttle van.

The driver reminded her of Andy Griffith. "So what brings you to Florida?" he asked.

"My grandmother's in the hospital."

"Nothing too serious, I hope," he said.

"Very serious," Lily replied. "She's in the ICU at Morton Plant." Her curt tone implied she didn't feel like chatting.

"Sorry to hear that," he mumbled. He returned his focus to the road and merged onto the ten-mile causeway, separating Tampa from Clearwater.

Lily stared out the window at the shimmering royal-blue waters of Tampa Bay. Suddenly, the shiny gray dorsal fin and broad back of a large dolphin broke the surface of the glassy water, triggering a memory. How thrilled Dylan had been when he learned they had arranged for him to swim with dolphins at Seaworld during their Florida vacation. She tried to hold onto the image of his joyful expression, but the painful knowledge that the adventure never happened – and could never happen – crushed the memory like a bug on a windshield. Lily sighed and rode the rest of the way to the hotel lamenting about what might have been.

A few blocks from the Belleview Biltmore, the driver pointed out the massive Morton Plant complex. "As soon as you get checked in, I can run you back to the hospital," he said.

"Thanks." Lily gazed at the hospital over her shoulder, unable to picture feisty, kindhearted Grams languishing in one of its rooms.

They slowed as the shuttle crossed the bridge to the resort's entrance. The security guard recognized the driver and waved as he raised the traffic arm.

Lily stared ahead at the sprawling white building, rising five stories in front of them. Despite her melancholy, the beauty of the Belleview Biltmore took her breath. She hadn't been here since she was a teenager, but the passing years had done little to make the building appear any less majestic. She still couldn't see the entire hotel without turning her head, first in one direction and then the other. Atop the bright green-shingled roof were dozens and dozens of peaked gables, vividly framed against a bright blue, cloudless sky. The grounds surrounding the enormous Victorian structure were dotted with towering oaks, dripping with Spanish moss; each tree encircled with a bed of red, orange, purple, and white impatiens.

The driver coasted to a precision stop, directly in front of the double-door entrance. He walked around to her side of the van, opened the side door, and extended his hand to help her out.

"You go on inside. I'll arrange for the bellman to bring your luggage in for you," he said.

Lily started to fumble in her purse for a tip, but the driver gave her a broad Andy Griffith smile and waived a dismissive hand. "I hope your grandmother gets better," he said as he turned away.

Lily felt guilty for having been rude to him. She turned and limped up the wide entryway, bordered on both sides with ornate concrete planters overflowing with colorful flowers. On either side of the huge glass doors, larger planters featured trellises of climbing bougainvillea, dripping with hot pink blossoms.

A doorman pulled the glass door open for her, and she shuffled inside. As she approached the long, mahogany registration desk, Lily's crutch made distinctive clicking sounds with every step in the otherwise silent lobby. She felt someone watching her – the cripple. She cast a contemptuous glare around the vast, domed entrance. There were several seating areas, each furnished with Victorian Era replicas, but the lobby was empty.

She tried to shake off the uneasy feeling and addressed the desk clerk. "I'm Lilyanna Thorne," she said. "I asked for a room near the entrance, but it was a last minute reservation, so they couldn't guarantee availability."

The peppy brunette's smile faltered as she scanned the map of vacant rooms on her computer screen. She bit her lower lip and narrowed her brown, almond-shaped eyes. "Well, one suite is available just inside the East Wing, if you could manage four steps."

"I can, as long as there's a railing." Lily replied.

The girl's smile returned. "All righty then," she chirped. She keyed in Lily's information, swiped her credit card and then opened a colorful, tri-fold map of the hotel on the counter. She circled Lily's room number and launched into a well-rehearsed spiel, pointing out the hotel's various amenities.

Lily raised her open palm. "Don't bother – I'm not vacationing. My grandmother's in the hospital down the street. I flew down to be with her."

"I'm sorry to hear that," the clerk said, switching tactics without losing a beat. "The hotel's complimentary shuttle can take you to and from the hospital." She flipped the hotel map over to reveal a list of phone numbers. "Just call the concierge fifteen minutes before you're ready to go." Then she handed an old-fashioned, brass room key to a uniformed bellman. "Ben will escort you to your room, Mrs. Thorne," she said, still smiling. "I hope you enjoy your stay."

"Thanks." Lily turned and eyed the bellman, who was checking the room number, stamped into her key.

"This way, please," he said, rolling the luggage cart toward the main corridor. "Did you know the Belleview Biltmore was used to house a battalion of Army Air Corps troops during World War II?"

Lily's lack of response didn't faze the bellman's enthusiasm. As they approached the four steps at the entrance to the East Wing, he stopped and pointed to three narrow phone booths, one on the left side of the wide staircase, and two on the right.

"These were installed by the Army so soldiers could call home." Then he pointed back toward the hallway. "The main corridor is called the Promenade and the Candlelight Ballroom is about halfway down, on the left. There's a bar in there with a trap door in the floor that leads down to a series of underground tunnels. During Prohibition, they say that bar was a speakeasy and Al Capone used the hotel's railroad to transport shipments of bootlegged alcohol. Supposedly, Capone's men knew whenever the police were planning a raid, so before the cops arrived, they dropped all the alcohol down through the trap door. Workers would hide the liquor in the tunnels or in one of the Pullman cars that were stored in the hotel's rail yard out back, so when the police showed up to raid the place, all they found were people sitting around sipping glasses of iced tea. Then, when the coast was clear, they brought everything back up through the trap door."

The moment Ben finally stopped to take a breath, Lily grabbed the handrail and pulled herself up the steps. The bellman followed, carrying her two suitcases. He unlocked the door for her and then stepped back to allow her to pass before bringing in her luggage.

Lily glanced around the spacious parlor. On one side of the room was a small round, mahogany table and four matching chairs. The other side was furnished with a burgundy, rolled-arm sofa, a coffee table, and an armoire that concealed a TV. She hobbled down a short hallway, past a black and white tiled bath and into the bedroom. The rich floral-patterned burgundy drapes and bedspread, glass door-knobs and other Victorian Era touches in the décor gave the suite an authentic aura. "This is a big suite," she said.

The bellman placed her suitcases on the king-sized four-poster bed. "Yeah. When they first opened this hotel in 1897, this suite would have actually been two separate rooms and you would have shared that bath with your neighbor."

Lily wrinkled her nose, causing the bellhop to chuckle. "Yeah, it's hard to imagine, but sharing a bathroom with only one other guest room was considered a luxury back in those days."

The laughter of children in the hallway caught Lily's attention.

"The pool is at the opposite end of this corridor, but don't worry – it closes at dusk, so the hallway is usually quiet at night." Ben grinned. "Unless you believe the people who claim ghost children play there late at night."

Lily stiffened. "Ghost children?"

"Yeah, but I don't believe in all that nonsense," he said with a shake of his head.

Lily relaxed. *"Silly ghost stories – every old hotel seems to have them,"* she thought. She muffled a yawn as the bellman made his exit. Then she dialed the Neuro ICU for an update on Grams' condition.

"Mrs. Bloom is undergoing a minor procedure right now," the nurse explained. "But she'll be back in about an hour."

Lily decided to unpack. By the time she finished, she could barely keep her eyes open. She sat on the upholstered bench at the foot of the bed to remove her leg brace. Then she hopped to the bedside and let herself fall back against two rows of fluffy pillows for a short nap.

Almost immediately, she drifted to sleep and tumbled into a thick cloud bank. She felt as light as a feather, spinning in the puffy swirls. Lily had never experienced anything like this before. She stretched out her arms, hoping to stabilize herself, but before she could, the clouds dissolved away.

Lily lurched, preparing for a fall to earth, but instead, she drifted gently until her feet reached a carpeted floor. She felt dizzy and nauseous, but these sensations subsided as she got her bearings and recognized the parlor of her hotel suite.

Then she noticed she wasn't alone.

Chapter Two

A stout, middle-aged woman, wearing a long blue dress with a floral print and high-neckline, sat at the round table. The woman's brown hair was captured in a neat twist beneath a wide-brimmed hat, decorated with blue silk flowers and a single white feather. Fair-skinned and holding a tea cup in her hand, she looked perfectly at home in the Victorian parlor.

Lily felt dizzy and confused. Before she had time to contemplate the woman in this dream, a man suddenly materialized next to the table.

Dashing was the word that came to Lily's mind. His short, dark hair was parted high on the side, and he sported a pencil-thin mustache above full lips and a square jaw. His dark gray, pin-striped suit had a matching vest, buttoned over a high-collared white shirt, and a narrow, red tie. He looked as though he had just stepped out of the 1920s. He even wore white spats with black buttons over his shiny black shoes.

He and the woman spoke in hushed tones, giving Lily time to contemplate her role in this dream. The couple's odd dress seemed to indicate a costume party was forthcoming. Lily glanced down at herself and nodded smugly, convinced her assessment of the situation was correct. Otherwise, why would she be dressed as a flapper?

Her bright red, fringed sheath dress was gorgeous, but it didn't match her state of mind. She closed her eyes and attempted to change her costume to something more fitting – like the Grim Reaper or a vampire. When she opened her eyes, she was surprised to see she was now dressed in her normal clothes.

Puzzled, she turned her attention back to the strange couple. They didn't seem to notice her, so she edged nearer, eavesdropping on their conversation.

"You're just so predictable, Clay!" the woman scolded. "You're drawn to women in pain, like a moth to a flame! The moment I noticed her in the lobby, I knew you'd be showing up here."

The man turned to Lily and shook his head; his dark eyebrows knitted together above sad, brown eyes. "Why did you change?" he asked. "Don't you want to be beautiful?"

Lily glanced down at the angry red scars on her forearms and the brace on her leg; perplexed.

"What makes you think you can help her?" the woman asked, her tone softening.

"I've done it before," he replied.

"Ah, but that was an extraordinary situation, wasn't it?" she prodded.

"I don't understand. Who are you two?" Lily asked.

The instant she spoke, Lily lost her footing and fell backward into the strange clouds. But this time, instead of floating, she dropped like a rock right through the mist.

She woke flailing in her hotel room bed, her heart thumping. The room was much colder than it had been when she fell asleep, but otherwise, the room looked exactly as it had when she dozed off a half hour earlier.

"Weird dream," she muttered, stretching. "And different."

She sat up, recalling every word, image and feel of the strange experience. She was used to dreaming. She did it all the time. But normally the fog in her dreams signaled the beginning of nightmarish hallucinations, and they *always* revolved around Dylan.

She shook her head. No matter. She didn't have time to dwell on it. Right now, Grams needed her.

Chapter Three

Lily rose, fitted the brace to her leg and limped over to adjust the thermostat higher before splashing water on her face. Feeling more like herself, she called the concierge desk to request a shuttle to the hospital, slipped on a windbreaker to cover her scarred arms, and peeked into the parlor. Once she was certain no one was in there, she stepped into the hallway and turned the brass key in the lock.

At the end of the hall, Lily eyed the narrow phone booths next to the stairs, recalling the trivia the bellman had shared with her. She shot a glance down the Promenade. *"With all that guy's talk of Al Capone just before my nap, no wonder I dreamed I was a flapper. Puzzle solved!"*

She hobbled past a broad, boxed-spiral staircase and cut through a cozy seating area, barely glancing at the ebony, baby grand piano in the center of the space. There was a time when Lily might not have been able to resist sitting down to play a few bars of a favorite melody, but those days were long gone.

The hotel lobby was busier than it had been earlier. Conference attendees, wearing matching name badge lanyards around their necks, clustered in overstuffed chairs, chatting and drinking martinis. Lily grew uncomfortable, anticipating their curious stares, but no one seemed to notice her.

A doorman pulled the heavy glass door open for her. She gave him a nod of thanks and headed toward the waiting shuttle. The same shuttle-driver who had ferried her from the airport, smiled at her and opened the front passenger door.

"This seat might be easier for you to manage," he said. "Morton Plant Hospital, right?"

"Yes. The Neuro ICU," she said, clambering into the van.

"That's in the main hospital building," he replied.

They drove the few blocks to the hospital campus in silence. As soon as the shuttle came to a stop at the entrance, Lily opened the door and started to climb out, but hesitated. This was exactly the kind of activity that reminded her how little strength her leg possessed and why her doctor recommended a bone transplant to further her recovery.

With the support of the driver's arm, she climbed down.

"Thanks," she said, managing a fleeting smile.

He handed her a business card. "My name's Pete," he said. "Call this number when you need a ride back to the hotel. I'll be working till eight, so I'll pick you up right here."

Lily tucked the card into the pocket of her windbreaker. "Thanks, Pete."

She turned toward the hospital and gulped, intimidated by the size of the building and frightened, knowing the severity of Grams' condition was about to become a reality.

"Just inside that door is an information desk," Pete said. "They should be able to direct you to your grandmother's room."

Lily nodded and limped through the automated glass doors. The lobby was well-appointed with paintings, plants and track lighting. The focal point of the vaulted space was a sleek information desk, staffed by two women. As she approached, one of the women noticed Lily's leg brace. "Do you need a wheelchair escort?" she asked.

"No, thanks. I can manage," Lily replied, with more confidence than she felt. "I'm here to visit my grandmother – Lois Bloom. She's in the Neuro ICU"

The other woman typed the name into the computer. She shared a solemn, knowing look with her co-worker and then gave Lily a sympathetic smile. "She's in room 4544."

The first woman pointed to a wide corridor. "Use the elevator bank at the end of this hall. The ICU is on the fourth floor."

As Lily made her way to the elevator, she passed a woman in a wheelchair, chatting with a man on crutches. Both wore robes over hospital gowns and both gave her a nod, as if they were comrades in the battle to regain the use of their limbs. Along with the antiseptic smell, the pair reminded Lily that no amount of elegant décor could disguise the fact that this was just another hospital, filled with people who didn't want to be here.

Lily took a deep breath as she pushed through the double doors of the ICU. When she reached Grams room, she hesitated just inside the door. A privacy curtain was pulled, hiding all but the foot of the bed and a portion of a large bay window beyond. She tensed and moved closer.

When she finally glimpsed Grams, Lily caught her breath. Her grandmother had lost so much weight that her pale, withered body barely put a dent in the mattress. The white sheet and blanket that covered her were unwrinkled, which was a bad sign. It meant she hadn't moved since the bed was made. An IV dripped into Grams' bruised left hand, and an oxygen line was wrapped around her short, silver hair and over her ears, to keep the tubes from falling out of her nostrils. A small black box, the size of a pack of cigarettes, rested on Grams' chest and the wires sprouting from it disappeared beneath her hospital gown. A heart monitor was clipped to her thin finger.

After the accident, Lily had become accustomed to ominous-looking medical equipment, but the sight of it attached to her grandmother troubled her.

"I'm here, Grams." she whispered. "I love you." A wave of guilt washed over her. "I'm sorry I've been so distant lately. I've had a rough go of it, but that's no excuse for ignoring you the way I have. It's just I couldn't bear to hear you talking about Dylan like he..." Lily stopped and studied Grams peaceful facial expression. She patted her grandmother's bony arm. "Never mind. I guess it doesn't matter now."

Lily kissed her cheek and took a seat in the blue vinyl armchair, under the window. For several minutes, she watched Grams' chest move up and down with each frail breath, until at last, the silence became unbearable. She needed to explain – and perhaps justify, her neglectful behavior.

"We used to talk all the time, Grams. Do you remember?" She took a deep breath, determined to say everything she had been holding back. "I never wanted to hurt your feelings because I knew you meant well, but after the accident, every time you told me that you knew exactly how I felt, I wanted to scream."

Lily paused for a moment to watch the monitors for any sign that Grams could hear her. No change. She took another deep breath and continued. "I mean, I know we both lost a child, but it's like you never recognized the differences between your loss and mine. You know, the day you lost your child, I lost my *mother.*" Lily bit her lower lip. "And while it's awful that Mom died, at least she was a grown woman who made her own choices. And another thing – your house wasn't utterly empty after she was gone. You had me. I mean, I know it wasn't easy to raise another child, but I think it made it easier for you to move on." Tears filled her eyes. "Dylan never got the chance to grow up. And my home is a tomb without his sweet laughter."

Lily gazed at her grandmother's still form, thinking about their relationship. After the accident, every time Grams encouraged her to *"move on"* Lily subconsciously added another brick to the wall she was building between them. When Grams started losing touch with reality, it was too much. They barely spoke at all during the last year.

A single tear escaped and rolled down Lily's cheek. She swiped it away with the back of her hand. "I'm sorry for deserting you, Grams. It's not your fault that Dylan died. And I know you were only trying to comfort me."

Lily sagged into the high-backed chair, hoping there would still be time to set things right. "To tell the truth, I think I'm going crazy, Grams," she said. "Lately, when I dream about Dylan, he morphs into strangers... and the nightmare is back, too. And today something else..."

Lily let out a long breath. "I'll be right here when you wake up, Grams." She rested her head against her fist and closed her eyes, returning to her earlier dream of tumbling through thick clouds. She tried to swim, but before she reached the edge of the fog, it dissipated, softly depositing her in the middle of a meadow.

She felt nauseous – the same way she did whenever she stared out the side window of a moving car for too long. She tried to focus. Two ladies were walking next to her. Lily was certain the older of the two was the Victorian woman from her earlier dream, but now she was clad in a long, black dress. The other woman appeared to be in her early twenties and was stunningly beautiful. Most of her short, red hair was hidden beneath a dark blue, bell-shaped cloche. Her loose-fitting frock was several shades lighter blue than her hat. Six inches below her waistline, the straight shift transitioned into a pleated skirt, hemmed just below her knee. Her clunky brown shoes had square heels and a big buckle closures.

"This field is perfect," the older woman said. "Just the spot for a hospital. My stepson, Morton, has enough money to build it. We just have to convince him to do it."

Without warning, the fog enveloped Lily and a few moments later, it evaporated again. There was no sensation of swimming this time. It was more like tumbling a few times in a dryer and then being dropped onto a chair.

Lily's eyes darted around in disbelief. *"How did I get here?"* she wondered, gazing around the parlor of her hotel room. Across the small, mahogany table from her were the two ladies she had seen walking in the field only seconds before. The young woman had removed her hat, revealing bobbed dark red hair, parted just above her right eyebrow and pressed into deep, symmetrical waves on either side.

"Hello, darlin' girl," the older woman cooed.

"Hello," Lily replied automatically.

"I am Missus Margaret Josephine Loughman-Plant. You may call me Margaret." She extended her upturned, open palm in the direction of the younger woman. "And this young lady is Missus Roberta Johnson Hamilton. Everyone calls her Bobbi. Now, I do apologize for my rude behavior, but I must counsel with Bobbi for just a moment."

Lily nodded, still a bit dizzy and definitely confused. *"Did I only dream I went to the hospital?"* she wondered. *"Am I still napping at the hotel?"* She closed her eyes, hoping she would float back into the fog, but nothing happened.

"Bobbi," Margaret said, "I see the similarities too, but I need to warn you. Clay has already made a connection with this one, so you may want to reconsider. Otherwise things could become rather complicated, wouldn't you agree?"

Lily heard a loud bang in the distance. When she turned to see where the noise had come from, the fog engulfed her and she plummeted through the clouds, falling again.

Chapter Four

Lily woke with a start. It took her a moment to get her bearings and remember that she was in her grandmother's hospital room.

A heavy black nurse was backing into the room, pulling an unwieldy equipment cart. After the cart banged into the door-frame a second time, the nurse pushed it back a few feet to straighten the wheels; then pulled it into the room.

"Time to check your vitals, Miz Bloom!" she called. When she turned and saw Lily, the nurse's eyes flew open in surprise.

Lily placed her finger to her lips in the universal sign for 'quiet.'

The nurse's expression changed to curiosity. She glanced at Lois Bloom and then back to Lily.

"Child, if I could wake Miz Bloom up just by saying 'hello,' it would make my day!" She moved closer to the bed, mumbling, "Yes it would... it would make my day!"

Lily dropped her finger from her lips, realizing she was only fooling herself – Grams wasn't merely asleep.

"My name is Opal," the nurse said. "Now, who might you be?"

"Lily. Lilyanna Thorne. I'm her granddaughter."

"You don't say!" Opal's gaze swept over Lily's braced leg, but she said nothing about it. "I didn't think Miz Bloom had any family... at least not nearby."

"Grams and I are all that's left of our family," Lily explained. "I just flew in from St. Louis. I'm staying at the hotel down the street until... well, as long as necessary."

Opal nodded. "I'll bet you're glad you wore a jacket. No matter how much we complain, the rooms in this ward are always too cold." Opal bent over the bed. "Did you hear the good news, Miz Bloom? Lily flew all the way down here to visit you. Isn't that wonderful?" She glanced up at Lily and shook her head. "I'm sorry. I spend so much time with patients who can't talk that I tend to do the talking for both of us." She chuckled, revealing a full mouth of large white teeth.

Lily smiled, unable to resist Opal's charm.

"Have you already spoken with your grandmother's doctor?" Opal asked.

"Not yet."

"I'll page Dr. Weston to let him know you're here, but he's probably gone for the night."

"Can you tell me exactly what's wrong with her?" Lily asked.

"I can tell you that she suffered a stroke and is comatose, but Dr. Weston will have to provide the details of her condition and prognosis," Opal said.

Opal turned her attention back to her nursing tasks, working with skill and confidence that suggested many years of experience.

"Miz Bloom, you'll feel a squeeze from the blood pressure cuff, but it's nothing to worry about." Opal said.

When she finished documenting Lois Bloom's vital statistics in her medical chart, Opal turned back to Lily. "I guess that will do for now." Her smile was genuine. "It was nice meeting you. If I hear from Dr. Weston, I'll let you know."

"Thanks." Then Lily's curiosity got the best of her. "Opal, tell me something... why do you talk to her like that... I mean, Grams can't hear anything, right?"

Opal paused, her hands on the handle of her equipment cart. "There are a lot of theories on the subject, but the truth is, we just don't know. As for me, I believe that as long as people are alive, we should treat them that way." She looked at Lois Bloom and then back at Lily. "Besides, talking to her can't do her any harm, right?" Opal smiled again and nodded to Lily. Then she backed out the door, pulling her equipment cart along with her.

For several minutes, Lily stood watching her grandmother, thinking about what Opal said. Then she slid the visitor's chair close to the bedside and sat down, taking her grandmother's small hand in her own, shocked at how fragile it felt.

"Grams," she whispered. "I'm sorry for what I said earlier. When you wake up, I'll try to do better." She paused, recalling happier times. "Dylan always loved visiting you. Remember that time you let him help you make homemade caramel corn?"

The image of Dylan as a toddler eating caramel corn flashed through her mind more vividly than Lily was prepared for – his sweet smile; his sticky fingers holding out a few kernels to share with her. Lily felt her heart break for what felt like the millionth time.

She closed her eyes. "I don't know how much longer I can take this, Grams. I mean, every morning I wake up dreading the thought of the day ahead. I just lie in bed wishing I could go back to sleep and dream that Dylan was still alive." She bit her lower lip. "But then when I do go to sleep, I just have nightmares about the accident. Or sometimes I dream that his head is attached to the bodies of all sorts of different people, and when he talks, his voice sounds like whichever body he's wearing at that moment. It's beyond creepy." She watched Grams for a moment. "I sure wish I'd told you about all of this before..."

Lily laid her cheek against her grandmother's weathered hand, wishing she would wake up. Finally, she raised her head and studied the old woman's ashen face, gulping back her tears. "You can't die, Grams. Not with so much left unsaid."

The nurse reappeared in the doorway. "I'm sorry, but Dr. Weston is gone for the day," she said. "His service asked me to let you know he'll stop by after his rounds tomorrow morning to answer any questions you might have." She gave Lily a comforting smile. "There's really nothing more you can do here tonight. Why don't you go on back to your hotel? If you leave your phone number at the nurses' desk, I promise to call if there's any change."

Lily nodded and struggled to her feet. She kissed the old woman's forehead and stroked her cheek. "Goodnight, Grams," she whispered.

Chapter Five

A few people were dining late, but the Terrace Cafe at the Belleview Biltmore was relatively empty by the time Lily was seated. While waiting for her French onion soup and Caesar salad to arrive, she sipped on a glass of Merlot and studied the décor of the large dining room. High-backed Queen Anne style chairs upholstered with gold brocade fabric, tables covered in crisp, white linen, a maroon carpet with a gold diamond pattern, gold chandeliers and dark, intricately carved china cabinets gave the room an authentic, Victorian charm. Next to a large, gilt-framed painting of a woman casually leaning against a piano, several sections of greenery-filled planter boxes separated the dining room from the Promenade. Across the wide hallway, well-dressed people were beginning to gather in an ornate lounge, featuring a huge mahogany bar. A photographer was trying to pose a wedding party on the massive box-spiral staircase nearby, but the bride was having trouble climbing the stairs in her tight, mermaid-style dress. The rest of the wedding party was enjoying a good-natured laugh about it.

Lily watched, feeling alien to the concept of joy. By the time her food arrived, she had emptied her glass of Merlot and ordered another. The hot crock of soup, covered with a thick slice of baked provolone, provided the comfort she needed. Lily enjoyed twisting each delicious bite of cheese around and around on her spoon, and scooping up soggy croutons to complete the taste experience. Her cool, crisp salad provided the perfect contrast. She relaxed and her eyelids grew heavy.

Lily barely remembered the walk back to her room or getting ready for bed, but the moment she fell asleep, Dylan appeared. This time, his little-boy face was attached to the body of a doctor.

"Mom, you shouldn't drink while taking pain medication," he said. "It isn't good for your health."

"You mean it could make me hallucinate and see the head of my thirteen-year-old son on a doctor's body?"

Dylan grinned. "It's a medical student's body."

Before Lily could respond, he faded into a thick, chilly mist. Then she was floating again…flying and tumbling through the fog.

She heard voices in the distance and tried to peer through the cottony white clouds. "Dylan?" she called. "Is that you?"

When the mist lifted, Lily was seated with the Victorian woman, Margaret, at the small, round table, near her parlor window, and the man Lily dreamed about when she first arrived at the hotel stood next to them. Ignoring her queasiness, Lily leaned forward, listening to their conversation.

"Are you absolutely sure you want to pursue this connection, Clay?" Margaret clucked. "Bobbi thinks it will take both of you to make this connection work. I tend to agree, but I'm concerned. I've noticed the two of you aren't getting along lately."

Clay's jaw tightened. "Bobbi's frustrated with me right now, but she'll come around in time."

"But you know how this works," Margaret admonished. "It will be as if no time has passed at all."

Clay twirled a fedora-style hat between his hands. "I can handle it if she can."

All at once, Bobbi, the young redheaded woman from her earlier dream materialized at the table. Lily gasped, but the trio acted oblivious to her presence.

"Hello, Long-Gone," the new arrival said; her voice cool and measured. "You've been making yourself scarce lately."

"I don't stick around when I don't feel welcome. Besides,

you've been spending most of your time at the hospital, and you know I hate that place," Clay countered.

"Deal with your personal issues later," Margaret snapped.

Bobbi pressed her lips together. "Time is short, but she needs to understand how everything started."

"Ladies first, then," Clay said. He tossed the hat onto his head, pinched the brim between his fingers and nodded to the two ladies. Then he vanished.

This time, Lily's gasp was more of a frightened squeal. Margaret and Bobbi turned to face her.

Lily closed her eyes tight. "You're not real," she said. "I'm hallucinating like I did after the accident. I'm stressed about Grams and I'm just..."

She opened one eye slightly, to peek. Margaret and Bobbi were still there, watching her.

"We're real enough," Margaret said. She lifted her cup of tea and took a sip.

Lily sighed. "I give up. Why, for the love of God, am I dreaming about you people again?"

"In all my years, I've never encountered such calm acceptance from a person during the initial stages of a connection," Margaret commented, returning her rosebud motif tea cup to its matching saucer.

"Well, this isn't my first rodeo," Lily replied, her voice void of emotion. "The psychologist at the hospital said that when I'm injured or stressed, I tend to dream that I'm having out-of-body experiences. He said it's my brain's way of helping me process shock and grief."

"Ah, psychology," Margaret enthused. "Dr. Sigmund Freud. I read his book, 'Interpretation of Dreams.' He theorized that dreams are simply a person's wishes come true as they sleep. I didn't think his hogwash was going to catch on, but – apparently it did."

"I'm not familiar with Freud's work," Lily replied.

"Interesting. If you were not already acquainted with Dr. Freud's book, then how is it possible that this is a dream?" Margaret challenged. "You can't acquire new knowledge in a dream, now, can you?"

Lily's eyes narrowed. It was a good point. "If this isn't a dream, what is it?"

"Perhaps we should finish the introductions I began earlier, when I gave you permission to call me Margaret. In life, I was the second wife of Henry B. Plant, the magnificent man who built this hotel in 1896."

"In life?" Lily echoed. "So that means you're ghosts?"

"Spirits, darlin', not ghosts. The living often confuse the two entities, but we are quite different," Margaret explained.

"You're both dead, aren't you?"

"Yes, but spirits retain their full consciousness. Ghosts don't. We are as different as you and your Grams are right now. While one could argue you are both living beings, your levels of consciousness are quite different, wouldn't you agree?" Margaret asked.

Lily considered this. "Okay, let's say you are spirits. Then why are you haunting me? Don't I already have enough problems without being spooked by you guys?"

"Oh, my," Margaret commented. "You do have an interesting outlook on matters. You have nothing to fear from us. We may even be able to help you – just stay silent and watch."

The clouds swiftly enveloped Lily. She fought to wake herself up, but couldn't. She was powerless in the mist.

Chapter Six

When the fog cleared, Lily was standing next to a large oval track made of crushed oyster shell. She gulped in air to quell her nausea and took in the scene. Directly in front of her was a set of bleachers, filled with spectators. Based on their attire, Lily guessed it was the early 1900s. Then she noticed Margaret approaching at the side of a man who was wearing a straw hat and had a bushy gray mustache. Despite Margaret's efforts to gain his attention, the man didn't acknowledge her presence any more than Lily's.

A small, redheaded child suddenly stood up in front of Lily. She wore a simple white dress with long sleeves, black leggings, and high-topped, brown leather shoes with buttons on the outside edge. An enormous, white bow was tied on top of her head, holding back her long, wavy hair.

"Good day, Mr. Plant! I would wager that Stilwell will take this race," she exclaimed, as the man in the straw hat took a seat in the front row, next to her. "His costume has a lightning bolt on it!"

The child sat back down, but wriggled in her seat, having a difficult time keeping her youthful excitement in check.

The man in the straw hat laughed. "Well, Bobbi, I suppose your logic for choosing a winner makes as much sense as the methods employed by many of these chaps." He reached across her to shake hands with the man seated next to her. "Good day, Emmitt. I dare say your niece is quite a sportswoman already."

"Hello, Morton. You're right on time. The racers are lining up just now. My money is on young Habersham, though his blouse has no lightning bolt." He winked. "Care to wager against him?"

"I believe I'll heed Bobbi's advice on this first race. Our usual dollar bet?" Morton asked.

Bobbi clapped her hands together, laughing with delight. The sound was enchanting. It reminded Lily of wind chimes, floating on the breeze.

Emmitt smiled. "Agreed –though I question the wisdom of accepting racing tips from a twelve-year-old."

Lily narrowed her eyes. *"Bobbi?"* She was confused. *"How had Bobbi turned into a small child?"*

Just then, a horn blasted and six men on bicycles took off around the track, bumping elbows as they tried to break free from the starting pack. The riders wore short-sleeved tunics and tight, wool shorts, hemmed just above their knees. Two competitors had stockings over their calves, but the others wore what looked like leather ballet slippers on otherwise bare feet. On the inside of the track, an announcer in a small tower used a megaphone to call out the progress of the race.

The race was three laps around the track and by the third lap, only three riders remained in contention. Habersham and Wilson were neck and neck, with Stilwell close behind. Bobbi couldn't keep her seat any longer. She stood and jumped in place, cheering for Stilwell. Her impetuous behavior endeared her to several nearby spectators, but none more than Morton Plant, who grinned at her antics.

On the final turn, it looked like Habersham would take the race, when suddenly Wilson's peddle caught in Habersham's rear wheel. Both bicycles spun out of control, taking their riders down to the ground in a heap. The crowd jumped to their feet as Stilwell swerved around the collision and crossed the finish line.

Bobbi cried, "Hip, hip hooray!" and imitated Stilwell, raising her arms with her hands balled into fists above her head in victory.

Emmitt flipped a dollar coin to Morton, shaking his head with amusement.

Lily's attention shifted to Margaret, who was trying to gain Morton's attention again. She noticed that Bobbi was also looking directly at Margaret. When Margaret began pounding her fists against Morton's chest, Bobbi's jaw dropped open.

While the two men continued chatting undisturbed, Bobbi stepped a few feet away. "Please don't do that, ma'am," she said in a soft voice. "You might hurt him. Besides, he can't see you."

Margaret looked directly at Bobbi, astonished. "You can see me, child? Tell Morton that I am here, straight away," she directed.

Instead, Bobbi called out, "I need to return to our room, Uncle Emmitt. I'll return shortly."

Emmitt gave her a slight nod, without breaking from his conversation.

Though Lily made no effort to move when Bobbi walked away from the bleachers, she began floating along at the child's side. Margaret followed after them, demanding that Bobbi stop and turn around.

Once they were a good distance from the track, Bobbi slowed. "What is your business with Mr. Plant?" she demanded, turning to face Margaret.

"Don't be impertinent, child," Margaret clucked. "He's my stepson. I'm Margaret Plant. I'm the widow of Henry Plant, Morton's father." She paused. "I'm dreaming that I'm invisible and I can't seem to wake. I'm hoping he can help me."

"He can't help you," Bobbi said, shaking her head.

A trio of older ladies, wearing long dresses with bustles, large feathered hats, and carrying parasols gave Bobbi a curious glance as they strolled by. No doubt they wondered why the child was talking to herself.

When Bobbi returned to her brisk pace, Lily realized they were approaching the Belleview Biltmore Hotel, but it looked different. They walked up a flight of wooden stairs onto a wide veranda, where a black bellman in a bright red uniform and small pillbox hat, opened the door for Bobbi.

"Good afternoon, Missy," he said as she passed.

"Hello, Washington," Bobbi replied.

Margaret continued to follow close behind, hurling question after question in Bobbi's direction, but the child didn't respond. When they reached the privacy of her uncle's room, Bobbi closed the door and moved to a small table, situated near the window, next to a bed and a small cot. Margaret watched with an irritated glare as Bobbi poured herself a glass of water from a pitcher.

"Impudent child," hissed Margaret. "Haven't your elders taught you to always serve guests before yourself?"

Bobbi wasn't intimidated by Margaret. "You have powers that I do not possess," she replied. "All you have to do is think of what you would like to drink, and it will appear before you. Try it, Ma'am."

"Don't be ridiculous," Margaret said, pinching herself on the arm.

"That won't work," Bobbi said. "You're not asleep. You are invisible to most people because your body has been buried and your spirit is the only part of you that remains."

Margaret scoffed. "Look at me. In this dream, I'm only thirty years old, at most. If I could wake, you would see that I am well into my sixties. I'm dreaming of my youth, to be sure."

"You appear as you wish to appear," Bobbi informed her. "Don't your sensibilities tell you that if you were simply dreaming about your youth, then Mr. Plant would still be a child?"

Margaret knitted her eyebrows. "Morton is actually only one year younger than I, but your point is taken. He does appear to be older than when I last saw him."

"Now, try to imagine a glass of water before you," encouraged Bobbi.

"Water is for fish," Margaret chided. "Civilized ladies drink tea."

When a silver tea set materialized on the table before her, Margaret stared it with wide eyes. She stretched out one finger and touched the teapot. Then she moved her finger to the water pitcher and tried to touch it. Her finger went right through the pitcher as if it were an illusion. Fascinated, she repeated the process a few times, then raised the teapot and poured steaming, dark liquid into a porcelain cup. She spooned sugar into the tea, tapped the spoon and laid it to rest on her saucer. Then she raised the cup to her lips, blew across the surface, and took a sip. She closed her eyes and sighed with satisfaction. "I certainly hope I can recall this fascinating dream when I awake!"

Bobbi covered her face with both open palms and shook her head. Lily was trying to suppress a giggle at the child's frustration when she heard a phone ring.

Chapter Seven

The instant Lily turned her head toward the ringing phone, she slipped through the heavy mist and woke in her hotel room bed. *"Haunting, my butt. It was just another dream,"* she thought. She reached an arm out from under the warm comforter and grabbed her cell phone.

"Good morning. Were you still sleeping?" Scott asked.

"Of course I was. It's only..." Lily looked at the clock radio on the nightstand. *"That can't be right."*

Scott finished her sentence. "It's 8:00 here, so it's 9:00 in Florida."

"But I don't understand," Lily protested. "I went to bed early last night."

"You slept all night? No nightmares? That's wonderful, Lily!"

Lily sat up, amazed. "I guess I did." She felt more rested than she had in months.

"I'm sorry I woke you," Scott said. "I just wanted to know what the doctor had to say about Grams' condition."

"Oh my God. I forgot. I'm supposed to talk to Grams' doctor this morning. I've got to go, Scott. I'll call you later." Lily hung up the phone. The room was cold and the bathroom floor felt icy under her foot as she hopped to the shower. She made a mental note to adjust the thermostat even warmer before she left for the day since it obviously wasn't working properly.

Twenty minutes later, Lily ignored her grumbling stomach and tightened the Velcro straps of her leg brace. As she reached for her crutches, her cell phone rang. She pulled it from the pocket of her wind breaker. Her heart sank when she saw the Caller ID read 'Morton Plant Hospital'. She answered, terrified by the thought that Grams might have died while she overslept.

"Ms. Thorne?" the friendly voice asked. "Dr. Weston asked me to call and extend his apologies, but he had a patient emergency this morning and won't be making his rounds until around noon."

Lily breathed a sigh of relief. "That's no problem. Has my grandmother's condition changed overnight?"

"No change," came the reply.

"Okay then, since the doctor will be running late, I think I'll have a bite to eat before I come to the hospital. Thanks for letting me know." Lily hung up.

She headed down the wide arched Promenade to the Terrace Cafe, stopping frequently along the way to rest her leg and to admire several huge pictures, depicting the history of the hotel. Halfway to the restaurant, she noticed the Candlelight Ballroom, with ornate wrought iron gates guarding its entrance. Remembering the story the bellman had shared when she first arrived, she smiled and peered in at the bar. The décor of the room was so authentic; she could almost picture Al Capone and his minions hosting a party with bootlegged whisky.

As she moved further down the hallway, her eyes locked on a rendering of the Plant family tree. "Oh my gosh," she whispered. "There really was a Margaret Plant."

"I wonder if I read about the Plant family when I was a kid and forgot about them until last night. But why would I dream about Margaret?" She pondered the thought until she reached the restaurant, near the end of the long corridor.

To give Terrace Cafe customers a sense of privacy this morning, several four-foot high planter boxes, each filled with a wide variety of stunning orchids, had been rolled across the Promenade to form a temporary wall. At the entrance, a sign directed patrons to *Please Seat Yourself.*

When Lily plopped down at the first table, a server hustled over to present her with a menu and fill her water glass. She placed an order for hazelnut coffee, strawberry crepes and bacon, and then pulled her iPad from her bag and typed the name 'Margaret Plant' into her search engine.

Lily found several articles and book references for the railroad and shipping tycoon, Henry B. Plant, but her search revealed almost no information about Margaret. Then she remembered what Margaret had said about Sigmund Freud and typed his name into the search engine. Lily scanned the timeline of his significant achievements and discovered he published a book in the year 1900, titled *"The Interpretation of Dreams."*

A shiver ran down her spine. *"What are the odds that I remembered both the Plant family and this old book in my dreams?"*

Her concentration shattered when her table jostled. Looking up, she discovered a man was sitting down at her table. His blond hair was cropped short, and he wore dark, round sunglasses, a tight black tee-shirt bearing a Harley insignia and blue jeans. She could see a partial tattoo on his right arm, but couldn't make out the design. Then she noticed his white cane.

Lily wasn't sure what to do. She opted to give a slight cough to make him aware of her presence.

The man jerked back in surprise. "Did my table come with company this morning?" he joked.

Lily admired his self-confident demeanor. It matched his overall biker appearance. Only the cane and glasses seemed out of place.

She chuckled. "I must have missed the *Reserved* sign when I sat down."

"Sorry," he said, "I've been here for a few days and usually sit at this table in the morning so I don't have to worry about bumping into everything else in the restaurant."

He started to stand up, but Lily reached across the table to stop him, placing her hand lightly on his well-muscled forearm. "Please stay. My food hasn't arrived, so I can easily move to another table," she volunteered.

"If you're eating alone, why not stay, and let me pretend I have a date?" He revealed a perfect smile and a dimple in his chin.

Lily couldn't think of a polite way to say 'no' without appearing to be uncomfortable about eating with a blind man, so she relented. When the waiter noticed the man's arrival, he came over with another menu and held it out to him. Then he noticed the dark glasses and white cane. He froze, not sure how to proceed.

Lily intervened. "The waiter's here. I'm having a strawberry crepe. Does that sound good to you?"

"When you're blind, you learn not to order anything with powdered sugar on it. I'll have black coffee, a ham and cheddar cheese omelet, fried potatoes, bacon and some wheat toast."

"Would you like some orange juice?" the waiter bellowed, as if being blind affected one's hearing.

"No! Thanks!" he replied in an equally loud voice.

The waiter flushed and turned on his heel, while Lily tried to not to laugh.

"I'm sorry," he said. "I hope I didn't embarrass you. I just get frustrated with people who freak-out around someone with a disability."

"Believe me, I understand." Lily tapped her leg brace with her crutch. "Bum leg. By the way, my name is Lily Thorne."

"Cast or brace?" he asked. "And my name is Seth Lyons."

"Brace – car accident three years ago. And you? Birth, injury or disease?"

"Bacterial infection. Five years ago." He gave her another grin. "It's cool to meet someone who understands medical condition shorthand."

Lily chuckled. "So what brings you to Belleair?"

"I'm going through a battery of tests to make sure I'm a candidate for surgery. With a little luck, I'll be ditching this cane within six months. How about you?" Seth asked.

"My grandmother is in Morton Plant Hospital. She's not doing well and I don't want her to be alone," Lily explained.

"Sorry. Are you two close?" Seth asked.

"Used to be. Long story," Lily said.

"I like long stories. Beats chit-chat any day."

Lily tried to sidestep the question. "Let's just say our relationship got complicated."

"Okay. How about your folks? Do they live around here?"

Lily sighed. "No. My mom died when I was little. I never knew my dad."

"Ouch. Goddamn. I'm dredging up all kinds of crappy memories for you, aren't I? Bet you're real glad you agreed to eat breakfast with me." He smiled again, but it was evident Seth felt bad about his gaffes.

"It's okay... and not nearly as dramatic as I made it sound. To make a long story short, my mom died of an overdose and afterward, I was raised by my grandparents. Grams was... I mean... she is... a good woman. She was always wonderful with D... with children, but we've grown apart in recent years." Lily noticed Seth cocked his head when she almost said Dylan, and she was grateful he didn't press the issue. "Now, what's your story?"

"I guess you could say I was born with a restless soul. I saved up enough money for a Harley and left my family's farm in Idaho as soon as I graduated from high school." he said.

"Farm in Idaho – let me guess... potatoes?"

"Apples, actually. And barley. My pop runs a good-sized farming operation near Twin Falls. He's a great guy... deacon at our church, loves his family – and for fun, he brews hard cider and distills whisky." Seth shook his head. "He wanted me to take over the operation one day, but the only part of his life that appealed to me was making cider and whisky." He grinned. "Pop understood. Besides, my three younger brothers love the farm. So I've been biking around the country ever since. Well, at least until I lost my sight."

"How do you keep a job if you're on the move all the time?" Lily asked.

"Reflexology," he replied.

Lily knit her eyebrows together. "What?"

"I massage various pressure points on peoples' feet and calves to heal their bodies. Unfortunately, reflexology doesn't cure bacterial infections, but I don't need vision to do my job, so it all works out," he said.

"Do you have your own reflexology shop?"

"Hell, no!" He shook his head. "I might as well have stayed on the farm if I was going to do that. No... I used to take part in motorcycle events all around the country and set-up my booth wherever we stopped for the night. But you can't drive if you can't see, so now I hitch a ride in one of the pick-ups that chase behind the bikes, hauling tool boxes, camping gear, and all that crap. I'm still able to make a living, but God, I miss riding my Harley."

Lily glanced up and saw the waiter approaching. "Here comes our food," she said.

Seth took his elbow from the table and sat back in his chair while the waiter served their plates and confirmed everything was cooked to order. Minding his volume, he asked, "Can I bring you anything else?"

"No, thanks," Lily said. She turned her attention to Seth, watching as he tapped his fingers on the table to locate his napkin, silverware and plate. "Your omelet fills the entire left side of your plate. Your bacon's at your one o'clock, potatoes are at your four, the toast is on a separate plate at your two, and your coffee is at twelve," she coached. "Oh, and the salt is to the left of the pepper at eleven o'clock."

"Okay – who taught you to do that?" Seth asked with a smirk.

"When I was in the hospital, one of my favorite roommates was blind. I used to help her with stuff like this," Lily explained.

They chatted amiably until the waiter returned to collect their empty dishes. Seth turned to look in his direction. "Everything was great, as usual," he said. "Please add a twenty percent tip and charge the bill to room 4323.

"You don't need to pay for my breakfast," Lily protested.

"I always pay for my pretend dates," Seth wisecracked. "Do you want to meet here again tomorrow at ten?"

"Maybe. We'll see."

"Doubt I'll see, but I'll be here," he teased.

Chapter Eight

While she waited for the doctor to make his rounds, Lily relaxed in the chair beneath the window, watching for any sign Grams might be coming out of her coma. The bright Florida sunshine warmed the back of her neck as she dozed off and floated into the familiar fog bank.

When the clouds parted, Lily stood in a garden at the Belleview Biltmore. Margaret and the child version of Bobbi were having a serious conversation on a bench nearby. Lily steadied herself, enduring another wave of motion sickness. After it passed, she observed the two more closely.

Bobbi was an incredibly beautiful child, with long, wavy red hair, wide green eyes and a broad smile. Margaret, looking the same age as before, was wearing an emerald green dress and a wide-brimmed hat, decorated with long feathers. She frowned. "Apparently, you're the only person who can see me here, wherever this is," she said. "So tell me about yourself. Why are you called 'Bobbi'?"

"Bobbi is short for Roberta. My father prayed for sons, but only got six daughters, so he calls us: Jo, Lou, Bobbi, Max, Fred and Henry. My older sisters' real names are Josephine and Louise, and my younger sisters are Maxine, Winifred and Henrietta."

"Your father should learn to accept God's will."

"Father is very pious," Bobbi protested. "He can always tell when people are being tempted by Satan, even when they don't know it themselves." She trembled and lowered her voice. "Sometimes he has to drive Satan out of us – especially when he studies his Bible with an uncorked bottle of whisky."

Margaret narrowed her eyes. "Sounds to me like a case of the pot calling the kettle black."

Without warning, the fog rolled over Lily, pulling her back into the thick, dense folds of mist. *"Why am I still dreaming about people I don't know?"* she wondered. She was still trying to decipher the puzzling question when the mist cleared once more.

This time, Lily found herself standing in the main room of a small house. A pregnant woman and a small, redheaded child were putting a meal together near the fire. Another child was asleep in a wooden bassinette and a large, burly man sat nearby, an open Bible in his lap. The front door opened and two girls, both with red hair like Bobbi's, stepped inside, removed their cloaks and hung them on a peg by the door.

"Mother," said the older girl, "Mr. Johnson and his son were at the market and asked Lou and me to extend their good tidings to you."

Without warning, the man slammed his Bible closed and jumped to his feet, a menacing scowl on his face. "How many times must I put you Jezebel sisters back on the path of righteousness?" he bellowed, crossing the room in three steps.

"Papa, I promise we did nothing sinful," the older girl pleaded, stepping in front of her younger sister.

He smacked her with the back of his hand, knocking her to the floor. He grabbed a fistful of her long red hair and pulled her face close to his. "Do you think I'm blind? Do you think I don't notice how you brush your hair back and lift your skirts as you walk? Do you truly expect me to believe your heart isn't black with lustful thoughts? Get on your knees, you harlot!" he screamed. "Repent before God the Almighty!"

The woman moved cautiously toward the girls, who were now both on their knees, sobbing. She handed the man his Bible and knelt down between the children, wrapping her arms around them. "Thank you, Abraham, for tending to your family with such devotion," she said.

Her voice calmed the man, and the Bible in his hands prevented him from continuing his physical assault.

"Edith, you know how beauty attracts the Devil," he railed. "If Jo and Lou won't conceal their looks, by God, I will destroy them! I won't allow the Devil to use my daughters to tempt good, righteous men into committing sin!"

Edith pulled her daughters closer. "Of course, you are right. Let us all pray together, Father. Bobbi – come pray with your family. Then perhaps a hymn..."

His family congregation kneeled in a tight semicircle at his feet with their heads bowed, as the drunk and belligerent patriarch closed his eyes to pray.

"Dear Lord, I understand that wide is the gate and broad is the road that leads to destruction. So when my wicked daughters head down the path to ruin, I know it is my duty as their father to convince them to turn away from Satan and return to the path of righteousness. I ask that you guide my hand as I provide them with a taste of hell tonight, so as to discourage them from continuing to commit sinful behavior. Amen."

With that, he removed a well-worn leather whipping strap down from a nail on the wall. As he raised the strap high, Jo and Lou tensed and arched their backs, knowing what was in store.

"Their mistake was so small, Abraham," Edith pleaded, pushing Bobbi out of harm's way. "Please don't make their punishment too severe."

Before the first blow landed, the fog gathered around Lily, sweeping her from the scene, shaking and horrified. She fought to wake up, but she was unable to break free of the clouds. Trapped within the mist, a tear rolled silently down Lily's cheek as her own childhood nightmares of abuse, neglect and abandonment resurfaced.

Before her death, Veronica, Lily's mother, had been serving drinks at a local bar and dreaming of Broadway fame, while her boyfriend, Roy, who detested and often abused four-year-old Lily, sold drugs out of their seedy Bronx apartment. Veronica died on Lily's fifth birthday, shortly after abandoning her child in Florida.

When the fog finally dissipated, Lily drifted into a chair at the table in her hotel room. Margaret, somberly dressed in black, poured two cups of tea and slid one over to Lily.

"These memories belong to Bobbi," Margaret said. She scooped three heaping teaspoons of sugar into her tea and stirred until it dissolved. "They may remind you of your own childhood, but they are not yours."

Before she could respond, Lily heard a man's voice call softly, "Ms. Bloom!" She turned toward the distant voice and immediately fell backward into the fog, as if falling off a cliff. She flailed her arms, trying to stop the free-fall, but she was out of control.

Chapter Nine

"Wake up, Ms. Bloom," the voice coaxed again.

Lily's eyelids flew open. It took a second for her to realize she was slouched in the chair next to her grandmother's bed, with a doctor standing over her. Embarrassed, she bolted upright and rubbed her hands over her face to clear her thoughts.

"I'm sorry," she said, "I dozed off there for a minute and I – I must have had that dream about falling."

The gaunt doctor absently tugged at the lapels of his white coat. The corners of his mouth turned up in a half-hearted smile. "Yes, well I'm sorry to wake you Ms. Bloom. I'm Doctor Weston – your grandmother's neurologist."

"I'm pleased to meet you, Doctor," Lily said, still flustered by the abrupt end of her dream. "I'm Lilyanna Thorne... Bloom was my maiden name."

"Well, Ms. Thorne, I'm sorry I'm running so late," he apologized, "but a patient emergency kept me away for most of the day." He pushed his black-rimmed glasses up his long, hawkish nose and then smoothed back the dark gray hair that fringed the sides of his otherwise bald head.

Lily glanced at the clock on the wall, amazed to discover the entire afternoon had evaporated while she napped. She shivered.

"You know, it's okay to ask for a blanket," Dr. Weston said. "We keep these rooms cool to help reduce the potential for spreading infection, but this room is downright cold and there's no reason for you to be uncomfortable."

"Thanks. I'll do that." Lily cleared her throat, willing her brain to become more alert as she met the doctor's gray eyes. "I know Grams had a stroke and that she's in a coma, but the nurse said you could help me understand her prognosis."

Dr. Weston looked over at Lois Bloom and then back at Lily. "Ms. Thorne, I wish I could give you better news, but your grandmother suffered a severe hemorrhagic stroke."

Lily tilted her head, wishing Dr. Weston didn't look so much like an undertaker. "What does that mean?"

"A blood clot burst, causing one of the blood vessels that carried oxygen to your grandmother's brain to rupture. This resulted in two critical complications," he explained. "First, her brain cells were deprived of oxygen. Second, she suffered an intracranial hemorrhage – bleeding in her brain."

Lily nodded, her mouth too dry to speak.

The doctor continued. "There's hardly any extra room inside the human skull, and pooling blood can occupy a lot of space. The results of a CT scan confirmed the hemorrhage was compressing your grandmother's brain-tissue and bleeding into the cerebrospinal fluid around her brain. I drilled a few miniscule burr holes to alleviate the pressure, and then consulted her cardiologist."

Dr. Weston pushed at his glasses again. "You do know your grandmother suffers from hypertension, right?"

Lily nodded. "Grams has taken medication for high blood pressure for years."

"Well, I'm so sorry, but given her age and other health issues, her cardiologist and I agreed she wouldn't survive neurosurgery to repair the torn blood vessel." Dr. Weston cleared his throat. "We don't expect your grandmother to regain consciousness but we can keep her comfortable as her body shuts down."

Lily couldn't stop the tears from welling in her eyes.

Dr. Weston handed her a cheap, one-ply tissue, from the small box on the nightstand. "Your grandmother isn't in any pain," he assured her. "And she won't feel any pain at the end. She'll just stop breathing."

A sudden wave of panic overcame Lily. "I won't let you unplug her," she blurted.

If Dr. Weston was surprised by the outburst, he didn't react. Instead, he calmly checked Lois Bloom's medical chart, slowly turning pages with his long, skeletal fingers.

"Your grandmother has a living will on file with the hospital," he said. "That means we can't take extraordinary measures to keep her alive. But as long as she is breathing on her own, we will continue to provide IV fluids and do our best to make her comfortable."

"How long can she live like this?" Lily asked, her voice trembling.

"There's no way to determine an exact timeframe, but her brain and internal organs are already starting to break down. It could be a few days; no more than two weeks."

Dr. Weston closed the chart and prepared to take his leave. "I'm sorry we can't do anything more, but I'll stop by every day. If there are any changes, I'll have someone contact you immediately." He extended his hand to Lily.

Lily nodded and accepted his cool, bony handshake. When he was gone, she stood and pushed her chair close to Grams' bedside. She sat and took one of the old woman's frail hands in her own. She brought it to her lips and kissed it, trying to accept that soon her grandmother, like Dylan, would exist only in her dreams.

"I can't believe your life is ending and you still haven't taken a single trip abroad," she lamented.

As long as Lily could remember, her grandparents planned elaborate trips abroad that never materialized. Even after her grandfather died, Grams continued to plan trips. She devoured books about exotic locations; learning about the history and inhabitants of chosen destinations, determining which sights she would most like to visit there.

Lily recalled a time when Grams planned a trip to Norway. For weeks, she met Lily at the door after school with traditional Norwegian greetings, laced with a not-so-traditional southern accent. She smiled at the memory and lay her head down next to her grandmother's on the pillow.

"Grams, I don't know what would have become of me if you and Gramps hadn't taken me in when Mom died, but I'm so sorry that raising me cost you guys your dreams."

She closed her eyes and suddenly Dylan popped into her mind's eye. In this hallucination, his face was embedded on the body of a plump black woman, wearing a red, orange and purple flowered muumuu. The black hair around his face was plaited with beads, and his expressive hands flashed bright purple fingernails.

"Mama, don't you worry none... On dis side, Great Grams can curl her toes in da white sand and sip on a daiquiri forever if dat what makes her happy. She can float on da breeze like a butterfly and sway to da music of steel drums... she can fly to wherever her dreams take her. I promise ya dat."

Lily tried to push Dylan's strange image from her mind; struggling without success to picture her little boy as he really was and recall the sound of his voice. As the black woman with Dylan's face faded from her mind, still swaying her hips to the island music, Lily mumbled, "God Almighty. What is wrong with me?"

"Nothing's wrong with you," a voice said from the doorway. "You just need a good night's sleep, that's all."

Lily snapped her head up and saw the friendly nurse, Opal, wheeling her equipment cart into the room. Lily blushed, embarrassed at being overheard.

"You heard what the doctor said," Opal continued. "He'll call you if there are any changes in your grandmother's condition. Why don't you go on back to the hotel for the evening? I promise Miz Bloom will still be here in the morning."

Lily squinted her eyes. "Isn't that a risky promise for you to make?"

"Not really. Her spirit tells me she isn't ready to let go yet."

Lily's jaw dropped. "Really? Her spirit talks to you?"

Opal smiled and shook her head. "No... no...I didn't mean it like that. It's just that whenever I take care of a patient for more than a few days, I get a funny feeling when their spirit is getting ready to leave their body, and I don't have that feeling about your grandmother." She moved to Grams' bedside. "Miz Bloom, I'm just going to check your blood pressure," she said.

Lily thought about spirits as she watched Opal check Grams' vital statistics. "Opal, do you think this hospital is haunted?" she asked.

The nurse eyed Lily with curiosity. "I don't know, but I guess it wouldn't surprise me. This is an old hospital and I'm sure hundreds of people have died here over the years. Why?"

"I just had a strange dream about Morton Plant and this hospital." Lily said, deciding the less she said about her dreams, the better.

"Well, I think the hospital is named after him because he donated a lot of money to help run it, but I haven't heard any rumors about him haunting the place."

Lily suddenly felt foolish. "It's not important. I probably just dreamed about him because I saw his picture in the hotel where I'm staying." She shook her head. "You know, I think I'm going to take your advice and call it a day." She stood and kissed Grams on her cheek.

"Don't you worry, child," Opal comforted. "Things always have a way of working themselves out."

Lily nodded. She called for the hotel shuttle, then picked up her crutch, wished Opal a good evening, and limped out the door.

By the time she reached her hotel room, Lily wondered if she might be coming down with something. She hadn't slept so much in years, and yet she could barely keep her eyes open. She decided to lie down and watch some television before dinner, but as soon as her head hit the pillow, she was engulfed by the fog once again.

This time, Lily decided not to fight the experience. She closed her eyes and concentrated on her breathing, as if practicing yoga. As she relaxed, she began to enjoy the peaceful sensation of gliding through space and time, weightless and unencumbered. When she felt the fog beginning to melt away, Lily kept her eyes closed until she felt her feet touch the ground. Slowly, she opened her eyes. Her stomach did a mild flip, but otherwise, she felt fine.

The peaceful feeling was short-lived.

Chapter Ten

"Demons!" the man howled. He slammed his half-empty bottle of whisky down like a fist on the table and slouched into his chair, filling the space at the head of the dining table. "My daughter chooses to consort with demons!"

Lily recognized the room. This was Bobbi's childhood home. The trembling child stood just inside the door, wearing the same dress and hair bow that she had been wearing at the Belleview Biltmore.

Lily shuddered; confused. *"Why do I continue to dream about this child?"* she wondered. *"Or, if Margaret is to be believed, why am I reliving Bobbi's memories?"*

As the eldest child, Josephine sat closest to their father on one side of the table. Next to her was an empty chair. On the opposite side of the table, Louise, Maxine, and Winifred sat together on a long bench. All of the children stared wide-eyed at their father except for the baby, Henrietta, whose cries went unattended in a nearby bassinette.

"Are you sure they aren't angels, Father?" Bobbi asked.

"Angels have wings," he sneered. "And they don't make a habit of appearing before dim-witted children, the likes of you." He picked up his cup and tossed its contents over his shoulder. Water splattered against the wall next to the bassinette and dripped to the wood floor. No one moved as he filled the cup with whisky.

"But this one wasn't like the others I've seen. She was a grown woman, Father," Bobbi clarified.

"Hush, Bobbi," her mother warned. She ladled some soup into

a bowl and set it in front of her husband. "Here, Abraham, it's your favorite – potato soup." She turned back to Bobbi with raised eyebrows. "One can overlook the zealous imagination of a child, but you must stop playing at such foolishness as you grow older. Now take your seat."

"Stay where you are!" Abraham commanded. He slurped his soup, considering the issue until both his bowl and cup were empty. "Perhaps she should kneel and pray throughout the night, to drive away these evil spirits and prove she won't be turned from God."

"I think if she went to bed early and said extra prayers, that would suffice," her mother said.

"Edith, you coddle the girl. It was you who allowed your brother to take her on this outing and now it's my duty to erase his wicked influence."

"Have some more soup, dear Abraham," she suggested, refilling his bowl.

While Abraham was distracted with his second bowl of soup, Jo tried to discretely slide the whisky bottle out of sight.

"Are you aiming to join your sister in her punishment, Jo?" he barked.

"No, Father. I meant no harm," she mumbled, dropping her hands to her lap.

Abraham uncorked his whisky bottle and poured another glass. He glared at his redheaded daughters, seated around the table. "And how about the rest of you? Lou, Max, Fred? Are your souls also in need of redemption?"

Maxine began to cry. Louise wrapped a comforting arm around her younger sister. Abraham shook his head in disgust and turned his attention back to Bobbi.

"On your knees, wretch," he slurred. "Admit to your sins and pray for forgiveness."

Bobbi knelt as directed, her bare knees against the hard wood floor. "Our father, who art in Heaven, hallowed be thy name..."

Abraham stared holes through her, while Bobbi repeated the Lord's Prayer over and over. Edith shuttled the rest of the children to the safety of their bedroom and returned to hover nearby.

Bobbi's voice started to crack with exhaustion. She watched with growing apprehension, as her father took several long swigs directly from the whisky bottle. Then he stood, picked up his Bible, and removed the leather whipping strap from the nail by the door.

"No, Abraham," Edith pleaded. "Roberta is a good and repentant girl. The minister told me that he believes her to be one of God's favorite children."

"And she'll stay that way as long as I don't spare the rod," he snarled. But before he could take aim at Bobbi's small back, he swayed, obviously too drunk to remain standing. He staggered to a chair near the fire and dropped into it with a heavy thud, his eyes half-closed. The strap slipped from his grasp, but he still clutched his Bible.

Edith sat on the floor by his chair and began to chant the Lord's Prayer. She signaled for Bobbi to move quietly to the table, where a bowl of soup waited for her. Abraham began to mumble the prayer under his breath, his head nodding against his chest until his words gave way to snores.

Lily was gawking at Abraham and Edith, when Bobbi's small voice startled her. "This was the last time I ever told anyone that I could see invisible people, but it wasn't the last time I saw Margaret."

"You can see me now?" Lily asked, incredulous.

The instant she spoke, Lily fell backward through the mist and woke with a start, back in her bed at the Belleview Biltmore.

"What the hell is happening to me?" she asked under her breath. She closed her eyes, hoping to return to her dream and get some answers, but instead, Dylan's face appeared.

This time, her son was wearing a white lab-coat and black-framed glasses. He also had large breasts. "Mom," he said, in the Midwestern voice of a young woman, "Your Post Traumatic Stress Disorder is probably responsible for the increase in the number of weird dreams you're experiencing. Research suggests emotional stress can trigger PTSD episodes even among people who received proper treatment after the initial onset of the disorder, which you never did. You should seek the help of a therapist when you get back home. Until then, you really need to relax. Maybe Dad can help."

"Stop it!" Lily wailed. "You're not real!"

She forced her eyes to open, vanquishing the illusion into oblivion. As much as she hated to admit it, transgender poltergeist Dylan was right about one thing. She could really use one of Scott's bear hugs right about now. She settled for placing a 'comfort food' room service order and calling Scott on her cell.

"Grams isn't going to get better," she told him.

"I was afraid of that."

"She – has – less than – two weeks," Lily said, choking on the words.

"Do you want me there with you?" he asked.

"No, I'm fine by myself. I'll call you if there's a change," she said, echoing the doctor's promise.

"That's our problem," Scott answered, sounding uncharacteristically aloof. "You're always fine by yourself and I'm not." He blew out a deep breath. "Listen, Lily – I can't keep living like this – waiting for you to forgive me and come home. If we're going to work things out, you need to accept that I did the right thing for Dylan."

"The right thing?" Lily retorted. "Letting them kill our son was the right thing for him?"

"I didn't *let* them kill Dylan," he hissed. "You need to stop saying that."

"I don't want to talk about this tonight." She closed her eyes. "And nobody's forcing you to wait for me to come home, either."

"Look, you're upset about Grams, so I'm going to hang up before we both say things we're going to regret. Good night, Lily. I love you." Scott hung up without waiting for her reply.

Lily flung her cell phone onto the bed and stared at it. Almost immediately, her anger shifted into self-loathing. *What's wrong with me? Why can't I stop pushing him away? He's going to find someone new, Grams is going to die and I'll be all alone for the rest of my life. God damn it – I wish it was me who died in that damned accident.* She curled up in a fetal position around the phone and sobbed.

Lily was engulfed by the fog without realizing she had cried herself to sleep. Too exhausted to resist its pull, she allowed the mist to carry her away, as if she were a feather floating on the breeze.

The booming voice belonged to Clay – the man Bobbi had called 'Long-Gone.' As the clouds parted, Lily saw him pacing the floor of her hotel room parlor. Margaret sat at the round table, next to the grown-up version of Bobbi.

"Any fool can see she needs a lot more than a peaceful resolution with her Granny," he snarled.

"You're right, Clay," Margaret chimed in. "But her situation is complicated. And I don't know what to make of her odd visions."

"You both know what we need to do to help her," Bobbi said, her voice barely audible.

Clay stopped pacing and gazed down at Bobbi. "Are you sure you can handle going through all that again?"

"I don't think we have a choice," she replied in the same, soft voice.

"Perhaps I could help resolve her issues with her grandmother, while the two of you work on the rest," Margaret suggested.

"I'm not a broken vase that needs fixing," Lily muttered. "Can't you all just leave me alone?"

A knock on her hotel room door brought an immediate end to the discussion. As fast as if she were flipping on a light switch, Lily fell through the mist and landed in her bed.

Wiping her tears, she hobbled to the door and let the room service waiter in. He carried the tray to her table and lifted the metal cover to reveal a large portion of shrimp fettuccini and garlic toast. Lily's stomach growled despite her lack of appetite. She gave the waiter a polite smile, signed his delivery ticket and closed the door behind him. Then she attacked her plate, for no other reason than to force all other thoughts from her mind.

When she finished eating, Lily changed into a nightgown, closed the drapes, climbed into bed and pulled the thick, down comforter up around her chin.

When the fog settled over her, she didn't resist. She needed answers.

Chapter Eleven

When the mist parted, Lily found herself seated at her parlor table with Margaret. Without a word, Lily stood and crossed the room to the short hallway that led to her bedroom.

"Aha!" she said, pointing at her bed. "See? There I am – still asleep. This is only one of my weird dreams, just like I said it was."

"This is not a dream," Margaret countered. "While your physical body sleeps, your consciousness visits those in the spirit realm with whom you have formed a connection. We're sharing some of our memories to help you."

"How is watching memories of an abused child supposed to help me?" Lily challenged.

"Situations have a habit of repeating themselves over time. Perhaps witnessing one story can change another story's ending."

"That makes no sense," Lily protested.

"Try listening more and talking less for a while," Margaret suggested.

Lily opened her mouth to issue another protest, but thought better of the idea. She settled back into her chair.

Margaret gave her an approving nod. "I can tell you that Bobbi was an exceptional child. Her open mind, gentle heart and intelligence drew people and spirits to her, as if sunlight radiated from within her soul. Unfortunately, Abraham, her father, believed God burdened him with raising six beautiful temptresses as a punishment for his having strayed as a youth. Over time, whisky began to influence his decisions more than the Bible, and his mission to raise virtuous daughters became a twisted obsession. All the girls suffered countless beatings for mostly imaginary transgressions, but Abraham never broke Bobbi's spirit."

The fog swallowed Lily with no warning. She focused on the sound of Bobbi's voice, coming from somewhere in the mist.

"To avoid becoming the target of my father's wrath, I spoke very little, worked vigorously, and almost always kept my wicked red hair wound tight and covered under a bandana."

Blurry images appeared along the edges of the mist. As they came into focus, Lily realized the pictures were flashes of Bobbi's childhood – her memories of the events she was describing – working in the fields with a bandana tied around her head, help-ing her mother, and hiding from her father. Lily was fascinated, even though she still believed this was just a dream.

"My hard work didn't go unnoticed," Bobbi's voice continued. "When I was fourteen, our minister recommended me for a posi-tion with old Doc Farthing, a member of our congregation who had been recently widowed. Father approved, as long as I turned over all of the wages I earned. I cleaned Doc's home, fetched his meals from the hotel and served as his nurse."

Pictures flashed by of the elderly doctor and the large East Gate Victorian Cottage, just inside the Belleview Hotel property, where he lived and worked. He had a thin face, hooked nose, large ears, unruly gray hair and wore spectacles over deep-set brown eyes.

"Doc Farthing wasn't much to look at," Bobbi said, "but his heart was made of pure gold. My daily chores were considerably lighter than what I had been accustomed to – especially when the hotel was closed for the summer. Most afternoons, Doc Farthing took a long nap and he insisted I take that time to enjoy myself. This was my first delicious taste of freedom."

Peaceful images flashed by of Bobbi strolling through the empty hotel grounds, sitting on the long pier, sketching the scen-ery, and sitting in a rocking chair on the porch, reading.

"When the hotel opened for the winter season, the Doc and I

were kept busy, as workers were often distressed by cuts and burns, and guests at the hotel suffered all sorts of maladies."

Finally, the clouds rolled away, taking the vignettes with them. Lily took deep breaths to quell her motion-sickness, while observing the scene before her. She knew she was inside the hotel, but couldn't pinpoint the exact location. Then she realized why. Bobbi and Doc Farthing were standing next to the stairs that led down to St. Andrew's Pub. In the present, this part of the hotel served as the Lobby Lounge, but in Bobbi's memories, it was the actual hotel lobby.

A bright flash of light caught Lily's attention and she turned, just in time to see a couple dressed in wedding attire descend the last few steps of the box-spiral staircase. A photographer pulled his head out from beneath the drape that covered the back of his camera and tripod. Both the groom and photographer sported stylish handlebar moustaches. The bride carried a small bouquet of colorful flowers and wore a long, loose-fitting white dress, overlaid with lace slipover. Her short, jet-black hair was covered with lace cap and long veil. The groom's black suit featured wide-legged pants, a long-tailed jacket, white bow tie and a top hat.

Lily recalled watching a wedding party pose on those very stairs only a few days before. She returned her attention to Bobbi and the doctor, idly wondering how many such photographs had been taken over the years.

"Bobbi, my dear," the old gentleman said, "I'm going downstairs to toast Mr. DuPont on his daughter's marriage. I'll come find you shortly."

"Certainly, Dr. Farthing," Bobbi replied. "I'll tend to your things." She took his black medical bag and watched as he descended the stairs to the gentleman's pub. Then she turned and walked down the busy Promenade, unnoticed by the wealthy guests. She stepped into a small, ornate lobby outside the entrance to the magnificent Starlight Ballroom, hoping to listen to the orchestra. Next to a grand fireplace that covered most of one wall, she noticed a small, partially open door. Curious, she peeked inside. To her amazement, a short staircase led down into a narrow room, where several children about her own age were lined up, learning to dance. Fascinated, she stood at the door until the instructor noticed her standing there.

"Come in, child. The lesson is just beginning. I'm Miss Abigail."

Bobbi's first instinct was to run. After all, how many times had her father warned her that dancing came from the Devil and led straight to sins of the flesh? But Miss Abigail's smile was warm and inviting and she didn't look one bit like the Devil. Bobbi set the doctor's bag on the landing and gingerly made her way down to join the other children learning the new dance craze, called *The Tango*.

The moment the music started, Bobbi's body began to sway. It was as though she were born to dance. Miss Abigail was amazed at how easily she mastered the intricate dance steps. Several times, she encouraged the other children to "watch how Bobbi moves to the rhythm."

Suddenly, Dr. Farthing appeared on the landing at the top of the stairs. Bobbi was too frightened to even breathe. She left the dancefloor at once, hoping no one would notice her creeping away. Just as she bent to snatch up the doctor's medical bag, Miss Abigail called out, "Doctor, your granddaughter dances wonderfully! Please bring her back for another lesson next Saturday evening."

Doc Farthing tipped his hat without correcting Miss Abigail. Bobbi flushed and rushed past him, too terrified to speak. She remained silent as they stopped at the kitchen for a teakettle of hot water, then exited the Belleview Hotel and walked back to East Gate cottage.

One thought occupied Bobbi's mind. *"What will Father do to me when the doc tells him he caught me dancing?"*

She rushed into the house to put Doc Farthing's bedtime toddy together – hot tea with a splash of whisky and honey – and then carried it to the doctor, who was enjoying his evening pipe on the front porch.

Whenever they worked late, the doc arranged for the hotel carriage to take Bobbi home from his house, but the driver had not yet arrived. Bobbi stared at her sinful feet, wishing she could undo the last few hours of her life.

"What's bothering you, child?" Doc Farthing finally asked. "Are you upset that we left the hotel before you finished your dance lesson?"

Bobbi felt her knees turn to jelly. "I didn't tell that woman I was your granddaughter," she blurted. "And I promise to work harder and never dance another step in my whole life, if only you will *please* not tell my father." She burst into tears.

The doctor stood and put his arms around her. "Oh, sweet girl. You did nothing wrong. Nothing." He patted her back as her body racked with sobs. "My wife and I had but one child. Alton was born to us late in life and he doesn't seem intent on marrying anytime soon, so I enjoyed pretending I had a lovely granddaughter. And if you don't want anyone to know about your dance lesson, it will be our secret."

Bobbi hiccupped, regaining control of her emotions. "But I *sinned*," she lamented. "Father says all sins must be punished."

"Fiddle faddle," he said. "I don't usually interfere with a man's family, but I'm not blind to your father's harsh discipline. You and your sisters attend church more often with black eyes than without, and I'll not contribute to a further injustice. Dancing is not a sin and you'll not be judged as though it were, if I have anything to say about it. Why, if I had more grace and energy, I would dance every night! Now, dry your tears, child." He handed Bobbi his handkerchief.

"Oh, thank you, Doc!" Bobbie cried, throwing her arms around the old gentleman and kissing his cheeks.

"Shush now," he said with a chuckle. "I see the driver coming up the boulevard and he'll be wondering what mischief we've been up to."

When the fog rolled in, gently lifting Lily from the scene, the voice of Bobbi's older self began talking to her again.

"Not only did Doc Farthing keep my secret, he insisted I continue taking Saturday dance lessons in the children's room at the Belleview Hotel. With Miss Abigail's help, I was ready to join the adults in the Starlight Ballroom after only a few weeks."

When the fog lifted at last, Lily saw young Bobbi, standing with Doc Farthing on the dancefloor, waiting nervously for the orchestra to begin to play.

"My first *real* waltz," Bobbi whispered.

Lily gazed up at the twenty-foot high ceilings of the Starlight Ballroom, noting how different the room looked all in white rather than its current burgundy décor. She was surprised to see large windows flanking both sides of the room and arched French doors opening onto a wide balcony, as these no longer existed. Before she had time to decide which room design she preferred, the music commenced.

Bobbi held her breath and stiffened as Doc Farthing took her hand. Her heart was pounding. *"What if I forget the steps?"* she worried.

Lily felt Bobbi's fears melt away almost instantly; replaced by exhilaration. Held in Doc's confident embrace, she began to glide around the dancefloor as gracefully as though she had wings. Lily was sorry when the mist gathered around her, carrying her away from this memory.

Bobbi's voice floated through the clouds. "By the end of that first waltz, I knew in my heart that Doc Farthing was right. Dancing wasn't a sin. It was one of God's joyful gifts to His children."

Lily smiled as more images appeared at the edge of the mist.

"That was a fine winter," Bobbi continued. "Doc Farthing bought me a proper gown and dancing shoes, and he let me keep them at his house, so father wouldn't find them. Then, once or twice a week, he allowed me to steal away and go dancing for an hour or two."

Lily smiled as images of Bobbi streamed by. Though still in her mid-teens, she looked more grown-up with her hair piled on top of her head, wearing a bright red dress and high-heeled shoes.

"Alton Farthing was attending medical training in Connecticut, but one night he arrived home for a visit, just after I had changed into my dancing clothes."

An image of a thin young man appeared at the edge of the mist. Right away, Lily recognized him as Doc Farthing's only child.

Unfortunately for Alton, he had his father's hooked nose, large ears and deep-set brown eyes.

"I was pleased to finally meet Alton, but I didn't want to miss an opportunity to dance, so instead of staying to chat, I rushed off to the Belleview. I had no idea that decision would change my life forever."

Chapter Twelve

When the fog dissipated, Lily was floating next to Bobbi as she skipped up the dirt path to the rickety porch of her home. An hour earlier, Bobbi watched in amazement as Mrs. Dillard's newborn son took his first breath. She burst through the front door, still flushed with excitement and beaming with pride over the fact that Doc trusted her to bathe and swaddle the infant.

Her father attacked her the moment she stepped over the threshold, slapping her face so hard, the force of it sent her reeling.

Lily almost screamed. She felt Bobbi's pain and confusion as Bobbi crumpled to the floor, stars dancing before her eyes. Abraham kicked the door closed and glowered at her, his face contorted with rage.

"Father, please! she begged. "Tell me what I've done wrong!"

"The Reverend talked with a man who did some work at the Belleview last week," he snarled.

This fact meant absolutely nothing to Bobbi. Terrified, she cowered as her father staggered closer, his bloodshot eyes radiating disgust.

"The man told the Reverend he saw my girl dancing there!" Abraham roared. "He said she was a real beauty in her red dress!" He snatched the bandana off Bobbi's head, grabbed a fistful of her long auburn hair and dragged her across the small room.

"You wicked harlot!" he screamed. "I'm gonna put an end to your seductive looks once and for all! Pray for God's mercy on your evil soul!"

Abraham grabbed his hunting knife from the mantle and swung it at her face. Adrenaline surged through Bobbi, the instinct for survival overriding her terror. She yanked her head back just in time. The knife missed her cheek, but slashed through the large swath of hair clutched in her father's fist. The miss cost him his grip on her.

Bobbi leapt to her feet, suddenly defiant and furious. Ignoring the throbbing pain in her face and the hank of hair on the floor at her feet, she glared at her father, trying to appear taller than her five feet, two inches. "How dare you?" she shouted. "The Reverend tells you some man saw a girl dancing at the Belleview, and then, without even asking me about the matter, or making sure the man wasn't talking about some other redheaded girl, you come at me with a knife? I am your daughter! And for months, I've been working every day – bringing home money to help support *your* family!"

The unprecedented outburst stunned Abraham into momentary silence.

"*You* should ask God to have mercy on *your* soul!" Bobbi spat. The bedroom she shared with her sisters was only two steps away. She ran in and slammed the door.

Breathing hard and shaking, she closed her eyes. Her knees went weak. She slid to the floor, waiting for her father to force his way in and kill her for her sinful behavior. Bobbi's thoughts raced back to the week before – the evening Alton Farthing arrived home just as she was on her way to the Belleview. *"If only I hadn't gone dancing that night..."*

If she was ever caught in the act of dancing, Bobbi planned to lie and pretend that she was someone else. She never anticipated someone would tell her father without first confronting her.

Seconds ticked by, turning into minutes. Finally, Bobbi started to hope. Maybe she wouldn't die tonight. She opened her eyes and found her sisters staring at her with a mix of fear, astonishment and admiration.

"I think you're safe until morning," Jo murmured. "Mother told me that on their wedding day, father swore an oath before God that he would never set foot in another lady's bedchamber. I doubt he'd break an oath, no matter how furious he is."

Still trembling, Bobbi moved to the small dressing table and picked up a tarnished mirror to examine her ruined hair and the angry crimson welt on her face.

"There's no hope for it," Jo said tenderly. "I'll have to cut the rest of it off."

Bobbi agreed, but when Jo started cutting what remained of her wavy auburn tresses, she gulped back tears and squeezed her eyes shut.

When Jo finished, she stepped back. "Oh, my," she said, admiring her handiwork.

Bobbi opened her eyes to discover the last vestiges of her girlish looks had fallen away with her locks. Reflected back from the depths of the mirror was the face of a beautiful young woman with fashionably bobbed hair.

Still smiling, Jo joined her sisters in bed, but Bobbi continued to stare at her reflection. Exhausted, she finally laid her head on the table and dozed off.

At dawn, her mother woke her. "Hurry, Bobbi," she whispered. "Run away before he wakes!"

"Please don't send me away," Bobbi pleaded.

Her mother dropped her gaze to the floor. "God and Doc Farthing will keep you safe."

As Edith reached for the doorknob, she and Bobbi gasped in unison. Abraham's hacking cough announced that he was waiting on the other side of the door.

"Just as well," Bobbi said with a tight-lipped smile. "He'd have punished all of you for helping me." She gave her mother a hug and cast a loving glance at her sleeping sisters. Then she took a deep breath, lifted her head high and emerged from the bedroom to face her father, come what may.

Even in his hung-over state, Abraham could tell Bobbi had undergone a metamorphosis during the night. Her short red curls licked at the edges of her face as though they were flames, and her green eyes sparked with defiance. Wayward curls at the back of her scalp inadvertently resembled two small horns.

A shadow of fear crossed his unshaven face. Holding his Bible out for protection, Abraham backed across the room and yanked the front door open. "Daughter of Satan!" he hissed. "Leave this righteous home and never return!"

Bobbi didn't understand what had come over him, but marched to the door, eager to obey his last command. "God will be my judge," she said. "Not you." She stepped into the dawn and didn't look back.

"Yes!" Lily cried, falling through the fog. A moment later, she woke in her hotel bed, recalling the horrible day just before her fifth birthday, when her mother left her on Grams' front porch. It wasn't abandonment. She could see that now. Her mother was protecting her from Roy's abuse. *"Hmmm,"* she mused, *"I wonder if that's the lesson Bobbi wanted to teach me."*

Energized, she showered and got dressed, then glanced at the clock. Nine thirty. She smiled, thinking about how much she had enjoyed breakfast with Seth the day before. With no history or future expectations, they had been free to relax and appreciate one another's company. Then her thoughts shifted to Scott. Feeling guilty, she decided to call and patch things up with him.

Lily was a little disappointed when Scott answered his phone. Leaving a message would have been easier.

"Any change with Grams?" Scott asked, in place of a greeting.

"No." She took a breath. "Listen, Scott, I'm sorry about our last conversation. I don't want to fight with you."

"It's okay. Forget it." His clipped tone seemed to indicate the opposite was true. "Listen – someone from Grams' nursing home left a message at the house yesterday. Apparently, they know about her prognosis. They want to know if we would rather pick up her things before next Saturday or pay for an additional month. What do you want to do?"

The question caught Lily off-guard. "It seems wrong to pack up her belongings before she's gone."

"I know, but you could take a few of her favorite things to the hospital. It might make her room feel a little homier."

Lily had to admit it was a good idea. "Let me think about it, okay?"

"Okay. And while you're thinking about packing stuff up, I have something else I want you to consider. You were only supposed to rent that apartment of yours for a few months, but you've been there almost a year now, and living in our house by myself is depressing. It's pretty obvious that you don't want to live here anymore, so maybe it's time... I mean, no pressure or anything – but maybe it's time to think about listing it for sale."

Lily sucked in her breath. She knew it wasn't fair to ask Scott to remain in a house that was too painful for her to live in, but knowing that Dylan's bedroom still existed provided her a measure of comfort.

"I can't – talk about that right now," she stammered.

"I'm not asking you to. Like I said; no pressure. I just want you to start thinking about it."

Lily didn't answer. "I better get going," she said.

"Okay. I love you."

"Love you, too," Lily echoed as she hung up. "No pressure," she mumbled, saddened by thoughts of past and future losses, and her apparent inability to alter the course of events. Then the digital clock on the nightstand caught her eye and a smile crossed her lips. 9:50. "Well, I do have control over one thing," she said, slipping on her windbreaker. "I can show up for my breakfast date."

Chapter Thirteen

"You came back!" Seth exclaimed when she neared his table.

"How did you know it was me?" Lily asked. She hadn't yet worked up the nerve to say "Hello."

"You forget that blind people develop Spidey-senses. You smell like flowers and soap. It's pretty... just like you are, I'll bet."

"Hardly," Lily said, glancing in the direction of her scarred forearms. "Hyper-sense of smell, huh? Bet that comes in handy."

"Yeah, except when I'm close to a trash dumpster," Seth replied with a grin.

"I guess no superpower is without its down-side," Lily kidded.

She read the highlights of the breakfast menu to Seth and then they placed their orders. They both opted for omelets, but while Lily ordered egg whites, veggies and low-fat cheese in hers, Seth asked for bacon, sausage, ham, grilled onions and peppers, and extra cheddar cheese.

"How do you stay in such good shape, eating like that?" Lily asked.

"I'm not sure how I feel about you ogling me when I can't recip-rocate," Seth teased.

"I wasn't..." Lily coughed, embarrassed.

Seth gave her a disarming smile. "To answer your question," he said, growing serious, "when I went blind, I became afraid of the dark. Not like a little kid is afraid, because a kid knows they can always turn on a light, or just wait a few hours and morning will come. When you know that morning isn't coming, it's a whole new kind of scared. I also realized how much of my life was centered around activities that required sight – and how slowly time passes when you have nothing to do."

Seth cocked his head to the side as if attempting determine what she was thinking.

"So you started body building?" she enthused, encouraging him to continue.

Seth chuckled. "Not even close. I started doing push-ups and sit-ups because they helped pass the time. Then my doctor prescribed rehab at the hospital fitness center. That got me out of the house and talking to people again. And once I realized how many of them were a lot worse off than I was, I decided to quit feeling sorry for myself and get on with life." He grinned. "But enough about me. Tell me about you. Do you work?"

"I haven't gotten on with my life like you have," she confessed. "I moved to an apartment and hide there as much as I can."

Seth nodded, pressing his lips together. "There's no one-size-fits-all magic formula. You'll work stuff out. It just takes time."

"Maybe. But I still wish I died in the accident." Lily slapped her hand over her mouth. "I'm sorry," she stammered. "I don't know what possessed me to say that."

"No problem. I'm sorry I didn't realize you were still in such a bad place. So much for my heightened senses." He smiled. "Let me try to redeem myself. Most likely, the reason you opened up like that is because I can't see you. That makes you feel anonymous. But if you did it because you were hoping to push me away, it didn't work. I like complicated people."

Lily decided to sidestep Seth's uncomfortably accurate theory by changing the subject. "Speaking of heightened senses," she said, "have you sensed anything unusual at this hotel?"

"Like what?" he asked.

Lily cringed, realizing Seth's blindness did make it easier to speak her mind. "I mean, can you sense if this hotel is haunted?"

There it was again. Seth tilted his head, trying to figure out what she *wasn't* saying.

"I don't think heightened senses work like that," he said. "But no, I haven't sensed anything unusual about the hotel, other than it feels kind of ancient – and I mean that in a good way."

"Maybe I'm just crazy."

"Maybe it's just easier to sense things when you already believe in them. For instance, I believe in fate. Because I do, it's easy for me to believe I was destined to meet you. Now, depending on what you believe, that either makes me crazy or enlightened."

"I'll have to think about that," she said.

Seth nodded. "Okay, I'll tell you what. Let's change the subject. Tell me something unusual about yourself. Quick now. Don't take time to think about your answer."

Lily's first impulse was to say, "*I dream about my dead son inhabiting other people's bodies*," but instead, she opted for, "I write a blog about dying."

"No shit." Seth knitted his eyebrows, his voice suddenly thick with concern. "Are you dying?"

"No. Not me," she explained. "I provide information of interest to people with terminal illnesses."

"Like what?" Seth asked, his curiosity piqued.

"The kind of services nobody advertises."

Seth made an exaggerated grimace. "Yuck. I'm almost afraid to ask."

"My blog's called *Way To Go*. I list and rate companies that provide end-of-life services, like those that furnish live-in companions, or provide legal guardians for pets." She paused. "I also post information about countries where suicide and assisted suicide are legal – and for people who embrace the morbid and want to hear their own eulogies, I provide ideas for hosting a 'Living Wake' and 'Mock Funeral.'"

"I see," Seth deadpanned. "Now that you explain it, it doesn't sound creepy at all." He stretched his lips back over clenched teeth, pretending to be horrified.

"Okay, it's your turn, smarty pants. Tell me something unusual about yourself."

"Well, I'm a wannabe writer. Actually, I started writing a book just before I lost my sight. I'm continuing to collect entries for it and hope to get it finished as soon I can see again."

"What's it about?"

"It will be what they call a coffee-table book, filled with pictures of amazing motorcycles and dumb warnings."

"Dumb warnings?"

"Yeah. You see, when I bought my first Harley, people were constantly telling me, 'those things are dangerous.' I thought that was a dumb warning. I mean, it's obvious motorcycles are dangerous. That's part of the thrill of riding one. Then one morning, I noticed a warning on my hairdryer that said it was dangerous to use it in the bathtub, and a few minutes later, the warning on my pack of cigarettes happened to catch my eye. It got me thinking about all the dumb warnings that are out there, and poof! The idea for my book materialized. I'm calling it *Motorcycles are Dangerous and other Dumb Warnings.* Each page will feature a picture of a spectacular motorcycle, along with a dumb warning."

"Can you find enough dumb warnings to fill a book?"

"More than enough. For instance, did you know most frozen TV dinner packages warn you that the food will be hot after you cook it? And you know those silver sunshields people use to keep their car cool when they park outside in the summer? Well, they have warnings, reminding people to remove them before driving their car!"

Lily laughed. "Really? Well, I think your book sounds great. I'd love to see it."

Seth grinned. "Thanks. You know you have a great laugh. You should do it more often."

Lily stopped; suddenly self-conscious.

"Oh, no!" Seth said. "I spoiled the moment."

"No, you just made me think... that's all," Lily said. "It's been a while since I've been able to enjoy a person's company so much."

The waiter brought the check and Lily charged it to her room over Seth's protests.

"I'm enjoying our breakfasts together," Lily explained, "and I'll feel guilty if I keep letting you pay."

Seth nodded. "Okay, then – tomorrow it's my turn."

Lily stood and picked up her crutch while Seth unfolded his cane. She thought he was going to shake her hand, but instead, he touched the side of her head, and then slid his fingers down her face, lifting her chin. Before she had time to react, he kissed her lightly on the lips.

Chapter Fourteen

Lily jerked back in surprise. "Um – see you – tomorrow, then" she stammered, trying to sound casual.

Seth smiled, showing no trace of discomfort. "Great! I'm looking forward to it already."

Lily turned and limped toward the lobby as quickly as she could manage. She was outside the hotel before she realized she hadn't called for the shuttle. A parking attendant ushered her to one of the white, wrought-iron benches by the covered drive, to await its arrival.

She sat and closed her eyes, still tasting Seth's kiss and feeling the echo of his tantalizing touch. *"Good grief, get a grip on your libido!"* she lectured herself, idly twisting her wedding ring on her finger. *"A blind guy gave you a peck on the lips. No need to make a federal case out of it."* She played the scene over in her mind, trying to convince herself of Seth's innocent intent. It wasn't working.

"Shuttle, miss?"

Lily's eyes flew open and she blushed; thankful the valet couldn't read her mind. "Thanks," she said, clambering into the shuttle. She glanced at the unfamiliar driver. "Morton Plant Hospital – main entrance, please," she said.

He nodded at her and then returned his attention to a baseball game on the radio. Lily was relieved he didn't feel the need to make small talk. Other than a groan when the opposing team scored, he drove to the hospital in silence.

Lily considered the implications of this morning's conversation with Scott as she disembarked and hobbled to her grandmother's room. Once there, she decided to follow Nurse Opal's example, and talk to Grams as though she were conscious.

"Hello, Grams," she said. She studied Lois Bloom's peaceful, unresponsive face, wishing she hadn't squandered so many opportunities to ask for her advice. "You know, Grams, I always thought Scott and I were perfect for one another, but I'm just not sure anymore," she confessed. "He wants me to come home, but I don't know if I can. I mean, I'm still so angry with him for giving up on Dylan – and he still doesn't think he did anything wrong." She sighed. "Maybe it's time for us to go our separate ways."

She pressed her lips together, stunned by her own words.

"God, Grams, if only we could go back in time and change what happened that night..." She shook her head. "But we can't."

Lily gave the old woman's hand a squeeze and then eased into the chair under the window. She watched the sunlight dance across the Intracoastal Waterway in the distance and began to daydream about Seth. Running her hands through his spiky, blond hair as he leaned in for another tender kiss, she wondered what color his eyes were. She lifted his dark, round glasses, but to her amazement, it was Scott's mahogany brown eyes that looked back at her. And when she glanced up, she found her fingers were now entangled in Scott's mop of wavy black hair.

Confused, Lily opened her eyes, only to discover she was adrift in the fog of the spirit realm. A moment later she heard Bobbi's strained voice from outside the mist.

"It's Henry – Mr. Plant's young son..." she shouted. "He's had an awful bicycle accident!"

The clouds cleared to reveal Bobbi, racing across the grassy expanse between the hotel and the bicycle track, carrying a teakettle and a large basket. Despite the distracting motion sickness, Lily marveled that she had no trouble keeping up with Bobbi's youthful strides. She studied the girl as they ran. Clearly, Bobbi was still a teenager. But her short, red hair was now covered with a nurse's cap. Her white dress and pinafore, emblazoned with a red cross, gave her an air of maturity.

When Bobbi reached the track, a small group of onlookers parted to let her through. The sight of the two crumpled bicycles turned Lily's stomach, but Bobbi knelt at Doc Farthing's side without flinching. She pulled a small basin from the basket, filled it with steaming water from the teakettle and handed it to the doctor.

Lily could only muster the courage to cast furtive glances at the wreck and poor Henry. She guessed the boy was about sixteen years old. His face was contorted with pain and he cried out when the doctor touched his leg, which was still entangled in the twisted wheel of his bicycle and clearly, the location of his most serious injuries.

The doctor poured some of the hot water over Henry's leg to get a better look and the boy howled, writhing in pain. His upper thigh was sliced open, perhaps cut by sharp metal, and two bicycle spokes pierced through his calf.

The doc signaled Bobbi, who nodded and applied a few drops of liquid to a folded towel. When the doc held the towel under Henry's nose, he immediately relaxed into sleep. Then Bobbi handed Doc Farthing a pair of heavy surgical shears, which he used to cut the spokes from the bicycle. As soon as Henry was separated from the wreck, some of the men helped move him onto a canvas stretcher. The doc pressed a towel to Henry's thigh as four men lifted the stretcher and marched toward the Belleview Hotel.

Lily looked up just in time to see Morton Plant kick the offending bicycles. "This is the last time someone will be hurt on this damned track," he bellowed at a group of workers. "Tear down the grandstand and plow the track under. Do it now!" Then he turned his back on the site and rushed to catch up to his son, just as the fog returned and whisked Lily away from the scene.

Almost immediately, the clouds parted again. Lily felt as though she had been spun through a revolving door, but tried to make sense of the scene before her.

Young Henry, still asleep, lay on a wooden table in the small dining room next to the kitchen. Bobbi tended to his minor cuts and scratches, while the doctor and Morton discussed treatment options.

"I'm not a surgeon," Doc Farthing reminded Morton. "But Henry might not survive the six-hour ride to the hospital in Tampa. I've slowed his bleeding, but..." He shook his head, the gravity of the situation clearly etched on his face. "I'll ring Tampa and arrange for a surgeon to come here to operate – but you should brace yourself – Henry might lose his leg."

Morton Plant made his decision in an instant. "Don't call Tampa; just do what you can to keep Henry comfortable. I'll send for my personal surgeon and a medical railcar."

He hurried away to place a call to New York.

"Doc, do you think a surgeon can save Henry's leg?" Bobbi asked.

"I don't know, but with our help, he'll stand a better chance," the doctor replied. "I have to take that tourniquet off, so we'll have to control Henry's bleeding by applying pressure. If he wakes, we'll give him laudanum for the pain." He glanced at the pile of blood-soaked rags on the table. "Take these away and fetch some clean ones. And have the kitchen bring me a pan of boiling water. It's going to be a long night, Bobbi."

Bobbi collected the bloodied towels and dashed through the servant's door, into the kitchen. After ordering the water, she descended a steep, narrow staircase to the basement, with Lily floating next to her. Bobbi ran through the labyrinth of tunnels that crisscrossed the underbelly of the hotel, following the sounds of washing machines to the huge laundry. There, fifteen women were busy cleaning and pressing linens of all description. She exchanged the bloodied towels for fresh ones and then raced back through the tunnels and up the stairs.

As she was about to reenter the dining room, Bobbi spotted Morton Plant leaning against the wall. He was holding an unlit pipe in his mouth, watching her.

"I'm glad you're here, Bobbi," he said. "You've always brought me good luck." He chewed on his pipe for a moment. "How would you bet on this race? Will the surgeon get here in time to save my son's leg?"

Bobbi lifted her chin and met the tall man's eyes. "Mr. Plant," she said in a reassuring voice, "I would bet on Henry to make a full recovery."

He smiled, wanting to believe her. "You know, my wife, Nellie, is quite ill. It will cheer her to hear there's hope."

Bobbi nodded and pushed open the door to the dining room.

Doc Farthing ministered to Henry without a break for the next several hours. Finally, Bobbi convinced the exhausted doctor to allow her to spell him while he took a short nap.

"Wake me in one hour – sooner, if you need me," he told Bobbi as he settled into a rocking chair.

A few minutes later, sounds of the doctor's snoring filled the room. Lily moved closer to Bobbi, watching as the young nurse applied pressure to Henry's wound.

Lily had to muffle a scream when Margaret Plant materialized right next to her.

Chapter Fifteen

"What has happened to my dear Thrice?" Margaret wailed.

Bobbi was also startled by Margaret's sudden appearance, but she recovered more quickly than Lily. "You mean Henry? He got hurt on the track – in a cycling race," she whispered. "Mr. Plant sent for a surgeon. He's expected to arrive by rail in the morning."

"Poor boy," Margaret fussed. "What idiot allowed a child to wander onto a race track?"

"He's nearly seventeen years old," Bobbi replied, keeping her voice low.

"Don't be ridiculous," Margaret blustered. "My grandson is still a boy."

"We met long ago, Mrs. Plant. Don't you remember?" Bobbi asked. "I'm the girl who told you that you're a ghost."

"Of course I remember your absurd assertions. You made them only a moment ago," Margaret said.

"No, I didn't," Bobbi persisted. "Look how much Henry has grown. Four years have passed since that afternoon."

Margaret ignored Bobbi's comments. "Perhaps God, in his mercy, is sending angels into my dreams to forewarn me so I can keep Thrice safe from harm."

"I used to think ghosts were angels," Bobbi muttered, "but this is the first time *I've* ever been mistaken for one." She laid a fresh towel over Henry's wound and pressed firmly to slow the flow of blood. Henry moaned and stirred slightly, but didn't wake. "Tell me, why do you call Henry *Thrice*? I've heard no one else call him by that name."

Margaret gazed at Henry with affection. "My husband, Henry, gave him that pet name because he was the third to bear the name 'Henry Plant.' Thrice brought us so much joy during the last years of Henry's life. I suppose Morton and Nellie have stopped using that nickname now that Henry is gone, but the precious lad will always be *Thrice* to me."

Suddenly Doc Farthing snorted in his sleep, drawing Margaret's attention back to the dining room. "You know, my Henry always said that a beautiful view and the warm sea air were the best medicines a man could ask for. That's why he named our hotel the Belle-*view* and our town Belle-*air*." But situations like this require real medicine. She frowned, her eyes still riveted on the doctor. "I know Morton houses the doctor in East Gate Cottage in exchange for his tending to Nellie and the hotel guests, but Belleair is growing. It needs more than just one doctor. Unfortunately, Morton is too obsessed with his golf course to think much about such things."

"A local surgeon would be a godsend," Bobbi agreed.

Margaret clapped her hands. "So that's the purpose of this strange dream! God wants me to convince Morton to build a hospital."

"A ghost can't..." Bobbi sighed with exasperation. A moment later, she flashed an impish grin at Margaret. "If you were awake, how would you go about convincing someone to build a hospital?"

Margaret rubbed her chin, thinking. "I suppose I would start by promising Morton the hospital would bear his name."

"Is Mr. Plant a vain man?" Bobbi asked.

"It's not about vanity," Margaret said. "It's about fathers and sons. Morton has lived his entire life in Henry's shadow. To most people, Morton is known as the only surviving son of the great Henry Plant – the man whose railroad opened Florida to the masses. There's even a city named 'Plant,' in Henry's honor." Margaret cleared her throat. "So the thought of seeing his own name on a building might be just the thing to convince Morton to open his wallet. As soon as I wake, I'll make that suggestion."

With that, Margaret disappeared from sight.

Lily gasped, staring at the empty place where Margaret had been standing only a moment before.

Bobbi shook her head. "I've encountered several ghosts who didn't know they were dead at first, but Mrs. Plant is a truly stubborn case."

The familiar, haunting sound of a train whistle in the distance suddenly caught Bobbi's attention. "Wake up, Doc!" she cried. "The surgeon is coming!"

At the same moment, something bumped against Lily's leg brace. Puzzled, she turned to see what hit her.

It was as if she stepped off a cliff. She spiraled down through the fog, fighting to stay aloft by waving her arms. Suddenly, the fall ended as abruptly as it had begun.

Startled, Lily opened her eyes. A hospital orderly was cleaning the floor of Grams' room, unconcerned that his mop was bumping against Lily's chair.

"Sorry," he grumbled, noticing he had awakened her. He continued working, nodding his head to the time of whatever music was playing through his earphones, until he mopped his way out of the room.

Lily watched him leave and then hobbled over to Grams' bedside. "I hope your dreams are more pleasant than mine, Grams," she joked. She gazed at her grandmother's deathly pallor, a lump forming in her throat. "Please, God," she whispered, "let her stay with me just a little while longer." Finally, she kissed her grandmother's cheek. "I'll be back in the morning," she said, pulling out her cell phone to call the hotel shuttle.

When the van pulled away from the hospital, Lily stared up at the huge, lighted, blue letters on the front of the building: MORTON PLANT HOSPITAL. She recalled Nurse Opal saying that Morton Plant donated money to run the original hospital. *"Did Margaret Plant's ghost haunt him until he built the hospital?"* Lily wondered. *"Or am I sculpting my dreams to match known facts?"*

When Lily arrived back at the Belleview Biltmore, she limped down the Promenade to the restaurant, hoping to bump into

Seth. Her leg was throbbing again. Despite several surgeries, she knew her tibia wasn't healing properly. Her doctor insisted a long-bone transplant was the best course of action, but she refused the surgery.

She didn't spot Seth, so she ordered a hamburger and carried it back to her room. Once there, Lily took a heavy dose of ibuprofen – the strongest pain medication she was willing to swallow, and sat on her bed to elevate her aching leg. She took a few bites of the burger and relaxed as the fog returned.

Lily only had a moment to wonder who would fill her dreams before the mist lifted. She felt her stomach flip, as if an elevator had come to an abrupt stop, and then she was sitting at the parlor table with Margaret, Clay Long, and the grown-up version of Bobbi. The trio was in the midst of a heated discussion.

"Tell, me," Clay demanded, "how are your memories of the boy's bicycle accident supposed to help her?"

"If you'd just be patient, you'd find out," Bobbi countered.

"The two of you are making my head hurt," Margaret complained. "Bobbi, Clay has a point. It's a complex situation and we don't have much time. You two need to share your stories as quickly as you can. Meanwhile, I'll try tweening with her grandmother."

"You're going to try to do *what* with Grams?" Lily asked.

Margaret nodded at Bobbi without answering Lily's question.

Bobbi returned Margaret's nod and directed her attention to Lily. "After I left home, my mother and sisters suffered relentless abuse at my father's hands. In one of his violent rages, he disfigured my sister Jo and then forced her to marry a man who shared his belief that all beautiful women possess wicked souls." She shifted her gaze to her teacup. "Eight months later, on the same night that Doc Farthing and I struggled to save young Henry's leg, my father used his hunting knife to kill my mother and two of my precious sisters – Winifred and baby Henrietta. Then he set fire to our home. Maybe he'd planned to kill himself too, but lost his nerve. Witnesses said he tried to escape the wild flames, but just as he reached the door, the roof collapsed, pinning him inside.

They say he cried out for God's mercy – screaming and repenting for the murders as he slowly burned to death."

Lily gulped, remembering how it felt to be burned.

Bobbi paused a moment, pressing her lips into a thin, white line. "I hope God sent him straight to hell, to burn forever." She looked at Lily. "Thankfully, Lou and Max were spared. Mother had sent them to Jo's home, to help her prepare for the birth of her first child. But when Jo's husband heard what happened, he blamed me for causing Father's madness and turned my sisters against me."

Bobbi picked up her cup and sipped her tea. "Even though it was horrible to lose my sisters, my sole regret about leaving home was that I never told my mother how grateful I was for the sacrifices she made on my behalf and how much I loved her. It's a miserable feeling to part from a loved one with such important things left unsaid."

"That's exactly how I feel about Grams," Lily said. "I don't want her to die before I set things right." She turned to Margaret. "Can you help me talk to her?"

"We'll try," Margaret replied as the fog engulfed Lily. "But be quiet now. Watch, listen and learn."

Chapter Sixteen

When the mist finally parted, Lily had no idea where she was. She fought the sensation of dizziness with deep breaths and closed eyes as she floated to a chair in a summer garden. Nearby, Margaret and young Henry sat together on a bench.

"I've missed you so much Grandmother," Henry said. "They told me you died."

"Nonsense, Thrice," Margaret replied. "You must have been dreaming. I know what that's like. I've had a few strange dreams myself recently."

"But isn't this Heaven?" Henry asked, pointing his finger downward.

When Lily looked where he was pointing, the grass disappeared beneath her feet. Far below, she saw Henry, lying unconscious on the dining room table, where he had been carried after his racing accident. The area around his thigh was drenched in blood. A man in a white coat was talking to Doc Farthing and Bobbi, while four other men lifted Henry's pale form onto a litter.

"Thank you for your offer, doctor," the man said. "But you've done your part. My operating room in the railcar has everything I'll need, including surgical assistants." He turned his back on the elderly doctor. "All right, lads – quickly now – let's save this boy's leg, shall we?"

When Lily turned back to Margaret and Henry, Henry was gone.

"This is all so strange," Margaret said as she faded out of sight.

Lily gave herself up to the fog, completely confused. She had so many questions; she didn't know where to begin. When the clouds cleared this time, she was alone with Margaret at the parlor table.

Margaret poured two cups of tea and slid one across the table. "I call it *tweening*," she preempted.

"Tweening?"

"Yes," Margaret said. "At the time, I didn't believe I was a spirit and I couldn't understand how Henry could exist in two places at once. But eventually, I realized that this had been my first experience with tweening. I have come to understand the phenomenon much better since that time." Margaret smiled. "You see, as a person's body prepares to transition from your realm, its spirit will try to float free of its body. But it can't. As long as the body is alive, it acts as a tether, holding onto its spirit. But that tether doesn't stop the spirit from peeking into the next realm and talking with other spirits."

"So you and I are tweening?" Lily asked.

Margaret scoffed. "No, no... we are connecting. Spirits don't just leave their bodies willy-nilly. Forming a connection is something altogether different. Tweening is simply a conversation between two spirits, one of whom is still tethered to a body that is teetering between life and death." Margaret took a small sip of her steaming tea and wrinkled her nose. She stirred three teaspoons of sugar to her cup and sipped it again. "That's better," she said.

"And when the body dies, the tether breaks?"

"Yes, and then the lighted path appears. But sometimes the person doesn't die after all. In those cases, the spirit returns to the confines of its body, as it did in Henry's case. Occasionally, people remember some of their experience in the spirit realm, but most of the time they don't."

Lily considered this. "Where does the lighted path lead?"

"That's a question not even I can answer," Margaret said. "I can tell you that most newly-freed spirits travel the lighted path willingly, content to take the next step in their eternal journey. But not all do. Some spirits remain in this realm for a short time; others for a long while – some accept their new reality quickly, and others refuse to acknowledge it for years." She smiled and shook her head. "It took me *ten years* to finally accept that I am a spirit, but I suppose I've always possessed a stubborn streak."

"You said you were going to try tweening with Grams," Lily said, remembering the earlier conversation.

"Yes. Tweening is a form of entertainment in the spirit realm and, as you can imagine, a hospital is quite a popular place for this activity. But in this instance, I believe tweening might serve a useful purpose. It may help us repair your relationship with your grandmother before she transitions."

"You mean, before she dies?"

"Only the body dies – your grandmother's memories will live on as she transitions into her spirit form and takes the next step on her eternal journey."

Lily toyed with her teacup while she considered Margaret's explanation. She was surprised to find she could feel the fine porcelain against her fingers. She picked up the cup and took a sip. She tasted the hot, bitter liquid moving down her throat. But she also knew, beyond the shadow of a doubt, that her body was asleep in the next room.

"I don't care whether I'm dreaming or talking to ghosts," she told herself. *"If I can use this tweening to tell Grams how sorry I am, I'm going to embrace it like it's made of chocolate."*

"How do we get started?" Lily bit her lower lip. "I mean, how close to death do I need to be before Grams' spirit can talk to me?"

Margaret widened her eyes. "You misunderstood my plan. I'm not even certain tweening would work between two tethered spirits. I plan to tween with your grandmother and discuss your concerns with her. Then I'll connect with you while you sleep, and show you my memory of her response. If it works, you'll be at peace when she transitions."

Lily rubbed her forehead. *"Great. Just what I need. Another level of crazy in my elevator. A ghost offering to convey messages to my comatose grandmother and report back to me in my dreams."*

"I'm a spirit, dear, not a ghost," Margaret interrupted.

Lily took a sharp breath. She hadn't said the word 'ghost' aloud. "I don't think I want you poking around in my head, checking out my memories."

Margaret chuckled. "Don't worry, your memories are yours alone – to share or keep private, as you choose. As I've already explained, it's difficult to form a connection with a living being – even when the spirit possesses *my* level of proficiency. And when connections form, we are able to share memories with the living, not the other way around. Now, if a person is dreaming just as a connection is made, the spirit can see the dream, and sometimes a spirit and a person can hear one another's thoughts while they are connected, but that's all. Tweening, on the other hand, is simply a conversation between a spirit and a tethered spirit. Memories can be discussed, but not shared."

Lily nodded.

"But you should be prepared." Margaret frowned. "Your grandmother may not respond as you hope."

"What do you mean?" Lily asked.

"It's just that your grandmother is more a part of the spirit realm than the living one right now, and things are different in our realm."

"Different how?"

"Well, the living tend to conceal thoughts and actions that would reflect poorly on themselves, or hurt someone's feelings. But a tethered spirit doesn't feel bound by social convention. While tweening, your grandmother will share her true feelings, with no regard for yours. That's one of the primary reasons tweening is considered such fine entertainment in our realm."

Lily considered this. The idea that Grams wouldn't lie to Margaret was oddly comforting. "Okay, what do you need to know?" she asked.

"If I am to try to mend this relationship, I must first learn what damaged it – and quickly. Even I don't know when your grandmother's spirit will be set free. What drove a wedge between the two of you?"

Lily gulped. "I lived with Grams from the time I was five years old. She and my Gramps postponed a trip around the world to take care of me until my mom could come back for me. But Mom died and they got stuck raising me." Lily fiddled with her teacup, examining the delicate pink rose clusters in its design. "Gramps died before they could take that trip. They gave up their dreams to care for me."

"I doubt your grandmother blames you for becoming orphaned and spoiling her travel plans," Margaret said.

A fleeting smile crossed Lily's lips. "No, but even though she gave up so much for me, I turned my back on her when she needed me."

At that moment, Lily's cell phone rang, sending her crashing through the fog.

Chapter Seventeen

"Ms. Thorne?"

"Yes." Lily tried to focus, blinking in surprise at the daylight. She glanced at the nightstand. Eight o'clock. *"I slept twelve hours?"* She threw back the comforter. *"In my clothes?"* She spied the half-eaten hamburger lying next to her and groaned.

"This is Sue Phillips, at Bay Manor. We are so sorry about your grandmother."

"Thanks."

"I'm calling to let you know there's a waiting list here at the Manor, so you can save a full month's rent if you'll permit us to lease your grandmother's room immediately."

Still trying to wake up, Lily didn't respond.

"We could pack her possessions and arrange to have them shipped to you," the woman added.

"Yeah, I was planning to call you today," Lily lied. "That sounds like the logical thing to do, but I want to stop by and pick up a few of her things first."

"Could you come this morning?"

"I can be there within the hour," Lily replied. *"And if I hurry, I'll be back in time for breakfast with Seth."*

She showered, dressed in record time, and then called for a cab. When she reached the box spiral staircase near the hotel lobby, she heard Seth's unmistakable laughter. She scanned the vicinity until she spotted him, chatting with a blonde woman near the concierge.

80

They made a stunning couple...Mr. and Mrs. Gorgeous Blond America. Lily looked away and fought back a wave of jealousy as she limped past, toward the entrance.

"Lily?" Seth called out. "Is that you?"

She turned around with a smile plastered on her face, ready to feign surprise at the encounter and welcome an introduction to the living Barbie doll. To her surprise, Seth was walking toward her. Alone. The blonde woman tossed an annoyed glance in his direction and then turned her charms on the enraptured young man behind the concierge desk.

"Lily?" Seth repeated, stopping a few feet from her. "Are you there?"

"Yes," she said, finding her voice. "You just caught me off-guard, that's all. How did you know I was here? Your sense of smell can't be that good."

"I recognized the clicking sound of your crutch... some sounds are as distinctive as fingerprints. Are you headed to the hospital?" he asked.

"No. I'm going to a nursing home to collect a few of my Grams' keepsakes –I'll try to be back in time for breakfast."

"Want some company? I'm bored," he said.

She felt an involuntary spasm in her lower abdomen; the thrill of being asked to the prom by the quarterback right in front of the head cheerleader – a mix of butterflies and a surge of estrogen, with just a twinge of married-woman-guilt.

"Seriously?" she asked. "You heard where I'm headed, right?"

Seth smiled. "It's the company on the journey; not the destination. Lead the way." He extended his arm toward her.

Lily caught his hand and laid it on her upper arm, careful not to let him touch her scarred forearms, hidden beneath the windbreaker. She didn't even mind the valet's curious stare as they climbed into the cab. Seth picked her, and that was all that was important for the moment.

At Bay Manor, Nurse Vicki volunteered to escort them to Grams' room. Plump and graying, the woman radiated warmth like a furnace. "I love your grandmother," she chirped. "She talks about you and your family all the time! She sure is proud of that great-grandson of hers!"

The nurse smiled and bobbed her head in greeting each time they passed one of the residents. "Of course, why wouldn't she be proud?" she continued. "You must be bursting with pride, yourself. I mean, earning an early entry into medical school is no easy feat!"

Lily cringed and changed the subject. "You know, Seth here is writing a book that contains all kinds of silly safety warnings that manufacturers put on their products. I'll bet you've come across some doozies in your line of work. Can you think of any?"

"An author! How wonderful!" Vicki gushed, switching topics with ease. "Well, back in nursing school, I did a rotation with an anesthesiologist and I found it strange that the anesthesia came with a warning that it may cause drowsiness, since the whole purpose of anesthesia is to put patients to sleep. Is that the kind of warning you mean?"

Seth chuckled. "That's perfect! Would you mind repeating that?"

He pulled a small tape recorder from a pouch on his belt and she obliged. "Oh – and there's a warning on my curling iron that says it shouldn't be used for curling eyelashes... as if anyone would ever try to do that." She shook her head.

Seth laughed. "That's another great one – thanks!"

Vicki stopped at Grams' door and unlocked it. "We always lock rooms when guests are away," she explained. She pushed down on the oversized, silver handle to open the door and flipped on the light. The fluorescent bulbs in the roof-mounted fixture flickered a moment, and then lit the room with stark, white light.

Lily's hand flew to her mouth. Directly in front of her were the computer and monitor she sent to Grams three years ago. Still in the box, they were serving as a nightstand.

Vicki noticed her reaction. "We offered to set that computer up for Mrs. Bloom, but she wanted to keep it in the box. She didn't seem to have any desire to learn how to use it."

Lily smiled. "Yeah, Grams doesn't think much of modern technology. I once bought her an oscillating fan and she refused to use the remote control. She had me set the speed on 'Medium' and whenever she wanted to turn the fan off; she pulled the plug from the wall."

"That sounds about right," Vicki said, nodding.

"I had just as much luck when I tried to introduce her to a microwave oven," Lily continued, unable to look away from the computer. "I don't think the thing was ever used unless I was visiting."

Lily shook her head. She had planned to teach Grams how to use e-mail, but the accident changed everything.

Vicki pointed to a football-shaped phone sitting on the computer box. "We always teased her about owning both the most expensive bedside table and the oldest phone at Bay Manor. We provide our guests with cordless phones, but she insisted that her great-grandson could only talk to her on that one." Vicki smiled. "Well, I better get back to work. Do you want the door open or closed?"

"Closed would be nice," Lily said.

Seth tapped his cane to find the bed and sat down on its edge. "Okay, now – be my eyes," he said. "Tell me about each keepsake you're taking and why it makes the list."

Lily stared at the football phone. It had been Dylan's. He sent it to Grams for the spare bedroom that she always called 'his room.' That felt like a million years ago. She cleared her throat. "I didn't want to tell Vicki, but everything Grams said about my son... his being in medical school and calling her on the phone all the time... well, that was all lies." Tears welled in her eyes. "I guess she felt so alone here that she had to make up stuff about her loving relatives."

"Don't beat yourself up," Seth comforted. "Shit happens. We all neglect people we shouldn't. And everyone decides for themselves how to deal with loneliness. Those are just facts of life."

"And what would you know about loneliness?" Lily teased, trying to lighten the conversation.

Seth raised his eyebrows in surprise. "I get lonely."

"Right – I saw the way that blonde bombshell was practically throwing herself at you back at the hotel. I bet that happens all the time."

"Wait a minute... that girl was blonde? And beautiful? Damn! If I would have known that..." Seth grinned. "Just kidding. In case you haven't noticed, all women look pretty much the same to me."

"You may be blind, but you're not stupid," she chided. "You can tell when a beautiful woman is flirting with you."

"Yeah," he confessed. "Pretty women like to flirt with blind guys. I think they consider it a challenge to attract a man without using their looks or boobs."

"I hadn't thought of that," Lily admitted.

"Yeah, I've learned a lot about women since I lost my sight. For instance, I never knew women get a lot more out of the sensation of touch than men do. Guys are more visual. They tend to only pay attention to the parts of a woman they like best. Women like that I have to 'see' with my fingertips. Since I have to feel my way along, all of their parts get equal attention. I'm going to try not to forget that about women when I get my sight back."

Lily nodded, recalling the feel of Seth's hand on her face. "It probably feels great to touch a woman who has smooth skin..." She glanced at her arms. "but not tattooed skin... or scars... or whatever."

Seth frowned. "I'm blind, Lily, but I'm still a guy. I only use my sense of touch to create visual images in my mind. And personally, I find women with tattoos and scars more interesting."

"Why?" Lily asked.

"Well, bikers say that every tattoo contains a story. Ask anyone about their body art and they'll tell you all about how they selected each design and what it symbolizes. Their stories say a lot about what kind of people they are – how they see themselves and what's important in their lives. And a scar – well, that's just a tattoo with a different kind of story behind it. Usually the bigger the scar, the more interesting the story."

"Yeah, right." Lily laughed self-consciously. "Enough talk. Let's get on with the job we came here to do, shall we? I'm going to take some of Grams' framed photos." Lily limped to the bookshelf and sighed. "Wow. Most of these pictures are pretty old."

"Describe them for me," Seth prompted.

Lily picked one up and stared at it. She, Scott and Dylan were standing by Grams, who was seated behind a birthday cake covered with 85 lit candles. Scott had set the timer on the camera and run back to take his place at her side, but he accidentally put too much time on the delay and they all got the giggles watching the candles melt as they waited for camera to snap the picture. The camera flashed just after the fire alarm sounded, sending them into fits of laughter.

Lily bit her lower lip and thought about the concept of time. The minute they spent waiting for the camera to flash lasted so long, yet the entire wonderful year afterward evaporated in an instant. Then there was the accident. And nearly every minute of every day since then ticked by as if in slow motion.

"Lily?" Seth said, "Are you okay?"

Lily snapped out of her reverie. "Yeah," she said, setting the photograph aside. She picked up a different one. "I'm holding a photograph of me when I was thirteen. I'm skinny, I have braces and I'm wearing bangs and a florescent pink tee shirt that's three sizes too big for me. Man, what a looker!"

"I'll bet you were," he said. He cocked his head to the side. "I really would like to know what you look like, you know. Would you mind?"

"You want me to tell you what I look like?" Lily asked.

"It's a two-person job," he said. "Come over here and sit next to me."

Lily limped to the bed and sat. He placed his hands on her shoulders and she stiffened.

"Relax," he said. "I promise this won't hurt a bit." He slid his fingertips to the top of her head and gently probed her scalp, trying to determine the size and shape of her skull. Then he let his fingers glide over the top of her head softly, tracing the part down the side of her hair to her forehead. He smiled. "What color?"

"Red."

Seth nodded, as if he were coloring in the hair on the picture he was creating in his mind. His hands slid down her long hair, rubbing tresses between his fingertips. "Thick – long – soft," he murmured. "I'll bet it's shiny, too." He grasped a large lock of her hair in his fist and held it under his nose.

Mesmerized, Lily watched him drink in her aroma.

"Nice. Strawberry red or orange?" he asked.

"More like dark copper." She swallowed hard.

Seth nodded again, adjusting the picture in his head. He let go of her hair and used his fingertips to trace over her facial features. His touch was light and gentle. She closed her eyes, fighting the urge to rub her face against his hand; like a cat asking for a scratch behind its ears.

"Freckles?" he asked.

"Nope." She took a quivering breath.

He nodded again and began tracing the outline of her full lips; first with one fingertip; then with two.

Caving to temptation, Lily slid her tongue between her lips to taste his fingers, but Seth pulled back as if she had bitten him. She blushed – embarrassed for letting him know she was turned on by his touch – and stung by his rejection of her advances.

A moment later, Seth returned his fingertips her still-moist lips. Lily closed her eyes and caged her tongue behind gritted teeth, hoping he would think she had been joking.

His touch drifted down over her chin and then back up to her cheeks. He felt the shape of her closed eyes; her long lashes; her eyebrows; her cheekbones. "Eye color?" His voice was so low, it was almost a whisper.

"Blue"

"Shade?"

"Aqua"

"Aqua blue," he repeated, allowing his fingertips to circle her eyes once more.

The color sounded delicious the way he said it. Though still embarrassed, Lily opened her eyes and watched his impassive face as his fingertips slid over the bridge of her narrow nose, high cheek bones, and small ears.

Lily sighed. "*Maybe he doesn't know I wanted to kiss him.*"

As if to dispel that notion, Seth nestled his lips against her ear.

"You are absolutely gorgeous," he whispered. "But..."

There it was – the one word that rendered the compliment meaningless. Lily pulled away, finishing his sentence for him. "But you're not interested."

Seth drew back in surprise. "Of course I'm interested," he said. "Buuttt..." he paused and crossed his arms over his chest to emphasize that she had finished his sentence incorrectly. "You're going through some real bad shit right now and you're vulnerable. A few years ago, that might not have mattered to me, but I'm trying to be a better person these days. So let's just relax, get to know one another, and then see what happens, okay?"

Lily blinked back her tears, knowing he was right. Consumed by anger, frustration, guilt and loneliness, she was close to falling apart. When she sniffled, Seth wrapped his arms around her and pulled her close. Lily collapsed into his embrace, unable to keep the hot tears from sliding down her cheeks.

"You know, you see pretty well for a blind guy, but ..." her voice cracked, "I can't talk about it... not to anyone."

"Don't worry. You don't have to tell me anything until you're ready. For now, we'll just be buddies, okay?"

Lily nodded against his shoulder.

Nurse Vicki interrupted the intimate moment with a light knock as she opened the door. "I was just checking to see if you needed anything." Then she noticed Lily's tears. "Oh, poor thing – it's hard to pack away a loved one's belongings, isn't it?"

Lily didn't attempt to correct the misunderstanding. She pulled a tissue from the box on the computer-turned-nightstand. "I'm just taking a few things with me today," she said, trying to steady her voice. "I'd like the rest of her belongings to be shipped to my home... except the computer. Can I donate that to Bay Manor?"

Vicki clapped her hands together, "Oh, my goodness, yes! I think the computer equipment in our media room is almost as old as some of our guests. We'd love to have a new one." She paused. "Are you sure you want to donate such a valuable gift?"

Lily nodded. "I'll trade it for the shipping costs – and a small packing box, if you have one."

Vicki beamed. "I'll run and get you one right now."

As soon as she left, Lily gathered a modest pile of possessions onto the bed, including Grams' favorite afghan and jewelry. She described a few pictures to Seth as she stacked them on the bed, but not all of them. Then the football phone caught her eye.

"I'll take that, too," Lily thought. *"After all, if it brought Grams comfort when she was lonely, she might like to have it nearby when..."* She froze, allowing the thought to sink in. *"When she dies – which will be soon. Her condition is terminal. God, I've written dozens of blog posts about how to prepare for an imminent death, but I still almost forgot the golden rule – plan details ahead of time."* She took a deep breath and then removed Grams' favorite outfit from the closet – the one she saved for special occasions – her navy blue, linen suit with a light blue blouse and a matching pillbox hat. She laid it on the bed, just as Vicki returned with a cardboard box and bubble wrap.

"Vicki, does your gift shop sell food?" Seth asked. "We missed breakfast at the hotel."

"Not really," Vicki replied. "But I can escort you to the dining hall and treat you to a complimentary breakfast as thanks for your generosity."

"Thanks," Lily said, "but..."

"That would be great!" Seth interrupted. "I'd love a ham and cheddar cheese omelet and some bacon."

"Well, actually," Vicki confided, "we use egg substitutes, fat-free cheese and turkey bacon – but you can hardly tell the difference."

Seth's smile dropped like a rock, much to Lily's amusement.

"I'm sorry, Seth," she said, coughing to cover a giggle, "but we really need to get back. We don't have time to eat."

"No problem," Seth replied with an audible sigh of relief. "Thanks anyway, Vicki."

While Lily finished packing Grams' memorabilia, Vicki called for a cab and then insisted on carrying the box to the exit for them.

As the cab pulled out of the drive, Seth gave an exaggerated shudder. "Fake eggs, fake cheese and fake bacon? Should we report them for abusing the elderly?"

Lily laughed. "It's just a heart-healthy facility, but I agree – it didn't sound very good." She leaned forward. "Driver, please pull into the first restaurant we come to that has a drive-through. We're starving."

"It may be cliché," Seth said, grinning mischievously, "But the way to my heart is definitely through my stomach and I just fell in love with you a little bit!"

Chapter Eighteen

The cab stopped to drop Lily off at the hospital before taking Seth back to the hotel.

"Breakfast tomorrow?" Seth asked.

"Wouldn't miss it," she said, giving his hand a squeeze. She handed the cab driver cash for the fare, then hoisted the small box of Grams' memorabilia onto her hip and struggled to the hospital doors.

"This time," she told the lobby volunteer, "I'll take you up on your offer to give me a wheelchair escort."

Opal was checking Grams' vitals when they arrived. "What happened to you?" she asked, eyeing the wheelchair.

"If I tried to walk all the way up here carrying this box of Grams' stuff, I'd probably wind up being your next patient."

"Did you hear that Miz Bloom?" Opal cooed. "Lily brought some of your things. Maybe that'll warm this place up."

The ponytailed volunteer took the box from Lily's lap and placed it on the table. Lily thanked her for the lift and then hobbled over to kiss Grams' cheek.

"You look like you've had a good morning," Opal said.

Lily blushed. "I was at Bay Manor," she said. "The people there are very kind."

"Uh-huh." Opal's expression said she believed there was more to the story, but she didn't pry.

Flustered, Lily started unpacking Grams' memorabilia. Opal

asked questions about the photographs, including Grams in the conversation, as if she were looking at them, too.

"My, oh my, Miz Bloom – your husband was a fine looking man," she told Grams. "And look at Lily... why, her sweet face looks the same as when she was a little girl."

Lily lined-up the photos on the windowsill, along with the football phone. Then she opened the closet and hung up Grams' navy-blue suit.

"Lily picked out a beautiful outfit for you, Miz Bloom," Opal said with a nod of approval that told Lily she understood the outfit was for Grams' journey to the Pearly Gates.

Lily smiled, grateful for her compassion.

Opal winked and rolled her bulky equipment cart back into the hallway. "You have a good day, Lily."

Lily stashed the empty box in the closet, took three ibuprofens, settled into the chair under the window, and snuggled under Grams' afghan. As soon as she relaxed and closed her eyes, the foggy mist gathered, carrying her into the spirit realm.

When the clouds cleared a moment later, Lily was sitting in one of four high-backed wicker rocking chairs lining the wide front porch of East Gate Cottage, next to the Belleview Biltmore Hotel. Doc and Alton Farthing occupied two of the chairs and Bobbi sat in the other.

"Son," Doc Farthing lectured, "if you were here last month, you would have learned far more about being a surgeon than you could in a fancy school. And that surgeon who saved young Henry Plant's leg learned his trade as I did – standing at the elbow of an experienced doctor." He picked up his clay pipe and knocked the ashes out. "It goes to show that anything more than two years of college serves no purpose other than to line the pockets of doctors who would rather preach in a classroom than work for a living."

"But, Father, there have been countless advances in medicine since you first took up the calling," Alton countered. "In fact, many hospitals have begun to *insist* their doctors attend four full years of college. And the Medical Institution at Yale College offers the highest caliber instruction available. With such an education, I'll be able to run circles around the Plant boy's surgeon."

"Balderdash," Doc Farthing muttered. He patted his pockets, looking for matches.

Bobbi picked up the box the doctor had left on the table and struck a match. She cupped her hand around the flame and held it close to his pipe as he puffed his tobacco to life.

"Doc Farthing, it staggers the imagination to think how much Alton could learn from all those brilliant doctors." She blew out the match. "Consider what fantastic medical discoveries might be made if every doctor received so much education."

Lily studied Alton. He gazed at Bobbi as though she possessed angel's wings, but Bobbi appeared oblivious to his lovesick adoration.

"Hmph," Doc Farthing replied. "A fancy medical education isn't much use here, son. We're miles from the nearest hospital."

"Well, on that point, we can agree, Father," Alton said. "Modern doctors need a hospital and proper equipment to utilize their education. Hopefully, they'll build one nearby before I finish school."

This time, the fog rolled over Lily like a tsunami, tumbling her over and over as it carried her away. It vanished as quickly as it had appeared, leaving her standing dazed in an open field, next to Margaret and Bobbi.

"When I wake up, I'll talk to Morton," Margaret said, raising her parasol to block the sun. "This is the perfect location for a hospital – just a stone's throw from the hotel and suitable for people living in Belleair as well as Clear Water Harbor."

"It's just called Clearwater these days," Bobbi replied. "And as I've told you a hundred times, you can't talk to Morton. You are a ghost."

"A specter with full use of its mental faculties?" Margaret scoffed. "That's preposterous."

"Never mind." Bobbi sighed. "I agree we need a hospital. Doc Farthing's son says educated doctors insist on having one nearby." She narrowed her eyes. "Margaret, can I help you convince Mr. Plant to finance one?"

Margaret smiled. "Well, Doc Farthing has become quite fond of you..."

"He's been like a grandfather to me... especially since..." Her voice trailed off; the memory of the fire still too raw to put into words.

"Then perhaps he would be willing to speak with Morton," Margaret suggested.

"Alton might be more convincing," Bobbi replied. "He's visiting next week."

The mist swirled around Lily again, tumbling her into a different scene just an instant later. She sank down on a high-backed, red velvet couch next to Bobbi and Alton Farthing, her head spinning with temporary motion sickness. Morton Plant sat in a wicker chair opposite the couch, smoking a cigar.

Looking around, Lily recognized the Belleview Hotel. She knew this section of the hotel had been the lobby for many decades, and when they eventually built a new entrance, they converted this area into the 'Lobby Lounge.' But it was one thing to know a piece of hotel trivia and quite another to experience it.

Guests clustered in small groups throughout the large space; ladies outfitted in long dresses and men clad in three-piece suits. Several people were gathered around a pianist, singing along with his rendition of "It's a Long Way to Tipperary," while workers scurried about, serving drinks.

"My dear fellow, you know I have the greatest respect for you and your father," Morton said, drawing Lily's attention back to the conversation. "And nothing would please me more than to have a hospital close at hand. But why, pray tell, would you expect me to finance such an undertaking? I am but one man, and I reside in Belleair for less than half of the year. Shouldn't you solicit local businessmen to support your cause?"

Alton Farthing gulped, unable to formulate a response to Morton's logical argument.

Bobbi watched with horror as the determination of her champion crumbled.

"I can tell you why," she blurted.

Both men turned to Bobbi, startled by her outburst.

"Mr. Plant," she continued, "the town is in sore need of a hospital, as you discovered yourself when young Henry was seriously injured a few years ago. And we're asking you to finance the endeavor because you possess five times the wealth of the entire town put together."

Morton considered Bobbi, a poker expression concealing his thoughts; his cigar frozen in place, several inches shy of his lips. Finally, he took a long puff of his cigar, but still said nothing. Bobbi held her breath and bit her lower lip as the silence mounted. Just as she was about to apologize for her blunt assessment of his finances, Morton spoke.

"Young lady, when you were just a child, I told your Uncle Emmitt you would be a handful when you grew up. It appears my prediction was correct." His tone was stern, but there was an amused glint in his eyes. "So I propose we make a wager, just as your Uncle Emmitt and I used to do, God rest his soul."

Bobbi sat forward on her seat and nodded, completely taken with the idea.

"All right, Bobbi," Morton challenged, "If you can raise twenty thousand dollars before the Belleview Hotel closes for the season, I'll provide an endowment for the hospital equal to five times that amount. But if you fail to raise the building capital, then you'll serve as my wife's private nurse for one full year."

"I accept the wager," Bobbi said without a moment's hesitation.

Alton jumped to his feet. "Thank you, sir, for a most generous offer, but I'm sure you realize the young lady has bitten off more than she can chew without comprehending the onerous consequences of her actions. Please disregard her impetuous behavior and let's reconsider the matter."

Without responding to Alton's plea, Lily extended her hand and Morton shook it, sealing their bet.

Then Morton turned to Alton. "Son, I think that if you're attempting to control Miss Roberta Johnson here, then it is you who has bitten off more than you can chew. Now, if you will excuse me, I promised to join some of my fellows for a friendly card game this evening." He saluted each of them with a perfunctory bow of his head and then turned to descend the basement stairs to St. Andrew's parlor.

Alton turned to Bobbi, wringing his hands. "Oh, Bobbi – what have you done?"

Chapter Nineteen

"How in the world do you propose to raise twenty thousand dollars in two and a half months?" Alton fretted. "I return to Yale next week, so I can't help you."

"Alton, dear," Bobbi replied, "Don't be a wet blanket. I don't know how I'm going to raise the lettuce just yet, but I'm certain I'll succeed. And just think how wonderful it will be to have a hospital nearby when you return!"

The clouds engulfed Lily, lifting her from the memory more gently this time. She relaxed, enjoying the peaceful floating sensation. *"How in the world will you pull this off, Bobbi?"* she wondered.

When the mist finally cleared, she was with Margaret and Bobbi, walking through an open meadow. Barely nauseous, Lily fell in step with the ladies.

"Margaret, if you wished to coax people into contributing substantial amounts of money for a worthy project, such as building a new hospital, how would you go about it?" Bobbi asked.

"That's easy," Margaret replied. "I would secure hefty donations from a few gentlemen who possess only modest financial holdings and make sure the news of their generosity spread far and wide. Wealthy men in the community would soon be stampeding to my door to demonstrate how much more charitable they could afford to be than their less prosperous acquaintances."

"But how would you persuade men of modest means to donate large sums in the first place?" Bobbi asked.

"Well, before I married Henry, my business provided services to several gentlemen in town – helping conceal evidence of numerous – shall we say – indiscretions. I'd meet with a few of those men, and if they didn't immediately offer sizable donations, I would encourage them to do so, by explaining how their generosity would engender an act of goodwill from me. In exchange for supporting my cause, I would give them the page from my accountant's journal, wherein the unfortunate incident was recorded – thus ensuring the misdeed would remain forever hidden from public scrutiny."

"Blackmail?"

"Such a nasty word, that," Margaret said. "I prefer to think of it as a mutually beneficial transaction."

"Where's your accountant's journal?" Bobbi asked.

"It doesn't exist, but that's not important. I would simply pen the details of the incident into an old journal and present the page in exchange for a donation."

Bobbi smiled. "Do tell, Margaret – which gentlemen you would solicit for donations?"

Margaret frowned, thinking. "The first man I would call upon would be Mathew Cummings. When he was a young man, he beat a prostitute nearly to death. In truth, Hannah survived the ordeal and became my accountant and dear friend, but he doesn't know that. He believes he killed her and that I arranged her funeral. Cummings still possesses a small part of the great fortune his father left him. Because he hopes to marry his equally wretched son into a prominent family, he'll pay a tidy sum to keep his name untarnished. Next, I would pay a visit to..."

Bobbi withdrew a paper and pencil from her drawstring bag and scribbled down notes, as the fog swept Lily away once again. She chuckled, hoping to watch Bobbi solicit donations from a few of the men on Margaret's list, but when the clouds finally parted, the ribbon-cutting ceremony for the finished hospital was taking place.

Morton Plant and several other distinguished-looking gentlemen stood in a semi-circle behind a podium, where a rotund man in a brown wool suit was speaking to a large crowd, gathered on the front lawn of the hospital. Bobbi stood off to the side, along with Doc Farthing, Alton, and a dozen less well-dressed men.

"Now, I can't think of a better way to begin the year 1916, or my term as Mayor of Clearwater, than to recognize the fine group of citizens standing behind me. Each of these gentlemen volunteered to reach deep into his purse, to help build the first hospital in northern Pinellas County – with twenty beds, five bassinets and an operating room!" The rotund man used his forefinger to brush the ends of his dark mustache off of his upper lip, waiting for the crowd's polite applause to subside. "And now, without further ado, please join me in welcoming to the podium, the primary benefactor of the hospital that will bear his name – Mr. Morton Plant!"

The audience clapped with genuine appreciation as Morton stepped forward.

"Thank you, Mayor Thomas, for those kind words." Morton turned to face the crowd. "Some of you may know that my son, Henry, was severely injured in an accident a few years ago. Fortunately, I was able to transport a surgeon and medical equipment to Belleair by train to care for him." He paused for a moment. "Although Henry recovered fully, that near-tragedy made me keenly aware of the need for a hospital in this growing community."

Morton glanced around the crowd; his eyes resting on Bobbi long enough to give her a quick wink. "I issued a challenge to the citizens of this fine community. If they could raise the twenty thousand dollars necessary to build the hospital before the end of the Belleview's winter season, then I would establish an endowment for its operation equal to five times that amount. Well, the gentlemen and lady standing before you answered my challenge, so I am proud to honor my promise and humbled that the hospital will bear my name."

"That's one way to explain the wager," Lily supposed. *"But it's a shame Bobbi received so little recognition for her hard work."*

The crowd cheered as Morton left the podium and joined the mayor at the door of the hospital to cut the ceremonial ribbon.

Before the ribbon hit the ground, the fog descended, pulling Lily from the scene.

This time, she woke up. She shifted in her chair as a recorded announcement played over the hospital speaker system; *'Visiting hours are now over.'* Lily shivered. It was always chilly in this room, but tonight it felt colder than ever before. Although visiting hours didn't apply in the ICU, she stood and covered her grandmother's frail body with the afghan.

"There now, Grams," she said. "I'll bet your favorite afghan will make you feel better. Maybe having your pictures here will help, too... and that silly phone." She scrutinized the old woman's facial features. "What are you dreaming about, Grams? I need to know that you're okay... that we're okay. Please."

She waited another minute and then kissed her forehead. "Alright, then. Goodnight, Grams. I'll be back tomorrow."

Lily sat on a bench outside the main entrance to the hospital, waiting for the shuttle, along with a few other guests of the hotel. She thought about the enormous size of the Morton Plant Hospital campus, and wondered if her dreams were true – that in 1916, local residents gathered right here to celebrate the opening of the hospital. *"Why am I having these hallucinations?"* she wondered. *"Is it because I believe Dylan would have lived if he had gotten medical attention sooner, like young Henry Plant did?"*

Just then, the hotel's shuttle pulled into the U-shaped drive. Lily limped to the van, dismissing the troubling thought. Pete, her favorite driver, opened the back door for the other guests and then helped Lily into the passenger seat. "Still no change?" he asked.

Lily shook her head.

"Well, maybe tomorrow," he said.

Lily smiled to acknowledge his kindness.

When they arrived at the hotel, she considered looking for Seth, but her leg was throbbing too much. She limped to her room and ordered room service. Before her food arrived, Scott called. Lily told him about her trip to Bay Manor, leaving out the part about Seth accompanying her.

"I'm so sorry you had to go through that alone," he said.

Lily flushed. "I didn't mind."

There was a long pause before Scott spoke. "Maybe it doesn't bother you, but I hate being alone. Are you still having the nightmares?" he asked.

Scott knew Lily woke up several times every night – often screaming from nightmares about the accident, or trembling from strange dreams, wherein Dylan morphed into various parodies of himself.

"Sometimes," she said. She didn't tell him about her recent dreams, for fear he would think she had completely lost her grip on reality.

"How's your leg? Have you given any thought to the surgery?"

Lily's physical recovery had stalled, yet she continually declined cosmetic surgery to lessen the scars on her arms and absolutely refused to discuss a bone transplant for her leg.

"It's fine," she lied.

Scott sighed, letting her know he didn't believe her. "You know I love you, Lily. I want you to come home. If you keep putting that off, I'm afraid we'll drift so far apart, we'll never be able to fix things between us."

Lily closed her eyes and pressed her lips together. A year ago, Scott suggested counseling, but she asked for a few months of separation instead. He had indulged her, but distance hadn't helped. She couldn't forgive him for allowing Dylan to die. The thought of moving back into what had once been their happy home, repulsed her.

Scott interrupted her musings. "If you have to take this long to think about your answer, I guess we've already drifted too far apart to fix things," he said. He let out a long breath. "When it's time, I'll fly down to Florida to help with Grams' memorial service and after we get back to St. Louis, we can file paperwork – to make it official." His voice cracked. "Goodnight, Lilyanna," he said. He hung up.

Lily gulped down the lump forming in her throat. Scott had never ended a phone call without telling her he loved her. Not when he was busy. Not when he was distracted. Not when he was in the middle of a business meeting. Not even when he was angry.

Not until now.

Chapter Twenty

"Love you, too," Lily whispered into the dead phone. She stared unseeing at her cell until room service knocked on her door.

She took a few bites from the large bowl of chicken and vegetable soup, then pushed it aside and curled up under the thick comforter, feeling miserable and alone. Tears rolled down her cheeks unchecked and when sleep finally overtook her, the old nightmare returned with a vengeance.

It always started with Lily staring through the windshield, struggling to see through the thick blanket of fog covering the already dark road. She tried to make sense of the thunderous crashing noises just outside of the car, desperate to steer the car out of danger, but not knowing which direction led to safety.

Time moved in slow motion. In one instant, Scott was asleep next to her. In the next, he was gone, along with the passenger-side door. A log, the size of a tall tree, slammed into the car. Followed by another. And another. Like murderous rain, giant logs hit the pavement, some ricocheting directly at the car with the force of battering rams.

"What the..." Lily's mind raced, seeking but not finding a logical explanation.

The car launched over some of the debris, momentarily taking flight until gravity pulled it back from the sky. It landed on two wheels and rolled onto its passengers' side, skidding down a steep embankment, bouncing off trees and boulders as it went. The airbag exploded. The headlights went out. The car smashed into a massive boulder and came to a halt. The engine died. Lily's head dropped to her shoulder as the inky night enveloped the car.

In the distance, she heard Dylan calling, "Wake up, Mom!"

She couldn't see in the dark and wanted more than anything to sleep a little while longer. Suddenly, a thin flame began to glow just behind the front seat, illuminating the car's interior. Dazed, she breathed a sigh of relief. *"That's better,"* she thought; grateful for the light. She glanced at the empty passenger seat. *"Where did Scott go?"* She shifted her gaze to the back seat and saw Dylan, still in his seatbelt and shoulder harness, his head resting against the ground where the window should have been. She smiled. He was such a sound sleeper – and bigger than all the other kids in his grade, even though he had celebrated his thirteenth birthday only a week ago.

The narrow ribbon of fire caught her attention. It was coming from a crack in the floorboard and it was growing. All at once, her mind cleared, the peaceful cushion of shock giving way to horror.

"Wake up, Dylan!" she screamed. He didn't move. "Dylan! We had an accident! Wake up! Scott! Somebody help us!"

There was no answer.

Lily tried to open her door, but with gravity working against her, the door was too heavy to push upward. She unfastened her seatbelt. As she fell toward the passenger side of the car, she felt the first real surge of pain and screamed. Her right leg was caught in the twisted wreckage.

"Dylan, wake up!" she cried again.

He didn't stir.

The rope of fire intensified. Hotter. Bigger flames. Her mind shrieked, *"Get out of here – now!"* Her adrenalin surged, giving her the strength to curl her body against gravity and use both of her hands to pull away pieces of what had been her car's interior until she finally freed her crushed leg. She lifted the useless limb over the console, and stood on her good leg.

There was no time to dwell on the odd sensation of standing on the ground where the passenger door should have been. She pushed against the driver's side door, trying to open it like a hatch above her head, but it wouldn't budge. Frantic, she reached her hands through the broken windshield and peeled back the shattered safety glass. Ignoring her excruciating pain, she pulled herself through the opening and fell to the ground.

She had to free Dylan from the fiery wreckage. That single thought kept her moving. It made the horrendous pain bearable.

By the time she reached the driver's side of the car and wrenched open the back door, the rope of fire had become a solid, six-inch wide column of blue flames between her and Dylan.

"Dylan!" she cried. "Please wake up! We have to get out of here!"

He didn't move.

"Oh my God," she thought, *"He passed out!"* All at once, she knew what she had to do.

She steeled herself and reached through the column of fire, searching frantically for the seat belt release button. She fought the instinct to yank her forearms out of the flames – to put an end to the agonizing torture. She smelled her flesh burning, but the flames hadn't yet reached Dylan, so she willed herself to keep going. Finally, the seat belt released. She shoved the harness over his head, grabbed his shirt with both fists and with a Herculean effort, threw herself backward out of the car, pulling his limp body with her.

As they fell to the ground, Lily's head hit a rock and her world went black once more.

Chapter Twenty One

The nightmare usually continued, but tonight was different. The acrid smoke of the wreckage disappeared; replaced in an instant by the puffy white clouds of the spirit realm. She relaxed, drifting free from pain and without a care in the world, wishing she could stay in this peaceful cocoon forever.

Then she became aware of a conversation just beyond the fog. As Lily strained to listen, the mist began to thin. She floated into a chair at the round table in her parlor. She felt a bit dizzy, as though she had just stepped off a merry-go-round, but the sensation was a far cry better than the cold sweats and night terrors that normally followed her nightmare.

"There, there, darlin' girl, it was just a bad dream," Margaret cooed. She poured a steaming cup of tea for Lily and slid it across the table. "You'll be right as rain in no time at all."

Lily's eyes widened with surprise. Bobbi and Clay sat next to Margaret, watching her with expressions filled with compassion. Neither spoke.

"All of you watched my nightmare?" Lily asked, slightly embarrassed.

"Yes. We tried, but we couldn't pull you out of it," Margaret said. "Your ability to focus your subconscious is remarkable. I think it's an inherited trait, which helps me understand how your grandmother can refuse to listen to me while she's tweening with that blasted Sharon woman."

Lily shook her head, trying to clear it. "What? Who's Sharon?"

"Sharon is a spirit who apparently traveled the world from hither to yon," Margaret replied, her tone icy, "and has a story about *every single* whistle stop along the way. Your grandmother is fascinated with her silly anecdotes. She keeps shushing me whenever I try to get a word in edge-wise, but don't worry, I'll keep trying." She rubbed her hands together. "Meanwhile, your nightmare made us realize why our connection is so strong... and why Bobbi and Clay must tell you their whole story." She nodded to Bobbi, relinquishing the floor.

Bobbi cleared her throat. "As the second decade of the new century came to a close, life changed in Belleair. Morton Plant caught a fever and died in 1919, God rest his soul, and immediately afterward, his wife... that is, his second wife – Maisy – sold the grand hotel to John McEntee Bowman. He added the Belleview to his collection of hotels and renamed it the Belleview *Biltmore*. I'm not sure I'll ever get used to that name!" Bobbi shook her head. "And there were many other changes, too... the Great War ended, women got the right to vote, and prohibitionists convinced Congress to ban alcohol." She paused, thinking back. "And I suppose I was changing, too."

Lily relaxed into the fog once again, allowing it to carry her like a twig floating in a brook until lively chatter and jazz music began filtering through the clouds.

When the fog dissipated, Lily surveyed her surroundings. She knew this was the small lounge at the entrance to the Candlelight Ballroom, but the usually quiet room had been transformed into a crowded, smoke-filled speakeasy. She, Bobbi, and a mousy-looking woman were seated at a minuscule table near the door.

While waiting for her light-headedness to pass, Lily studied Bobbi, who had blossomed into an exquisite woman. Her red hair, still cut in a wavy bob, was encircled by a black headband with a small feather decoration at the center of her forehead. She wore a sleeveless, knee-length, royal blue shift with a scooped neckline, and a long string of pearl beads hung around her neck. Smoke wafted from a straw-length cigarette holder resting between her fingers and a short glass of amber-colored liquor sat on the table in front of her.

"You're a doll, Bobbi," the woman remarked, scanning the crowd. "Why, you could have your pick of beaus."

"Horse feathers," Bobbi replied, turning her gaze in the direction of the bar, where a tall, broad-shouldered man was unloading liquor from a wooden crate for the bartender's inspection. Clearly, he was a working man, but his face was clean-shaven and his clothes were neat and well-fit. His thick, sandy-blond hair dipped in an unruly wave over his forehead, enhancing his wide smile, and the sleeves of his white shirt were rolled up, exposing tanned, muscular forearms. His brown wool pants were held up by suspenders and his boots were scuffed, but Bobbi thought he was far more attractive than any of the finely dressed men in the room.

"He'll be out of work soon, now that Prohibition is the law," Bobbi commented, without taking her eyes off the man. "Lawmen in some parts of the country are already destroying every bit of liquor they can lay their hands on."

The woman shot a glance at the bar. "I think our sheriff has the right idea – let people drink up the existing stockpile. If you give folks time to get used to not having liquor, there'll be less trouble when it's gone."

Bobbi lifted her glass and rocked the golden liquid back and forth. "You know, May, liquor never tempted me until it became illegal."

"Me neither. Think it's the lure of forbidden fruit?" May asked.

"Yeah." Bobbi nodded. "I'm sure we'll forget all about liquor once it's gone, but for now, I plan to enjoy the way it makes me feel."

Lily wanted to tell Bobbi that Prohibition wouldn't turn out as she anticipated, but remembering Margaret's warning that a memory would dissolve instantly if she spoke, she remained silent.

Bobbi returned her gaze to the man at the bar. "I do believe that is the most handsome man I have ever laid eyes on," she said.

May smiled. "Who cares about a rag-a-muffin when the place is chock-full of swells?"

"Yeah, but he's the real McCoy," Bobbi said. "I can tell."

Having completed their business transaction, the bartender served the man a beer and they eased into congenial conversation.

May spied a thin man across the dancefloor waving his handkerchief, trying to catch Bobbi's attention. "Looks like someone's carrying a torch for you," she teased.

The man's black hair was parted down the middle. A liberal application of hair oil glued two tight curls against his pale forehead and the ends of his handlebar moustache were waxed to form two additional curls. He began snaking his way through the crowd toward Bobbi.

"That's George Applegate," Bobbi said. "I offer him absolutely no encouragement, but I'm afraid he's pursuing me, none-the-less."

"He looks pretty keen to me."

Bobbi closed her eyes and took a deep breath. Lily could sense her revulsion at the thought of spending time with George. It was as if Bobbi were speaking out loud, even though she wasn't.

When Bobbi's eyes reopened, they were sparkling with mischief. "He's all yours, May." She stood, balancing on high heels, and made her way to the bar, the alcohol relaxing her inhibitions.

Lily enjoyed the sensation of floating along beside Bobbi, invisible and pain-free, as she took a spot at the bar, close to the stranger, whose back was turned to her.

The burly bartender, Frankie Muldoon, smiled when he noticed Bobbi approaching. "Your usual?" he asked, flipping a bar towel across his shoulder.

Bobbi gave him her best smile and nodded. He placed a short glass of sweet iced tea in front of her, spiked with half a shot of sipping whisky.

"Thank-ie, Frankie. You're a real champ." Bobbi smiled. She reached into her drawstring bag for a dime.

"This one's on the house, Bobbi," Frankie smiled. "Beauties like you keep the men drinking – trying to work up the courage to ask you for a dance."

Bobbi nodded and smiled again. When Frankie rejoined his previous conversation, the stranger turned enough that Bobbi could see his profile. She listened as they talked about whisky sales... how much was left in storage and how it wasn't the government's business to decide how a man should relax after a hard day's work.

Bobbi appraised the stranger out of the corner of her eye. Even under close scrutiny, he took her breath away.

"Are ya ready for another frothy, Bear?" Frankie asked.

Bobbi raised her eyebrows. "Bear?" she repeated, making sure her voice was loud enough that the man would hear her. "Why, he doesn't look like a bear at all!"

The stranger turned toward her; a slow, sexy grin spreading across his face, revealing straight white teeth. "Well, hello there." He tipped an imaginary hat at Bobbi. "Bear is short for a long, snooty name that doesn't suit a fella like me."

Lily felt Bobbi's excitement, as Bear pulled himself to his full height of over six feet.

"We haven't been properly introduced," he said, extending his hand. "Let's fix that. I'm Barrett Nathaniel Hamilton... Bear to my friends and beautiful redheads."

Bobbi smiled, silently evaluating his approach *"Not too cocky and extremely likeable."* She accepted his handshake. "Roberta Johnson... Bobbi to those who know me."

His touch was electric. She didn't want to let go of his hand. "Pleased to make your acquaintance," she murmured.

Just then, George Applegate pushed between Bobbi and Bear, in a blatant attempt to divide the two. Without acknowledging Bear, he leered at Bobbi.

"Didn't you see me trying to hail you, Bobbi?" he asked. "You should have waited for me. You know I like to buy your drinks." He extended his arm. "Come on – if we get a wiggle on, we can make it to the dancefloor before they start the next number."

Bobbi took a step back to put some distance between herself and the intruder. "I'm afraid my dance card is filled-up this evening, George." She crossed her fingers behind her back and peeked over his shoulder at Bear, begging him with her eyes to play along with the ruse she was concocting. "George Applegate, I'd like to introduce my dear, dear old friend, Bear Hamilton." She cleared her throat. "Bear just made me shake on a promise to dance with no one but him the rest of the evening, since we haven't seen each other for so long." She bit her lower lip. "Isn't that right, Bear?" She smiled, hoping he wouldn't reveal her scam.

Bear smiled disarmingly and stepped around George, just as the jazz band began to play. "That's right," he said. "Sorry to spoil your plans there, Applesauce, but I truly can't remember the last time I saw Red." He placed his broad hand at the small of Bobbi's back and guided her towards the dancefloor.

"Okeydokey," George called after the pair as they disappeared into the crowd. "A few dances between two old friends. No harm in that – I'll just wait here for you... and it's Applegate; not Applesauce."

Bobbie giggled, pleased to escape George's advances, even for a little while. She stepped onto the dancefloor, hoping Bear knew a few basic dance steps and wouldn't stomp too heavily on her toes, but to her amazement, he twirled her around the dancefloor as if they'd been dancing together for years. When the song ended, Bobbi stared at him in awe.

Sensing their vibrant chemistry, Lily felt a mix of excitement and sorrow. She and Scott had once shared a similar state of bliss. *"How is it possible the two of us are talking about divorce?"* she wondered.

The fog gathered, sweeping Lily back into its folds and ending her contemplation. Bobbi's memories of the evening floated by like video clips at the edge of the clouds. Lily watched the happy couple spinning around the dancefloor, while George Applegate scowled and nursed drinks at the bar.

All too soon, the jazz music of the Candlelight Speakeasy disappeared into the fog.

A moment later, Bobbi's voice floated through the mist. "After we met that night, Bear and I were inseparable. He was an amazing man. And despite his appearance, he had a little nest egg saved from when he served as a doughboy with America's First Army in the Great War. The whole time Bear was in France, he saved his pay, so when he came calling on me, he was driving his very own Model T Touring Car."

Chapter Twenty Two

Although she knew nothing about automobiles, when the fog cleared and Lily found herself bouncing down a crushed oyster-shell road in the back seat of a car, she was certain it was a Model T Touring Car.

Bear was at the wheel, singing a silly ditty that Lily didn't recognize. Bobbi laughed, while holding onto her hat with one hand and the picnic basket in her lap with the other.

Bear finished his song by lifting his chin, pursing his lips and howling like a wolf. When they both stopped laughing he said, "Okay, your turn!"

"But I don't sing as well as you do," Bobbi protested.

"Now, don't be a flat tire, Red... sing the Barney song."

"Sing it with me. You know the words as well as I do."

When the couple began singing, Lily recognized the tune to "My Bonnie Lies Over the Ocean" but the words were clearly a parody of the famous song; its lyrics altered to poke fun at a cheating soldier.

My Barney lies over the ocean; My Barney lies over the sea; My Barney lies to foreign women; Just the same way that he lies to me...

Suddenly, the right side of the car dipped sharply into a rut, caused by rainwater erosion. Bobbi gasped as Bear grabbed her arm, pulling her toward him, while simultaneously fighting the car back onto level roadway.

Lily was terrified, thinking the car was about to tip over. Her own accident flashed through her mind. She wanted to wake up, but before she had time to figure out how to make that happen, Bear had righted the car and everything was fine. Lily's heart was pounding.

"Are you okay?" Bear slowed the car.

Lily nodded before realizing he was talking to Bobbi, not her. One glance and Lily understood why Bear was so concerned. Bobbi was ashen-faced. Suddenly, Lily understood. She was experiencing Bobbi's emotions as well as her own and she wasn't sure which of their hearts was pounding the hardest.

Bear pulled the car to a stop. "Did I hurt your arm?"

"No, Bear. You didn't hurt me." Her eyes filled with tears. "It's just that when you grabbed me, it brought back bad memories, long buried. This may be the first time a man used the strength of his hand to protect me, rather than do me harm."

Bear's eyes narrowed as the meaning of her words sank in. "You tell me the name of the bastard who laid his hands on you and I swear I'll make him sorry he was ever born."

Bobbi wiped her tears. "He's already gone," she said. "And I don't like to talk about my past, remember?"

"After four months, you should be able to trust me with your secrets, Bobbi," he said.

Bobbi stared into her lap.

"Hey, I have an idea," Bear said. "I'll drive, while you tell me all about your life before I met you. That way, you can let all the memories you don't want to keep blow away on the wind."

"I'd rather not."

"Come on, Bobbi." Bear put the Model T in gear. "I'll show you how." As soon as the car began moving, Bear said, "I don't want to remember seeing that look of fear on Bobbi's face." He pretended to grab the thought from his head and tossed it into the wind.

Bobbi hesitated a moment longer; then decided to try. "My mother once took a blow that was aimed at me. I don't want the memory of seeing her fall at my feet."

It worked! She continued recounting the events that shaped her tragic childhood, giving up each ugly memory to the wind.

Bear gripped the steering wheel as she spoke, staring through the windscreen as if the road ahead were a movie screen where he was watching her story unfold. His knuckles turned white when she talked about her father's abuse, disguised as attempts to instill her and her sisters with pious virtues.

After recounting the memory of her last night at home, she patted her head instead of tossing the memory into the wind. "I need to remember that one," she said. "I don't want to ever forget that I survived and became a stronger person because of that ordeal. I only wish I could have saved my family, too."

Bear slowed down and turned off the main road onto a one-lane path, marked only by tire ruts cutting through a field. All around them was a sea of tall grass and southern pines. They bounced in their seats as Bear maneuvered the car between slender trees and over the tops of a few young palmetto shrubs, until they finally reached their secluded destination. He stopped the car under the shade of a fat oak tree and turned off the engine, but made no attempt to get out of the car. It was clear he wanted Bobbi to finish her story.

Bobbi licked her lips. "When I left home, it drove my father mad. He killed my mother and two baby sisters, and then perished when he set fire to our home afterward."

Bear's jaw dropped. "Jesus Christ, Bobbi... I had no idea..."

"I've come to terms with it for the most part, but sometimes I still regret that I didn't stay and try to be more obedient to him – that I didn't love my mother enough to stay by her side. And a part of me worries my father was right – that dancing is sinful – and their deaths are punishment for me enjoying it so much."

"Hogwash!"

Bobbi blinked, jolted from her reflections. "Pardon me?"

"Bobbi, your father was wrong. It's that simple. He should never have tried to shame you for being beautiful. He should have cherished your zest for life. Had he only opened his eyes and looked into your heart, he would have seen that God resides there. It's obvious to everyone who knows you."

He took Bobbi's hand and cradled it between both of his own.

"And I don't believe for one instant that God would bless mankind with music and a sense of rhythm – and then deny them the pleasure of celebrating those two blessings together, in the form of dance."

Lily could feel Bobbi's heartbeat quicken and her emotions swelling until she was certain of one, undeniable fact: Bobbi was head-over-heels in love with Bear.

As if Bear sensed the magical moment too, he lifted her hand to his lips and kissed it. "Marry me, Bobbi. Make a home with me. Let's teach our children to dance. Let's fill our lives with so much laughter that sorrow never finds room to sprout."

"Yes," she whispered, tears shimmering in her eyes. "Yes, I will marry you."

He lifted her chin and gave her a gentle kiss. Then he kissed her again – harder.

Chapter Twenty Three

Bobbi and Bear quickly discovered the front seat of the Model T wasn't designed for lovers. As Bobbi shifted her body awkwardly into Bear's embrace, the picnic basket started to slide from her lap. Instinctively, she whirled back to catch it, breaking the magic spell of his kisses.

Her cheeks flushed with embarrassment as she imagined what her father would have said about her brazen behavior. "Bear, we must resist temptations of the flesh until we are wed."

Bear smiled. "I tend to believe kisses are like dancing – the good Lord intends for us to enjoy them or he wouldn't have made your lips so soft. But I'll respect your wishes." He got out of the car, opened Bobbi's door and carried the picnic lunch to a clearing, overlooking a bubbling stream.

After he helped Bobbi spread a blanket on the ground, he pulled off his boots and socks, rolled up his pant legs, and waded into the stream to cool off.

"Come in the water with me," he called.

"You know very well that I didn't bring a bathing costume," Bobbie retorted.

"It's not deep… your dress won't get wet."

"Very well – turn your back, so I can remove my stockings," she said.

Bear turned away and scooped cold water over his face and arms. When Bobbi squealed, he turned back around and smiled.

She stood little more than ankle-deep in the stream.

In addition to her shoes and stockings, she had removed her belt. Her light yellow sundress alternated between billowing out in the gentle breeze, and then sucking close against her shapely body.

"This water is freezing!" she cried.

"The water bubbles up from an underground spring," Bear explained, trying not to stare at her figure. "So, no matter the season, the water in the stream is always the same temperature."

"Where does the spring come up?" she asked.

"Over there." Bear pointed to a spot up the stream, where the water was a brilliant aqua color.

Bobbi stepped gingerly towards the spring. "I hope there are no snakes in here," she said.

"The water's too cool for snakes, but be careful. The moss on the stones can be slip..."

She fell before he could finish his warning, landing squarely on her bottom. Her head and shoulders stayed above the water, along with her dress, which floated in a circle around her like an open umbrella. Everything below the crystal clear water was completely exposed.

Time seemed to move in slow motion. Trying to be a gentleman, Bear moved toward her with his eyes squeezed shut. "Grab onto my arms and I'll help you to your feet," he called.

His plan might have worked, had he not stubbed his toe on a rock as he neared her. Instinctively, he pulled his foot up out of the water, which threw off his balance. Not only did he fall, but he landed on top of Bobbi, plunging them both under the icy water.

In their struggle to stand up, they became even more entangled. Bear kept his eyes closed and reached for her shoulders, but his hands landed on her breasts, sending them both into a panic. Bobbi gasped and sputtered as she pushed him away.

Lily was amused, watching the debacle, but she understood that such a scene wouldn't have been a laughing matter, back in 1920. If Bobbi was severely humiliated, she might even break off their engagement.

Bear finally got his footing. He grabbed Bobbi under her arms and pulled her to her feet, clearly expecting her to be furious.

Instead, Bobbi laughed and placed her open palms against Bear's chest. Before he had time to react, she pushed hard, sending him sprawling. His shocked expression sent her into another fit of laughter.

Bear sat in the stream, appraising her with a mixture of awe and relief. "So, that's the way it is?" he teased. Using his stiffened arm as a paddle, he shot a large spray of water in her direction.

Bobbi yelped and made for the shore, while Bear got to his feet. He caught her waist just as she reached the water's edge and pulled her back; both of them laughing at her feeble attempts to get away.

Then Bear noticed she was shivering. He carried her up the bank and over to the waiting blanket. He lay down next to her on one side of the blanket and pulled the other half over the top of them.

Lily could read Bobbi's thoughts as clearly as if she were speaking. Bear's embrace was simultaneously warming her body and exciting her passion. She was torn. She wanted more of Bear's kisses, but years of her father's preaching still echoed in her ears. Sins of the flesh lead to fire and brimstone eternities. Period.

Bobbi contemplated their situation for a long moment and then steeled her resolve. "I've read the Bible from cover to cover more than once," she murmured, "and nowhere does it say that marriage vows have to be exchanged in a church while wearing a white dress."

Gazing into Bear's eyes, she put her palms together in prayer. Bear nodded his understanding and followed her example. If they were man and wife, then laying together wouldn't be a sin.

"I, Roberta Alice Johnson," Bobbi began, "do vow, with God as my witness, to take Barrett Nathaniel Hamilton as my husband, from this moment forward. I will honor him, obey him, be faithful to him, and do my best to make a home for him and his children, until death do us part."

"And I, Barrett Nathaniel Hamilton, promise to devote the rest of my life to Roberta Alice Johnson." Bear smiled. "I vow to always keep her warm and dry, even at the cost of my own peril." As he studied her porcelain features, he grew serious, the depth of his love obvious. "And I solemnly swear before God that I will cherish her love and be her faithful husband from now until death do us part."

"You may kiss the bride," she whispered.

He gave her a tender kiss; then pulled back. "Are you absolutely certain about this, Bobbi?"

"As your wife, I give myself to you wholly and without reservation."

"I love you, Mrs. Hamilton."

Bobbie smiled, enjoying the sound of her new name. She unbuttoned the four large, white buttons that held the shoulder straps of her yellow sundress in place, then laid her arms at her sides and held her breath, uncertain what to do next.

Bear kissed her, and then tugged her wet dress and cotton slip down to her waist. He admired her flawless, porcelain skin, peeking from beneath a simple white cotton corset, held closed by white ribbon laced over small hooks. "Beautiful," he whispered. He bent and showered kisses over her neck to the tops of her breasts.

Bobbi sucked in a sharp breath and twitched, reveling in the tantalizing sensations, but Bear misunderstood her reaction. He pulled back and waited, wordlessly seeking her permission to continue.

When she reached up and untied the bow that held her corset closed, Bear's hazel eyes flashed with lust. He unlaced the ribbon, crisscrossing her body until at last; the corset fell open, exposing her ample breasts.

Bobbi suddenly felt shy and ignorant. She had gained a vague understanding of sex while working with old Doc Farthing, but she didn't know any of the *particulars.* No man ever laid eyes on her naked body before, let alone *touched* it. She closed her eyes, wondering exactly what Bear was going to do to her.

Bear balanced his upper body on one forearm; and used the fingertips of his other hand to outline her ribcage, gliding his hand lightly back and forth over her skin, inching up until he cupped her left breast. His breathing was uneven as he lowered his mouth to taste her nipple.

Bobbi gasped; the power of his touch sending tingles racing throughout her body. Her pinkish nipples stiffened into small, hard nubs. She arched her back and curled her toes. Her hands flew to his head, her fingers fisting his hair, as wave after wave of electricity pulsed through her.

Lily wanted to look away, but was spellbound by the couple's sizzling interaction. She thought of Scott and remembered the first time they made love. The feelings were so powerful that it was difficult to determine which of the strong emotions belonged to Bobbi and which came from her own memories. For the first time in a very long time, Lily wished a man was holding her close and discovering her body. She gave herself over to Bobbi's memories, allowing herself to experience all of Bobbi's thoughts and emotions.

Bear pulled away from her left breast, shifted slightly and then sucked her right nipple into his mouth. Bobbi writhed, each of her breasts craving the attention of his tongue. The rush of cool air against her wet nipples made her long for the feel of his warm skin against hers. She pushed her hands in-between their bodies and tried to unbutton his wet shirt, but her normally deft fingers felt clumsy and incapable of handling the simple task.

Bear sat up and pushed the suspenders from his shoulders. Then, without bothering to unbutton his shirt, he pulled it over his head and dropped it to the ground. Next, he unbuttoned his short-sleeved union suit and pushed it down to his waist, revealing his naked torso.

As Doc Farthing's nurse, Bobbi had glimpsed the naked figure of an ill or injured male patient on occasion, but Bear's muscled chest looked nothing like those men.

When he laid back down and resumed sucking her nipples, his naked chest touched against her bare belly. Bobbi didn't want to breathe, for fear the slightest movement might cause the exquisite feeling to stop.

Bear tried to tug her wet dress off, but it clung to her still-damp body. He got to his knees for better leverage, and pulled, sliding her dress over her legs. He tossed it onto the grass next to the blanket and eased himself back down, running his hands over her naked flesh.

Bear ran his finger across the top edge of her short knickers, sending a torrent of mixed emotions charging through Bobbi's brain. Curiosity. Embarrassment. Longing. Fear. Desire.

Suddenly, fear took charge. She covered Bear's hand with hers, to prevent him from removing her last shred of clothing, but he mistook her hesitation for desire. He untied her last bow and slipped his hand inside, cupping her mound. Bobbi's hesitation vanished as he parted her hair and stroked her with his fingertips.

She lifted her bottom and let Bear tug her knickers off. Then he rolled to his side and unbuttoned his pants, attempting to push them off with one hand. The wet fabric refused to cooperate. He cursed under his breath, then stood up and peeled his pants off, along with his union suit, turning them inside out in the process.

Bobbi had never seen a man's erection before. It was terrifying. She had a vague notion of what he planned to do with it, and she was certain there was no way it could possibly fit into her body. All desire drained from her.

When Bear lay down beside her, naked, Bobbi's lower lip trembled and tears sprang to her eyes. She closed her legs and pressed her knees tightly together.

Bear tried to kiss her, but she turned her head.

He kissed her cheek and whispered into her ear. "I love you, Bobbi Hamilton. I will always love you. And I will be gentle. Trust me." He kissed her neck and nibbled at her earlobe. His hands caressed her breasts and slid over the soft contours of her body.

Bobbi closed her eyes and began to relax, responding to his tender touch and deep kisses. Without even realizing she was doing so, she opened her legs for him.

Bear held himself back, touching her only with his fingers, carefully parting her red hair and fondling her until he felt her begin to push herself up, into his hand. He stroked at her warm core with his middle finger until he felt her moisture blossom from within. Then he slowly inserted his fingertip, pushing it a bit further inside, each time her hips moved; enjoying the feel of her warm, silky flesh.

When he was sure she was ready, Bear moved into position between her legs and eased the head of his penis inside of her. Bobbi sucked in a quick, startled breath. He paused for a moment; then slid himself into her just a little further. She rotated her hips to ease her discomfort as Bear pushed a bit further inside of her body.

Suddenly Bobbi jerked back and cried out, as a sharp twinge of pain tore through her.

"There, now," Bear whispered. "It's done. The worst is over."

After a long moment, Bobbi began to relax. A strange feeling settled over her – she wanted Bear to touch her deepest parts. Her legs snaked around his torso, attempting to pull him closer, but he refused to move. She opened her eyes and was shocked at the grimace on his face.

"Are you hurt?" she asked, worried.

"No," he whispered through clenched teeth. "It's just – I'm trying to stay still so that I don't cause you any more pain."

"It doesn't hurt anymore, so you can try moving around a bit – if you want to."

"Promise you'll tell me if I hurt you," Bear choked in a gruff whisper.

Bobbi nodded. He began to move in and out; each thrust penetrating more deeply than the last until the full length of his shaft was buried in her velvety body. Unable to stop himself, he exploded deep inside of her and then collapsed, quivering against her chest.

"What happened?" Bobbi gasped. "Are you alright?"

Bear chuckled at her innocence. "I'm in heaven." He rose up and kissed her. "The next time will be better for you. I promise."

Bobbi couldn't imagine anything feeling better than holding Bear's warm, naked body next to hers, knowing he was her husband. "I believe I could stay right here, forever," she purred.

Eventually, the setting sun and hunger won out. They dressed and feasted on their picnic of cold fried chicken and soft bread with strawberry jam before climbing back into the car.

"I think we should make our marriage official at the courthouse tomorrow afternoon," Bear said on the ride back to town.

Bobbi nodded. "And perhaps we could have dinner with Doc Farthing at the Belleview afterward."

"Would you mind sleeping at Doc's house one last night?" he asked. "It'll give me time to get my house ready for my bride." He paused. "Say – do you think I should have asked the Doc for your hand? After all, he's been like a father to you for a long stretch now."

"I think he'd love that gesture." Bobbi grinned. "But then perhaps we shouldn't tell him we're already married."

Then the mist folded around Lily, carrying her away from the bouncy Model T.

Lily woke, envious of Bobbi and Bear for being in love, and aroused from having watched them have sex. She hugged one of the extra pillows to her body, frustrated in the chilly, pre-dawn darkness, recalling a time when she and Scott had been in love like that.

"Of course, Scott wants to move on," she thought. *"We haven't had sex for three years."*

The thought of Scott making love to someone else made her heart ache. But at the same time, she couldn't stand the thought of bringing him pleasure. Not after what he had let them do to Dylan.

Lily closed her eyes, determined not to think about Scott or sex. When she finally fell back to sleep, she met with partial success. The pillow in her arms was no longer a substitute for Scott. The man in her sultry dream had blond hair. And tattoos. And dark, round glasses. And a motorcycle.

Chapter Twenty Four

When the alarm went off, Lily groaned and hit the snooze button, hating to let go of the pleasant fantasy. She closed her eyes, hoping to recapture it, but instead, her earlier visions of Bobbi and Bear resurfaced.

"How strange," she thought. *"I remember every detail of that dream, but nothing about the one I was having when I woke up."*

Then she remembered how her conversation with Scott ended. Unless she could figure out how to forgive him soon, their marriage would be over. Thoughts about her marriage and her dreams jumbled together as she showered, dressed, and walked down the Promenade to the Terrace Cafe. Seth was already seated at their special table when she arrived.

"Which is worse," she asked, "to be crazy or to be haunted?"

"Don't people from Missouri start conversations with 'hello'?" Seth teased.

"I'm sorry. Good morning." Lily took a seat across from him. "It's just that I keep having visions of people I've never met. That's just not normal – even for me."

Seth cocked his head. "Visions?"

"Well, sort of. They happen while I'm asleep, but they aren't dreams."

Before Seth could reply, the waiter approached to take their order. Lily ordered a bowl of oatmeal with bananas, rye toast, and coffee.

"That's it?" Seth smiled. "Did you forget it's my turn to buy?"

"I'll make up for it next time," she said, still distracted.

"Well, I'll have eggs benedict, biscuits with gravy, bacon, and a tall glass of orange juice."

"Good choice," the server said with a smile. Then he turned and disappeared into the kitchen.

Lily resumed their conversation. "You probably think people who have visions are nuts, right?"

"No, but even if I did, why would my opinion matter?"

"I don't know," Lily admitted. "I guess because you're the only person I can talk to about it."

"Don't you have a husband?"

Lily's eyes widened. She hadn't told Seth about Scott. "How did you know that?"

Seth smiled. "No blind voodoo or anything. I felt your wedding ring when I took your hand at the nursing home."

Lily shot a glance at her left hand. "Yes, I'm married, but things are – complicated. We're not living together and..." She faltered, unsure how to explain their situation.

"Let's go to the pool after breakfast," Seth suggested. "We can get some sun while we talk."

"I can't. I have to go to the hospital."

"Just for an hour or so," Seth persisted.

Lily struggled; searching for an excuse. "I don't swim."

"You don't have to swim. The pool is really quiet during the week. It'll be easier to talk about whatever's bothering you out there, rather than in the middle of a restaurant."

"Okay, after breakfast, I'll call to check on Grams and if everything's okay, I'll meet you at the pool for half an hour."

"Fair enough." Seth smiled and changed the subject. "Hey, guess what – my doctor found a dumb warning for my book. He said one of his other patients showed him a prescription bottle that had the *'use caution when operating a vehicle'* warning on the bottle, but the prescription was for the guy's dog!"

Lily laughed, her mood already brightening.

An hour later, Lily limped down the corridor leading to the pool. *"How did he talk me into this?"* Despite the warm weather, she wore a light pink windbreaker over a long, cream-colored gauze skirt and a scoop-necked, lilac top. She hoped Seth was right about the pool being empty on weekdays. She hated gawkers.

Just outside of the French doors at the end of the hallway, she stopped to admire the breathtaking landscape of the hotel. Queen palms punctuated a grassy courtyard; each surrounded with a bed of bright yellow daylilies. Fuchsia azalea hedges surrounded each wing of the massive white hotel, and hanging baskets, over-flowing with colorful impatiens and petunias, accented its wide, covered verandas. Pink and yellow hibiscus bushes bloomed at the base of the steps and the red brick walkway to the pool was edged with purple, Mexican heather.

In the distance, the sparkling pool was surrounded by unoc-cupied white chaise lounge chairs and tables, shaded by blue umbrellas. Island music wafted from the poolside bar, where Seth sat, chatting with the bartender. He was wearing flip flops, baggy black swim shorts and a sleeveless, unbuttoned white shirt.

"Jesus, he's absolutely gorgeous," Lily thought, working her way down the brick path.

The bartender smiled as she approached. "She's here," he an-nounced. "That'll be one dollar, please."

"Lily!" Seth cried. "I bet Dave that you wouldn't show up because I never win bets and I really wanted you to come." Grinning, he pulled a dollar bill from the pocket of his shirt and slapped it on the bar.

"I like a man who pays his debts," Dave joked. Then he smiled at Lily "What would you like to drink?"

"Coke, please."

"Put it on my tab – and I'll have another Rumrunner," Seth said. "Would you mind bringing them to us by the pool?"

"No problem," Dave assured him.

Seth put his hand on Lily's arm and she led him to the pool deck.

"Do you want to go in the water?" Seth asked.

"No, but I can walk you to the steps if you want to go in."

"Maybe later. Let's just lie in the sun and talk for now. Are we close to the lounge chairs?"

"Three steps to your left – they're all empty."

Seth used his cane to locate the two nearest lounge chairs. He shrugged off his shirt, stretched out on one chair and patted his hand on the one next to his. "Come sit."

Lily lowered herself onto the lounge, trying not to stare at his abs. "The circle tattoo on your arm is the Hindu symbol for the circle of life, right?"

"Sort of – it signifies the concept of Zen and enlightenment – setting your mind free – that sort of thing."

"And the band of flames on your other arm?"

"Not flames," he said, turning his arm so she could see it better. "They're tiny yin and yang symbols, encircling my arm to remind me that without balance, all is lost," he said.

Just then, Dave arrived and handed Lily her drink. "Here you go," he said, putting Seth's drink in his hand. "Just wave at me if you need another round."

Seth raised his plastic cup. "Cheers."

When Lily touched her cup to his, the back of Seth's hand grazed against the sleeve of her windbreaker. He tilted his head; curious. "Why are you still wearing a jacket?"

"Scars. Big, ugly, horrible scars."

"Don't you remember what I told you? Scars are just tattoos with more interesting stories behind them."

Lily didn't respond.

Seth set his drink on the deck and leaned toward her, sliding his hand up the side of her face. Lily tensed, but didn't move away. He brushed his fingertips gently over her left temple until he found a small pock mark.

"I felt this scar the other day, when we were at the nursing home," he said, running a finger lightly over the small indention. "Tell me its story."

She closed her eyes. "I caught the chicken pox when I was two years old. My mom said this blister was too close to my eye for medicine, so I kept scratching it and wound up with a scar."

He nodded, moving his hand over her face again. His light touch stopping at a short row of bumps, hidden on the underside of her lower lip. "And this one?"

"That one," Lily sighed, "is a reminder not to stick my tongue out at a school bully when he's holding a fork."

"Ouch!" he said. Then he dropped his hand to her abdomen and started to slide his hand inside her shirt.

Her hand instinctively covered his to stop him. Seth paused, but didn't move his hand away.

"Please trust me. I promise not to go too far."

After glancing around to confirm they were still alone, she dropped her hand.

He ran his hands over her upper abdomen, exploring.

Lily closed her eyes, trying to imagine how her body felt to his touch. His fingers traced several fine lines on her sides, below her ribs.

"What caused these?"

"Those are stretch marks," Lily said. "My son was a big baby and even though I used cocoa butter, I still got a few marks..." Her voice trailed off, as she fought to keep memories of Dylan from surfacing.

Seth slid his fingers just below her waistband and traced the thin scar running down from her navel. "C-section?" he asked.

"I developed complications during delivery..." Tears welled in Lily's eyes. She took a shaky breath. "My doctor had to perform an emergency hysterectomy."

"I'm sorry that happened to you." Seth gently patted the scar and then withdrew his hand. Shifting positions, he pushed her skirt up over her knees and slid his fingers over her good leg, stopping at a scar on her knee. "How did you get this one?" he asked.

Lily was relieved to change the subject. "I was riding an old bike and hit a tree, but it's actually a funny story."

"Tell me," Seth encouraged.

"I didn't know the brakes were broken on my old bike until I was zooming down a hill, with pieces of our picnic lunch bouncing out of my handlebar basket. I tried to slow down by steering onto the grassy shoulder and managed to hit the only tree on the entire road." She chuckled. "I wasn't hurt except for my skinned knee, but when my husband tried to pick my bike up, he discovered it was broken in half. Then our son caught up to us and managed to run right over what was left of our lunch!" Lily's voice trailed off, remembering how often she and Scott had laughed over that ill-fated picnic. "I guess you had to be there," she mumbled.

Seth smiled politely, but pain stabbed Lily's heart with the realization that 'being there' was what made hundreds of memories she shared with Scott so precious. All of those memories were about to become meaningless... collateral damage of a divorce.

Margaret's voice suddenly filled Lily's thoughts, "When precious memories are shared between individuals, it's as if an orchestra is playing beautiful music that only those who share the memory can hear. No matter how hard you try, you can't describe that music to anyone who didn't hear it for themselves."

Seth moved his hands to Lily's shoulders and began to slide the windbreaker from her arms, jolting her attention back to the present. Her hands flew to his, stopping him.

"Please," he said. "I want to see."

Chapter Twenty Five

Lily glanced around, relieved to find they still had the pool area to themselves. She shrugged the jacket off her shoulders and down her arms.

Seth slid his fingertips down her arms, slowly caressing the wide pink scars and wrinkled, damaged skin that covered the majority of her forearms. He shook his head and slowly blew out a breath. "Okay, now tell me this story."

Lily's mouth went dry. "No."

"Tell me," he repeated.

Lily swiped at the tears rolling down her cheeks and pulled her windbreaker back on. "I don't want to. They're from the night Dylan died."

Seth nodded. "Okay. Tell me about Dylan, then."

Lily hesitated. "My son. He had wavy black hair and... he was beautiful."

"What sort of things did he like to do?"

"Dylan loved everything," Lily said. "He kept a list of all the adventures he was going to have one day, tacked on a bulletin board in his room. He wanted to climb a mountain, fly in a hot air balloon, scuba dive, go on safari, learn to fly a plane, ride a camel, dig for dinosaur fossils – you name it."

Seth smiled. "My kind of guy."

"I was always a homebody," Lily continued, "but we started including Dylan's adventure list in our vacation plans. We wanted to help him check off as many adventures as possible before he – he grew up." Lily closed her eyes and took a deep breath. "So, right after Dylan turned thirteen years old, we drove to Florida to visit Grams, and we arranged for him to swim with the dolphins at Sea World while we were there. He was so excited..."

"It sounds like you were a wonderful mom," Seth said.

"Right up until I killed him," she thought. "I don't want to talk about this anymore, Seth. I mean it. Besides, I need to get to the hospital."

Seth cocked his head to the side. "Okay – but before you go, tell me why you think a ghost is haunting you."

Lily finished her Coke. "Not one ghost – three ghosts – I mean three spirits."

"There's a difference?"

Lily bit her lip. "Yeah... see, that's exactly the kind of thing that puzzles me. I would never have thought there was a difference, but Margaret says a ghost is just a fragment of a spirit."

"Who's Margaret?"

"She's one of the spirits. I think she wields some authority over the others... or at least they respect her. She was Henry Plant's second wife."

"Who's Henry Plant?"

"He built this hotel," she explained. "Listen, I know this sounds crazy, but it all started in the hospital after my accident. I had some incredibly realistic visions and my doctor explained that hallucinations are my brain's way of helping me cope with... with everything that happened." She tilted her cup and shook a small ice cube into her mouth. "Sometimes I still experience visions of Dylan. They're weird, but he always tries to help me. So when Margaret first showed up in my dreams, I figured my brain added a new wrinkle to help me cope with my guilt about messing up my marriage and my relationship with Grams." She shook her head. "But I'm not sure anymore."

"What changed?" he asked.

"Well, for one thing, after I dreamed about the hospital getting built in 1916, I did a little research and found out that everything

I dreamt was true – and my dream contained way more details than I can find in any historic records." Lily took a deep breath. "So, either I'm reliving a spirit's memories in my dreams or I've crossed the line into Crazy Town."

Seth frowned. "I've always heard that working issues out in your dreams is a sign of intelligence, not insanity."

"I don't know about that," she said, reaching for her crutch. "But what I do know is I have to get my butt over to the hospital." Putting all of her weight on her good leg, she stood.

"Okay. Let's talk more at breakfast tomorrow," he suggested.

Lily sighed, eyeing Seth's tanned, muscled body and movie-star face. "I'm so messed up, Seth. Why in the hell do you want to spend more time with me?"

"Are you kidding?" He grinned. "Compared to you, everyone else around here is downright boring!"

Chapter Twenty Six

At the hospital, Lily gazed at her grandmother, considering the blurred lines between life and death, and wondering what divides reality from imagination, and imagination from insanity.

"Can spirits chat with people who are near death – tweening, as Margaret calls it, or is it just my twisted brain, conjuring up encounters with an imaginary spirit world? How can I know for sure, Grams?"

Lily kissed her grandmother's cheek and then limped to the blue vinyl chair by the window. She pictured Bobbi and Bear planning a future together and envied their innocent optimism – their belief that love was strong enough to carry them through any storm. She wished she still believed in naive concepts like *forever*. Lily closed her eyes and wasn't surprised when thick fog materialized, sweeping her away.

When the mist suddenly vanished, Lily gulped air to calm her stomach. Bobbi and Bear were climbing out of the Model T, parked in front of East Gate Cottage. Lily floated next to them as they entered the house.

"Bobbi," Doc Farthing called from the front parlor. "Come see who decided to surprise us with a visit!"

Doc and Alton Farthing were sitting in a pair of black leather wingback chairs. Alton grinned and stood up when she entered the room.

Bobbie clapped her hands in delight. "Alton – it's so good to see you!" She rushed over and gave him a welcoming hug. "Bear, come meet Doc's son!"

Although Alton kept smiling, Lily saw the joy disappear from his expression when Bear stepped into the room.

"Alton has been attending medical school in Connecticut for almost four years," Bobbi explained. "So his visits are rare."

Bear strode across the room and shook Alton's slender hand. "It's good to meet you, Alton. Bobbi speaks highly of you. And your timely arrival makes this day even more special than it already is."

Old Doc Farthing's body was growing feeble, but his mind and hearing were still sharp. "Have I forgotten some special occasion?" he asked.

Bobbi stepped to Bear's side. Lily sensed her nervous excitement.

"Doc, I've asked Bobbi to marry me and she accepted, provided we have your blessing, sir."

"I told Bear that you and Alton are like family," Bobbi said, smiling.

Doc Farthing's eyes glistened as he smiled at Bobbi with fatherly affection. He took her hands in his own. "Is this what you want, child? Do you love this man enough to wed him?"

Bobbi swallowed a lump in her throat. "Yes, Doc – I love him more than anything."

He nodded and turned to Bear. "I hope you know how lucky you are that she chose you," he said.

"I certainly do, sir," Bear replied.

"Then you have my blessing." He brought Bobbi and Bear's hands together between his own, nodding his approval. "Well, now – I suppose I'll need to find a new nurse and housekeeper."

Lily glanced at Alton, who was staring at the floor; his lips pressed tight together. Despite his obvious dismay, he forced a smile to his face and offered the couple his congratulations.

Once the excitement died down, Bobbi fetched a crystal pitcher of tea from the small icebox in doc's office. She poured drinks for everyone and then took her place next to Bear on a burgundy couch, facing the wingback chairs.

"Well, as long as we're making announcements, I have one of my own," Alton said. "I've decided to accept Yale Hospital's offer of employment."

Doc Farthing turned to his son in surprise. "But I thought you planned to return to Belleair. You know East Gate is reserved for the hotel's doctor. I hoped you'd take my place when I retire."

Alton swallowed. "Yes, but Bobbi's announcement changes things. When she moves out, you'll be able to assign her rooms to a local medical practitioner."

"I suppose that's true," Doc Farthing replied.

Alton continued, gaining confidence as he spoke. "Some well-deserving individual will earn a valuable medical education at your elbow. Meanwhile, I'll be able to further my studies at Yale and establish a surgical practice, comforted by the knowledge the people I love are being well-cared for back home."

Doc Farthing nodded, accepting his son's decision. "Will you be able to stay in town long enough to help me select a new apprentice?"

"Absolutely, Father. And I'll visit more often, to make sure everything remains copacetic."

Bear raised his glass of tea, "Cheers to your new venture, Alton. Bobbi and I wish you grand success in Connecticut."

Bobbi lifted her glass. "And we're thrilled you'll be here to help celebrate our wedding."

Doc Farthing glanced at her. "So you'll be marrying right away, then?"

"Yes," Bear said. "We're planning to go to the courthouse tomorrow."

"I'll not hear of it," Doc Farthing said. "If you want my blessing, you'll get married in church. Besides, I want to see Bobbi walk down the aisle in Mildred's wedding dress."

Tears filled Bobbi's eyes. "You'd allow me to wear Mrs. Farthing's wedding gown?"

"Oh dear," Doc Farthing said, rubbing his chin. "I didn't tell you? After Mildred died, I packed her special things in a cedar chest and stored it in the attic. Later, when your family's home burned down,

Alton suggested we bequeath the chest to you. I thought it was a sterling idea, but I must have become distracted and forgotten to tell you." He shook his head. "Sometimes, I think I would forget to eat, if it weren't for my stomach rumbling to remind me."

Bobbi jumped to her feet, radiating the excitement of a child on Christmas morning. "Oh, thank you, Doc!" She clapped her hands together. "This is just the berries! Let's go fetch it down right now."

As Bobbi bounded toward the attic stairs, the clouds engulfed Lily, pulling her away from the memory.

Although she couldn't see them, Lily could hear Bobbi and Clay arguing beyond the fog.

"Damn it, Bobbi," Clay said. "I've tried to be patient with you, but we don't have time for you to relive every single memory of your life."

"It's important that she understands about my life before," Bobbi argued.

"She's not empty-headed," Clay said. "She gets the picture. You were in love and the world was perfect."

Margaret's voice cut through the mist as Lily strained to hear. "Shush, both of you."

When the haze melted away, Lily found herself seated at the round table in her parlor, between Bobbi and Clay. Bobbi's green eyes shot daggers at Clay, who sat unflinching; his arms folded tightly over his chest. Across the table from Lily, Margaret finished stirring some sugar into her tea and then tapped her spoon against her cup, as if calling a meeting to order.

"Lily, my dear, I have a bit of good news," Margaret announced. "Your grandmother and I were tweening for a few minutes earlier today." Then she frowned. "Unfortunately, what she said made no sense. There's no dementia in the spirit realm, but she seems to think your son visits her regularly and they're planning to take a trip to Europe. Before I could ask her to explain, that idiotic Sharon interrupted us and started listing all the places your grandmother should visit in Europe. Once the two of them started tweening, they ignored me completely." She rested her spoon on her saucer. "But don't be alarmed. I'm sure I'll get better results tomorrow. Now, if you'll pardon me for just a moment, Lily, I need to address this latest squabble."

Margaret turned to face Clay. "You're acting like a child, Clay Long – and don't think for a moment that I don't know what's behind all of your blustering." She shifted her gaze to Bobbi. "And Bobbi, dear, although I do understand that this is a special connection, Clay's right. Time is running short. Perhaps you could use memory snippets to move things along."

Bobbi gave Margaret a submissive nod. Before Lily could ask what a *memory snippet* was, the fog closed in around her.

Chapter Twenty Seven

Bobbi's voice filled the air inside the clouds. "Bear and I married at the Midway Baptist Church and then dined with our friends at the Belleview. It was a fitting place to celebrate, since Bear and I fell in love while dancing in the Candlelight Ballroom."

Lily saw moments from the wedding celebration popping up, one after another at the edge of the fog. *"Memory snippets are like short video clips,"* she realized.

Bobbi made an exquisite bride in Mildred Farthing's wedding dress – a white linen relic of the Victorian Era, with intricate lace designs on its high collar, long sleeves and the bustle in back. Her short red bob peeked out from beneath a long tulle veil, trimmed in lace and pinned into place with pink roses.

Lily smiled at the well-wishers in the memory vignettes. She spotted George Applegate leaning against a wall, still scowling at the happy couple. She felt sorry for him, remembering how hard he had tried to win Bobbi's affection the night she met Bear Hamilton.

One clip showed Bear carrying Bobbi into their first cottage, and another showed them dancing together in their kitchen. Lily could tell they were happy, despite having only meager possessions.

In each of the next four scenes, a new child joined the family. After the birth of her fourth child, Doc Farthing sat next to Bobbi's bed, watching her cuddle the new infant. "This is our last child," she confided.

Doc lit his pipe and stretched his long legs out in front of his chair. He shifted his glance to Bear, who was standing in the doorway, rubbing his whisker stubble and smiling. "That so?"

"Yep," Bear replied. "Bobbi always wanted four kids and I wanted at least two sons and two daughters. So with Nathaniel, Fred, Henrietta and now little Belle there, we both got what we wanted. And I reckon Bobbi's gonna make me behave from now on, if I want to keep sharing her bed." He gave Bobbi a wink.

"Just as well," said Doc. He coughed several times, and then re-lit his pipe. "You have enough mouths to feed and steady work is getting harder to come by all the time. But the only surefire way to prevent pregnancy is for Bobbi to take an aspirin every night – and go to sleep with it held tightly between her knees."

Bear chuckled as the image faded away.

The next memory made Lily tear up. It was Doc Farthing's funeral. Alton Farthing stood at the graveside with Bobbi and Bear. Bobbi held infant Belle in her arms, and Nathaniel, Fred and Henrietta held hands beside her. A sizeable crowd of mourners stood behind them, paying their final respects to the fine old man.

Bobbi's voice floated through the clouds as brief memories continued to appear and then fade away at the edge of the fog. "We used the money Doc Farthing left us to buy a truck for Bear, but soon after that, local delivery jobs started drying up. Bear had to accept long-distance hauling jobs that took him away from home for weeks at a time. And no matter how much we scrimped, we still had to rob Peter to pay Paul every month."

Lily watched as Bear's dirty black truck with wooden side-rails pulled up and parked in front of their small clapboard cottage. Only Bobbi, Nathaniel and Belle came out to greet him.

Bobbi's voice continued. "My sister, Maxine and her husband were well-off, but they were unable to have children. She volunteered to take Fred and Henrietta for a few months to help us out, and for the children's sakes, I agreed. I took a job doing piece work in a garment factory. A woman who lived near the factory looked after all the seamstresses' children while we worked, but she was too busy to do a good job of it, so after school, Nathaniel would pick up Belle and look after her until I arrived home in the evening."

"But Nathaniel's only eight or nine years old," Lily thought, aghast. Images of the garment factory floated by at the edge of the mist. It was dimly lit and hot, with row after row of women, hunched over sewing machines, incorporating an assembly line approach to manufacture men's shirts. Next to each station were two baskets: one filled with pre-pinned pieces that were to be sewn together; and one to hold completed work. Bobbi sewed one collar after another until her piece basket was empty. Then she carried the completed work to an inspection station, where a man evaluated it. Every time he approved a piece she had sewn, he placed a check by her name in his logbook. Each time a piece was rejected; he marked through one of those checks.

"Working hard on the farm throughout my childhood prepared me for long hours at the factory," Bobbi said. "I was paid a half-penny for every collar piece I set onto a shirt, so if I worked hard, I could earn nearly five dollars a week to help our family. We had enough to eat and Bear still took me dancing at the Belleview sometimes."

One snip of memory showed Bear climbing out of his truck with little red-headed Fred and Henrietta. Lily smiled, watching the reunited family hug one another – the quintessential picture of joy. But in the very next scene, Bobbi was holding back her tears and waving goodbye, as Bear and the two children drove away again.

The next few clips showed Bobbi making children's clothing. "I enjoyed sketching designs I saw displayed in store windows. After Bell and Nathaniel were in bed, I transferred my sketches onto newspaper to make patterns and used fabric scraps from the factory to make fashionable clothing for them. Max and her husband provided for Fred and Henrietta, so all of our children were well dressed. And it wasn't long before Cricket, the factory foreman, took note of my ability and put it to use. He paid me extra to help design clothing for children, in addition to my normal sewing responsibilities."

The images faded away, but the fog didn't part.

"The stock market crash put an end to Bear's long-distance hauling work," Bobbi's disembodied voice recalled. "It was awful. Bear took whatever odd jobs he could find, but the only wages we could count on were what I earned at the factory – and even there, wages were cut in half."

The fog dissipated, plopping Lily into a seat at the kitchen table in Bobbi and Bear's cottage. The couple was engrossed in a conversation with a burly man. He looked familiar to Lily, but she couldn't place him.

"Lawmen are taking Prohibition more seriously than any of us ever thought they would," the man said.

"But don't most revenuers just go after moonshiners who are making folks sick with their rotgut?" Bear asked.

"Yeah, and we usually avoid trouble with coppers and politicians by sweetening their pensions, but lately, a few of our competitors are getting greedy. Some of our shipments have been hijacked and what makes it worse is that we think the heists might be inside jobs."

"And you can't go to the cops about it," Bear noted.

The man tapped his forefinger against the side of his nose. "Exactly. Which is why we need men we can trust working for us." He lowered his voice, "An honest man like you could make good money without traveling too far from home, Bear."

"I don't know, Frankie. I promised God that if he let me survive the war, I'd never raise another weapon."

Frankie smiled. "Yeah, but you wouldn't object to having someone riding shotgun, would you? I mean – just to keep the highwaymen at bay."

Bobbi stood up; nervous about the direction the conversation was headed. "Can I fetch you men some coffee?"

Frankie grinned. "*You* offering to serve *me* a drink – how's *that* for a switch?" He winked at Bobbi. "Maybe next time, doll. I have to be getting back."

"That's where I've seen him," Lily realized. *"He's the bartender at the Belleview Biltmore."*

Bobbi smiled. She had always liked Frankie.

Frankie turned his attention back to Bear. "We're in a tough spot tonight and we need a driver. Help us out. We'll pay you enough to put meat on your table for a month, and then tomorrow you can decide if you want to keep the job."

"What happens if I decide I don't want it?" Bear asked.

Frankie pushed back from the table and raised his hands, palms up. "No problem. These days, it's easy to find fellas who need work. I just offered it to you first because we go way back and I trust you."

"Okay, Frankie. I'll give it a go."

Bear stopped on the way out the door to give Bobbi a quick kiss. "Don't worry, Red. Everything's gonna be fine."

The fog engulfed her so fast that Lily tumbled over several times before she could stabilize herself by stretching out her arms as if she were flying.

She heard Bobbi whisper in the mist. "I should have put my foot down..."

Chapter Twenty Eight

Lily woke in the hospital, wondering what Bobbi meant. She tried to fall back to sleep, but couldn't. Frustrated, she stood and moved to her grandmother's bedside.

"Grams, do you remember when I came out of my coma and told everyone that Dylan visited me at the hospital? The doctors said my skull fracture caused me to hallucinate. But what if they were wrong? I mean, what if spirits are real? What if Dylan really did visit me?" She gave her grandmother a wistful look. "I wish you could wake up and tell me if I'm crazy or not."

Lily turned and gazed out the window at the clear, late afternoon sky, recalling the sound of Dylan's voice waking her from a deep sleep at the hospital.

"Wake up, Mom," he pled.

Lily had tried to focus, but it was no use. She thought Dylan was standing next to her, but she couldn't make out the details of his face.

"Is that you, sweetie?" Lily asked; her mind still thick with sleep.

Dylan smiled. "Yeah. I just wanted you to know my underwear was clean."

She was confused. "That's good. Is this a school day, Sweetie?"

Dylan shook his head. "No – it's summertime... don't you remember? We were driving to Florida."

"Driving to Florida." Lily repeated. "*We must have stopped at a hotel for the night.*" The logical thought comforted her. "Okay,

141

then," she said. "Why don't you go watch some TV until Dad and I wake up?"

"I don't think I can stay much longer, Mom."

"What?" Lily said, trying to concentrate.

"They're operating and I think they're almost done with me," Dylan said.

"Dylan, you're not making any sense." Everything was so fuzzy. "What are you talking about?"

Even with blurry vision, she marveled at how much Dylan and Scott looked alike – tall, with thick, wavy black hair and big brown eyes. Dylan had grown three inches this year and was putting on muscle. Even though he had just turned thirteen, he was already bigger than some her adult friends.

"In a few years," she thought, *"the school's football and basketball coaches will be fighting over him."*

"Don't you remember?" Dylan asked, interrupting her musings. "You always told me to make sure my underwear was clean in case I was in an accident. Nobody else seemed to care, but I wanted you to know." He paused and looked away for a moment; then returned his attention to her. "They're all done with me now. I think I'm supposed to leave. There's a bright light over there..."

Dylan started drifting away from her.

Terror tugged at the edges of Lily's consciousness. *"An accident?"* She tried to recall what they were doing just before she went to sleep, but her memory was blank. She began to panic. "Don't go, Dylan!" she cried. "Please stay here with me. I don't understand..."

Dylan returned to her bedside. "Okay," he said. "I'll stay. I promise. But you have to wake up soon, okay?"

"Sure," she said, closing her heavy eyes. "Just a few more minutes. Then I'll wake up and we'll figure everything out."

As the darkness closed around her, he whispered, "I love you, Mom."

"Love you, too," Lily murmured.

As the vivid memory evaporated, the Florida skyline reappeared outside the hospital window.

"Grams, is it possible that Dylan's spirit is still here? That he talks to you on that old football phone? That he's still waiting for me like he promised?" Lily shook her head and lowered her voice. "More likely, I'm losing it again. Otherwise, why would I be asking a comatose woman for answers?"

She pulled out her cell phone and called for the hotel shuttle, then bent to kiss Grams' cheek and slipped out the door.

She was the only passenger. As Pete drove the shuttle out of the hospital parking lot, he pointed to the darkening skyline.

"It's going to be a great sunset," he said. "Want to stop and watch? The ball should drop in about ten minutes."

"Sure. Why not?" she said.

"Great."

Across from the hospital, a short, steeply-sloped road dead-ended at the Intracoastal Waterway. A spacious gazebo dock rested on the water, providing an ideal view of the water and barrier islands beyond. Pete pulled the shuttle to the curb and parked.

"You're in luck," he said. "This is usually a popular spot at sunset, but tonight it looks like you'll have the view to yourself."

Pete helped her walk up the wood ramp into the gazebo. Then he leaned against the entrance and settled his gaze on the reddening sun. Lily walked to the section that extended farthest out over the water and watched the sunlight reflecting off thousands of ripples on the water's surface like twinkling lights on a Christmas tree. As the sun sank, its reflection cast long streaks of red and gold light over the waves. Above the water, the sky resembled a painter's palette of reds, oranges, pinks and purples.

When Lily first came to live with Grams, they often watched sunsets together. Grams told her that if she sat cross-legged, took deep breaths, and listened very carefully, she might hear the sizzle when the fiery sun touched the water. A few times, Lily could have sworn she heard a hissing sound. Much later, she realized Grams was teaching her yoga and breathing techniques to use as tools to control her nightmares.

A stiff sea breeze caught hold of a swath of Lily's long, copper hair, and blew it across her face. She caught the wayward strand, but before she could tuck it firmly behind her ear, another one escaped and soon several of her unruly locks were dancing on the wind. The strong airstream blowing through her hair reminded her of riding in Bear's Model T.

"Why not?" she thought. She stared at the sunset, took deep breaths, and focused on her scariest childhood memory. She had spilled her milk and was cowering in a corner. Roy, her mother's last boyfriend, was coming at her with his belt – liquor on his breath and hatred in his eyes. Using Bear's technique, Lily pretended to pull the horrible memory from her head and let it go on the wind.

She smiled, actually feeling better. *"Maybe my brain conjured up spirits to help me remember lessons that I learned as a child, but have since forgotten."*

By the time the sun sank beneath the horizon, Lily felt calm and relaxed. She continued watching until all that remained of the sunset were pink streaks on the horizon. Then she turned and hobbled back to where Pete stood waiting for her.

"Thanks, Pete. That was beautiful."

"My pleasure. Nothing like a good sunset to set the world right." He extended his crooked arm and escorted her back to the shuttle.

They rode back to the Belleview Biltmore in congenial silence and parted as friends. Energized, Lily decided to walk down the grand Promenade and have dinner at the Terrace Cafe.

As she passed by, she noticed the elegant, white wrought iron entrance gates of the Candlelight Lounge were closed, indicating the ballroom was reserved for a private event. Lily thought about Bobbi and Bear. *"Did real people fall in love while dancing in this room, or did my imagination invent them?"* She puzzled over the dilemma until she reached the restaurant.

The café was full, so Lily added her name to a waiting list for a table. She spied a young couple at her regular table, sitting close together, sharing a bottle of wine and laughing – oblivious to the rest of the world. Lily turned her back on them, ignoring a pang of jealousy.

Across the Promenade corridor, dozens of hotel guests gathered near the huge mahogany bar. It was an eclectic group – some dressed in shorts and tee-shirts; others in elegant evening wear. Some guests sang along with a three-piece band's rendition of "Mustang Sally", while others attempted to carry on conversations over the music.

Lily tried to picture everyone dressed in 1920s' attire and visualize the lounge area as it was when it had been the main entrance and hotel lobby. But try as she might, it was impossible for her to picture anything except what currently existed.

"How can I imagine people and their surroundings in such detail in my dreams, when I have no such ability while I'm awake?" she wondered.

As the band finished the song, she thought she detected the sound of Seth's laughter. Startled, she scanned the lounge and spotted him at the end of the bar, chatting with the bartender and a cocktail waitress.

She smiled. *"Maybe I won't have to eat alone after all."*

Chapter Twenty Nine

Lily hobbled over to the Lobby Lounge before she lost her courage.

"Fancy meeting you here, Seth," she said, trying to sound casual while yelling over the din of the lounge. "I was about to grab a bite to eat and I'd enjoy some company, if you haven't already had dinner."

"Lily!" Seth grinned in her direction. "Hey, you guys... this is the woman I told you about." He pawed the air, trying to locate Lily.

"What exactly did you tell them?" she wondered as she took his hand and placed it on her upper arm.

"Lily, this is Jessica, and the guy behind the bar is Randy. They told me some amazing stories about this hotel."

In lieu of a greeting, Lily smiled at the pair.

"Listen, guys... I'm starving, so I'm going to jump on her dinner invitation. Besides, I can hardly wait to tell her about this place."

He reached into the right front pocket of his jeans, pulled out a twenty dollar bill, and laid it on the bar to pay his tab. "Keep the change, Randy."

Randy continued filling Jessica's serving tray with martinis. "Thanks, Dude. Stop back over when you're done eating and I'll make you a nightcap."

"Wait," Jessica said. "I thought you were blind. How did you know that was a twenty?"

Seth shrugged. "I felt the number on the bill. Can't you do that?"

Lily punched his arm. "He's teasing you. He keeps different denominations in separate pockets."

"Way to destroy my mystic aura, Lily," he said with a grin.

"That's really smart," Jessica said, impressed. She hoisted the tray of martinis above her head, balanced on her open palm. "Nice meeting you," she called over her shoulder as she began weeding her way through the dense crowd toward her thirsty customers.

"Let's eat outside," Seth suggested. "There's never a wait and besides, it'll be easier to carry on a conversation out there."

The hostess led them across the restaurant and through French doors to the nearly empty veranda dining area, where soft jazz music wafted through the warm, moist air. The heavy wrought iron chairs scraped against the stone floor as Seth and Lily seated themselves. Almost immediately, a young, Asian woman arrived to offer them menus.

"I already know what I want," Lily said. "I'll have a bowl of shrimp and lobster bisque, a chicken Caesar salad, and a glass of Chardonnay."

"Make that two. Except I'll have another beer instead of wine," Seth added, holding up his nearly empty bottle.

"That makes my job easy," the congenial server remarked, turning away. "I'll be right back."

"Wow... it's peaceful out here," Lily said.

"Describe it for me, okay?"

"Well, we're seated at a table near a wide, curved stairway that leads toward the pool. The outer edge of this veranda is enclosed with a white half-wall and let's see – one, two, three... eight carved pillars support the roof. Enormous baskets of pink and purple flowers are hanging between each of the pillars, and that breeze is coming from huge ceiling fans with blades shaped like palm leaves. Oh, and the tables have white tablecloths with crystal candleholder centerpieces. It's really pretty."

"Damn, you're good," Seth said with an approving smile. "By the way, how's your grandmother doing?"

"No change."

"At least she didn't get worse." Seth paused briefly before attempting to change the subject. "Are you up for learning about the history of this place?"

"I already know some of it. We used to come here when I was a kid. I even wrote a school report about Henry Plant, the guy who built this place. After all these years, I still remember that he built railroads and fancy hotels along the west coast of Florida, while his competitor, Henry Flagler, did the same thing on the east coast."

"I wasn't talking about that kind of history. Randy and Jessica told me that this is one of the most haunted hotels in the country."

Before she could respond, the server reappeared with their meals. Lily looked up and checked her nametag. "Have you worked here very long, Sarah?" she asked.

"For about three years," Sarah replied.

"What's your opinion – is the Belleview Biltmore haunted?"

Sarah smiled and began placing dishes on the table. "I've never seen anything myself, but some of the kitchen staff swears a ghost haunts the kitchen, messing with the lights and temperature." She shrugged. "Who knows? Can I bring you anything else?"

"No, thanks – I think we're set," Lily said.

Sarah nodded and turned away to tend other customers.

"I didn't hear about a kitchen ghost," Seth said, "but Randy told me he's had tons of reports from people who say they've seen a ghost by the entrance to the Lobby Lounge. You were right about Margaret Plant being Henry Plant's second wife. People say she loved this hotel so much, her ghost still greets people when they come inside. And get this... a few people swear she talked to them while they were sleeping." Seth raised his eyebrows above his glasses. "Sound familiar?"

Lily frowned. "I'm sure Randy was just playing along after you described my weird dreams."

"That's the best part, Lily. I never told him about your dreams." Seth grinned like a mischievous little boy. "Do you want to hear more?"

Lily took in a sharp breath. "Yes, I most certainly do."

"I thought so." Seth took a swig of beer. "According to Randy, there are tons of ghosts in this hotel. A couple of the big ghost hunter TV shows even filmed here and they say this place is haunted, too."

"I don't know if I'm seeing ghosts, Seth. I mean, ever since my accident, my imagination conjures up all sorts of crazy stuff."

"Funny you should say that," Seth said. "Jessica told me that most folks chalk-up reports about ghost encounters to overactive imaginations, but she said she's worked here a long time, and what she notices is that a lot of them describe the same ghosts."

"Are there any reports about ghosts from the Roaring Twenties?"

"They didn't mention any," Seth said. "Jessica said a lot of people claim Morton Plant's second wife, Maisie, roams the halls, looking for an expensive pearl necklace she lost... and even more people claim they made contact with a little boy who drowned in the old swimming pool back in the 1930s."

"A little boy?" Dylan flashed through Lily's mind.

"Yeah, and there's a creepy bride who jumped to her death from a fourth floor balcony, after her fiancé was killed in a car accident. People say she just floats around in her wedding gown, looking all sad."

"That one sounds like a ghost story someone would tell around a campfire," Lily joked.

Seth shrugged. "I'm just repeating what Randy and Jessica told me. They also said the front desk gets lots of reports from people complaining about little children laughing and playing in the hallways late at night, but no matter how hard the staff searches for kids, they never find them."

"The bellman told me that one when I checked in, but I haven't heard anything. Maybe people hear stuff because workers like him plant ideas in their heads."

"Okay, smarty-pants – what about these..." Seth ticked off the next few stories on his fingers: "Some people swear they've seen a Victorian couple dancing in the ballroom. And supposedly, there's a bad-tempered ghost on the fifth floor, who gets a kick out of scaring the hell out of people, and there's a window that keeps opening by itself, even after a maintenance guy nailed it shut." Seth slowly shook his head. "Man, they told me so many stories, I can't even remember them all."

He gulped down a long swig of beer. "Lily I know I said I don't believe in ghosts, but goddamn. So many stories make me wonder. I mean, being blind and all, how can I even be sure that when I strike up a conversation with someone, it's a person and not a ghost?"

Lily stifled a giggle. "Maybe you should refuse to talk to anyone until they let you feel-up their face."

"Ha. Ha. Very funny. I must say, this is not the reaction I expected," Seth said "Are you okay?"

Lily took a sip of wine. "I'm fine."

Seth cocked his head to the side. "Really?"

"Okay, maybe I'm not totally fine. I mean, I thought my dreams were just that – dreams. Now you say I'm being haunted by real spirits. What's the *right* way to react to something like that?"

"I don't think there's a right way, but who knows? Maybe these ghosts can teach you how to get rid of the ghosts from your past."

His words struck a nerve. Lily waved to Sarah, signaling the server to bring the check. "Listen, Seth, we can talk more about this in the morning. Let's call it a night, okay?"

"I'm sorry; I didn't mean to upset you," he said.

"You don't have anything to be sorry for. I'm just tired and you've given me a lot to think about." After charging the meal to her room, Lily grabbed her crutch, and stood. "Come on, I'll take you back to the bar for that nightcap Randy promised you."

"Are you sure you don't want me to walk you back to your room?" Seth asked.

"No, thanks. I'll be fine. Really."

After resisting a few more of Seth's attempts to get her to join him at the bar, Lily limped back to the sanctuary of her room. She changed into a nightgown and slipped into bed, her heart aching for the days when she was a happy wife and mother. There was only one person in the world who shared those distant memories. She dialed Scott's number.

"Hello?" a woman's voice answered.

Chapter Thirty

Lily jerked the phone away from her ear to check the caller ID. The bright display confirmed she had dialed their home – or technically, Scott's home.

"Um... is Scott there?" she asked.

"He's in the shower, but I'm sure he'll be out in just a minute. Can I take a message?"

"No..." Lily struggled to put a sentence together. The woman sounded so casual about Scott being naked. It was a kick in the gut. "It's... nothing important. I'll, uh, call back tomorrow."

She hung up and turned off her cell, pushing it across the nightstand as if it could bite. Then she unplugged the hotel phone for good measure. She turned off the light and pulled the comforter around her chin, holding it there with both fists. *"God, why didn't you just let me die in that goddamn accident?"*

Without realizing she was falling asleep, Lily drifted into the fog. She heard Margaret's voice before she materialized at the parlor table.

"The biggest lie the living tell one another is that you get all the answers when you die. That simply is not true. All you get is a new set of questions."

"What do you mean, new questions?" Lily floated to the table.

Margaret stirred sugar into her tea. "What happens if I take the lighted path? What happens if I don't? Where are the people I once loved? Can I still affect the world of the living? Am I supposed to try?" She tapped her spoon against her cup and laid it on the saucer. "I ask myself these and a thousand other questions all the time." She took a sip of tea. "You see, men of faith tell the living they know what happens after death, but they don't. They may *believe*, but they don't *know*. It's the same on this side. There are spirits who insist they know what waits down the lighted path. But they don't have any more knowledge than the preachers of your world. The only ones who know are those who actually travel the lighted path and none of them have ever come back to tell us."

"Can't you just tell me what I'm supposed to learn from these dreams?" Lily asked.

"You can't rush the lessons you learn from a spirit's memories. Be patient. The answers will come."

The fog engulfed Lily before she could reply, and almost immediately she heard Bobbi's voice floating through the folds of the mist.

"Prohibition laws didn't apply beyond three miles offshore." Bobbi's voice sounded close, even though Lily couldn't see her. "So boats came from Cuba and the Bahamas loaded with sugar cane rum and anchored just beyond that point, in legal waters. Folks started calling it the *rum-line*, and in the dead of night, so called *rumrunners* would go out there and buy as much liquor as their boats could carry to shore. Rumrunners sold the liquor to bootleggers, and they hired men like Bear to transport shipments for distribution."

Lily listened, curiosity aroused, as Bobbi continued.

"George Applegate ran the Chicago Outfit's bootlegging operation in these parts. His right-hand man got himself pinched for almost killing a poor sap in a barroom brawl, so Butch Torrio got promoted to handle purchases and distribution. That first night, Bear said Butch paid a rumrunner with the biggest wad of cabbage he'd ever seen. Then they loaded Bear's truck with booze, covered it with lumber and delivered the shipment to Frankie at the Belleview Biltmore."

Lily expected the fog to part, but instead of opening to a new memory, a snip of memory appeared at the edge of the mist, depicting Bobbi waking Bear up to eat dinner with her and the children.

"I worried about Bear because I knew George disliked him from the day they met. But it was wonderful to have him home so often – even if he was usually asleep when I was awake, and awake when I was asleep."

The next vignette showed Bear gulping down his dinner and then kissing Bobbi and the children goodbye as he headed out the door. When he was gone, Bobbi wrapped the remainder of their meal in newspaper and handed the package to Nathaniel, who carried the little bundle outside and placed it on top of their mailbox.

"With both of us working, we had plenty to eat," Bobbi said. "But it kept getting harder for men to find steady jobs. Every night we left food scraps out for the needy and every morning, they were gone without a trace."

Another clip appeared, showing Bobbi in her tiny kitchen, wearing a sleeveless red dress with black beadwork on the collar. A wide black sash adorned with a red silk flower encircled her hips, and her short red hair was parted down the middle, crimped in neat waves. She twirled to the music on the radio, while keeping watch out the window. When Bear's truck pulled into the yard, she dashed outside and climbed into the cab, between Bear and a man who was built like a wrestler and armed with a Tommy gun.

"Sometimes when Bear and his armed guard, Willie, were scheduled to make a delivery to the Belleview Biltmore, they'd agree to pick me up along the way. On those special nights, the children stayed with a neighbor, and after Bear finished his work, we danced." She sighed. "Those evenings are some of my most treasured memories."

The next image featured the speakeasy at the hotel. It was crowded, smoky and loud, but Bear and Bobbi were all smiles as they danced the Charleston. When the lights flashed off and on three times, an organized chaos ensued. Patrons raced to the bar to dump their drinks into a small galvanized washtub and waiters filled their empty glasses with sweet tea. Behind the bar, a trapdoor opened in the floor. Frankie dropped bottles of liquor, followed by the galvanized tub, into waiting hands below. Then he slammed the trapdoor shut, pulled a rug over the opening, and struck a casual pose. A few minutes later, police poured through the door and began weaving throughout the room searching for, but not finding, alcohol.

Bobbi laughed. "The Belleview was the perfect place for a speakeasy. It sat on a high bluff and was surrounded with extensive gardens, so lookouts could easily spot cops approaching, no matter which route they tried. There was always plenty of time to hide everything before they could make it to the Candlelight or to the men's pub in the basement. In minutes, the liquor was stacked onto railroad handcarts and hidden in the maze of basement tunnels, or moved through a tunnel to the train yard. Pullman cars belonging to influential people were perfect for hiding booze. It was all a big game, really. Once the police left, the men brought the liquor right back in and the party would start all over again. That horrible mix in the galvanized tub was called *witches brew*. It was great fun to make bets and watch the comical faces people made when they accepted dares to drink the vile concoction."

The vision faded away. "Prohibition didn't stop people from drinking alcohol," Bobbi mused. "It just changed the route the liquor traveled to get to their glasses. Money blurred the lines between gangsters, politicians, cops, doctors, clergymen and the regular folks, who were just trying to get by. Lots of men got rich, but lots more wound up dead."

As the fog cleared, Lily recognized the pub in the basement of the Belleview Biltmore. The quiet atmosphere provided a sharp contrast to the Candlelight Speakeasy upstairs. Men in three-piece suits sat drinking whisky and smoking cigars. A few played poker.

Lily floated onto a chair next to Bobbi, who was still wearing her red dress. Bobbi and Bear eyed one another nervously, trying to ignore the heated discussion at the bar and pretending not to notice that men armed with submachine guns guarded the doors.

Lily squinted, trying to make out the faces at the bar. One looked amazingly like Al Capone. Another was definitely George Applegate.

George's face shone with sweat. "Cops and politicians always have their hands out, so it costs more to make problems go away than it used to. Plus, we're losing more shipments to highwaymen." He shot a sour glance in Bear's direction.

"I don't want to hear your goddamn excuses," the man replied, his voice eerily calm. "Find the sons of bitches who are stealing from me and rub them out or you're going to discover lead poisoning can be contagious in this racket." He waved his hand, dismissing George, and then took a drink.

It was obvious George wanted to continue the discussion, but when the armed giant standing next to the man snarled at him, he buttoned his lip and walked away.

When the man turned around and waved his hand, summoning Bear, Lily saw the three knife scars on his left cheek. She gasped, her suspicion confirmed. The man was indeed Al Capone – called Scarface by his enemies.

"Wait here," Bear whispered.

Bobbi nodded, but leaned forward, straining to hear the conversation.

"Bear, is it?" the man asked, holding out his meaty hand. "I hear good things about you from men I trust. And you're a family man. I like that. Means you've got roots to protect. So in spite of George's concerns, I'm giving you a promotion."

The fog rolled in again, carrying Lily away from the memory.

"Bear's new job involved hauling rum to Chicago and bringing Canadian whisky back to Florida," Bobbi said. "He was gone a few days each week, but he was paid very well. We could finally afford for me to quit working, and we brought Fred and Henrietta back home. It was wonderful having our family back together."

A vignette of Bobbi and her family, gathered around the kitchen table for a pot roast dinner, floated by at the edge of the mist.

"George wasn't pleased that I found happiness with another man, so he told Bear he didn't want anyone riding along on deliveries except his armed guard. Bear usually obeyed, but on our anniversary, he decided to break that rule so we could dance in the Candlelight after he dropped off his shipment at the Belleview Biltmore – just like we did on the night we met."

The clouds parted just as Bear's truck pulled up in the yard.

Bobbi ran out to greet him, wearing her knee-length, red dress and high-heeled dancing shoes. This time, the hip sash of her dress was decorated with a row of black fringe and she wore a tiara of black feathers in her short auburn bob.

Lily lifted her face toward the full moon and swallowed to settle her stomach, while Bobbi climbed into the truck. An instant later, she found herself seated next to Bobbi.

"Roberta Hamilton, I'm one lucky man," Bear said. "You're still the most beautiful woman I've ever seen."

Bobbi grinned and scooted closer to Bear, rewarding his compliment with a kiss.

"Where's Willie?" she asked.

"He wanted to check on his sick mother. Since the Belleview isn't very far, he asked if he could bail out a few miles back. I was happy to oblige since I didn't want him to know I was picking you up."

"I love you," Bobbi purred.

They shared another kiss before Bear put the truck into gear and turned down a dark, twisty back-road.

"I'm glad you chose this back road," Bobbi said. "I mean, I know you did it because there's less chance of getting caught by the police, but being out here all alone with you feels romantic."

She was reminiscing about their *two* weddings when Bear jerked his head sharply toward his rear view mirror.

His jaw tightened. "Bobbi – get on the floor. Now!" he commanded.

The frightened look on Bear's face told her not to question his order. As she scooted away from him, Bobbi stole a quick look through the rear window. A car was approaching fast and she knew that meant trouble. Whether it was the cops or highwaymen, Bear needed her out of harm's way, so he could concentrate on driving the truck as fast as he could on the dangerous road. Bobbi slid to the floor and curled up in a ball, her knees under her chin, her arms wrapped tightly around them.

Lily knew she was just an apparition in this scene, but she could feel Bobbi's fear and read her thoughts. A sense of dread settled over her. She tried to wake up.

The truck tires bounced in and out of chuckholes on the old road. Bobbi could hear the liquor bottles rattling in the back of the truck. She knew Bear wrapped each bottle in cloth scraps before packing them snuggly into wooden crates. She had always wondered why, but now she understood. How often had Bear had been in danger on these back roads? How many times had he outrun cops or men hoping to hijack his shipment?

"Is someone after the whisky?" she asked.

"Maybe, but this truck can handle rough roads better than a car." He tried to give her a quick, reassuring smile before skidding around a curve.

The back of Bobbi's head slammed against the dash. She wanted to cry out in pain, but managed to muffle the sound. She maneuvered around until her back was resting against the passenger seat, figuring she would be less likely to bounce around if facing forward.

Bear glanced at her and then over his shoulder at the cargo. A split second later, all hell broke loose. There was a loud bang and the rear window exploded, sending shards of glass flying all over the passenger compartment. Bobbi saw that Bear had cuts on the side of his face.

"What happened?" she cried.

"It's okay, Bobbi. Don't worry. Sometimes windows break on rough drives. It's happened before." Without taking his eyes off the road, he reached behind his back and pulled out the folded army blanket he used for back support. He tossed it to her, getting his hand back on the wheel just in time to slide around another sharp curve. "Cover yourself so the glass won't cut you."

He shot a glance out the side window and began swerving back and forth across the road while Bobbi covered herself. The wool blanket was saturated with Bear's scent, giving her a sense of calm despite the terrifying circumstances.

There was another bang and the passenger window blew out. From under the blanket, Bobbi thought she heard Bear grunt and wondered if he had gotten cut by flying shards of glass. When she heard another bang, her blood ran cold with understanding. Someone was shooting at them.

Bobbi felt the truck veer sharply to the right, hit against something, and then swerve back to the left. Another shot rang out. This time, she heard a voice yelling outside the passenger window.

"How'd you like that applesauce, you son-of-a-bitch?"

Bobbi knew the yelling was coming from the black car – and sensed it had pulled up next to them. She also knew the road was too narrow for two vehicles to travel side by side for long.

Two more shots rang out. The truck hit against the side of the car – harder this time. From under her blanket, Bobbi heard the car drop back. It was behind them now. Bear hit the accelerator and took a sharp turn to the left. The truck struggled to remain on four wheels, but failed. The driver's side lifted off the ground and the passenger door fell open. Bear grabbed for Bobbi just as she started to slide out of the opening, blanket and all. He caught her around the waist, but lost control of the truck.

Before a scream could escape Bobbi's lips, the truck careened off the road, and into a tree-lined ravine. Bear managed to hold onto her, even though one of her legs was hanging out the door.

Neither of them saw the massive oak tree – dead ahead.

Chapter Thirty One

Lily let out a blood-curdling scream and covered her eyes, refusing to look at the wreckage. She tried to pretend this was just a bad dream, but she knew it wasn't. This was a memory – Bobbi's memory. An instant later, she was engulfed by the fog and pulled away from the scene.

She struggled to wake up, without success. When the fog parted, Lily sat at the parlor table, trembling. Margaret pushed a cup of hot tea across the table to her.

"Why did I have to see that?" she cried. "What possible good can come from seeing more lives destroyed in a car accident?"

"I'm sorry the memory upset you." Margaret took a sip from her teacup. "I know the circumstances were similar to your own tragedy, but you must remember that these are Bobbi's memories, not yours. I'm quite certain she wouldn't be willing to relive this horror, unless she believed doing so could provide great benefit to you." Margaret pointed at Lily's tea. "Drink deeply and collect yourself. Then you must go back. She's waiting for you."

Lily shivered, still reeling. "But why do I have to see it?" She wrapped her hands around her warm teacup. "Can't Bobbi just tell me about it?"

"I don't know why," Margaret said. "It's not my story; it's hers. You need to trust Bobbi to discern which memories you must witness." She studied Lily. "And no matter what you observe, I want you to remember this simple truth: No matter what happens, it is *never* as important as what happens *next.*"

Lily took a deep drink and wiped her teary eyes as the fog gathered in thick folds around her. She hoped she wouldn't have to witness any more of the accident, but braced herself, just in case.

When the mist began to clear, Lily heard two men's voices in the shadows. She bit her tongue, fighting the impulse to scream. Her eyes were open, but it was too dark to see more than blurry shapes.

"Jesus Christ," one of the men barked. "You said he was alone."

"He ought to a been. This here is his own fault," the other man replied. "I know you wuz lookin' forward to comfortin' his hotsy-totsy widow, but ain't no use crying over spilt milk."

A train whistle blew nearby. "I've always loved that sound," Bobbi murmured.

Surprised, Lily tried to peer into the darkness. She was certain Bobbi wasn't actually speaking, yet she could hear Bobbi's voice as clearly as if they were chatting together.

"The whistle reminds me of when I lived near the hotel's rail-road tracks," Bobbi's voice continued.

When a memory snippet appeared of old Doc Farthing, smoking his pipe on the porch of East Gate Cottage, Lily finally understood. *"Bobbi's reminiscing. I'm sharing her thoughts."*

She watched as other memories of Bobbi's life drifted through her mind, flashing past like photographs. As each new image appeared, the previous one faded away. Bobbi was enjoying the visions, but the conversation between the two angry men was distracting. Like a mosquito buzzing in her ear, it kept drawing her attention.

"Come on… let's scram before somebody sees us," the first man said.

His voice sounded familiar, but it was too difficult to concentrate. Bobbi stayed quiet, hoping the men would go away and let her enjoy her memories in peace.

"What about all that there hooch?"

"Leave it. I don't want to risk getting copped for murder."

"Murder?" Bobbi echoed. *"Did they kill someone?"*

Lily continued to feel only what Bobbi felt and see only what she saw. Nagging thoughts and discomfort pulled Bobbi away from her sweet memories, toward the voices. She tried to move, but couldn't. Something heavy held her down.

"Maybe they could help me up," she thought. She tried to call out, but her mouth felt full of sharp pebbles and her jaw wasn't working properly. She pushed a pebble out with her tongue. Somewhere deep inside, it occurred to her that the pebbles felt like broken teeth sliding over her lips, but she continued nonetheless, hoping that once they were gone, she could speak – or at least be comfortable enough to return to her dreams.

It worked, but she was too tired to shout. As she slipped back into unconsciousness, the soothing memories resurfaced. She was at the Belleview Biltmore, learning to dance. She could hear the music of the waltz and see old Doc Farthing smiling down at her. *"One, two, three, one, two, three... don't watch your feet. Let Doc lead you around the floor...one, two, three..."*

"Bobbi, wake up. We hit a tree."

The ballroom vanished into the darkness.

"Bear, is that you?" Bobbi asked, rousing herself awake. She was certain her eyes were open, but she couldn't see. Everything felt cold and wet and dark.

"I feel zozzled," Bobbi thought, trying to keep calm. She blinked, but still couldn't see. *"Something must be covering my eyes."* She tried to raise her hands to her face, but she couldn't move one of her arms at all, and her other arm was partially pinned down by something heavy. She felt around the object as much as she could, in an attempt to figure out what was holding her captive. To her horror, she realized that Bear was wedged across her body at a peculiar angle.

"Bear! Wha 'appened?" She shouted. Her voice didn't sound right – as if her tongue was swollen and numb.

Bear didn't move. Bobbi listened carefully... for the sound of his breathing... for the other voices... for a car ...for anything that would let her know that she was not alone. She knew they were in serious trouble, but she couldn't stay awake.

"I'll rest a few minutes and then try again," she thought. She closed her eyes and sank back into unconsciousness.

Suddenly, Bear appeared, just beyond her reach. His expression was grave, but a beautiful light glowed behind him.

"Oh, you're all right," Bobbi said, breathing a sigh of relief. "Come closer."

"You have to wake up, Bobbi," he said. "I know you're hurt real bad, but the children need you."

Bobbi tried to think, but the pain was too great.

Bear gazed at her, his eyes filled with sorrow. "I know this is hard, but you're the smartest, strongest woman I ever saw. You can handle whatever comes. Get a message to Butch Torrio at the hotel. He'll help you." He looked at something in the distance and then turned back to her. "I love you, Red. Never forget that."

"I don't understand," Bobbi whimpered. "What's happening?"

"I have to go to Heaven, but someone's coming to help you," Bear said. "Now, Bobbi... you must wake up and call out. Now!" Then he disappeared, along with the bright light.

Bobbi's world turned dark again. "Bear!" She cried. She heard a stranger's voice in the dark, but ignored it. "Bear! Come back!"

Chapter Thirty Two

More than anything, Bobbi wanted to float away with Bear to the gates of Heaven. But a man's voice pierced the darkness again, imprisoning her in life.

"God, oh God..." he gasped.

A sea of clouds wrapped around Lily, pulling her from the awful memory. Before she had time to be grateful, she was startled by another voice inside the fog.

"Bobbi's memories from right after the crash aren't too good, so I'll share mine with you," Clay Long said.

The scene of the crash reappeared at the edge of the mist, but this time, Lily was viewing it from the top of the ravine. It was no less terrifying at a distance. She stared at the truck, smashed against the giant tree, knowing that Bear and Bobbi were still inside the mangled cab.

"Is this how Bobbi died?" she wondered. She took a deep breath and tried to relax, hoping she wouldn't have to view any more memories from the terrible event unfolding at the bottom of the ravine.

Clay's voice was deep and soothing. "I was a happy-go-lucky bindle stiff... minding my own business, riding the rails, making myself at home in empty boxcars... until I had the bad luck to catch a ride on the train that ran alongside this road. The sun was just coming up and the train was moving slow, so I decided to jump off and walk to town, to see if there was any work to be had in these parts... or maybe find a friendly game of poker. I noticed some fresh tire tracks in the dirt between the rail and the road, and wondered if some fellas were operating a still out here. I decided to take a look around. That's when I spotted the truck."

Lily looked at the wreck, imagining what it must have been like to make such a gruesome discovery.

"I fought in the Great War, so it wasn't the first dead man I'd ever seen," he said. "But I wasn't prepared to see a woman torn up like that."

The clouds parted swiftly and then Lily was floating next to Clay as he half-walked; half-slid down the ravine to the truck.

"God! Oh God," he repeated, as he peeked into the cab. Bear and Bobbi were trapped inside; their bloodied bodies tangled together. Clay swallowed hard and pulled the partially ajar passenger door the rest of the way open.

Lily flinched when she noticed the calf of Bobbi's leg had been crushed in the door. Bear's right arm was wrapped around Bobbi's waist and his torso lay across hers. Lily heard Clay's thoughts. He was hoping they had died quickly.

"Oh God," he said, unable to find any other words. He fought the urge to vomit.

Bobbi was confused. "God?" she asked.

"Jesus... you're still alive!" Clay sputtered. "Rest easy, lady... I'll go get help!"

Bobbi remembered what Bear had told her. She struggled to form words. "Children."

"Children!" Clay screamed. "Are your children in the back of the truck?"

Bobbi moaned. Clay bent closer to hear what she was saying.

"Liquor... tell Butch... help my children."

Her words, issued through the broken hole in her face that had once been her mouth, were difficult to understand, but Clay got the gist of it. He glanced back at the tarp-covered truck bed, trying to deduce what had happened. "You were hauling moonshine?" he asked.

"Belleview... tell them... Bear hijacked..." Exhausted and near death, Bobbi allowed the soft blackness to engulf her once again.

Clay eyed Bobbi, trying to decide if she was finally dead. "She should be," he muttered. Her face was crushed. What remained of it was swollen, bloody and bruised. Her eyes were barely in the sockets and her nose lay against her cheek. Her teeth were broken or knocked out altogether. Bits of them were caught in the coagulated blood on her chin and a few more were embedded in the dash, where her face had taken the full impact of the crash.

"Lady? Hey there... Lady?" Clay asked. She didn't move. He eyed her closely, looking for any sign of life. "I doubt anything's left to sell," he said. "But I'll check."

Leaving the passenger door open, he stepped to the back of the truck.

With her heart aching for Bobbi and Bear, Lily floated along as if she were Clay's shadow. She could see Bobbi, but no longer saw things from her perspective. Instead, she saw things as Clay saw them and shared his thoughts.

Clay pulled off the tarp and found, to his amazement, the truck bed was completely filled with wooden crates. Each crate contained twelve bottles of fine Canadian whisky, individually wrapped in rags. Straw was stuffed between the bottles, preventing them from bumping against one another. Miraculously, the entire shipment appeared to be intact.

Clay gave a low whistle, trying to calculate the whisky's worth. *"Enough to see me through a few months of fine living, for sure,"* he thought. He was already spending the money in his imagination when he heard Bobbi moan again.

"Good God, woman. How can you still be alive?" he muttered as he walked back to the passenger door.

"Listen, lady," he said. "When the cops get here, they're going to confiscate all that liquor, and if you live, you'll be charged with bootlegging and your children will be put in an orphanage." He studied her, trying to determine whether she heard him. "I'm going to do you a favor and take all the whisky before they get here. That way, no one will ever know the truth."

"Please...help my children," Bobbi pleaded. A single tear rolled down her mangled cheek.

Clay was touched by her devotion. When he was four years old, his mother had left him at a convent and never looked back. It didn't seem right to allow a good mother to die believing she had failed to provide for her children.

"I'll tell you what," he said. "I'll unload the truck and stash the liquor. After we get you some help, I'll go to the Belleview and tell Butch what happened."

Bobbi moaned and Clay moved closer to hear her.

"Your word.... give me... your word," she begged.

"Sure...yeah... you have my word."

Bobbi took a long, rattling breath and focused. "Break your vow... I'll haunt you... drive you... insane."

Clay stumbled back several steps. "Damn," he mumbled. "I was trying to be nice and here she goes and puts a witch's curse on me!" He tried to shake off her words as he went to work on the truck's cargo, carrying one case after another twenty yards away. He covered the whisky with weeds and brush, as well as the path he inadvertently created by walking back and forth so many times.

Then he circled back around to the passenger side of the truck, fully expecting Bobbi to be dead. "Hey lady," he said, "You didn't really put a witch's curse on me, did you?"

To his utter amazement, Bobbi replied, "Yes."

Before he had time to react, Clay heard a truck in the distance. It was the first vehicle to pass along this road since he arrived, so he scurried to the top of the ravine and waved it down, certain the driver would be willing to take two poor souls to the hospital... or undertaker. He smirked. If he was lucky, he could hitch a ride to the Belleview Hotel, find Butch, and sell him the liquor before leaving town.

Lily froze, aghast. Clay Long had no intention of giving any portion of the liquor profits to Bobbi's children. As the fog gathered around her, she left the memory grieving for Bobbi and disgusted with Clay. *"No wonder Bobbi's always fighting with him!"*

When the clouds parted a moment later, Clay was cleaned up and having a drink at the bar in the basement pub of the Belleview Biltmore.

"Good thinking, saving the whisky." Butch clapped Clay's shoulder. "Bear Hamilton was a good man... and a good driver. Bad luck that Willie wasn't with him... and a real pity that Bobbi was. Wonder why the highwaymen left the booze behind? Maybe you spooked 'em."

"Could have," Clay agreed, still thanking his lucky stars that Butch told him the booze belonged to Scarface and offered him a handsome reward *before* he tried to sell it.

Lily noticed George Applegate watching the encounter, his thin, spectacled face, void of emotion. Although his hair was beginning to gray, he still wore it parted down the middle; with two tight curls plastered against his pale forehead in opposite directions. He signaled to Clay. "Butch, send your new friend on over here," he said. "We have business to discuss."

Clay sauntered over and eyed George, sizing him up.

"The name's George Applegate," he said. He waved at a chair, indicating where he wanted Clay to sit. "So, you're ab-so-lute-ly positive my driver and the dish are dead?"

Clay placed his freshly brushed, black Fedora hat on the leather-covered poker table and sat. He started to nod, but something about the look in the man's beady eyes stopped him. He decided to clarify the situation. "Well, the man was dead, for sure... probably killed instantly in the wreck. And I don't see how the woman could still be alive. Her whole face was crushed." He grimaced at the memory and swirled his hand over his face, trying to paint a picture of Bobbi's injuries. "I doubt she was still alive when they got to the hospital."

"You didn't take her to the hospital?"

"Well, I was going to, but since we were driving past the Belleview Biltmore and she had said the liquor shipment belonged to you fellas, I figured I better stop and take care of business. After all, there's nothing I could do for the dame. Like I said, I'm sure she was already in the Lord's hands."

George's thin lips curled into a partial smile. "Well, Then you probably did the right thing." He paused and rolled the ice cubes around in his rocks glass. "Lucky you were able to spot the truck at the bottom of that ravine. Are you sure you didn't have something to do with it going off the road in the first place?"

Clay swallowed, his practiced smile covering his unease. He had told Butch that the truck crashed into a tree, but he didn't think he had mentioned the tree was in a ravine. "Like I said, I jumped from a boxcar to take a whiz in the trees, and I spotted the truck. No one else was around. Just lucky I found your shipment before the cops did, I reckon."

"Yeah – lucky. And the broad didn't recognize the highwaymen?"

"She didn't talk much. If she knew, she took it to the grave."

George removed his glasses, took out his handkerchief, and rubbed the lenses. When he finished, he put them back on and studied Clay. "Well, we might be able to use a fella like you... able to keep his priorities straight in the midst of a bad situation."

"Yeah?" Clay sat up straighter. "I wouldn't mind having dough in my pockets more regular."

"Okay. You'll start out loading and guarding boxcar shipments. Prove to me that you know your onions, and I'll move you up the ranks."

"Sounds copacetic," Clay said.

George Applegate moved his jacket aside, intentionally revealing a shoulder harness and pearl-handled revolver. "You can bunk with some of the other men here at the hotel. Butch will get you settled in. And one more thing..." He closed his jacket, patting the revolver. "Don't ever forget who you work for. That mistake could lead to a fatal case of lead poisoning."

The fog dropped over Lily like a blanket, carrying her from the memory. The moment Bobbi spoke, everything shifted back to her perspective.

"After the accident, I floated between worlds, trying to find Bear," Bobbi said. "Instead, I found Margaret Plant. The moment she appeared, it dawned on me that I hadn't seen any ghosts since I got married."

A memory snippet suddenly opened in the mist next to her, causing Lily to jerk in surprise. In the memory, Bobbi looked as if the accident never happened.

Margaret smiled. "How appropriate that we reunite in the hospital you helped me build."

Bobbi smiled at the sight of her old friend. "Hello, Mrs. Plant. I'm glad to see you've finally accepted the fact that you're a ghost. But your memory is fuzzy," she teased. "It was *you* who helped *me* build the hospital."

Margaret chuckled. "Perhaps we're equally deserving of praise, though neither of us received any."

"I've missed you, Mrs. Plant."

"For heavens' sake, Bobbi – you're a grown woman now. Call me Margaret. And I'm a spirit, not a ghost."

Bobbi knitted her eyebrows together. "Am I a spirit, also?"

Margaret glanced down. Lily followed her example and was startled to see Bobbi's body lying in a hospital bed below them, her head wrapped in bandages.

"You're not dead, Bobbi, but you're badly injured. I'm certain you can survive, but the nurse who just left your bedside isn't, so if you want to live, you must wake up, Bobbi. Now!" Margaret clapped her hands and vanished, along with the fog.

"Bear said the same thing," Bobbi said, as the fog parted.

Lily tried to make sense of the scene before her. She and Bobbi's spirit were floating above Bobbi's hospital bed, inspecting her body as if examining a car she was thinking about buying. Except for narrow openings for her mouth and nostrils, Bobbi's head was bandaged in blood-stained gauze. Her injured leg, also wrapped in gauze, rested inside a three-sided, wooden box, and her left arm had been immobilized with plaster-coated bandages. After surveying the damage, Bobbi's unblemished spirit floated down and melted into her battered body.

For Lily, it was as if someone had turned out the lights. She could see nothing, but could hear everything. She couldn't feel Bobbi's physical pain, but she experienced her growing sense of alarm.

Bobbi tried to talk, but her mouth wouldn't form words and her jaw throbbed. She attempted to wave her arms, but they wouldn't move. Her leg radiated excruciating waves of pain. She moaned.

A woman's voice murmured softly, "There, there now... don't try to move. You're in the hospital. I'm a nurse and I'm going to give you a shot to help you sleep. The pain will soon be gone."

Bobbi felt a sting in her thigh, similar to that of an insect bite. As she drifted willingly into the inky void, the fog enveloped Lily. She floated for only a moment before the mist parted again, returning her to the parlor table, where Margaret waited.

"Did Bobbi die?" she blurted.

"As I've told you before, Bobbi's story is not mine to tell," Margaret said.

"Can you tell me if you were tweening with her in the hospital?"

"Yes. That's a memory from my own story, and I'm willing to share it with you."

"You said Bobbi wasn't ready to die. How did you know that?" Lily asked.

"I didn't. But as long as her spirit was still tethered to her body, I wanted her to try to live."

"I must have been tweening with my son, Dylan, after the accident." Lily started to cry. "Maybe, if I'd told him to wake up, he would have lived. But I didn't."

"Tweening occurs when a person is hovering between life and death. It's impossible for a spirit to tell who will survive and who won't," Margaret consoled. "If a body is too damaged, it will die, no matter how much its spirit wants to live."

A knock on her hotel room door sent Lily falling through the fog. She woke with a start, her face wet with tears.

"Lily, it's Seth. Are you in there?"

Chapter Thirty Three

"Seth?" Lily sat up. "Just a minute." She wiped her tears with the back of her hand and hopped to the door. She turned the glass doorknob, relieved that Seth couldn't see what a mess she was.

"Are you okay?" Seth asked.

"Sure. Why wouldn't I be?"

"You said you'd meet me for breakfast, so when you didn't show up, I got worried." Seth frowned. "Did you change your mind?"

"What – what time is it?" Lily asked, confused.

"Eleven thirty."

Lily's jaw dropped. "I'm sorry, Seth... I overslept. I don't know what's wrong with me lately. Did you eat without me?"

"No, I just had a cup of coffee. Three cups, actually."

"We could have lunch together before I head to the hospital, if you want."

"That'd be great," he said, relaxing his shoulders. "Maybe the concierge will know of a place nearby where we can still order breakfast."

"Why don't you go check? I'll meet you in the lobby in a few minutes."

"Or you could let me in while you get dressed," Seth said, feigning innocence. "I promise not to peek."

Lily coughed. "Nice try, but no."

"Okay, if you insist. But hurry, okay? I'm starving!"

Thirty minutes later, they were seated in a corner booth at Ted's Luncheonette. It was a modest diner, but it was clean and bright, and offered a surprising variety of breakfast options. A young waitress, brimming with southern charm, helped Seth choose a meat-lover's omelet with home fries and a stack of pancakes. Lily ordered French toast and sausage links.

"I've been thinking," Seth said. "There are way too many reports about ghosts at the hotel for all of them to be fakes."

"Yeah. As much as I hate to admit it, I came to the same conclusion. They're real. Now I just have to figure out what they're trying to teach me."

"What makes you think they're trying to teach you anything? I mean, ghosts usually haunt people because they want to get a message to someone, or catch their killer, or something like that, right?"

"Not ghosts. Spirits."

"Is there a difference, or is that just the politically correct term these days?"

Lily laughed. "Don't be a smart-aleck. It has something to do with how much of a soul's energy remains in this realm. Margaret says a spirit's energy is intact, but a ghost is just a fragment of its former self."

"Where does the rest of the ghost's energy go?"

"Apparently, that's a big mystery. Some lighted path shows up and the dead person decides whether to follow it or not. Margaret says no one on this side knows for sure where the path leads."

"Sounds like the ending in that Patrick Swayze movie."

Lily laughed. "No, it's not like that – at least not in my case. These spirits are sharing their memories with me. They're trying to teach me something, but I can't figure out what."

Lily didn't realize how hungry she was until she looked up and saw the waitress approaching with their order. "Yum," she said, eyeing her breakfast. While cutting her sausage link with the side of her fork, she glanced at Seth's meal. "Your omelet is at nine, potatoes are at three and your pancakes are on a separate plate to the right." She popped the bite of sausage into her mouth, immediately wishing she had blown on it first. "Hot!" she warned, juggling the bite around in her mouth until it cooled enough to swallow.

"Thanks for the warning," Seth said, blowing on a bite of pancake. "You know, maybe the key to figuring out what the spirits are trying to teach you, is to figure out what you need to learn."

"How do I do that?"

"Maybe I can help, if you tell me more about yourself. For instance, I know your body is still healing from the wreck, but what about your head?" He jabbed his fork into a large bite of omelet. "You know, I lost my sight five years ago, and sometimes I still get mad when I think about what I've lost and the unfairness of it all… Christ, even if I get my sight back, I'll probably still be pissed that it happened in the first place – and I'll always worry it might happen again. And you lost a hell of lot more than I did."

They ate in silence for a several minutes before Lily found her voice.

"You know I lost my only child – my son," she finally said.

"Yeah, and I can't even imagine how awful that must have been," he said. "But it was an accident, right? I mean, it's not like you had the power to prevent it – just like I couldn't avoid catching a stupid virus in my eyes."

"I was driving. That makes it my fault."

"Bullshit," he said. "If it was your fault, you would have gone to jail for manslaughter. Did you go to jail?"

His logical response caught Lily off-guard. "No."

"Did you get charged with the accident?" Seth persisted.

"No. A logging company was charged."

"Keep talking," he said.

"Because they overloaded a truck, the tie-downs didn't hold when the truck jack-knifed on an overpass."

"So it wasn't your fault, Lily."

"Yes, it was. I could have insisted that we stop for the night."

"More bullshit." Seth swallowed a large bite of his omelet. "What if you had stopped for the night and there was a fire at the hotel, causing the exact same outcome? Would you blame yourself for stopping? You're not omnipotent, Lily. Tell me more about the accident." He wolfed down his pancakes, waiting for her to speak.

"I can't." Lily paused. "I mean... I don't remember much about the accident, except what I see in my nightmares. Scott handled all the legal stuff because I couldn't bear to listen to testimony and all that."

"Scott is your husband?"

"Yes."

"Was he in the accident, too?"

"Yeah, but I don't want to talk about this anymore, Seth."

"Okay, let's talk about what happens when the gho... the *spirits* come calling. How do you know they're there?"

Lily thought about it. "Well, when I fall asleep, a thick fog bank surrounds me. I float in the clouds like I'm weightless. It's relaxing – kind of like Xanax, but in a dream world. Then the fog fades away and I watch something that happened in their past."

She described a few encounters and patiently answered Seth's questions. "Last night I saw some pretty disturbing memories. I wanted to wake up, but Margaret insisted they were important."

"What did you see?" Seth asked.

"They showed me a truck accident from a long time ago. Bear died and Bobbi is probably going to die, Clay turned out to be a heartless criminal, and now I have a second, even more horrible accident to think about when I go to sleep." Lily drew in a deep breath. "How can knowing all of that be a good thing?"

"Wait a minute. A bear died?" Seth asked, confused.

"No, Bear was Bobbi's husband's nickname. He died because highway men were trying to steal some bootlegged liquor and his truck crashed into a tree and then..." Lily stopped, suddenly realizing how absurd she must sound.

Seth frowned. "Okay, I'm starting to feel like I walked in halfway through a movie. When we get back to the hotel, I think it would be good for you to write this all down so you don't forget any of it. Maybe the lessons they're trying to teach you are like calculus. You have to see all the parts of the equation before you can figure out the answers."

"Maybe so," Lily said. "I forgot to tell you something else. Margaret Plant's spirit is trying to talk to my Grams for me."

Lily smiled at the shocked look on Seth's face. She let the new information sink in while the waitress refilled their coffee cups.

"How can Margaret talk to your grandmother? Isn't she – you know – pretty far gone to be dreaming?" Seth asked.

"Margaret calls it *tweening.* It's when a spirit talks with people who are hovering between life and death. She said lots of spirits enjoy hanging out at hospitals, tweening with people."

"If spirits can jump into people's dreams, why bother waiting until someone's almost dead to talk to them?" Seth asked.

"According to Margaret, it's really hard for spirits to connect and share their memories with the living, and after people die, their spirits usually go straight into the light. But when people are in-between – they're almost, but not quite dead, their spirits begin to pull away from their bodies and that's when other spirits can talk to them."

Seth nodded. "So all the spirits have to do is go to the hospital and look for people who are hooked up to life support equipment, right?"

"Something like that," she said.

"Do you think that accounts for the near-death experiences people talk about?"

"Probably not all of them, but definitely some."

Seth cocked his head to the side. "And Margaret Plant is going to talk to your grandmother?"

Lily waited to respond while the waitress cleared their dishes and moved off to check on her other tables.

"Grams and I grew apart during the last few years. I want to make sure she knows how much I love her and appreciate her giving up so much of her life to raise me."

"The last few years?" Seth repeated. "You mean, since your accident?"

"Yeah. It's totally my fault."

"You sure are eager to accept the blame for everything," he said.

"Well, it *is* my fault," she insisted. "Everyone has their own way of grieving and I wasn't able to accept hers. It was easier to just break off communication with her."

"Oh," Seth said. "Was she one of those people always says stuff like, 'you have to accept what's happened, and move on with your life'?"

From the way he spoke, Lily was certain Seth had received a lot of this type of well-meaning advice after he lost his eyesight.

"Actually, that type of attitude might have been easier to deal with. Grams kept insisting that Dylan wasn't dead. According to her, he called regularly and was having all kinds of great adventures."

"Like earning an early admittance into medical school?" Seth asked. "Isn't that what the nurse said at Bay Manor?"

"Exactly," Lily said. "You see, Grams and Dylan used to plan adventures they would have together after he finished college. I'm pretty sure dementia was setting in and it probably made Grams feel better to pretend he was living an incredible life out there somewhere, but I couldn't handle it. I hoped she would give it up after a while, but she didn't. As a matter of fact, she got worse. One minute she insisted he was a doctor, the next he was a musician. When she started talking about Dylan's children last year, I finally snapped and refused to talk to her anymore. Scott came down and moved her into Bay Manor. I planned to reconnect as soon as I was stronger, but I waited too long."

"Listen – are you absolutely positive that your grandmother was imagining everything? Maybe Dylan was able to reach out from great beyond like Margaret and..."

"Can I bring you folks anything else?" the waitress interrupted.

"Just the bill," Lily said, pulling out her phone to call for the shuttle.

The waitress tore the ticket from her pad and held it out to Lily.

Lily glanced at the amount and handed her a twenty. "This meal's on me for standing you up this morning, Seth."

As they left the restaurant, Seth's unanswered question echoed in Lily's thoughts. *"What if Grams really did have a connection with Dylan's spirit?"*

Chapter Thirty Four

Pete stopped to drop Lily off at the hospital before driving Seth back to the hotel.

"Do you want to get together later?" Seth asked.

"Maybe – let me call you when I get back to the hotel, okay?"

When she entered her grandmother's hospital room and kissed her cheek, Lily immediately felt a wave of guilt for arriving later than normal. Grams' breathing was more labored and her skin was so pale it appeared almost translucent. *"It won't be long now,"* she thought.

Lily pulled a chair close to the bed and sat down, taking the old woman's frail, wrinkled hand in her own. "I love you, Grams," she murmured. "I'm so sorry you had to sacrifice your dreams to take care of me. You and Gramps deserved so much more happiness than I was able to give you. I wish I had taken better care of you this last year." She gave her grandmother's hand a light squeeze. "Maybe you can find Gramps and Dylan on the other side and have wonderful adventures together, just like you planned."

Lily laid her head down, her cheek resting on her grandmother's hand, and began to cry. *"Everyone I love is either already gone or leaving me."* Her tears dissolved into sobs, racking her body so hard, it was difficult to breath.

"It's okay, Lily," a voice soothed.

Lily jerked up, momentarily believing Grams had spoken.

Nurse Opal, drawn to the sound of her weeping, repeated, "It's okay."

She knelt beside Lily and held her heavy arms open wide. Lily leaned against the kindly nurse, still crying, and allowed Opal to rock her like a child until she had no more tears.

"She's not in any pain, honey. And she's had a good life, filled with love."

Lily moaned. "I don't think she knows how much I love her."

Opal smiled and shook her head, wiping Lily's tear-stained cheeks with a tissue. "Oh, Lily... she knows. I'm positive she does. You wouldn't have cried like that if you didn't. And you couldn't have kept so much love a secret from her. It would have shown itself in a thousand ways. And besides, Miz Bloom isn't thinking about the fights you had or the time you spent apart. She's dreaming about her entire lifetime and all the special moments that made it worthwhile."

"How do you know that?"

"Look at her face. Miz Bloom's in a good place. Go on... really, truly look at her."

The big nurse grabbed the side rail of the bed and pulled herself to her feet. "Uh-huh," she confirmed, nodding at Grams. "That's the look of someone who's at peace, all right."

"Opal's right." Lily gazed at Grams. *"She looks like she's enjoying a good dream. Maybe she's having a nice conversation with Margaret."*

"Well, I best get back to work now," Opal said, turning to leave. "Thanks for..."

"Nonsense," Opal waved hand as she reached the doorway. "It does me good to know that my patients are loved so much."

Lily sagged back into her chair, emotionally exhausted. She closed her eyes and thought about Grams until the mist settled over her, carrying her into the peaceful buffer between worlds.

She hoped Margaret would be waiting for her with a message from her grandmother, but when the fog dissipated, there was only darkness and the sound of a man's quiet, reverent, chanting.

Lily immediately realized she was with Bobbi – seeing only what Bobbi saw and sharing her emotions.

"Through this holy unction and His own most tender mercy may the Lord pardon thee whatever sins or faults thou hast committed by sight..."

Bobbi felt light pressure over one of her eyes, then the other. The touch conveyed a sense of peace.

"...sins or faults thou hast committed by hearing..."

Bobbi felt pressure against one ear, then the other

"...sins or faults thou hast committed by..."

"Stop that!" an angry man interrupted. "This one doesn't need last rites, Father. She's not going anywhere just yet."

"She's beyond saving," a woman's voice snapped. "Now, be respectful and leave, so Father Jacob can continue."

"I'm sorry, my son," the gentle voice intervened. "But Nurse Parker is trained in medicine and knows when death is approaching."

"Well, she's wrong this time, Father," the angry man insisted. "This woman's not dying."

"You can't stop death," Nurse Cowell said. "You're not God."

"And neither are you. Now both of you – get out," the man ordered. "Bring me the man who's in charge here."

Lily heard footsteps receding.

"Bobbi," the man said. "It's Alton Farthing. I'm here now and I'll take care of you. Rest, my darling. You'll live if I have anything to say about it."

Bobbi felt the bandages being removed from her head, but she couldn't clear her thoughts. It was as if she were drunk beyond the ability to function. *"Why is Alton Farthing taking care of me instead of Bear?"* she wondered.

Finally, there was light.

Bobbi couldn't move or open her eyes more than tiny slits, but through her eyelashes, she could make out shadowy images. *"Is this really happening?"* She couldn't decide. Sleep kept trying to claim her, but she fought to stay awake.

She heard more footsteps.

"There he is," the nurse said, pointing at Alton.

"I'm Waldo Rothberg, Administrator of Morton Plant Hospital." The thin man's nasal voice was shrill with fury. "Who do you think you are, coming into this ward and making demands?"

Alton Farthing rounded on him, matching Rothberg's anger. "I'm Dr. Alton Farthing of Yale Hospital. And what I'm demanding is that your patient's condition be treated rather than simply sedating her until she dies."

"Dr. Farthing?" Rothberg instantly reversed his demeanor. "*The* Dr. Farthing? I'm terribly sorry, sir – I didn't recognize you. I knew your father, and I've followed your remarkable career in the medical journals. I recently read about your innovative research – to combine Sir Harold Gillies' skin grafting techniques with surgeries to treat battlefield injuries. Remarkable."

"Splendid. I'm pleased to hear you take the time to at least *read* about advanced medical techniques," Alton sneered.

Rothberg didn't react to the cynicism in Alton's tone. "Yes, we're a small hospital, but we do try to stay informed." He returned his attention to the matter at hand. "Do you know this patient, Dr. Farthing?" he asked.

"This *patient* is Roberta Hamilton. And if it weren't for her friendship with Morton Plant, this hospital might never have been built! She should be commanding the attention of your finest physicians... not this..." Alton waved his hand at the nurse and the open ward. He shook his head with disgust.

"I don't know the lady, but I've been told that keeping her sedated is the kindest thing we can do for her. When she was admitted two days ago, the attending physician determined it would be impossible to save her life, even if she had the ability to pay for her care, which she does not."

"The ability to pay?" Alton shouted. "I don't know about you, but I took an oath to care for my patients, without regard to their *ability to pay*. And if your physician had done a thorough examination, I'm certain he would have discovered that her vital organs appear to have suffered no damage whatever. I see no injuries that would prevent her survival."

"But even if she survived, what sort of life would she have?" Rothberg protested. "You've seen her face... and with head injuries like that, no doubt her brain is damaged."

"I'll know more about those injuries after I examine her," Alton said. "I have a proposal for you, Mr. Rothberg. In exchange for you allowing me to provide Mrs. Hamilton's medical care at no charge,

I'll extend the benefit of my education and experience to your staff until she is released from this hospital."

"You'd be willing to instruct and consult with my staff for free?" Rothberg was incredulous.

"Yes. And as long as Mrs. Hamilton is moved to a private room and no one interferes with the course of treatment I prescribe, I'll permit your staff to observe my methods. That might enhance their ability to more accurately diagnose and treat such cases in the future."

"You have a deal, Dr. Farthing," Rothberg gushed. "I'll make arrangements to have the patient... err, Mrs. Hamilton – moved immediately."

When Rothberg and his entourage were gone, Alton took Bobbi's hand. "Listen to me, Bobbi. You must live." His voice cracked. "I can't be content devoting my life to medicine unless I know you are well and happy. Live and I swear I'll move Heaven and Earth to make you whole again."

The fog gathered, pulling Lily from the memory. She thought about the hazy days immediately following her own accident. In addition to burns and her leg injury, Lily had suffered a skull fracture and a severe concussion. To help prevent brain damage, her doctor kept her sedated for more than two weeks, and like Bobbi, Lily often couldn't tell reality from hallucinations. To this day, she couldn't be positive whether her visions of Dylan were real or drug-induced.

Lily didn't notice the fog was parting until she heard Alton Farthing's soothing voice. He was standing at Bobbi's bedside, flanked by three dark-haired young men in white coats.

"How did this happen, Bobbi?" Alton's question was rhetorical, as Bobbi was still drugged and incoherent. "You curled into a ball to protect your body before the accident, but didn't have enough time to avoid it. And, while there's no doubt that your face hit the dashboard with great force, had you been looking straight forward, your nasal bone would have been driven into your cranium. You must have turned slightly to your right – perhaps to look out the window? And how did your leg get crushed? That makes no sense at all."

One of the dark-haired men cleared his throat. "Pardon me, Dr. Farthing. But what good does it do to try to figure out how an injury occurred?"

Alton glanced at the three young doctors. "At Yale, doctors stitch their surnames on their coats, so I don't have to remember them. I expect each of you to implement this practice by tomorrow. Until then, tell me your name each time you speak."

"I'm Dr. Mark Whiting, sir," replied the man who had asked the question.

"Well, Whiting, by visualizing what happened, not only can I make some assumptions about what injuries might have been sustained that are not readily observable, but I can also begin to formulate a plan to reverse the course of events."

The square-jawed Whiting nodded, admiration evident in his wide brown eyes. Lily thought he looked more like a movie star than a doctor.

"What are some of the issues we might expect to encounter during Mrs. Hamilton's facial reconstruction surgeries?" Alton asked.

"I'm Phillips," said the shortest of the three. He had a curly hair and an overbite. "She has too many breaks. There's no way to hold them in place as they heal."

Alton nodded without responding.

"I'm Ross," said a tall, thin man with round glasses. "There may be loose bone and tooth fragments that could cause additional damage if not removed."

Alton nodded again.

"Whiting, again. She needs to breathe and eat, but facial movement would hamper her recovery."

"All of you are quite right," replied Alton. "Additionally, we need to consider how to make the repairs in a manner that won't have negative cosmetic consequences."

"How is that possible, sir?" asked the handsome doctor. "I'm Whiting," he added.

"I'll operate in stages," Alton said. "First, I'll restore function – make the repairs that will allow her to breathe and eat. And I'll restore her orbital sockets to improve her vision. Once these surgeries are healed, I'll begin a second series of repairs to refine those functions and to remove temporary bracing structures necessary for the first repairs. I'll continue in this manner every six to eight weeks until her facial features are fully restored."

"Ross. Will she resemble her former self?"

"Her skin remained mostly intact, so my goal is to make Mrs. Hamilton look almost exactly the way she did before this accident." Alton said.

"Whiting, again. What about her leg?"

"A three-inch section of her fibula and tibia were crushed during the accident. Immobilizing the leg without using a plaster bandage provides the best chance for restored blood flow. If this approach fails, the leg will have to come off just below the knee, but either way, the crush injury is irreversible. Mrs. Hamilton will never walk again."

Lily felt a chill at the similarities. *"Is Bobbi trying to teach me that Dylan might have been saved if a doctor had intervened on his behalf, or that I should take advantage of modern medicine to repair my leg?"* She pushed these thoughts away and concentrated on scene before her.

"Mr. Rothberg believes you three are promising surgeons," Alton said. "Therefore, I will allow each of you to assist me tomorrow, as I complete the first phase of Mrs. Hamilton's facial reconstruction."

The three young men grinned at the news.

"As you are well-aware," said Alton, "I've spent several years studying surgical techniques and repairing debilitating facial injuries sustained on the battlefield and in manufacturing plants. Facial reconstruction requires superb surgical skills, artistic ability, a passion for precision, and the ability to develop a surgical plan as if playing chess – visualizing several moves ahead. Some of the finest surgeons I've ever known are incapable of this type of work, and this is the most complex case I've ever attempted." Alton took a deep breath and blew it out, shifting his gaze from one doctor to the next. "I won't tolerate anything less than perfection in my operating room.

Do you understand? "

The three young doctors bobbed their heads.

"Good. Tomorrow, I'll evaluate your surgical talent and select which one of you will continue to assist me moving forward."

"Whiting, here. How can we make her look like she did before, if we have no idea what she looked like?"

Alton gazed down at Bobbi. "I normally obtain a photograph from the patient's family, but I already know every contour of Mrs. Hamilton's face."

Bobbi's voice drifted through the mist, pulling Lily from the memory. "They never knew I heard them talking. It was distressing to learn my face was so broken, and even more devastating to realize that I would never dance again."

Chapter Thirty Five

"I drifted between the worlds of the living and the dead for many days after the accident. I wasn't certain in which I belonged," Bobbi's disembodied voice said.

As Lily floated along, two ethereal beings appeared in the mist. One was Bobbi; the other was a plain, young woman. Neither of them noticed Lily.

"Have you ever been to New York City?" the young woman asked.

Lily studied the woman. She was probably no more than sixteen, although her tawny hair, pulled into a haphazard bun and baggy brown dress made her look much older.

"No. I never saw any reason to travel. I've met people from all over the world at the Belleview Biltmore Hotel and they always tell me Belleair is the most beautiful place they've ever seen."

"I wish I saw New York City," the woman replied. "I was dead before I learnt spirits can only go places they already visited, or where they's buried. I spent my whole life on our farm. Well – till Papa fetched me to this hospital on account of I got the yellow fever." She shook her head. "He buried me in our orchard, but when the farm burnt down a while back, he done moved away. So nowadays I just stays here, talkin' to people. Folks should travel whilst they can."

"If get better, I should travel – perhaps take a train to New York City."

A voice came through the mist. "That's right, Bobbi, make plans for your future. Get better and I'll buy you that train ticket to New York."

Lily looked down. Through the mist, she saw Alton Farthing standing beside Bobbi's hospital bed. She drifted through the fog and watched, fascinated, as Bobbi's spirit reentered her body.

"Bobbi," Alton continued, unaware of the rejoining, "I'll be taking you into surgery in a few minutes, but before we go, the man who saved you is here to see you." Alton walked to the door. "Come on in, Mr. Long, but don't expect too much. Her mind seems to come and go. She's able to speak, but what she says doesn't always make sense. Her mouth is seriously injured, so you have to listen carefully to try to make out her words. I'll be right back."

Lily heard footsteps approaching and smelled the scent of a cigar, but before Clay Long appeared, she was pulled back into the fog and heard his voice.

"I came to the hospital to make sure Bobbi was dead before spending the money I got for the booze. I nearly keeled over when they told me she was still alive. And when they asked me if I'd like to see her, there wasn't much else I could do but say 'yes.'"

An instant later, Lily returned to the memory, but now she saw everything from Clay's perspective and felt his fear and revulsion as he approached Bobbi's bedside.

Bobbi's eyes were wrapped with gauze and the rest of her face was so swollen, it looked as though her discolored skin might burst open. Her deformed nose still lay against her cheek and her missing teeth and broken jaw made it appear as though she didn't have a chin.

"Mrs. Hamilton, I doubt you remember me, so I'll just be getting along now," he said. "I just wanted to wish you well."

Clay didn't understand Bobbi's response. "How's that again?" He lowered his ear near her mouth.

"Care for my children or die."

Her voice was low and her diction garbled, but Clay understood her perfectly. His eyes opened wide as he stumbled back from the bed, his heart pounding. "Jesus Christ, you really are a witch!"

Clay eyed the door and considered running, but thought better of the idea. He licked his lips and edged back to her bedside. "Come on, now, lady. You don't want to be all hateful and such. It's Unchristian-like. Why don't you go on and let the angels carry you off to Heaven like you already should of?"

Again, she mumbled an unintelligible response. Clay cringed as he bent closer. "How's that again?" he said.

"Take money and children to my sisters... or I'll haunt..." Exhausted, Bobbi lapsed into unconsciousness.

The fog dropped over Lily, pulling her away from the memory. She was disgusted with Clay and admired Bobbi for doing everything she could to make sure her children were cared for. The clouds parted so suddenly, she had to bend over and gulp air to keep from being sick.

Standing next to Lily, Clay knocked on the black door of a modest, white clapboard home. The woman who opened the door wore a faded blue, high-collared print dress that was several inches longer than the current fashion. She had a long, ugly scar on left side of her face and her auburn hair was pulled back into a severe bun at the base of her neck, but she was obviously related to Bobbi.

She sized Clay up while drying her hands on the corner of the white apron, tied around her waist. "Take whatever you're sellin' and move on down the road, mister."

"I wish I could, ma'am, but I was told two of Bobbi Hamilton's sisters live here, and judging from that red hair of yours, I think I'm at the right house," Clay said.

A booming, male voice came from somewhere within the house. "Who's at the door, woman?"

"Some fella's looking for Bobbi," she called.

"I'm not looking for her – I have bad news about her," Clay corrected.

"She dead?" the male voice was closer now – just behind the woman's shoulder, but he was still too far in the shadows to see clearly.

"Nearly," Clay responded. "She's in bad shape at the hospital. Her husband's dead and she asked me to let you know so you could look after her children."

"To hell with that harlot and her Devil-children," he snarled. "I always knew she'd come to no good."

Clay was caught off-guard. He turned to the woman, who had grown pale and folded her arms tightly across her chest.

"You're her sister, right?"

"I'll thank you not to talk to my wife," the man snarled. He grabbed the woman roughly by the shoulder and yanked, pulling her back. She let out a whimper, but said nothing as he stepped into the doorway. Clay tensed, but held his ground.

Lucian was short and obese, with grey hair that formed a ring around his balding skull. His untamed eyebrows curled wildly above beady, shark-like eyes. "This here's a house of God-fearing people," he bellowed. "We've had nothin' to do with that Jezebel since she dishonored her father and turned her back on the Lord."

Just then, a second auburn-haired woman descended the stairs just inside the house. Her face was in the shadows, but she appeared to be a younger, softer version of the woman at the door. "Lucian, Josephine and I can't be expected to ignore our sister's dying request."

The man rounded on her, his fists balled. "Damn it, Louise – how many times have I told you – as long as you live in my home, you'll do as I say! And I say it's high time your pagan sister reaps what she sowed."

"But it might not be too late to bring her innocent children back into the Lord's flock," she countered.

Lucian considered this possibility for a moment; then shook his head. "I won't risk bringing demons into my home. Besides, taking in more members of your penniless family is too much charity to ask of one man."

He started to close the door.

"They have a little money," Clay blurted, still fearing Bobbi's curse.

Lucian paused, waffling between his religious principles and greed.

"I can go look after the children and see to Bobbi's affairs," Louise volunteered. "Surely, it's the Christian thing to do. Besides, valuables shouldn't be left unattended in her house while she's hospitalized."

Lucian scowled and rubbed his chin. "All right, Louise. You go with this fella over to Bobbi's house. Search the place for cash and anything else of value and call Maxine to see if she wants the brats. If not, have the police take them to the Pinellas County Orphan's Home. Then you get yourself back here. No dawdling, ya hear?"

"Perhaps I should go with her," Josephine suggested.

"Perhaps you should shut your mouth and tend to my supper," Lucian growled.

Lily shuddered as the fog gathered around her. She couldn't imagine being married to such a repugnant man. Scott was always kind to everyone. She felt a stab of pain in her heart, knowing she treated Scott so cruelly that she had practically pushed him into the arms of another woman. When Lily heard voices through the thick clouds, she forced her thoughts back to the present.

The mist parted to reveal Louise and Maxine arguing in Bobbi's tiny kitchen. Clay was sitting backwards in a high-backed chair, his chin resting against his folded arms. Across the table, the four children sat huddled together, looking haggard and scared.

"There are four children and two family homes," Max said. "It's only fair that each of us take responsibility for two children. Duncan and I can take Fred and Henrietta, but you and Jo must take Nathaniel and Belle."

Lily's heart ached for Bobbi, knowing she was helpless to keep her family from being torn asunder.

"Lucian won't allow it. Surely you and Duncan can make room in your big home for all four children," Lou said.

"Fred and Henrietta look enough like me that people will believe they're my children. But Nathaniel and Belle – well, they look like their father. If Lucian won't take them in, then you should stay here and care for them yourself."

"Lucian won't allow that, either," Lou said.

"Ye gads, Lou –he's Jo's husband, not yours. Lucian may have taken us in when our parents died, but you're a grown woman now. You don't have to submit to his demands anymore."

Lou opened her mouth to protest, but no words came out.

"This is your chance to be free, Lou," Max continued. "Stay here." She patted her sister on the shoulder. "Now, come along, children," she said, wiggling a crooked finger at Henrietta and Fred.

The children looked to Nathaniel for guidance.

"Do as Auntie Max says." Nathaniel stood and held his arms out to his siblings. "Henrietta, give me a hug and dry your eyes. Mama and Papa would want you to be brave. Besides, we'll be back together again before you know it."

He wiped Henrietta's tear-stained cheeks and brushed her shiny auburn hair behind her ears. Then he held his hand out to shake Fred's hand. The red-headed boy ignored the extended hand and wrapped his arms around his brother's neck. Nathaniel hugged him tight.

"There, there, Fred. You're twelve years old now... almost a man. You take care of Henrietta until Mama gets better and I'll take care of little Belle. That's what Papa would want us to do, right?"

Lily's eyes brimmed with tears as she watched the heart wrenching farewells. Clay watched Nathaniel with open admiration, but he didn't move from his chair as the two children reluctantly left with their aunt.

"Whatever am I to do with you two?" Lou wailed. "I suppose it would be best to do as Lucian instructed. I'll fetch the police to take you to the children's home."

Nathaniel took Belle by the hand. "Please don't call the police, Aunt Lou. Stay here with us. I'm fourteen. That's plenty old enough to take care of myself and one five-year-old girl. We won't be a bother. I promise. You'll barely know we're here."

Lou shook her head. "And how would I pay for groceries and electricity?"

Clay flipped his Fedora upside down and pulled five, twenty-dollar bills from the hatband. He laid the cash on the table.

Lou stared at the cash. "I've never seen so much money," she whispered.

"You'll tell that prick brother-in-law of yours to go screw himself," he said. He pointed to the cash, "There's plenty sugar there to pay the bills for at least a month. That should be enough time for you to find work."

Clay shook Nathaniel's hand and then strode to the door. He tipped his hat at Lou and turned to leave, when little Belle ran to him and hugged his leg. He stiffened at the unexpected show of affection.

"There, now little girl – go back to your brother," he said, patting the child's blonde ringlets with a flat hand.

Belle held fast. When Clay bent down to pull her arms away, she grinned at him, her bright hazel eyes twinkling. With lightning speed, she let go of his leg and put her arms around his neck. Clay jerked upright, but she didn't let go. Instinctively, he put his arms around her back as she wrapped her chubby legs around his waist. She laid her head against his broad shoulder. "I've got you now!" she said, giggling at her victory.

Lily smiled; certain this was a game Belle had played with her father when he was getting ready to leave home to make a long-distance delivery.

Clay couldn't remember ever holding a child in his arms before. Growing up at the convent, the nuns had always discouraged open displays of affection. But holding the small child felt nice, and Belle's bubbly laughter was contagious. He chuckled before reluctantly lowering her to the floor.

He tipped his hat to Lou once more, nodded at Nathaniel, winked at Belle and then slipped into the night as the fog engulfed Lily.

Clay spoke to Lily as she floated within comforting folds of the mist. "All the way back to the Belleview Biltmore, I tried to convince myself that I could finally wash my hands of Bobbi and her family. I figured she wouldn't make good on her threat to curse me, since I got her sisters together and gave all that money to her kids."

Lily heard Clay inhale, and a moment later, she smelled cigar smoke. After a long pause, he continued.

"I probably could have forgotten all about them kids if Maxine had taken all four of them. But I kept thinking about the two she left behind. I mean, that boy had so much spunk and the little girl – well, she was like a princess. The harder I tried not to think about them, the more they haunted me. After a month, I decided Bobbi must have cursed me out of spite, and I knew she wouldn't leave me alone until I checked up on them kids."

Chapter Thirty Six

Lily woke to the sound of a woman crying somewhere down the hospital corridor; the images of Bobbi's children hugging one another goodbye still fresh in her mind.

"Maybe Bobbi's trying to show me what it would have been like if I lost Scott in the accident instead of Dylan," Lily thought, picturing Bobbi's eldest son. At fourteen, Nathaniel was only one year older than Dylan had been, but he seemed much older. *"Did kids grow up faster back then, or with his father gone, did Nathaniel have no choice but to fill the vacancy?"*

She watched Grams' chest until she detected the slight rise and fall of her breathing. Her thoughts shifted to the memory of Bobbi tweening with the spirit of the woman who haunted the hospital. *"Poor Grams will never get to travel,"* she realized. *"And what about Dylan? If Scott sells our home, would Dylan have to spend eternity in the hospital where he died?"*

All at once, Lily knew she had to call Scott and convince him to keep their house for Dylan's sake. But the lilting voice of the woman who had answered his phone the last time she called Scott still burned in her ears. Lily couldn't bear the thought of Scott moving on – especially right now. She alternated between gazing at the sky and watching Grams until the sun began to set. Then she called for the hotel shuttle.

Lily paused in the nearly empty hotel lobby, admiring the towering domed ceiling and ornate crown molding before limping to Maisie's Sundry Shoppe to buy a cola and a bag of chips. She glanced at the white wrought iron soda shop seating and debated pulling up a chair. *"Stop procrastinating,"* she admonished, looping the plastic shopping bag over the handle of her crutch.

After making her way back to her suite, Lily sat at the small parlor table munching her snack and staring at her cell phone, wishing Margaret would appear and provide some of the answers she so desperately wanted. An advertisement on the bag of chips caught her eye. Big bold letters declared: *You could be a winner! No purchase necessary!* Then, just below, it read: *Details inside.* She laughed. It wasn't exactly a dumb warning, but she knew Seth would enjoy the contradictory label, none the less. *"I'll have to tell him tonight,"* she thought.

Instantly, a wave of guilt washed over her. It was driving her crazy to think about Scott seeing someone, yet she had dinner plans with another man. She turned on her cell phone and dialed. Scott answered on the second ring.

"Lily... I've been trying to call you. I was getting really worried. How are you holding up?"

"I'm fine." Tears filled her eyes, arguing the contrary. "Grams' slipping away a little more every hour, but she's still breathing."

"Is there any chance she can come back? I mean, people surprise doctors all the time..."

"Not this time," Lily said with a heavy heart. "There's too much damage. They say she's going to stop breathing soon, and when she does, they won't do anything to help her because she has a do-not-resuscitate order on file."

"I'm sure she knows you're there with her," Scott said.

"I hope so." She paused, glad he hadn't mentioned the other woman. "Listen, Scott... I've been thinking about the house. I can't explain it right now, but I don't want to sell it. I understand if you don't want to live there, but maybe I can buy it from you or something."

"Lily, if you want to live here, the house is yours. It was paid for as part of the settlement. I can find an apartment someplace."

"I don't know if I want to live there, to be honest," she said. "I just know that we have to keep the house – at least for now."

"Come on, Lilyanna. If you want to stay here, that's one thing, but I don't want to hold onto it just as a shrine to Dylan's memory."

"I know, but..." Lily hesitated. *"But what? What if Dylan's spirit needs a place to hang out other than the hospital?"* She shook her head. "I'm just not ready."

"Okay. I'll stay here for now," he said. "But we need to come up with a permanent solution soon, okay?"

Lily agreed and then hesitated, choosing her next words carefully. "Scott, have you ever seen...I mean, since Dylan's been gone, have you ever – you know... thought he's still in the house?"

"Sometimes. Once, I woke up thinking how great it would be to surprise him with a couple tickets to a Cardinals' game. And another time, I started rearranging my work schedule so I could go watch his baseball practice before I remembered he wouldn't be there. But that kind of stuff happens less often as time goes by."

"That's not what I mean," she said. "Do you ever *feel* him with you while you're awake? Does he ever visit you while you're sleeping?"

Scott sighed. "Come on, Lily – don't start this again." It wasn't a suggestion.

Lily took a deep breath, trying not to become defensive. "I wish you'd believe me. I saw him. I talked to him." She bit her tongue. *"I still see him. I still talk to him."*

"The doctor explained how that happened. The medication they used to keep you sedated caused you to hallucinate. That's why you stopped seeing him after they moved you to the rehab center here in St. Louis."

"I know that's what they say, but..."

"Lily – are you sure you're okay? I mean, the thought of losing Grams is bound to set you back. Dr. Pope would probably refill your prescription if you called..."

"I don't need anti-depressants, Scott. Don't worry. It won't happen again."

She tried to fight it, but the memory flashed through her mind with the force of a freight train. A month into her rehabilitation, Scott agreed to bring Dylan's ashes to her, hoping the sight of the small urn would help her accept their son's death. Instead, grief-stricken Lily opened the urn and rubbed a portion of Dylan's ashes into her chest, desperate to bring him back. They stopped her, of course, and sedated her.

Dylan's spirit did visit her that night, even though his face was on the body of a young man who kept strumming a guitar. *"What if it wasn't just the drugs?"* she wondered. *"What if it's true that spirits can go wherever their remains are, and Dylan's ashes were with me?"* Lily shook her head. *"But that doesn't explain how I saw him before that night, or why I still see him."*

She couldn't expect Scott to understand until she had more answers. "I've been discussing some interesting theories about the afterlife with someone I met down here. It's helping me deal with my issues."

"Okay." Scott's voice remained skeptical. "But please be careful, Lilyanna. There're lots of wackos out there."

"I will – I promise. I'll call you tomorrow, okay?"

She hung up, relieved the subject of their relationship hadn't come up. She called Seth's room and left a message: "If you're still up for dinner, I'll meet you in the lobby at seven. If not, I'll see you in the morning."

Chapter Thirty Seven

"Pizza?" Lily laughed. "All that build-up about finding a great restaurant and you bring me to a pizza joint?"

"Aw, come on, Lily," Seth protested. "Pizza Hut is a pizza joint. Cristino's makes authentic Italian pizza in a coal-heated oven. Besides, it's within shuttle distance of the hotel."

Lily chuckled and took a swig of her Corona. She had to admit the little restaurant was charming, and their server was friendly and attentive, without being intrusive. They were seated at an outdoor table, on a patio surrounded by palm trees and lit with strings of lights that crisscrossed above, reminding Lily of a street festival. Beyond the man-made lights, a perfect crescent moon hung in the starry sky, completing the décor. She described the setting for Seth. "I wish you could see it for yourself," she said.

"Soon," Seth replied. "By this time next year, I'll be able to drive here on my Harley. That reminds me..." He reached into his pocket and withdrew a folded sheet of paper. "One of the desk clerks volunteered to type up some of the dumb warnings from my tape recorder. Want to read them before I send this to my folks?"

"Sure." Lily took the paper and unfolded it. "'Number one. Found on a chainsaw: Danger – Do not hold the wrong end of the chainsaw and do not attempt to stop chain with hands.'" She laughed. "You've got to be kidding. Is this is for real?"

Seth nodded "Yep. I guess the manufacturer is worried that some idiot will chop off his fingers and sue."

Lily laughed again. "'Number two. Found on an iron: Warning – Do not attempt to iron clothes while wearing them.'" She nodded. "Come to think of it, I knew a girl who used to iron the tails of her shirt while she was wearing it."

"See? That's why they have to label things." Seth grinned.

"'Number three. Found on a packet of silica in new jacket pocket: Warning – Do Not Eat.' Yuck! Can you imagine eating one of those things?" Lily giggled. "'Number four. Found on a skateboard: Warning – does not have brakes.'" She laughed and shook her head. "Yet another reason not to take up skateboarding. And lastly, 'Number five. Found on the bottom of a cereal bowl: Warning – Do not use without adult supervision.'" She frowned. "So, it's dangerous to eat Cheerios without your parents standing guard?"

"Apparently." Seth chuckled.

"Well, those are going to make great entries for your book." She refolded the paper and placed it in Seth's outstretched hand.

He grinned and slid the paper into the pocket of his blue jeans.

She glanced up, still smiling. "Oh, here comes our food."

When he sensed the server's presence, Seth smiled in her general direction. "So tell us, what's the dumbest warning label you've ever read? We're collecting them."

The perky brunette smiled and slid his folded white cane over just enough to make room for their pizza on the table. "Dumb? Oh, I know one – we bought some Korean knives a while back and each knife blade had a sticker that read: 'Warning – keep out of children.'" She giggled. "I'm sure they meant to say: 'Keep out of children's reach', so it was more of a lost-in-translation thing, but it cracked us up." She rolled her eyes. "Oh... I have another one. We were replacing some of the twinkle lights in the bushes out here and the box said, 'Warning – For indoor or outdoor use only.' I remember thinking, 'where else could we use them'?"

Seth laughed. "Those are good. Mind if I add them to my collection?"

"Be my guest." She turned to leave, but called over her shoulder, "Don't forget to save some room for gelato."

Seth pulled the tiny tape recorder from the pouch on his belt, repeated the warnings, including where he had heard them, and then put it away before diving into their meal.

After only one bite of the thin, crisp pizza, Lily knew it would be difficult to save room for gelato. They barely spoke as they wolfed down slice after slice until the serving platter was almost empty.

"So, have you seen any more spirits since breakfast?" Seth asked, patting his full belly.

"As a matter of fact, yes I have." Lily recounted the memories she'd seen while at the hospital. "I keep seeing similarities between me and Bobbi, but I still can't figure out what I'm supposed to learn from this experience. I'm certain it has something to do with the accident, but I don't know what."

"I was thinking. You told me you don't remember much about the accident, but you also said you have nightmares about it all the time. How is that possible?"

"In my nightmares, I only see scary, surreal flashes of the accident. I remember Dylan waking me up – and the fire. I remember freeing him from the seatbelt and pulling him from the car. That's about it." She took a drink of beer. "The police report says it was a freak accident. A logging truck was on the overpass right above us when it swerved to avoid a stalled car. The truck jack-knifed and his load of logs broke loose and fell onto the road below. The force of the logs knocked our car off the road into a thicket of trees and boulders, so no one knew another car was involved in the accident until firemen discovered our car was the source of a fire they had been sent to extinguish. They tell me I fell and hit my head on a rock, fracturing my skull. The next thing I know for sure, it was two weeks later and I was waking up in a hospital."

"That must have been tough," Seth said. "What happened after you woke up?"

"I don't like to talk about it," she said.

"No kidding," he cracked. "But can you give it a shot? I think it might help us figure out what your spirit buddies are trying to teach you. What's the first thing you remember?"

Lily let out a long breath and closed her eyes. "When I woke up, a nurse told me I had been injured in a car accident. She told me to lie still and she would bring Scott to see me. I asked if Dylan was alright but she didn't answer – she just disappeared through the door without looking at me. I guess I should have known that was a bad sign."

Seth listened intently, his muscular arms crossed loosely over his chest, just beneath the Harley wings, emblazoned on his tight, black T-shirt.

"When the nurse returned, she was pushing Scott in a wheelchair with one of those extended foot supports and a doctor was with them. Scott's right leg was in a cast all the way from his thigh down to his ankle and he was crying. I never saw him cry before, except for once when he watched a sad movie about a dying football player." Lily gulped a swig of beer. "Anyway, the nurse rolled his wheelchair next to my bed. Then Scott took my hand and told me about Dylan."

Lily could still hear Scott's words ringing in her memory and see the anguish in his eyes. "I'm so sorry baby, but Dylan is gone. They couldn't save him."

"I didn't understand. I mean, it was Dylan who woke me up right after the accident. He talked to me after I pulled him out of the car – before I passed out. He couldn't have been brain-dead like they say he was. I'm sure of it. But I was in a coma and Scott believed the bastards, so he signed the papers, allowing them to..."

She couldn't speak the thought that occupied her every waking moment and haunted her dreams. Scott had donated Dylan's precious organs and had the remainder of him cremated while she lay in a coma, unable to prevent it or even say goodbye.

"Anyway, I guess I flipped out. The next thing I remember, I was waking up again. Scott was in the wheelchair next to my bed, looking like hell warmed over. He warned me to stay still so I wouldn't reinjure myself, but talk about your dumb warnings... I couldn't move. My upper arms were secured to the sides of the bed with restraints, my hands were encased in giant mittens that looked like they belonged to Mickey Mouse, and my leg was in traction. Scott said they had to sedate me. Apparently, I had been determined to get out of bed and go find my son."

"Whoa," Seth murmured.

"They all stuck together and swore Dylan was already brain-dead when he arrived at the hospital, but that's bullshit. They might have tried harder to save him if they knew they had nothing to gain by letting him die. But Scott signed their papers, giving them permission to use our son for spare parts. If I'd been awake, Dylan might still be alive."

Lily slammed her beer bottle on the table harder than she meant to. Seth flinched, his body tensing instinctively. Their server glanced at them from a few tables away.

"I'm sorry," she mumbled. "I didn't mean to get so emotional."

"It would be strange if you could talk about that kind of stuff without getting emotional. It must have been awful to be tied down like that – helpless."

"Yeah. And unfortunately, things got worse," Lily said.

"Are you guys ready for some gelato?" the server interrupted.

"No," Lily replied, annoyed at the interruption. "I'm too full."

"Wait. Not so fast." Seth turned his face toward the server, offering her one of his sexy smiles. "The concierge at the hotel says the gelato here is amazing. Is he right, gorgeous?"

"It's the best in town," the girl chirped, turning her back to Lily. "And by the way, one of our cooks has a dumb warning for you. She says she bought a shirt for her son, and the tag said 'remove child before washing.'"

Seth gave her a wide grin. "That's perfect. Wait a second." He pulled out his tape recorder. "Tell me again. I want to save it in your sweet southern voice."

The brunette swatted his upper arm playfully, enjoying the flirtation. "Don't be silly," she protested, but then she obliged him.

Lily frowned at way the waitress enhanced her southern accent for the recording, clearly under the spell of Seth's sensual charm.

When she finished retelling her story, Seth thanked the girl again. "Now, about that gelato. Do you have chocolate?"

"We surely do," she replied, with an even stronger southern accent. "We have twelve flavors for y'all to choose from."

Seth cocked his head toward Lily. "Bring me a small chocolate. I'll bet I can coax my date into sharing it."

"Alrighty then. I'll be back in a jiffy."

The server shot Lily a patronizing glance before turning toward the large gelato display inside the restaurant. Lily wrinkled her nose in silent reply.

"Oh my God. Am I jealous?" She tried to cover the unexpected rush of emotion with humor – making a tisk-tisk sound with her tongue against her teeth. "What an incorrigible flirt!"

"What?"

"You were flirting with the waitress... not that I care or anything."

Seth grinned at her, recognizing a lie when he heard one.

After scraping the last of the gelato from the dish and paying their bill, the pair headed to the side street to wait for the hotel shuttle. Seth attempted to slide his hand down from Lily's upper arm, over her crutch to her forearm, but she stopped him as abruptly as if he had tried to put his hand up her skirt.

"They're just scars, Lily," he said. "Everyone has scars."

"Nobody understands."

"Tell me and I'll try."

"Fine." Her voice dropped low – a detached monotone. "They're a constant reminder of my failure as a mother."

"You didn't fail anybody, Lily. It was an accident."

"The shuttle's here," she said, watching the driver come around to open the passenger doors.

She didn't know this driver. He was a short, Asian man who greeted them in broken English. His nametag read: Akio. He held the front door open and nodded to Lily, smiling.

Lily returned his nod, but made no move to climb into the van. "I failed in the gravest way possible, Seth," she said. "The most basic responsibility of motherhood is to protect your child from death. I failed to do that."

Akio moved closer to the couple, offering each an arm. Lily lifted Seth's hand from her bicep and placed it in the crook of his elbow. Then she climbed into the front seat of the van and closed her door while Akio guided Seth to the side door.

During the silent ride back to the hotel, Lily thought about Dylan. At first, she had dreamed about him often – sitting next to her hospital bed, alive and unharmed. But then she started having macabre nightmares about the accident and about doctors with scalpels, waiting like vultures to feed on his body. Over time, she dreamed about her son less often, and when she did, his face was always attached to other people's bodies, as if he were wearing ghoulish human costumes. Her doctor prescribed drugs to help her sleep, but they seemed to enhance the strange dreams, so instead of taking them, Lily slept as little as possible.

Chapter Thirty Eight

By the time they disembarked from the van at the hotel, Lily had her emotions under control. "I'm okay," she assured Seth. "That all happened a long time ago."

She placed his hand on her upper arm and they walked inside. On the far side of the lobby, they paused in an alcove to listen to an entertainment duo. An elderly tuxedoed man played an ebony black piano and sang 'My Girl', while his partner, a middle-aged woman in a shimmery, full-length silver gown, sang harmony and occasionally offered her microphone to good-natured onlookers, encouraging them to sing a line or two.

By the time the couple finished a pleasant rendition of 'How Sweet It Is to Be Loved by You', both Lily and Seth were in better moods. When the duo started singing 'Proud Mary', Seth tugged on Lily's elbow.

"Want to get a drink and talk some more?" he asked.

"I'm talked-out for tonight," Lily said.

"Okay – how about we get a drink and don't talk, while you decide if you want me to walk you back to your room?"

Lily's heartbeat quickened at Seth's not-so-subtle suggestion. This was the second time he had picked her company over that of other available women, and that made her tingle in all the right places. "*Not that I would sleep with him. I haven't been with anyone else since I met Scott over twenty years ago.*" Images of her husband popped into her mind. She had never even come close to being unfaithful to her marriage vows. *"But things are different now, aren't they?"* she mused. *"After all, Scott plans to file for divorce after Grams' funeral, and a woman answered his cell phone while he was in the shower"*

"Lily? Did you hear me?" Seth asked.

She blushed. "Sorry, I was trying to make up my mind."

"And?"

"A drink? Yes. More talk? Maybe. Anything else? Well... we'll have to wait and see about that."

Seth grinned. "Let's go," he said.

A cocktail waitress brought their rum and Cokes to the veranda. Lily described their white bench-swing, and how it overlooked gardens and trees, glowing with twinkle lights. For a while, they rocked silently – listening to tree frogs chirping in the moist night air – savoring the sweet drinks and mounting sexual tension. Two couples occupied rocking chairs at the opposite end of the long, covered porch, but otherwise, they were alone.

Finally, Lily broke the silence. "It's cool to think that during Prohibition, people probably shared a swing and drank rum and Coke on this very same porch. No. Wait. Did they have Coke back then?"

"I think so. Man, wouldn't it be awesome to have a time machine, so we could go back and see what it was really like back then?"

"That's sort of what happens when the spirits show me their memories," Lily said. "It's like I'm there – every detail with nothing missing. That's what finally convinced me that I'm not just dreaming... I mean, my imagination just isn't that good."

Seth nodded. "Yeah – I asked my bartender buddy, Randy, about the rum line and rumrunners. He said all that stuff was true. And they really did have a speakeasy here, next to the Candlelight ballroom. The trap door to the basement is still there, behind the bar."

Lily smiled at Seth's increasing enthusiasm.

"He also said Canadian whisky dealers made concave liquor bottles during Prohibition, so Americans could strap them to their calves or tuck them into their boots, out of sight. They called them bootleg bottles, and the name caught on. Pretty soon anyone who transported hidden liquor was called a bootlegger. Get it?"

"Got it. I wonder if Margaret Plant knows that."

"Speaking of Margaret – now that you're a medium of sorts, maybe you can start blogging about ghosts. That would be more fun than blogging about dying people."

"I'm not a medium. And besides, my blog helps people."

"Maybe it does. But it's gotta be hard to see the future when you spend so much of your time writing about dying. Besides, you probably started your website back when you wanted to die, right?"

Lily gulped. Her blog had started out as a cover story, to keep people from wondering why she was so interested in learning about the legalities of suicide. But almost overnight, her blog, *Way to Go* attracted a throng of followers, many of whom asked questions that she felt obligated to answer. Therefore, in addition to listing countries where suicide is legal, she started posting ideas for video memoirs and last-fling vacations. She created how-to guidelines for making advance funeral arrangements and recently, she even started blogging about the importance of medical directives, wills and estate planning.

"How did you know?" she murmured.

"What – you think you're the only person who went through that shit? When that virus took my sight, my world fell apart, Lily. It might not seem like a big deal to some people, but my whole life revolved around riding motorcycles cross-country. My friends, my job, my passion – I lost it all and there was nothing I could do about it. For months afterward, I wanted to kill myself."

"What changed?" Lily asked.

Seth chuckled. "A woman I knew called me on my bullshit. She introduced me to Zen concepts and helped me realize that I didn't lose as much as I thought I did. The rest of my body and my brain still worked just fine, and with a few adjustments, I could still enjoy almost every aspect of my life – and maybe even become a better person."

"Perhaps I should get her number," Lily snarked.

"I have faith. You'll find your way."

Seth slid his fingertips down Lily's cheek to her mouth and used his forefinger to gently trace the shape of her lips. He cupped her chin, tilting it up as he leaned forward to taste a gentle kiss. Then he pulled back and touched his forefinger to her lips again, waiting for her reaction – waiting for permission.

Lily licked his finger and Seth smiled. His next kiss was deeper. His warm tongue tasted of rum and Coke as it teased her into submission. When he slid his arm around her, Lily melted into his embrace.

Near the porch swing, a door suddenly burst open and a dozen people poured onto the veranda, their laughter and chatter ruining the moment. Lily scooted away from Seth as quickly as a teenager caught kissing on her parent's couch. She recognized some of the newcomers from the crowd at the piano and surmised the entertainment duo had finished for the evening.

"Come back," Seth said. "There's no rule against kissing in public."

"Maybe not in your rulebook," Lily said. "Mine says a married woman isn't supposed to kiss anyone but her husband."

"I thought you and your husband were separated."

Seth tilted his head to the side, studying her from within his dark world. Normally, Lily found this habit endearing, but tonight, it annoyed her.

"We are, but technically, we're still married and that means the rules still apply."

"There's an old joke about rules. It goes something like this. Some Catholic school kids were moving through a self-service lunch line. Next to a bowl of apples was a little sign that read: *Follow the rules. Take only one. God is watching.* Further down the line, next to the platter of chocolate chip cookies, some kid posted a sign of his own that said: *Forget the rules. Take all you want. God's watching the apples.*" Seth grinned. "I say let's be like that kid and forget the stupid rules."

"Maybe God isn't watching us, but a whole crowd of people is," Lily replied.

"Ahh… another benefit of being blind. I can't tell when people are watching, so I never worry about it." He held his open arms out to her.

Lily slid closer to him and rested her head against his shoulder, trying to ignore the onlookers. "You never seem to worry about anything."

Seth wrapped his muscular arms around her and rubbed his cheek against the top of her head. "That's not true. I'm worried right now."

"Worried about what?"

"That you don't want to kiss some more," he teased.

"Seriously. Tell me something you worry about."

"Well," Seth said. "I worry about my upcoming surgery – that something will go wrong and that I won't get my sight back. And I worry that if I do get it back, the world won't look the way I remember it and I won't like what I see."

"Those worries sound pretty normal." Lily said.

"I worry about weird shit, too – probably because I watched too many episodes of the *Twilight Zone* when I was a kid. Sometimes I worry that my new eyes will be evil. I mean, what if I get the eyes of a murderer, or the memories of someone who has been murdered? Or what if I get the eyes of a woman who was obsessed with her hair and she makes me start worrying about how bad my hair looks after a long ride?"

Lily was confused. "What are you talking about?"

"You know… what if the donor eyes they use are possessed by their former owner and after my surgery, they start to control me like a puppet…"

Lily jerked away. "Transplants!" She spat the words. "The surgery to restore your sight is…"

"It's a double corneal transplant. How did you think they were going to restore my sight?"

Lily flushed. "I thought they were going to correct the damage the virus did."

"My corneas can't be fixed. They have to replace them. I thought you knew that." Seth tilted his head, attempting to understand the problem. "I was just kidding about the whole 'possessed' thing."

"People shouldn't be harvested for parts," she cried, her voice loud enough to draw a few wary glances from people, clustered near the veranda rail. "Those doctors would have tried harder to save Dylan, if people like you hadn't been standing in line, begging them to hurry up and pull the plug."

As Lily struggled to her feet, Seth caught her arm. "Whoa, Lily... hold on... Where's all of this coming from? I thought you, of all people, would understand how much I appreciate that someone was selfless enough to donate their corneas to give me a second chance at sight."

"Well, you couldn't be more wrong."

"You know, Lily, I care about you, but you ask for a lot of understanding, and you offer damn little when it's your turn to give some understanding in return. Can't you try to put yourself in my place and understand how much I want to see again?"

"Let go, Seth. I can't be around you right now."

Seth released her arm. "Lily, please don't leave. Let's talk about this."

"Not now." Lily took a step toward the door, noticing several pairs of eyes watching her. Obviously nothing was wrong with *their* vision. The irony was too much. She hobbled inside and headed for her room as fast as her injured leg would carry her.

Chapter Thirty Nine

Lily managed to hold back her tears until she reached the door of her room and began fumbling for her key. By the time she was inside, her shock had turned to anger at the betrayal.

"Just when I was ready to trust him with my heart, he turns out to be a transplant recipient!" She tore her leg brace off and fell onto the bed. *"The people who accepted his organs are just as guilty of Dylan's murder as the doctors."*

She turned off her vibrating cell phone, refusing Seth's call. A moment later, her hotel room phone rang. She unplugged the handset, thrust it into the nightstand drawer, and got ready for bed as if on automatic pilot. Then she turned out the light and cried herself to sleep.

One of her nightmare visions appeared the moment she drifted off. A young, Indian doctor stood at the head of a long dining table with a carving knife, preparing to slice Dylan up as if he were a Thanksgiving Day turkey. The doctor sharpened his knife, smiling benevolently at the people gathered around the table, eagerly waiting to receive Dylan's precious organs. The doctor's face momentarily morphed into Dylan's and then changed back into his own Indian features.

Lily had this nightmare many times before, but this time, something was different. This time, Seth was among those seated at the ghoulish table, holding out his plate to the smiling doctor.

Unnerved by the nightmare, Lily didn't realize the fog of the spirit realm had descended until the mist lifted and she was in Bobbi's hospital room.

Bobbi's entire head was wrapped in gauze, except for small openings for her eyes and mouth. Alton and a uniformed police officer were standing by her bed.

"Mrs. Hamilton," the policeman said, "I've come because I have my suspicions that you and your husband were involved in illegal doings, and the truck accident and his death were a direct result of those deeds."

Bobbi could see and hear, but she could not speak. Her jaw was wired shut as part of the facial reconstruction process. Still, Lily could understand her nervous thoughts as if she were speaking aloud.

"Listen, Officer," Alton said. "I may be her doctor now, but I've known Mrs. Hamilton for most of her life and can attest to her good character. What's the basis of these accusations?"

"When her husband's body was examined, it was discovered he had been shot. The coroner said he would have died from the wound, even if he hadn't driven his truck into a tree."

Bobbi let out an anguished moan.

Alton rested his hand on her shoulder, alarmed. "I won't have you upsetting her this way, Officer. Her recovery could be seriously jeopardized. I'm sure she's an innocent. If you can satisfy your doubts with a few questions that she can answer with yes or no responses, I'll allow you to proceed. Otherwise, I'm afraid your investigation will have to wait for at least a month... maybe more."

The policeman nodded his consent. The words 'No' and 'Yes' were painted on a small board that Alton placed on her stomach, where she could see it. Then he put a pencil into her good hand and nodded at the officer.

"Did someone hire you to transport illegal alcohol, Mrs. Hamilton?" the officer asked, "Yes or no?"

"No one hired me," Bobbi thought, using the pencil to point to the word 'No.' *"They hired Bear."*

"Did you know your husband was shot?" he asked.

Bobbi stabbed the word 'No' so hard, she broke the point off the pencil.

The officer nodded, considering her reaction.

"Officer," Alton asked. "Did you find illegal alcohol in the Hamilton's vehicle?"

"Well, no," the officer replied. "But we found a couple broken bottles of Canadian Whisky in some bushes quite near the accident and there were signs that a lot more of it had been stashed there. We think someone carried it off before we learned her man had been shot and went out to investigate."

"Well, there you have it, officer. If the Hamiltons had been transporting liquor, the broken bottles would have been in their truck, not on the ground some distance away. Mr. Hamilton probably had the misfortune of driving down a back road and stumbling upon murderous bootleggers, who shot him to keep him from reporting their crime to the authorities. After his truck crashed nearby, they no doubt made quick work of moving their criminal operation to a new location. That makes a lot more sense than supposing these upstanding folks were involved in such lowbrow affairs."

The policeman rubbed his chin. "Is he right? Were you and your husband attacked, Mrs. Hamilton?"

Bobbi moved the broken tip of the pencil to "Yes."

"Did you see the men who attacked you?"

Bobbi jabbed the word "No" and moaned again.

The officer frowned. "Well, I suppose there's nothing more to be done about it." He gave Bobbi a polite nod. "I wish you well, Mrs. Hamilton."

Alton took the policeman by the elbow and guided him toward the door. "Thank you, Officer. I'm sure she'll rest easier knowing her family name has been cleared of suspicion."

The fog gathered, pulling Lily from the scene, but she didn't get the sensation of flying that she usually enjoyed while moving between memories. When a small porthole opened in the clouds, Lily peeked through.

Chapter Forty

Lily knew this memory was different right away. Usually, when watching Bobbi's memories that involved Margaret, she could tell that Margaret was a spirit and Bobbi was a living being. This time, Bobbi and Margaret sat together at on a red velvet settee, both bearing the *not quite solid* appearance of spirits.

"Helping you acquire funds to build the new hospital marked the first time I was able to affect change in the living world since becoming a spirit."

"I was glad to have your help." Bobbi smiled. "Even though you kept insisting you were dreaming."

"Ah, yes. It was difficult to accept my – shall we say – new status. But we still became good friends, did we not?"

"Yes, indeed we did," Bobbi said. She glanced around in silent contemplation, her smile fading. "Margaret, am I dying? Is that why I am able to visit with you again?"

"No, my sweet. While it's true that most poor souls who are near death can see me, this is different. I have come into your dreams. I'm still learning about this realm of spirits, but I think this type of connection requires a special familiarity. I can't do this with most living beings."

"Is Bear in the spirit realm too?" Bobbi whispered.

Margaret shook her head.

Bobbi dabbed her eyes. "He came to me for a moment, just after the accident. He said he wanted me to stay with our children.

Then he faded into a bright light."

Margaret nodded. "I've seen several spirits follow that lighted path. I believe it leads to Heaven, but I'm not ready to go there just yet. You mustn't waste your days mourning Bear's death, Bobbi. Time matters in the living world. Cherish what little of it you're blessed with."

The window closed in the clouds and Lily began drifting; the sense of flying returning to her. She remembered Dylan calling out to her after the accident. *"Could it have been his spirit that woke me up?"* She dismissed the idea. *"Dylan was alive. I'm positive he was."*

Her musings were interrupted by the voice of Clay Long. "I fit right in with the crew working there at the Belleview Biltmore. The busier I got hauling booze, the easier it was to push Bobbi out of my mind. But I couldn't seem to stop thinking about those two kids I left with her sister, Louise. She was so damn skittish. After about a month, I decided to check on them – secretly."

When the fog cleared, Lily was standing next to Clay in the shadows, watching Bobbi's house. A dim light shined through the window; flickering as if it was coming from the fireplace.

Suddenly, the front door opened and woman strutted out onto the small porch, wearing high heels and a short, red dress, with a white bell-shaped hat pulled down over her hair. The long string of white beads that hung around her neck bounced and her hips swayed as she walked down the two wood-plank steps, past the unkempt rose bush and across the dirt yard.

Clay blew out a silent whistle and started forward, but he stopped short when the driver's side door of a parked car opened and a man stepped out.

"Good God, Lou-Lou! Aren't you the cat's meow!" He sauntered toward the woman with a cocky swagger.

"If you're looking for a kiss, you can check it," she said.

"What's the matter, doll?" he asked, opening the passenger's door for her.

"My beef's with you. You keep claiming to be this big cheese who can take care of me, but my electricity got turned off today."

He bent in for a kiss, but she pushed him away. "I'm telling you, this bank is closed."

"I'm sorry, Lou-Lou. But I'm on the level – honest. Just hang on a few more days and I'll be rolling in dough – just you wait and see."

"Where is all this money supposed to come from?" she asked.

"None of your beeswax. Now be a good girl and give me a kiss."

He pulled her to him and kissed her.

"You better not be feeding me a pile of baloney," she said, pouting. "Are you planning to hold up a train or something?"

He laughed. "Pretty close! I'm going to help Applegate steal a boxcar full of hooch and he's going to see to it that some other guy gets pinched for it."

"Who's the fall guy?"

"Some palooka named Clay something or another. It doesn't matter. Pretty soon we'll be living high on the hog in New York City, just like I promised."

"That sounds swell," she said, sliding into the passenger seat.

The man smiled, closed her door and returned to the driver's seat. A minute later, the car pulled away, leaving a cloud of dust behind.

Clay stood in the dark, reeling as the fog swept Lily away.

"It took me a minute to realize that Lou-Lou was actually Louise, Bobbi's older sister," Clay's voice said. "I guess by releasing her from her self-righteous brother-in-law, I sort of opened Pandora's Box. I didn't recognize the fella who was with her, but I was sure the *palooka* he mentioned was me."

The fog faded as quickly as it had appeared, instantly returning Lily to the same memory. The sight of a man creeping toward the door of Bobbi's home brought Clay out of his stupor.

Lily floated along like Clay's shadow as he moved closer, watching the man place a small package on the porch. The man tapped on the door and then raced back down the steps and across the yard, almost slamming into Clay in the dark.

"Jesus God Almighty!" the man hissed under his breath. He gave Clay a quick once-over, trying to size him up, and then turned to watch as Nathaniel opened the door and scooped up the package.

"God bless you!" the boy called into the darkness before closing the door.

The stranger turned back to Clay. "These folks don't need no more hard luck, fella. I'd be much obliged if-in you would git on about your business and leave 'em alone."

"First, tell me what was in the package," Clay said.

"Just table scraps. I'm returning the favor what was done for me a while back when I was so hard-put that I near starved to death." The man shook his head slowly. "If it weren't for that boy's mama leavin' me some scraps every night, I wouldn't have lived through last summer. I finally got a job takin' care of the widow woman's orchard next door, so's when I saw that boy pickin' through her garbage for food, I knowed it was my turn to give back some of what I had got."

"What the hell..." Clay shoved his hand inside his jacket, causing the man to step back several paces and raise his hands. "Don't get all excited. I'm not gonna hurt you."

The man relaxed his arms, but continued to eye Clay with suspicion.

"Here," Clay said, holding out his hand. "To help you take care of the boy and his sister."

The man came closer and Clay put a ten dollar bill into his hand. The man's eyes grew wide. "God bless you, mister," he said. "Those kids'll have milk in the morning. I swear they will."

Clay turned and walked back into the night without another word as the mist engulfed Lily.

The next time the clouds parted, the sun was burning high in the clear blue sky. Lily took deep breaths to quell her dizziness while watching Clay knock on the worn, wooden door of Bobbi's home.

Inside the house, a woman's voice wailed, "Answer that and get rid of whoever it is."

A moment later, the door creaked open and Bobbi's son, Nathaniel, peeked out. Lily noticed with satisfaction that his upper lip held the unmistakable traces of a milk-moustache.

"Good morning, Nathaniel. I'm Clay Long. I don't know if you remember me, but..."

Nathaniel cut him off. "I remember you. You brought her here." He jerked his thumb over his shoulder, toward the closed bed-room door.

"And money," Clay stammered. "Remember? I left money so she could take care of you and Belle."

"Yeah, I remember. That lasted right up until she went through Mama's closet and found her dancing clothes. We haven't seen much of her or the money since then."

Lily looked at Nathaniel's face more closely. Maxine was right. He did look like his father. He was a handsome boy – tall, with sandy hair and big hazel eyes. But now his eyes were dull with dark circles beneath them, and his cheeks had lost the rosiness that Lily recalled from when she had watched the family dancing in the tiny kitchen. Her heart sank, imagining what the child's life had been like since his mother was hospitalized and his father killed. Then she saw Belle, peeking out from behind her big brother's legs, her round face filled with curiosity.

"Long's a good name for you – Long *gone*, that is," Nathaniel continued. "Just like all them other fellas who called themselves my Papa's friends."

"Long gone, long gone, long gone, long...." Belle sang softly, putting the two words to the tune 'Twinkle, Twinkle, Little Star.' "Long gone, long gone, long gone, long!"

Clay shifted uncomfortably from one foot to another. "I didn't know your daddy, son," he said. "I'm the man who found your parents after the... after they got hurt. I got your mama a ride to the hospital and I brought your aunt here to take care of you. I gave her money out of my own pocket for food. I would think you'd be a little more grateful."

"I thank you for saving our mama," Nathaniel said, ignoring his sister's childish chant. "But that's all."

Just then, the bedroom door opened. Louise trudged into the kitchen and picked up a pitcher, filling a glass with water without acknowledging Clay's presence. Her tight bun was gone, replaced with a short hairdo that was currently sticking up in all direc-tions, and her face was smeared with last night's make-up. When she turned around, Lily noticed the lapel of the cotton robe she wore was embroidered with the letter *B*.

Louise squinted her eyes against the sunlight pouring through the open door. When she recognized Clay, she tried to improve her appearance by quickly running a hand through her hair and wiping a wetted forefinger beneath her eyes, but she couldn't disguise the dreadful hangover.

"I'm sorry I didn't greet you properly, but I'm not feeling well today," she said. "Please do come in." She pushed the children aside and opened the screen door. "Hush-up, Belle," she hissed.

Lily could tell that Louise hoped Clay would pull out another hundred dollars for her to spend. But before he stepped inside, Clay bent down and picked up a wooden crate.

"I asked the grocer to put together a week's worth of groceries for you to cook," he said.

Lou-Lou's smile died on her cracked lips. "How kind of you," she replied, barely glancing at the crate.

"There's some coffee in there," Clay went on, pretending not to notice her disappointment. "Why don't you make us a cup and let's have a chat."

"I can make coffee," Nathaniel said, grabbing for the wooden crate as if to keep it from disappearing.

Clay nodded at him, releasing the box. "Thank you, son. You'll find some doughnuts and oranges in there, too." He winked at Belle, who grinned at him in return. Then he walked over to the table and pulled out a chair for Bobbi's sister. "Please sit, Louise," he commanded. "Wait, you don't go by that name anymore, do you? Lou-Lou, is it? I'm not sure if you remember my name... it's Clay. Clay Long, not *long gone* like everyone else Bobbi trusted. And I'm not as much of a *palooka* as some folks think I am, either."

Lou-Lou's puffy eyes widened.

As the fog gathered around her, Lily couldn't help smiling. Her opinion of Clay Long had just taken a turn for the better.

Chapter Forty One

The next time the clouds parted, they were back in Bobbi's hospital room. Dr. Farthing smiled at Clay and then at Louise who, other than her short hair, looked like her old self in a plain dress and wearing no make-up.

Alton beamed at Louise. "Hello, Miss Johnson! It's good to see you. I'm Alton Farthing. You might not remember me, but I helped my father treat your measles when you were a child."

"I remember. My father was furious Mother called for the doc. He believed illness was a test of faith and that the only cure was prayer."

Alton coughed politely. "Yes, well... I'm glad to see you here. I know it's difficult for Bobbi to be away from her family. She can't speak, but we've given her a school slate and chalk, so she can respond a bit."

Clay glanced around the room, trying to avoid looking at Bobbi. His eyes fixed on a train ticket, propped up on her nightstand. "Is she going to another hospital?" he asked, pointing to the ticket.

Alton chuckled. "No, no... that's a promise. Before Bobbi recollected her wits, she kept going on about wanting to take a train across the country. I told her that when she's better, I'll buy her tickets to anywhere she wants to go. That ticket to New York City is to remind her that I mean it." He smiled at Bobbi.

"I'll leave you to enjoy your visit, but please don't stay too long. Bobbi tires easily."

"Let me step out with you, doctor," Clay said, "So these sisters can spend a few minutes together."

In the hallway, Clay lowered his voice. "Is she really going to get well enough to travel and such, Doc?"

"Truthfully, I don't know yet," Alton confessed. "I'm trying to encourage her to keep her chin up."

"What chin?" Clay asked, immediately regretting doing so. "I'm sorry, but remember, I'm the one who found her after the accident," he explained. He covered his eyes for a moment, as if to block out the memory. "Her face was gone."

Doctor Farthing nodded. "I understand your concerns, but I've studied with some of the finest reconstruction surgeons in the world, and I've developed a few techniques of my own. I'm hoping that, with enough time and God's good grace, a combination of these procedures will allow me to restore Bobbi's facial features."

"How long until she can go home to her children, Doc?"

"Not for a long while, I'm afraid. She'll be here for the better part of a year. And even if I'm successful, she'll never stand on that leg again. More than ten centimeters of the bone was crushed." Alton held his fingers up about four inches apart to demonstrate the length of the injury. "I think the best we can hope for is that her leg will heal enough that it won't have to come off."

"So she'll still need a lot of help even after she goes home." It was a rhetorical statement. Clay didn't wait for an answer. "Thanks for giving it to me on the up and up, Doc."

"I should be thanking you," Alton replied. "Bobbi is dear to me and out of the goodness of your heart, you not only saved her life, but you continue to help look after her family." Alton shook his head with wonder. "Your own family must be very proud of you."

Alton's description was so far from the truth that Clay almost choked. Instead, he swallowed hard and put on his best con-artist preacher's face. "Well, God calls on each of us to help his suffering lambs if we can."

Alton nodded solemnly while Clay tried to gather his thoughts. *"How in the hell did I get into this mess and how in the hell am I going to get out of it?"* he wondered.

Lily could read Clays thoughts, but it was difficult because his mind was racing. His dream was to make some quick money bootlegging liquor and then retire to Cuba, where he'd live the easy life, drinking rum and watching scantily-dressed island girls play on the beach. Invalids and needy children didn't fit into his plans at all. And he still had to figure out how to avoid getting framed for the heist that George Applegate was planning. On that score, it had been easy to get Louise to spill everything she knew about the set-up. The problem was, she didn't know much – just that the guy's name was Spike Reed, he was from Chicago, and he was about to come into some big money.

"Louise faltered a bit with regard to caring for the children during her first few weeks," Clay said, "but we had a talk and I'm sure she'll do better now."

He smiled, feeling proud himself, thinking about the way he had set Louise straight earlier that morning. He informed her that her dancing and drinking days were over. She was to cook, clean, care for Nathaniel and Belle, and visit Bobbi at the hospital at least once a week to regale her with stories about her wonderful children. Otherwise, he would take her back to her tyrannical brother-in-law, Lucian.

Alton and Clay glanced into the hospital room simultaneously. Louise had moved closer to Bobbi's bed, but her discomfort was obvious. Her eyes kept darting around the tiny room in an attempt to avoid looking at her grotesquely injured sister.

"Are you sure?" Alton asked.

"I am," Clay said, his confidence only mildly shaken. "I told Louise she wouldn't be free to go off on her own until Bobbi was well enough to care for the children. From the look of her, I'd say she's figured out that's not going to happen anytime soon. I'm sure she's disappointed, but she knows good Christian sisters are obliged to look after one another. I'm sure she'll accept her lot in time."

"I hope so." Alton shook Clay's hand. "Thank you again, Mr. Long." Then he turned and walked away.

Clay groaned and closed his eyes, *"Damn it. I promised Louise I'd pay for their food and electricity until Bobbi gets better. Jesus*

Christ. Cuba's drifting farther away every goddamn minute!" He sighed and trudged back into Bobbi's room.

Bobbi held up her slate: "Tell my children I love them."

Louise glanced at the message and nodded. "I will, but they already know that. I must be going now, Bobbi."

Bobbi put down the slate and reached out with her good arm to give her sister's hand a gentle squeeze. Louise responded with a weak smile. Then she stalked past Clay into the hallway.

Clay watched her walk out, pleased that her mood seemed to be improving. He congratulated himself on his ability to handle women. *"She's fiery, but I can control her. And she's a real looker, too,"* he thought. *"With her cooking my Sunday dinners, maybe everything will work out all right."*

He turned to Bobbi and tipped his Fedora. "Goodbye, witch," he joked. "By the way, I'd appreciate you casting one of your spells on George Applegate to keep him from framing me for robbery."

Bobbi drew a question mark on the slate.

"It's a long story, but don't worry... I'll figure something out."

Bobbi scrawled on the slate.

"Frankie Muldoon?" Clay read, confused. "You mean the bartender at the Belleview Biltmore?"

Bobbi wrote, *"Tell him."*

Just then, the fog rolled in, carrying Lily from the memory. As she floated in the mist, she contemplated the expression on Louise's face as she exited the hospital room and wondered how soon Clay would discover that he hadn't tamed that shrew after all.

Chapter Forty Two

Clay's voice suddenly boomed in the mist as if he were right next to Lily. It was a bit unnerving at first, but as she concentrated on what he was saying, the odd sensation that he was invading her personal space vanished.

"I didn't have anyone else to turn to, so I took Bobbi's advice and talked to Frankie. He listened to my sob story like any good bar-keep would do, and then he told me I ought to just keep my head down and do my job. He said he never heard of this 'Spike' fella, and that he probably just made up a pile of bull to string Lou-Lou along. I figured he was probably right. After all, Louise lived her whole life under the control of hard-nosed church-goers until I unintentionally gave her a taste of freedom and plenty of money to enjoy it. A naïve gal like that would be a pushover for a creep with a good story and no principles. The only thing that kept nagging at me was that Spike had used George Applegate's name... and mine."

As he finished speaking, the fog cleared, revealing his next memory. Lily squinted, waiting for her eyes to adjust to the dark and for her queasiness to subside. She was with Clay again, but this time they were standing next to an open boxcar – and they weren't alone. Three armed men stood nearby, keeping watch. The Belleview Biltmore was just a few hundred feet from where they stood. Only a few lights burned inside the hotel, giving it an odd, deserted appearance. Recalling that until recent decades, the Belleview Biltmore was only open during winter months, Lily deduced the hotel was closed for the season.

"Not totally closed," she observed. The guest room wings were dark, but she could hear the faint music of a jazz band coming from inside, indicating the not-so-secret speakeasy was still open for business.

Just then, a truck stopped at the entrance to the service path that led into the hotel's railroad depot and Pullman car storage yard. The driver flashed his headlamps on and off, three times. Clay picked up a dimly-lit oil lantern and turned the flame up and down three times, in response. The truck pulled into the yard and stopped next to Clay. He nodded silently at the driver, who returned the solemn greeting.

They worked quickly, unloading the truck and prying the lids off the crates for Clay's inspection. He held each bottle in front of the light, inspecting the color, label and seal, to make sure it contained top grade Cuban rum before returning it to the crate. When Clay finished inspecting a full crate, another man nailed the lid back on and loaded it into the boxcar. Lily smiled when she noticed the crates were clearly labeled *'Lysol Disinfectant – Lehn & Fink'* Once all the liquor had been inspected and loaded into the boxcar, Clay took a packet of money from the strongbox at his feet and gave it to the driver.

No sooner had the first truck left, when another truck pulled off the road and flashed his lights. The entire process was repeated three more times, with crates labeled, *'Clorox Bleach,' 'H.D. Poor – Orange Vinegar,'* and *'No Grit – Machinery Cleaner.'* When the entire cargo of precious rum was loaded, the three armed men hopped inside the boxcar. Clay followed them and closed the door.

Lily guessed it had taken several hours to load the boxcar, but to her, the time seemed to pass in only a few minutes. She was fascinated by the spectacle. The four men settled down on the floor of the boxcar, near the door and started playing cards, using one of the liquor crates as a table. An oil lantern sat on one corner of the crate; providing just enough light that the men could read their cards. They played stud poker with penny bets, but they were so serious, one would think the stakes were much greater.

In less than an hour, the train slowed to a stop. Clay looked from man to man, concern etched on his face. "It's way too soon for us to be there," he said. He pulled up his pant leg and retrieved a pistol from his ankle holster while the other men took hold of tommy guns.

Lily felt Clay's nervousness shift to fear, but he didn't let it show. He whispered for the men to get ready, then he put out the lantern and stood next to the door, coiled like a spring, trying to be ready for whatever happened next. Lily felt goosebumps rise on her arms. The tension increased exponentially as the seconds ticked by. Then came the moment Clay dreaded. Someone opened the boxcar door.

Clay's stomach flipped over when he saw the men's faces, well-lit by several lanterns. There were five of them, plus Lou-Lou's date, Spike, who appeared to be their leader. Clay figured seeing four well-armed guards inside the boxcar would be enough to cause the thieves to scatter, but Spike's men stood their ground.

He had no choice. Clay raised his pistol and aimed directly at Spike's forehead. He yelled, "Shoot, men!" and pulled the trigger.

Click, click, click... His pistol didn't fire. The submachine guns didn't fire, either. Clay glanced around, trying to figure out what was happening. His jaw dropped when he saw his men aiming their guns, not at Spike's crew, but at him!

He spun back around, firing his pistol again. *Click, click, click...* Goddamn Spike just grinned at him.

"Come on down here, ya dumb rube," Spike said. "If you haven't guessed by now, you aren't the one calling the shots... Hey, I made a joke... calling the shots, get it?"

It was difficult for Lily to decipher Clay's thoughts, as dozens of them were flashing through his mind, all at once, but one thought dominated the others. Clay knew he was about to die. He wondered if Spike was going to kill him here or elsewhere. He thought about

Cuba, sad that he would never get the chance to see the beautiful island of his dreams. He wondered if anyone would miss him – maybe Bobbi and her kids would. He was glad he had dropped off their week's groceries that afternoon. He wondered what it would feel like to die and hoped it wouldn't hurt too much. Then his jumbled mind focused on one last coherent thought. *"Come on, Witch; cast a spell on these guys. Get me out of this mess and I swear I'll take care of you and your kids for the rest of my life."*

In desperation, he tried once more to fire his pistol at Spike.

Spike just laughed. "You know, when you bunk in a hotel suite with guys you don't know that well, you really ought to sleep with your gun under your pillow so nobody can remove your firing pin," he taunted.

Clay's arm suddenly felt as though it were made of lead. It dropped to his side, still holding the useless pistol. He straightened his back and waited for the shot, determined to stay on his feet till the end.

"I believe I told you to get out of the boxcar, rube." Spike nodded toward the three, smirking men standing behind Clay; their submachine guns now hanging loosely at their sides. "Help him find his legs, fellas."

The largest of the three stepped up behind Clay and shoved him hard. Clay fell to the ground.

"You won't get away with this," he said. "I told some people what you were up to. If anything happens to me, they'll know who did it."

Spike looked at him with mild curiosity. "Who did you tell…Lou-Lou and her sister's brats? The sister? Well, don't worry; they won't be around long enough to miss you. I understand there's going to be a terrible house fire tonight… a real tragedy. I mean, Lou-Lou had the makings of a first-rate flapper. And oh yeah, the sister in the hospital should already be dead by now, too. Mr. Applegate thought about letting her live, since one of the cops on our payroll said she didn't know it was him who killed her husband, but he decided against it. I mean, who needs the headache of wondering if she might remember him later on?"

Clay struggled to his feet, "You bastard! I'll kill you!" He lunged at Spike, but one of the men in the boxcar used the butt of a tommy gun to hit him on the back of his head, sending Clay sprawling again. He hit the ground harder this time, but managed to roll over and stare up at the three traitors. He rubbed his head, trying to clear the stars and stall for time. "You rotten sons-of-bitches. You were paid damn fine wages to protect this shipment, so do it!"

"I reckon loyalty is for sale like everything else," replied Spike. "And our boss paid them more for it than yours. Now...it's time for you and me to take a ride. It's important that your body is never found. After all, you're the one who's going to take the blame for stealing this shipment of fine liquor." He gave the man standing next to him a curt nod. "Yep, you stole all this rum... right after you killed your own men in cold blood."

Lily gasped as the man next to Spike blasted his submachine gun, riddling Clay's men with dozens of bullets. Men, who just minutes before, had been playing penny poker. Men who were so shocked by the turn of events that they fell without getting off a single shot of their own.

"Come on, get on your feet," Spike ordered.

"You do all Applegate's dirty work?" Clay asked, still trying to stall for time – looking for an escape.

Spike didn't answer.

"I'm just asking because Capone is closing in on him and as soon he starts feeling the noose tighten around his chicken neck, Applegate's going to start pointing fingers. As a matter of fact, I'm willing to bet you'll be going for a ride yourself pretty soon."

"You're full of horse shit. No one's gettin' wise to us," Spike sneered.

"Are you sure about that?" Clay asked. "You know, I hear that when Capone catches a traitor, he doesn't just kill him straight-up. He tortures him to death, real slow... and then he scatters his body parts in the ocean for fish food – except his dick. He cuts that off and mails it to the fella's boss with a note that says, *'suck this.'*

"More horse shit," Spike said. Still, he seemed to be losing some of his swagger. "Gag that son of a bitch and put him in the car," he ordered.

The moment a man moved toward Clay, a gunshot split the night and the man went down, blood oozing from a hole in his back.

"What the hell," Spike screamed, jumping behind his men for protection. "Where'd that shot come from?"

In response, more shots rang out and the rest of Spike's men crumpled to the ground. Spike lifted his pistol and started shooting wildly into the dark night sky, but it was as if his assailants had vanished into thin air. Spying the barrel of a machine gun poking out from under one of his men's bodies, he threw down his empty pistol and started for it. A single shot rang out, stopping him in his tracks. Spike shrieked with pain and collapsed into the dirt, grabbing his shattered kneecap and writhing in agony.

A voice called out of the darkness, "You okay there, Clay?"

Clay blinked, straining to see. Then a smile spread over his face. Frankie Muldoon jumped down from the next boxcar, along with a dozen well-armed men.

"Sorry we had to let this play out, Clay, but we had to find out how many of them were working for O'Banion back in Chicago. And don't worry about Bobbi and her family, either. We've been watching over them ever since you told me she knew what was going on. You know, her husband was a good friend of mine. I'm glad we finally caught the son-of-a-bitch who killed Bear."

Spike was moaning – his pain excruciating, but Frankie just glared at him with disgust.

"Clay, I know you were just trying to stall this asshole by spewing a bunch of crap about how the boss cuts our enemies into little pieces, but I really like the idea of cutting off Spike and George's tiny dicks and mailing them to O'Banion. I think we just might have to do that."

Frankie smiled as Spike's howls grew louder.

When the fog engulfed her, Lily sighed with relief. She couldn't leave this awful memory quickly enough.

Clay's voice filled the mist again. "It turns out Frankie Muldoon was married to the sister of one of Al Capone's most trusted men, and he'd been keeping an eye on Capone's local interests for a long while. He suspected the hijacked trucks were inside jobs, but until I told him what I had overheard, he never suspected George Applegate." Clay paused. "George and Spike disappeared that night and were never heard from again."

Lily shivered, thinking about what horrors the two men probably endured during their last hours of life.

Chapter Forty Three

Lily's unpleasant thoughts vanished with the mist, as a new memory appeared. This time, she was sitting next to Clay in a shiny, bumble-bee black and yellow, Stutz-Bearcat sports car. He was wearing a new gray suit with white pinstripes and his beloved Fedora sat at a jaunty angle on his head. He was humming a cheerful tune as he drove.

Lily closed her eyes, waiting for the nausea to pass. She smiled when Clay began singing Belle's little chant, repeating the words *long gone* over and over again, to the children's' tune, 'Twinkle, Twinkle, Little Star.'

"Long gone, long gone, long gone, long. Long gone... Clay suddenly stopped singing and growled, "What the hell?" He pulled the car to the side of the road and yanked on the brake.

Lily opened her eyes, wondering what had caused his mood to shift so quickly. Then she saw two men, trying to push open the door of Bobbi's home.

"Let us in there or I swear I'm gonna give you a good pounding, boy!" one of the men yelled.

Clay leapt from the car and ran toward the men so fast that Lily didn't even have time to think about the fact that she was running alongside of him, feeling no pain.

"Hey, there!" he yelled. "What do you think you're doing?"

The men turned around to face him. They were both short, fat, middle-aged men and neither looked particularly fierce in their worn coveralls.

"We aren't looking for trouble," one of the men said, his puffy cheeks red with anger. "We just come to pick up the things we paid for and this boy won't let us inside."

"What things?" Clay asked; his anger turning to confusion.

"Lou-Lou sold us her furniture and stove last night. She told us she was leaving town and didn't need them anymore. We borrowed us a truck, and now we're here to take what's rightfully ours."

"Sorry, boys, but this isn't Lou-Lou's house and the furniture isn't hers to sell. You've been had. How much did she take you for?" Clay asked.

"Forty dollars," the man said, still furious.

"Let's go for the cops," the other man suggested. "Let them deal with these swindlers. We have a receipt." He pulled a scrap of paper from his pocket and waved it in the air.

"Yeah, well I could write you a receipt for the White House, fellas, but it wouldn't give you the right to lay claim to President Roosevelt's desk," Clay said. He felt a little sorry for the two men. "Don't feel too bad, fellas. Lou-Lou had me fooled, too. I knew she was cold, but I didn't think she'd stoop this low. I'll tell you what I'll do," he said, reaching into his pocket. "Here's twenty dollars of your money back. The other twenty will have to serve as a lesson to you... never trust a woman unless you meet her in church – and even then, hold onto your wallet."

The men hung their heads, realizing they had been duped. After a bit of commiserating about Lou-Lou's character, they thanked Clay for the money and left.

Clay turned back toward the house and saw Nathaniel peeking through the window. "You can open the door now," he said.

Inside, he heard the sound of furniture scraping across the floor. Finally, Nathaniel opened the door and Clay slipped inside.

"Holy Mother Mary!" he cried. "It must be two hundred degrees in here! Open the windows and let this heat out."

"I figured if I could make the stove hot enough, they wouldn't be able to carry it off, even if they managed to get in here somehow," Nathan said, moving to the closest window and pushing it open.

Clay tried to hide his smile, but failed. No denying it – this boy was smart as a whip. "Good thinking," he said. He removed his jacket and laid it with his hat on the table. Then he rolled up his sleeves, dragged the table and chairs back to the middle of the kitchen, and sat down. Once Nathaniel had opened the windows, he joined Clay at the table.

"Tell me what's been going on here. Did you know Louise was up to something? And where's Belle?"

Nathaniel's face clouded over. "Aunt Lou-Lou said she wasn't about to trade one jail cell for another," he began. "She and the fella who was sleeping with her in mama's bed were supposed to leave night before last, but he never showed up. She went to visit Mama yesterday, and when she came back, she had the police with her. She said Belle and I had to go to the orphanage because she was off to New York City." He wiped at angry tears with the sleeve of his shirt.

Lily remembered the train ticket Dr. Farthing bought to motivate Bobbi and was certain Louise stole it while visiting her sister at the hospital.

"They didn't have room for us at the orphanage," Nathaniel said. "So the coppers took us to stay at the quarantine clinic until some beds opened up." He lifted his chin defiantly. "They aren't used to keeping track of healthy kids, so I hot-footed it out of there as fast as I could. I figured I'd get some money together and then go back for Belle. I got home just a little while before those men showed up."

Clay listened in stunned silence until Nathaniel finished his story. "Have you eaten?"

Nathaniel shook his head.

"Go get the box of groceries out of the car. We'll eat and then figure something out, okay?"

Nathaniel gave him a weak smile and darted out the door.

"Okay, witch... you saved my life the other night, so I plan to keep my part of the bargain. But I may need more of your magic to fix this mess," he thought.

After they wolfed down ham sandwiches, Clay drove to the quarantine center.

"Wait here," he instructed Nathaniel. "It's more likely they'd try to take you instead of letting me take Belle."

"But Belle trusts me. What if she doesn't recognize you? What if she tells them you aren't really our uncle?"

"Don't jinx me," Clay said, opening his car door.

The sign on the door unnerved him:

WARNING: DIPTHERIA QUARANTINE CLINIC –
ENTER AT YOUR OWN RISK!

A bell sounded as he opened the door and entered the large house. He eyed the desk in the foyer that currently served as a make-shift lobby. A thin, middle-aged nurse looked up from her paperwork, with a no-nonsense expression. "Can I help you?" she asked, looking over the top of eyeglasses, perched on the tip of her nose.

The nurse reminded him of a particularly strict nun at the convent where he had been raised. He felt like a kid again, trying to fib his way out of some mess he had gotten into.

"My niece was brought here by mistake. Belle Hamilton. My sister was taking care of Belle while her mother, another sister of mine, is in the hospital. My sister had to leave town – um – unexpectedly and couldn't delay her departure until I arrived. My nephew – a real rascal – sneaked away from here yesterday to let me know what happened, so I'm here to take Belle off your hands."

"And your name is?"

"Clay Hamilton," he said.

The nurse's eyes narrowed as she examined him from head to foot. Clay couldn't stop picturing her in a nun's habit.

"I thought these were your sister's children. How is it that you have the same name?"

"Damn, I forgot Hamilton is her married name." Clay doffed his hat and bowed his head, thinking. "I'm sorry, I tend to get flustered in the presence of beautiful women," he lied. "My sister's name is Bobbi Hamilton. My name isn't Hamilton, of course. It's Clay – *"What had Doctor Farthing called Louise?"* — Johnson! My name is Clay Johnson. Our father's name was Johnson, too."

The nurse eyed him suspiciously. "Uh huh. Are you really Belle's uncle?"

"Of course," Clay said, tugging at his shirt collar. "She loves her Uncle Clay."

"We'll see about that," she said, getting to her feet. "Come this way."

She led him into a small, dark room. Belle was lying in a crib, even though she was clearly too old to need one. The nurse must have sensed his surprise. "We're short on beds," she explained.

Belle sat up. Her blonde curls were tangled and she had been crying. She looked at Clay with a blank expression. Before the nurse saw through his ruse, he said, "Belle, it's me... good old Uncle Clay. I've come to take you home, honey."

Belle blinked and rubbed her swollen eyes, but her expression didn't change.

Desperate, Clay began to sing her 'Twinkle, Twinkle Little Star' ditty: "Long gone, long gone, long gone, long..."

A smile spread over Belle's face as she scrambled to her feet. "Uncle Clay!" she said, stretching her arms out to him.

The nurse watched in amazement as he walked over and lifted the child out of the crib. Belle wrapped her arms and legs tightly around him and in little more than a whisper, cooed, "I've got you now!"

He laughed, feeling oddly content. "Yes, I'm afraid you do."

Chapter Forty Four

The fog tucked Lily into its folds and carried her away, still smiling. She wasn't sure how long she floated between memories, but all at once, the mist cleared and she was back in Bobbi's hospital room. Nathaniel stood next to his mother, but little Belle clung to Clay's leg, refusing to go anywhere near her.

When Bobbi reached out her good hand, beckoning her baby daughter, Belle let out an ear-splitting shriek that brought a nurse racing into the room. "Children aren't allowed in here!" she barked. "Take them out immediately."

"I'm sorry," Clay said, scooping Belle up to silence her. "But these kid's aunt just run-off, and before she left town, she told them they were orphans. They needed to see for themselves that was a lie." Clay nodded at Bobbi, who was still wearing a helmet of gauze, with only small slits for breathing and vision. Then he gave the homely nurse one of his most endearing smiles. "Another one of their aunts should be here to fetch them real soon. You'd be doing God's work if you let us wait here until she comes."

The nurse stood transfixed for a moment, mesmerized by Clay's devilishly handsome face. The thick lenses of her spectacles made her eyes look oddly magnified and she smiled with her lips closed, hiding crooked teeth. Torn between duty and Clay's charm, she scanned the room, sizing up the situation. "Is the little one angry or frightened?" she asked.

"Probably a little of both," Clay replied. "The tot's had a rough go of it and she doesn't believe her mama's really under those bandages."

"Maybe I can help." The nurse touched Belle's cheek. "Do you like sweets young lady?" she purred.

Curious, Belle rocked her head toward the woman, without lifting it from Clay's shoulder.

"I have some rock candy at my desk. Why don't we go get it and then we can sit outside until your aunt gets here?"

Belle eyed the nurse warily.

"Don't worry, Mother," Nathaniel said. "I'll take good care of her." He kissed Bobbi on her hand and whispered, "And I'll be back to visit you, even if I have to sneak in." Then he walked over to Clay. "It's okay, Belle. Let's go with her. She isn't like the nurses at the quarantine clinic. She's nice."

The nurse rounded on Clay. "Quarantine Clinic?" she asked, alarmed.

Clay handed Belle down to Nathaniel and gave the nurse another broad smile. "It's nothing," he assured her. "Now, go along with the pretty nurse, children."

Nathaniel took the nurse's hand and led her through the door before she could ask any more questions.

Bobbi watched them leave, her eyes filling with tears.

Her anguish wasn't lost on Clay. "Don't worry, Witch. That boy is smarter than lots of grown men I've known. He can take care of his sister."

Bobbi wrote on her slate. "Jo agreed to take them?"

Before Clay had time to respond, Jo entered the room. She looked older than her thirty-three years, with a red checked scarf folded in a triangle and tied beneath her chin, partially hiding the gruesome scar that ran down the side of her face. Her auburn hair was pulled back into a tight bun, just above the collar of her long-sleeved, high-collared white blouse. Her heavy black walking skirt was hemmed just barely off the ground. The perspiration above her lip revealed that her cumbersome, old-fashioned outfit was every bit as hot and uncomfortable as it appeared.

She stared at her younger sister, her mouth gapping at the unrecognizable body lying on the bed. After a moment, she turned to Clay. "Are you the man who called about Lou? About her running off, I mean?" she asked.

"Yes, ma'am," he replied.

Jo nodded. "Lucian is furious. Do you know where she's gone?"

"New York City."

Jo clasped her hand over her mouth as if Clay just announced Louise decided to become a prostitute.

"Lucian's furious. He said he's protected Lou from the Devil's influence for years, but after just a few weeks of living under Bobbi's roof, she surrendered to Satan's evil temptations."

"That's bullshit," Clay sneered. "More likely, she's wanted to fly the coop for years, and when she finally saw her chance, she grabbed it."

Jo shot a quick look at Bobbi before dropping her gaze to the floor. "Be that as it may, I'm sorry, Bobbi, but Lucian won't allow your children in our home and you know I can't defy him." Dabbing a handkerchief at her eyes, she darted from the room.

"Doesn't that beat all?" Clay muttered, shaking his head. "You want me to go after her?"

"No good." Bobbi scrawled on her tablet.

"Well, how about your other sister – Maxine. She's already got two of your kids. You think she'd take in the other two?"

"She must!" Bobbi wrote.

"Listen, I'll stay with them tonight, but I have to go out of town tomorrow. I'll catch Jo and tell her to call Max. Meanwhile, I'll make sure they have food enough to last until she comes for them and arrange to have your neighbor check-up on them. It's the best I can do, Bobbi."

Bobbi blinked her eyes, clearly worried, and then wrote, "Thank you, good man."

Clay reddened and left without answering. For the first time since he found her, he was more worried about what would happen to Bobbi and her children than he was about her ability to put a curse on him. He had his doubts that Bobbi's younger sister,

Maxine, would take custody of Nathaniel and Belle. Together with her politically-motivated husband, the barren woman had been happy to take Fred and Henrietta, whose green eyes and auburn hair matched her own, but not the two who favored their father.

With an increasing sense of dread, Clay gathered the blond, hazel-eyed children from the nurse's station and drove them home. For dinner, he opened the fuel door of the wood burning stove and handed each of the children a green stick for toasting bread over the fire. Then he poured a squeeze of honey on a plate.

"This is for dipping," he explained, ignoring the children's dubious glances.

Then he heard the sound of someone sneaking up the porch steps. Still unnerved from his near-death experience, Clay flung open the door with his pistol drawn. It was the children's mysterious benefactor, back to drop off more supper scraps.

Clay lowered the gun to his side and grinned. "Come on in, Santa Claus. It's high-time the children met you."

He ushered the big man into Bobbi's small kitchen. In the light, Lily could tell that he once had black hair, but now it was far more *salt* than *pepper*. His leathery skin was tanned from working in the sun, and his wide, drooping jowls brought the face of a bulldog to mind. Despite the man's fierce appearance, his dark brown eyes darted around nervously, as if he had been caught in the act of committing a crime rather than a kindness.

"Nathaniel, this is the man who's been leaving food on your doorstep. What's your name, big fella?"

"Mumper," he mumbled. "James Mumper."

"Thank you, sir," offered Nathaniel, "for all of your kindnesses."

"Just repaying a debt," James said. "Your mama's a good woman."

"Strange how you seem to know when these kids need food," Clay observed. "I figure you and your wife must live pretty close by."

"Widower," James said. "Going on six years."

Clay frowned. "You know how to cook and such?"

"Had to learn. Got tired of beans. Don't like it much – don't do it well." James glanced at the children, standing by the stove with their sticks of burned bread, and then narrowed his eyes. "Why?"

"Look, these kids need someone to stay here and look after them until either their aunt comes to fetch them or – more likely – until their mother comes home from the hospital," Clay said. "And since you're beholden to their mother..."

James walked over to the stove, still carrying the small package of food in his large hand. "Hard times. I'll help out tonight. I know a woman. One of my pickers. Her husband and young'un died of fever a while back. Harvest is about over. She'll be needin' a place to stay. Might trade cooking for room and board."

The mist gathered around Lily, pulling her from the scene. "The woman James mentioned was Amy Karr," Clay's voice said. "She wasn't much to look at, but she was kind, quiet as a mouse, and loved to cook. James liked her, too. When I stopped by to check on the kids, I'd usually find the two of them sitting on the porch like an old married couple; Amy working on a basket of vegetables or sewing, and James reading the paper, sharing the interesting tidbits with her."

When the clouds parted, Lily was with Clay in his bright yellow car. He was parking in front of Bobbi's house. She smiled at the way the children ran to the car with shouts of glee, as if Clay really was their favorite uncle.

Suddenly, a tapping sound drew Lily's attention. The moment she turned to search for the origin of the noise, the clouds disappeared and she plummeted through the mist.

She woke with a start, her arms flailing. Someone was knocking on her hotel room door. She tried to close her eyes and return to the spirit realm, but instead, memories of the previous evening came flooding back.

She had behaved badly. She knew that. Still, she wasn't ready to see Seth just yet. She stayed quiet, hoping he would go away.

"Housekeeping," a woman's voice called.

"Damn. I forgot to put the 'Do Not Disturb' sign out," Lily realized. "Please come back later!"

"Very well," the maid replied.

Lily glanced at the clock. The large blue numbers flashed 9:30. There was plenty of time to shower and meet Seth for breakfast and she knew it would hurt him if she didn't show up. Still, she lay staring at the clock, watching the minutes tick by.

Fifteen minutes later, she forced herself to shower and get dressed. She walked down the hallway to the four stairs and descended them more slowly than necessary. Then she stopped, trying to decide whether to turn right, toward the Terrace Cafe and Seth, or left, toward the hotel shuttle and Grams.

Finally, she turned left, trying not to think about Seth.

Chapter Forty Five

When Lily arrived at her grandmother's hospital room, the door was closed. She pushed it open and was shocked to see five muscular orderlies gathered around Grams' bed.

"Oh no..."

Before Lily could finish her thought, Nurse Opal rushed over. "Miz Bloom's condition hasn't worsened, Lily," she said. "We're just transferring her to a bed with an automatic air mattress. It'll shift her body weight from one side to the other, so she doesn't develop bed sores." The nurse smiled. "You're early today."

Lily realized she was holding her breath. She let it out and returned Opal's smile. "That makes sense. And you're right – I am here a bit earlier than usual."

"It's pretty crowded in here, so I'm going to have to ask you to step out until were finished. You can get a cup of coffee in the surgical waiting room down the hall. This shouldn't take more than twenty minutes or so."

"No problem." Lily stepped into the hallway and started for the waiting room. The clicking of her crutch against the tile was the only sound as she slipped into the room.

It was a typical waiting room: chairs lined against the walls, a few magazine tables and a small TV mounted to the wall. Directly across from the door, beneath a framed print of a beach landscape, a table held complimentary coffee, tea and breakfast pastries.

Lily's stomach growled in protest over missing breakfast, so she stopped to pick up a cup of coffee and an apple Danish. She carefully balanced the little dessert plate on top of her coffee so she could carry them in one hand, and lean on her crutch with the other. She had to concentrate and move slowly to avoid spill-age, but managed to make it to a nearby chair. She settled into a chair and with a sigh of relief, lifted the paper plate off of the cof-fee and brought the pastry prize to her lips.

Just as she took her first bite, she heard a woman sniffle. She glanced up in surprise and saw a couple sitting directly across from her. They were seated behind the open door, hidden from sight when she first entered the room.

Lily tried to focus on her Danish, but found it difficult to keep her eyes averted. The slight woman's dishwater blond hair hung in strings around her shoulders and her pale face was blotchy from crying. Her flowery blouse had come untucked from her navy slacks. She rested her head against a huge man who was squeezed into the chair beside her. Judging by his longish grey hair, jeans and blue denim shirt, embroidered with the name, *Hank*, Lily guessed he was a mechanic. His head rested against the wall and his eyes were closed, but he kept one of his enor-mous arms wrapped protectively around the woman's shoulders.

"They've had a long night," Lily thought. She picked up a maga-zine and hid behind it, pretending to read.

A middle-aged woman with glasses appeared at the door, wearing a long, white lab coat over a gray blouse and black skirt, her brown hair pulled back in a French braid. She glanced at the clipboard she was carrying, and then from one side of the room to the other.

Instinctively, Lily knew she was looking for the couple and pointed in their direction. The woman understood and stepped into the room far enough to be able to see around the back of the door.

"Mr. and Mrs. Patterson, my name is Mary Justus," she said. "I'm the transplant coordinator for the hospital. Dr. Thompson sent me. I have the consent forms he told you about."

Mrs. Patterson acknowledged the new-comer with a stiff nod while twisting a tissue in her hands. Her husband rubbed his eyes and then his five o'clock shadow, trying to hide his tears.

Mary Justus swung a chair around to face the couple and sat. She kept her voice down, but in the otherwise silent waiting room, Lily still heard her.

"I am truly sorry for your loss, but I want to thank you for making the heroic decision to donate Tracy's viable organs. Do you have any questions before giving your consent?"

Lily's jaw dropped. *"This can't be happening,"* her mind screamed. *"Not to another child..."*

Lily closed her eyes, wishing she could disappear. She tried not to listen, but her ears betrayed her. Instead of tuning out the voices, they focused, making sure she heard every syllable.

Mary continued, explaining the forms and getting the required signatures. "I can take you to say goodbye to your daughter now. Are you ready?"

Mrs. Patterson started crying, her breath coming in jagged heaves. Mary pulled a small package of Kleenex from a pocket of her lab coat and handed it to her. She watched silently as the distraught woman wiped her eyes and nose, pulling herself together.

Hank Patterson tightened his muscular arm around his wife, pulling her close to comfort her. "How bad does Tracy look? I want to be prepared."

Mary nodded. "Tracy's head is heavily bandaged and supported by a neck brace. The portions of her arms and legs that suffered cuts and abrasions in the accident are also bandaged. As Dr. Thompson explained, when the motorcycle went down, the back of her head hit a concrete curb, resulting in a severe skull fracture and catastrophic damage to her brain. Life-support equipment is keeping her heart beating and doing her breathing for her, so you'll see several wires and tubes running between her body and those machines." Mary looked directly at Mrs. Patterson. "It's important to remember that Tracy is in no pain whatsoever."

"How can you be sure?" Kathy Patterson whimpered.

"Her brain is no longer functioning. It can't communicate with her nerves or distinguish sensations like pain," Mary explained.

Lily bit her lip. She pictured a woman like this one, talking to Scott after the accident – convincing him to give up on Dylan. She scowled with revulsion.

Hank Patterson gave his wife a tender hug. "I think we're ready," he said in a gruff whisper.

Mary nodded and stood up. "She's in room 4551, just down the hall."

Hank Patterson got to his feet; then helped his wife balance on her wobbly legs.

"While you're saying goodbye," Mary said, "try to remember that Tracy's last accomplishment on earth will be to save the lives of other people. That knowledge will comfort you in the difficult days ahead."

Hank nodded and then slowly led his wife from the waiting room. Mary started after them, glancing over her shoulder to give Lily a courtesy-nod goodbye.

Whispering, Lily hissed, "Liar!"

Mary's eyes flew open. She didn't appear angry; just confused and perhaps, curious. "I'm sorry, did you say something?"

"I said you're a liar," Lily repeated, keeping her voice low so the Pattersons wouldn't hear. "Those people will always regret that they didn't fight to keep their child alive."

Mary glanced at the Pattersons. They were almost to the door of their daughter's room. She returned her gaze to Lily, clearly torn. "Those people need me right now. We can talk more later, if you like."

Sensing her sincerity, Lily's anger fizzled, leaving behind an empty void. "Just go away," she mumbled.

Mary nodded and hurried to join the Pattersons. A moment later, Lily heard the sound of Kathy Patterson's heartbreaking wails. She snatched up her crutch and headed for the silence of Grams' room as quickly as she could manage.

Opal and her team were gone by the time Lily arrived. She watched Grams' chest rise and fall ever so slightly, wondering if she liked her new bed. Every few minutes, a small motor clicked on; causing some sections of the air mattress to inflate, while others deflated. When the motor shut off, the silence was deafening, but Lily was still too disturbed to try for a nap.

After what felt like an eternity, Lily heard voices in the hallway. Seeking a distraction, she hobbled to the door and peeked out, just as two men, dressed in blue medical scrubs, slipped through the double doors at the end of the corridor. They were each carrying a small, red and white cooler, marked with a red cross.

Lily shuddered, certain that when they returned, those coolers would contain organs... Tracy Patterson's organs. She wondered how long Kathy and Hank Patterson would have to wait before someone came to tell them their daughter was *officially* dead. Lily knew she would never forget their faces, contorted with anguish.

She stumbled back to Grams' bedside and sank into her chair, her heart pounding. She was still contemplating the unfairness of life when someone knocked on the door.

"May I please come in and talk with you, Ms. Thorne?"

Lily glared at the organ donation coordinator. She knew it was irrational to blame the woman for opening old wounds, but her anger continued to boil. "I'm not planning to donate my grandmother's organs," she snapped, "so I don't think we have anything to discuss."

The woman ignored the jab. "My name is Mary Justus. I asked about you at the nurses' station. May I call you Lily?"

Lily shrugged, crossed her arms and stared out the window.

Mary dragged a lightweight, plastic chair close to Lily and sat down. "With a name like Lilyanna Rose Bloom-Thorne, I'll bet you're a natural in a flower garden," she teased, trying to lighten the mood.

Lily scowled. "Not really. Your name's Mary. Do you tend sheep?"

"Fair enough," Mary replied. "Listen, I'm sorry if this morning's encounter was difficult for you."

"I'm sure it was more difficult for the parents of the child you disemboweled," Lily replied.

Mary refused to take the bait. "No one ever tells you how long the grieving process can last after you lose a loved one, but..."

"Thanks, but I don't need any more grief counseling." Lily sneered.

Mary glanced at Lily's leg brace and then scanned the room. "What I told those grieving parents was the truth, Lily. Most families I've worked with tell me the knowledge that people were saved because they chose organ donation makes the loss of their loved one more bearable. Am I safe to assume you were in an accident and lost someone dear to you?" she asked.

"Lose someone?" Lily snarled, "No. I didn't *lose* someone. My son was *taken* from me. He was talking after the crash. After I pulled him from our burning car, we both lost consciousness. The doctors should have saved him. But instead, they told my husband Dylan was brain-dead at the scene. They coerced him into giving them permission to carve our beautiful boy into pieces. By the time I woke up, he was gone."

Mary shook her head. "That must have been a horrible ordeal."

Lily was shaking. "If Scott wouldn't have given his consent, I'm sure the doctors would have tried harder to save Dylan, but they stopped trying as soon as they found out they could have his organs." Lily re-crossed her arms over her chest, trying not to cry.

"Lily, I've been a transplant coordinator for more than a decade now. Everyone I work with believes organ donation is a selfless and heroic choice made by people who have just suffered the tragic loss of a loved one. We *never* discuss the option of organ donation with the family until we're absolutely certain the injured person has no chance of recovery."

"Doctors make mistakes." Lily's voice was barely audible, but still defiant.

"You're right about that... doctors aren't perfect and if someone made an error regarding your son's prognosis, it needs to come to light." Mary studied her for a moment. "I worked as a lead nurse on a trauma surgery team for many years. I'd be willing to review your son's medical records, and if I see anything suspicious, turn them over for an impartial medical review."

Lily froze, dumbfounded. After three long years, someone was finally offering to help her prove that Dylan could have been saved. She nodded her head, unable to speak.

"Okay then," Mary said. "I'll need to get some information from you – and you'll have to sign a consent form, granting me permission to access a copy of your son's medical records." She opened her portfolio and withdrew some paperwork.

After Lily completed and signed the release forms, Mary stood and prepared to leave.

"How long will this take?" Lily asked.

"I'll request a copy of your son's records today. If the hospital stores their files in electronic format, they might be able to respond to my request immediately. If not, it might take several days. I'll let you know when the file arrives, and if there's any question about your son's diagnosis, or if it looks like mistakes were made during transport or after he arrived at the hospital, I promise to request an investigation."

"Thank you."

After Mary left, Lily sat in the chair under the window, trying to digest the events of the morning. She wished for the hundredth time that her grandmother would wake up. "Did you hear all of that, Grams? I might finally be able to prove Dylan could have been saved." She shook her head. "Not that it will make any difference."

Watching her grandmother's rhythmic breathing, Lily's racing thoughts slowed down and her eyes grew heavy. Soon she dozed off and the clouds of the spirit world rolled in around her.

Chapter Forty Six

Lily floated through the familiar fog, contemplating the coexistence of her world and the spirit realm, and wondering what lay beyond the lighted path, until the clouds parted.

She knew she was with Bobbi, even though she couldn't see anything. Someone was gently shaking Bobbi's shoulder.

"Wake up, Mrs. Hamilton. Dr. Whiting is here to remove your bandages." The woman sounded excited.

Bobbi made some unintelligible noises.

A man coughed. "This is a big day for you, Mrs. Hamilton. Let Nurse Anna help you to the side of the bed so I can get those bandages off. Dr. Farthing will be along in just a moment to conduct your post-surgical examination."

Bobbi groaned, more from exhaustion and frustration than pain, but she allowed the nurse to help her sit up and support her injured leg as she moved. Once she was in position, Dr. Whiting went to work. His touch was gentle as he carefully removed layer after layer of bandages from Bobbi's head. After unwrapping several inches of bandages, he stopped.

"All right, Mrs. Hamilton. Let me stop here and notify Dr. Farthing. I know he'll want to remove the rest of this himself," Dr. Whiting said. "And don't be alarmed, but eight doctors, including myself, are following him today. We're all itching to witness the outcome of this procedure."

Lily listened to the sound of receding footsteps, feeling sorry for Bobbi, whose disposition felt as dark as the world she inhabited at this moment.

"After six long weeks, I'm sure you can hardly wait to get those bandages off of your eyes and those tubes removed," the nurse said.

Bobbi grunted and shrugged her shoulders.

"I know you're discouraged, but I'm sure your moxie will soon return," she chirped. "Better days are ahead."

Bobbi growled.

"I know I'm a stranger to you, but we've met before. I'm Nurse Anna Parker. I was here when you first arrived at this hospital in such a pitiful state almost a year ago. I sat with you for three days, administering pain medication, certain you were dying. You looked Irish, so I even had a priest come to administer last rites."

Bobbi grunted, as if to say, "Wrong on both counts."

Nurse Anna chuckled. "Yes, you have gumption all right." She patted Bobbi's arm. "You know, my own dear husband died not long before yours. When you were brought to the hospital, I thought you would be rejoining your husband very soon and I envied you for that." Anna took a deep breath. "But then you refused to die. And when Dr. Farthing arrived with such zeal and optimism, I realized I couldn't help others if I no longer cherished life. I left the hospital and booked passage on the transcontinental railroad."

Anna sighed.

"At first, I stared out the window, seeing nothing but my own sorrows. But gradually, I ran out of tears for all I had lost, and began to notice the splendor of the world outside. Whether we were charging through the countryside or rolling through large cities, beauty was everywhere – from snowcapped mountains on the horizon, to the smile on a child's face as he watched the train pass by. Eventually, I understood that my husband's love wasn't gone. As long as I treasure it, his love will live on in my heart, just like my memories of those lovely landscapes."

She paused, listening to the doctors gathering in the hall outside. "When I returned to work a few days ago and discovered that you're doing so well, I swore to God that I'll never give up on another patient."

Bobbi only grunted with distain, but Lily heard her thoughts as clearly as if she spoke out loud. *"Doing so well?"* She wanted to scream. *"My husband's dead, I'll never walk again, and my face is so disfigured, it frightens my own children."*

Nurse Anna stopped speaking when Alton Farthing and his protégés entered the room.

"Hello, Bobbi. How's my favorite girl feeling today?" he asked.

Bobbi grunted. *"Like one of Doctor Frankenstein's experiments."*

"I understand you're frustrated," Alton replied, patting her hand. "But today I hope you'll start to see that everything I've put you through was worthwhile. Just bear with me a few moments longer, Bobbi."

He patted Bobbi's hand and turned his attention to the group of doctors crowding the tiny room. "This patient suffered extensive facial injuries in a car accident almost a year ago. Repairing the damage required numerous restorative surgeries. Slivers of ivory were implanted to serve as internal splints, providing stability to her facial structure while her fractures mended. I also employed the services of Dr. Huck, a dental surgeon, to install porcelain jacket crowns over each of her broken teeth. The combination of on-going dental work, ivory implants, a shaved hairline and various surgical processes have been both painful and unattractive."

Alton rested his hand on Bobbi's shoulder. "But the dental surgeon completed the final phase of his work two months ago. Two weeks later, I operated to remove the ivory splints and temporary implants. I made all incisions inside the patient's natural hairline and beneath her chin. To minimize scarring, each incision was also closed with small, internal sutures."

Lily could sense that Bobbi was fighting a growing urge to reach up and yank off the last layers of bandages.

Alton felt Bobbi fidget. "I'm almost finished – I promise," he said, giving her arm another pat. "Doctors, I subscribe to the theory that complete immobilization following surgery allows facial structures and nerves to regenerate more rapidly, even though this type of recovery period is extremely difficult for the patient.

Her entire head was immobilized with a helmet of thick bandaging. Tubes were inserted to keep her nostrils open for breathing, and another tube was placed in her mouth to allow for liquid nourishment. We kept her calm by administering mild doses of chloroform on a frequent basis, and we did not permit visitors. Today, I hope to offer proof that the theory of immobilization has merit."

Alton turned to Bobbi. "Are you ready, pet?"

"I'm afraid," Bobbi mumbled, even though she knew he couldn't understand her garbled speech.

"If this procedure didn't work, I'll try something else," he whispered, unwinding the final layers of bandages. "I won't give up until your face is restored." When the last of the gauze had been removed, he carefully pulled the tubes from Bobbi's nose and mouth.

Bobbi heard the doctors shuffling around, trying to improve their observation vantage points as Alton plucked the cotton balls from her eyelids. Lily felt a sense of relief flood through Bobbi. Her vision was blurry, but it was marvelous to see light after being in total darkness for six weeks.

"Nurse," Alton ordered, "Get some gauze pads so I can wipe the petroleum jelly from her eyes."

"Here they are, Dr. Farthing," Anna replied, anticipating his request.

Once the protective Vaseline had been removed from Bobbi's green eyes, Alton's face came into focus. The pride in his expression and excited murmurs from the crowd were encouraging, but Bobbi was afraid to get her hopes up.

"All right, Bobbi, try to blink your right eye," Alton instructed. "Very good. Now, blink your left eye."

Once she had blinked each eye several times, he continued. "Squeeze both of your eyes shut tight. Good girl. Now wrinkle your nose; open your mouth; move your jaw..." The commands seemed endless. Finally, Alton said, "Now smile, Bobbi."

When Bobbi smiled, Alton held up a hand mirror. For the first time in almost a year, the face Bobbi saw reflected in the glass looked vaguely like her own.

Alton wrapped her fingers around the handle of the mirror. "Do you approve?"

Bobbi nodded, unable to look away. She ran her fingers lightly over her still puffy nose and cheeks and opened her sore mouth to study her teeth. She examined the hot-pink surgical scars beneath her chin, along both sides of her face and on her scalp, where a portion of her head had been shaved.

Alton's eyes sparkled with pride. "That swelling and bruising will go away, and those incision scars will fade over time. When your hair grows back, you won't even see the one on your scalp."

When the buzz of their audience erupted into applause, Bobbi blushed, feeling like a caged exhibit. Lily was thrilled for Bobbi, but also happy because she was finally free to look wherever she pleased.

Alton noted the color in Bobbi's cheeks and gave her a wink. Then he glanced at Nurse Anna. "You can wash her head, but take special care around the incisions. And if she feels up to it, let her try eating some broth and tapioca pudding." Next, he addressed the enthusiastic onlookers. "Doctors, let's adjourn to the courtyard for a well-earned cigar and allow Mrs. Hamilton to get some rest."

As they filed out of the room, the young doctors began bombarding Alton with questions about his surgical techniques and the use of photographs in the reconstruction process.

Bobbi and Lily watched the men leave and then eyed the short, trim nurse. Lily thought the nurse's physical appearance matched her soft voice. She wore a crisp white cap and uniform, and her attractive, heart-shaped face featured large, expressive brown eyes, long lashes, a button nose, dimpled cheeks and a kind smile. A few wild curls of ebony hair had escaped the bun at the nape of her neck.

Bobbi returned her gaze to the mirror. "Humpty Dumpty," she told her bruised and swollen reflection. "He's trying his best, but all the king's horses and all the kings' men couldn't put me back together again."

"Humpty Dumpty is it?" Anna clucked. "Well, I've always believed that if all the king's men had kept their horses out of it and just focused on repairing one small crack at a time instead of being overwhelmed by the enormity of the task, Humpty Dumpty might have been put back together right as rain. Lucky for you, Dr. Farthing is a brilliant surgeon who seems to possess the same belief, so..." Anna froze mid-sentence and flushed scarlet.

Lily and Bobbi turned and saw Alton standing in the doorway. The amused look on his face indicated he had overheard Anna's commentary.

"I forgot my clipboard," he said, retrieving it from the bedside table. He grinned at the mortified nurse. "Perhaps I should call this new facial restoration process the *Humpty Dumpty Method*." He chuckled and disappeared through the door, just as the fog began to gather, carrying Lily away from the memory.

Lily floated through the clouds, thinking about Bobbi. She still had a long road of recovery ahead of her, but at least she wouldn't have to live with a horribly disfigured face. She glanced at the burn scars on her forearms. *"Plastic surgery techniques have progressed light years beyond those crude, experimental surgeries Bobbi endured. They could probably fix most of this damage, if I let them. But I just can't."*

Chapter Forty Seven

The clouds parted suddenly, ending Lily's musings and leaving her dizzy. She gulped air to settle her stomach while taking in the scene around her. Clay and Nathaniel were standing next to Bobbi's hospital bed.

"You're beautiful again, Mother!" Nathaniel exclaimed.

Lily couldn't help noticing the boy looked much older than his fourteen years.

"When I tell Belle, she'll be sorry she stayed home with Mrs. Karr today," he said. "Wait till you see her, Mother. She can be such a scamp. Why earlier today, she even tried to pack herself in Mrs. Karr's suitcase when..."

Nathaniel stopped short and shot a glance at Clay. "Sorry, Uncle Clay, I didn't mean to..." he mumbled.

"Nathaniel, why don't you go with Nurse Anna so I can chat with your Mama?"

Lily noticed Clay was holding his Fedora with both hands and avoiding eye contact with Bobbi. Nathaniel nodded, forced a smile and kissed his mother's cheek.

Bobbi gazed at her eldest child. "I'm sorry for all you've been through this year, son. But I know your father would be very proud of the way you've handled yourself." She swallowed hard. "Now, run along with Anna and don't forget to give Belle my love."

The nurse smiled at Nathaniel, wrapping her arm around his shoulders. As she turned to leave, she called over her shoulder,

"Fix one crack at a time, Humpty Dumpty. Your daughter will be back in your arms before you know it."

Bobbi smiled at her friend. When she turned back to Clay, she was unnerved by the look in his eyes.

Embarrassed at being caught staring, Clay began studying the brim of his hat.

Lily swiveled her head from Bobbi to Clay, realizing that by focusing on one or the other, she could read their unspoken thoughts.

Bobbi was remembering when Clay discovered her in the wrecked truck. She knew her face had been so injured as to be frightening, and that every time Clay had seen her since that time, her head had been wrapped in gauze. *"How odd,"* she thought, *"that I've become friends with a man who has never seen my face."*

When Lily concentrated on Clay's thoughts, she discovered that, even with a partially-shaved head, residual swelling and fading bruises, he thought Bobbi was pretty. *"Before the accident, she must've been a real stunner,"* he thought, envisioning her bright green eyes peeking from beneath a head full of wavy auburn hair.

Finally, Clay broke the silence. "You must have strong magic, witch," he said, only half-kidding. "Because the day I found you, hanging onto life by a thread, I never would've believed..." He shook his head. "But look at you now. You're the cat's meow. "

Bobbi smiled. "You're a good man, Clay Long. You try to hide it, but you can't fool my children."

"Sure, little girls think I'm the bees' knees. It's the older ones I have trouble with."

"Not just Belle... Nathaniel, too," Bobbi said.

"That one's got good character. Folks can count on him even when the chips are down."

"Perhaps, but please keep him out of the booze racket, Clay. He's just a boy, even if he doesn't act like one, and it's too dangerous. I'm worried he'll be drawn to the excitement and easy money – especially if it means he can spend more time with you. You have to protect him."

"Because you'll curse me if I don't?" Clay shifted uneasily from one foot to other.

Bobbi shook her head. "Because you care about him and you know the bootlegging business is teeming with gangsters the likes of George Applegate. Nathaniel admires you. He'll listen if you tell him to steer clear."

"Hell, I think I liked it better when you just threatened to haunt me."

They chuckled and fell back into comfortable silence.

All at once, Clay smacked his forehead with the heel of his hand. "I forgot to tell you the reason we're here today. James Mumper and Amy Karr went and got hitched yesterday. The widow that James works for asked him to manage her orchards in Miami, so they're headed down there tomorrow. Amy said to tell you she was sorry for having to leave so sudden."

"Oh, no," Bobbi groaned. "I mean, I wish them well, of course – but who will take care of my children now?"

Before Clay could tell Bobbi he had called her older sister for help, Josephine knocked on the open door.

"It's a miracle," she whispered, gawking at Bobbi with wide eyes and a slack jaw as she moved to her bedside.

"Hello, Jo." Bobbi smiled. She showed Jo the various incisions and explained how Alton Farthing's team of doctors had accomplished the resurrection of her face.

"Unfortunately, I won't be able to go home for several weeks yet, and even then, I'll be confined to a wheeled chair," Bobbi continued. "And I've just learned that the woman who's been caring for Nathaniel and Belle is leaving tomorrow. You know that Max is only willing to care for Henrietta and Fred, and with Lou living on her own in New York – well, I have nowhere else to turn. Jo, I need you to take care of Nathaniel and Belle until I get home."

"I'm sorry, Bobbi, but Lucian absolutely refuses to take them in."

Bobbi's stricken expression bothered Clay more than he cared to acknowledge. "I'll speak to Lucian," he said. "After all, he's a good Christian man. I'm sure I can make him understand that it's not right to turn his back on family – especially children."

Lily glanced from one face to the next. Jo looked uncomfortable, Bobbi was worried, and Clay was obviously angry. An unhappy silence hung thick in the air until finally, Jo cracked.

"Perhaps another Christian man's perspective would be helpful in convincing Lucian to take them in – at least until we can reach Maxine," she said. "Thank you, Mr. Long."

Lily smiled as the fog rolled in, pulling her from the scene. She was certain Clay wasn't planning to convince Lucian to cooperate by quoting scripture.

Before long, she heard Clay's voice. "None of what happened next was my fault. I just want you to know that in advance. I don't think the witch believes me even to this day, but I think the good Lord stepped in and finally had his way – that's all I'm saying."

Chapter Forty Eight

Before Lily had time to wonder what Clay meant, the fog began to clear and she heard a woman screaming, "Help me, Help me!"

Lily strained her eyes to see through the mist. She was standing beside Clay's shiny, black and yellow Bearcat. His door was open and he was just starting to climb into the driver's seat, when Jo ran out of her shabby white house, waving her arms. "Help!" she cried.

Clay shifted his eyes from Jo to the house, his hand automatically moving to the handle of his pistol, concealed in a shoulder holster just inside his pinstriped jacket.

Lily gasped, reading Clay's thoughts. He expected to see foul-tempered Lucian charge out of the door, chasing after his wife, and he was trying to decide if he should shoot him.

"I think he's dying! Help me!" Jo shrieked.

Clay dropped his hand from the gun and slammed his car door closed. "Who's dying?" he yelled. "Did that son of a bitch hurt Nathaniel?" Without waiting for a response, he sprinted for the house.

"It's Lucian! He's dying!" Jo cried.

Clay burst through the open door before the meaning of Jo's words sank in. He almost tripped over Lucian, who was sprawled on the living room floor, his obese body covering the majority of the small space. Nathaniel stood on the far side of his uncle, clutching Belle – her hazel eyes the size of saucers. Lucian and Jo's five children clung to one another in the doorway between the living room and kitchen.

"Call for a doctor," Clay ordered as he dropped to one knee, next to Lucian. He scooped off his hat and put an ear to Lucian's chest. After a few tense seconds, he nodded, his ear still pressed against the large man's shirt. "His heart's still beating." He pulled back and began loosening Lucian's bowtie and collar.

Jo stood just inside the open door, wringing her hands. "He was mighty upset about the way you spoke to him. As soon as you left, he turned on me. He said that if I didn't get rid of Bobbi's children, he'd put *all* of us out in the street. I begged him. I said they could sleep in Lou's empty room…" Jo paused, took a deep breath and shook her head. "I don't know why, but that idea infuriated him. He whirled on me with his fists balled and I was certain I was in for a bad beating. I closed my eyes, but the first blow never came. Then I heard him crash to the floor. I didn't know what to do…"

Clay sneered at Lucian with blatant contempt. Lily felt him swallow hard, trying not to give in to his urge to re-tighten the unconscious man's tie or say what he was thinking. *"The coward didn't have the guts to fight me, but as soon as my back's turned, he commences to beating on a defenseless woman."* Clay stood up. "It's alright, Jo. Did you call for a doctor?"

"I did," a tiny voice replied.

Clay glanced at the kitchen doorway and saw a girl of approximately sixteen, who bore a striking resemblance to Bobbi. The four younger children clung to her in much the same way Belle held onto Nathaniel.

Clay was about to ask the girl her name, when Jo dropped to her knees beside Lucian and began to pray. All five children immediately followed her example. Clay shook his head. He stepped over Lucian, scooped up Belle, put his other arm around Nathaniel's shoulders, and without another word, he escorted the two children outside, leaving Lucian's family praying over his motionless bulk.

"Shouldn't we pray with them?" Nathaniel asked as they stepped outside.

"This ain't church, and besides, I'm afraid that man is beyond prayers," Clay said. "Let's just keep an eye out for the doctor."

They heard the wail of a hand-cranked siren. Moments later,

an ambulance arrived in front of the house. The moment the canvas-covered truck came to a stop, one man jumped out and headed for the house, while the other stopped to grab a canvas stretcher from the back.

"They're gonna need our help," Clay observed. "Those two won't be able to carry Lucian on their own. Belle, I need you to sit in my car until we get your Uncle Lucian into the ambulance. Can you do that for me, honey?"

Belle nodded, without lifting her head or letting go of her death grip on him. Clay walked to his car, opened the passenger's door and gently lowered her onto the black leather seat. Before closing the door, he brushed a kiss against her forehead. "That's a brave girl. I'll be back in a flash."

Belle brightened. "Not gone long, Long Gone?" She grinned at her own joke.

Clay smiled back at her, tapped her button nose with his forefinger, and then turned his attention to the problem at hand. *"Can we fit through that doorway while carrying the fat bastard on a litter?"*

The fog descended like a curtain, engulfing Lily and pulling her away from the memory. A moment later, Clay's voice filtered through the mist.

"All right, maybe it was partly my fault for getting the old goat all riled up, but if you ask me, he got what was coming to him."

When the clouds cleared, they were back in Bobbi's room at the hospital. Bobbi frowned at Clay, who stood at the foot of her bed, his head bowed, staring at his hat as if it might try to escape at any moment.

"I *knew* it was a bad idea for you to speak to Lucian," Bobbi wailed. "The man has hard pulse disease. He's bled on a regular basis, for goodness sake – and you threatened him in the sanctity his own home?"

"Bleeding must have been used to lower high blood pressure before the advent of medication," Lily reasoned.

"Now, Bobbi," Clay cajoled, "– threaten is a strong word. I never raised a hand to him. Besides, how was I supposed to know he would go and have a stroke? I didn't know he was sickly. And remember, I only went over there because I was trying to look out for *your* children."

Lily sucked in a sharp breath at hearing Lucian's diagnosis. Stroke was a medical condition she had become very familiar with since returning to Florida. She refocused her attention on the conversation, trying not to think about Grams.

"Of course, you threatened him! Jo said you called him a cheap, hypocritical prick and showed him your gun!"

"Maybe so. But I didn't say anything that wasn't the truth, and you know it. And besides, I started off real friendly-like, holding out my hand for a shake and everything. It was Lucian who started yelling right from the giddy-up. He called Nathaniel and Belle demons, for God's sake. *Demons!*"

Bobbi flinched at the crass insult, but she wasn't about to let Clay off the hook. "And you thought threatening him with your pistol would change his mind about that? Honestly, I think it would be more helpful if you lived up to your nickname from time to time, *Long Gone.*"

Clay's mouth turned up in a half-smile. If Bobbi was truly angry, she wouldn't have referred to him by Belle's pet name.

Jo drifted into the room before they had a chance to discuss the matter further. She was disheveled and exhausted, making her appear even older than she had the day before.

"Jo – come sit on the side of my bed," Bobbi said, patting the mattress. "What does the doctor say?"

"He'll live," Jo replied, sinking down next to her younger sister. "But he can't move and he can't talk. I don't think he even knows who I am right now..."

"I'm so sorry, Jo." Bobbi squeezed her hand.

Clay continued to fumble with the brim of his hat, avoiding eye contact with the sisters. "Maybe I should be going."

"Please stay," Jo said. "I don't blame you for what happened, Mr. Long. Lucian couldn't control his temper so this was bound to happen sooner or later. I'm thankful you were there to help."

Clay nodded and cocked an 'I-told-you- so' eyebrow at Bobbi. "That's real nice you, Jo, but Nathaniel and Belle are waiting in my car. I figure I'll take them to the hotel for supper and sleep at Bobbi's tonight. I have to go out of town tomorrow morning, but they should be all right until your other sister comes for them."

Bobbi bit her lower lip.

"You're worried Maxine will refuse to take them, aren't you?" Jo asked.

"Well, someone had better damn-well take responsibility for them," Clay said. "I've got a job to do and I can't be dallying around here acting like some goddamn wet-nurse!"

"You're right, Mr. Long," Jo said with a thoughtful nod. "My place is here at the hospital with Lucian, but I'm sure my girl Rebecca wouldn't mind caring for two more children at our home." She turned to Bobbi. "You'll probably have to find someplace else for them when Lucian comes home."

Tears filled Bobbi's eyes at Jo's unexpected offer. She leaned forward and hugged her sister tight – something they hadn't done since they were children.

"All right, then," Clay said, his voice cracking. "I'll go tell the kiddies." He ducked out the door, almost bumping into Doctor Whiting.

The young, attractive doctor stopped short at the sight of the two sisters clinging together. "Is everything all right?" he asked.

Jo pulled away from Bobbi's embrace and stood up, embarrassed he had witnessed the emotional exchange. In the rush to get Lucian to the hospital, she had forgotten to put on her scarf, so her hideous facial scar was clearly visible.

"Oh, my," said Dr. Whiting moving close to her. "What happened there?"

Jo tried to hide her face with her open palm, but the doctor brushed her hand away.

"It's from an accident when I was a child," she lied.

Bobbi looked away. She understood Jo's reluctance to admit the injury was intentionally inflicted by their father during one of his alcohol-crazed religious rampages. He had hacked off Jo's hair and sliced her face open with his knife, claiming the only way to protect her from temptations of the flesh was to rid her of her beauty once and for all. He had attempted to do the same thing to Bobbi a few nights before, but she had escaped his clutches and the following morning, left home for good.

Dr. Whiting tilted Jo's face toward the light of the bedside lamp, examining the inch-wide scar that marked her left cheek near her jawline, from just below her eye, down to her chin.

"This scar is far more severe than it might have been, had you received proper medical attention immediately afterward," he observed. There was no judgment in his voice and his examination was purely clinical; a combination of factors that allowed Jo to relax. "Stitches would have helped prevent infection and sped the recovery, as well as greatly lessening the width of the resulting scar."

"What's done is done," Jo replied, her voice flat. She attempted to turn away from the light, but Dr. Whiting held her chin firmly.

"Not necessarily. Working with Dr. Farthing, I've learned surgical techniques to repair this type of damage." Dr. Whiting smiled at Jo's wide eyes and released her chin. "Mrs. Cabot, your case would provide me an excellent opportunity to gain valuable surgical experience in this procedure. I would make an incision, remove the scar tissue and lift your undamaged skin toward your ear. Then I'd close the incision with fine, internal stitches. You'd still have a scar, but it would be a thin, straight line behind your jaw, where it would be far less noticeable. Would you allow me to perform the surgery? At no charge, of course."

Jo's lips moved, but no words came out.

"Do it," said Bobbi, grinning at her sister.

"Lucian would never approve," Jo whispered to Bobbi. "It's vanity."

"It isn't vanity. It's correcting a sinful deed while helping Dr. Whiting improve his surgical skills. And you're already staying at the hospital with Lucian. I say kill two birds with one stone."

"When?" Jo asked, absently touching the thick, ugly scar.

"Tomorrow morning," Dr. Whiting replied.

The fog dropped over Lily like a blanket. A moment later it pulled back again, depositing her into a chair at the small round table in her hotel suite. Margaret stood nearby, wearing a white, high-necked Victorian blouse, tucked into a black skirt. Bobbi suddenly appeared, dressed like a 1920s flapper, in a knee-length blue dress, featuring a long-waisted bodice and pleated skirt, and the two women drifted into chairs on either side of Lily. Once seated, a tea set materialized in front of Margaret and she poured three cups.

"Jo's surgery was a smashing success," Bobbi said. "Dr. Whiting removed the same amount of skin from both sides of her face so the tightness of her skin would match." Bobbi pushed back the skin on her cheeks to demonstrate the effect of removing excess skin. "Not only was her scar gone, but Jo looked much younger than before. She looked so beautiful in fact, that several women have approached Dr. Whiting, requesting surgery to tighten their own skin!"

Margaret clucked as she stirred three teaspoons of sugar into her small teacup. "If women paid as much attention to the development of their brains as they spend trying to appear youthful, they might discover a truth men have known for eons: wealth and power transforms even the most homely person into an attractive one."

"I suppose that's true, but still, I was pleased for Jo," Bobbi replied. She took a sip of tea and turned to Lily. "But things didn't go as well for Lucian. His mind cleared, but his physical maladies showed no improvement. The stroke left him unable to move his limbs, and when he spoke, no one could understand him. His doctors advised Jo to take him home, so she turned Lou's old bedroom into a hospital room of sorts. It was the practical thing to do, of course, but it also meant there wasn't enough space in Jo's home for Nathaniel and Belle."

Chapter Forty Nine

As the fog rolled in, the hotel room vanished, along with the teacup Lily was holding, and seconds later, it parted again. Lily gulped air to battle a wave of nausea.

"Alton thinks I'll be able to go home soon," Bobbi confided to Nurse Anna. "But he said I'll be confined to a wheeled chair for the rest of my life."

"That's exactly what I wanted to talk to you about," Anna said. "I know your leg was crushed too severely to expect it to support your body's weight, but..."

"But, what?" Bobbi demanded.

Anna fluffed Bobbi's pillows. "I have an idea." Anna eased over to the door and peeked down the hall to make sure they were alone. "But I don't know if it will work."

Bobbi sat up straight. "Tell me."

"I don't want to get your hopes up, but I know a blacksmith who might be able to fashion a brace for your leg, with a flat metal plate underneath your foot and a sort of saddle seat at the top. I think it would allow you to stand without putting weight on your leg. With crutches for balance, I think you could stand, and even walk short distances."

Bobbi squinted, trying to visualize the contraption Anna described.

"Let me show you." Anna pulled a small notebook from her pocket and showed Bobbi a rough sketch.

"Can I borrow your notebook and pencil?" Bobbi asked. She drew a second diagram of the brace. Then she drew one that showed how her leg would fit into the device.

"My goodness, Bobbi – you're an artist!" cried Anna.

"Not really," Bobbi said without looking up, "but I can draw clothing patterns and this is similar. How soon do you suppose your blacksmith friend could get started?"

"I have a confession," Anna said. "I asked him to come over to speak with you this afternoon. In fact, he might already be waiting downstairs."

Bobbi laughed. "Well, Then you might as well go and fetch him. The sooner he gets started on this contraption, the sooner we can start fixing another one of Humpty Dumpty's cracks."

Anna grinned and darted out, just as Jo and her oldest daughter, Rebecca arrived.

Lily stared at Jo in awe. She was beautiful and looked at least ten years younger than the last time Lily had seen her. The wide, jagged scar was gone from her cheek and her blue bonnet, tied in a bow beneath her chin, hid the thin, surgical scars. But other vestiges of her old self-image still clung to her. She wore her hair in a prim bun at the base of her neck and both she and Rebecca were wearing high-necked blouses and long, heavy skirts.

"How can they stand wearing those long black skirts in this heat?" Lily wondered.

Rebecca hurried to Bobbi's bed and kissed her cheek. Bobbi smiled, giving Rebecca's hand an affectionate squeeze. She had always been fond of sixteen-year-old Rebecca, though she hadn't seen her often until recently. With thick auburn hair, green eyes, and inquisitive mind, Rebecca reminded Bobbi of herself at that age.

"I'm sorry my hand is wet, Aunt Bobbi. I'm sweating something fierce." The girl tugged at her high, tight collar.

Jo clucked at her daughter. "How many times must I tell you, Rebecca – horses sweat and men perspire. Ladies *glisten*."

"Of course, Mother. You're quite right." Rebecca winked at Bobbi and smiled, her eyes twinkling with mischief. "What I meant to say is that I'm *glistening* so much you could probably wring water from my blouse."

Bobbi and Rebecca giggled as Jo let out a loud, "Harrumph!" Then Jo cleared her throat. "Bobbi, I've come to a decision," she began.

The serious tone of her voice set Bobbi nerves on edge.

"As you know, Lucian needs constant care, and with my home bursting at the seams with boisterous children, the situation has become intolerable. They require so much of Rebecca's attention, she has no time to help me care for her father." Jo paused, giving her daughter a disdainful glance.

Bobbi gave Rebecca's hand a thankful squeeze for making the children her priority, despite her mother's obvious disapproval.

"Since she's so keen to be a nanny, I think it would be best if Rebecca and the children, with the exception of my Sarah, went to live at your house for the time being."

This time, it was Rebecca who squeezed Bobbi's hand; a pleading look in her eyes.

"That's a good plan, Jo," Bobbi enthused. "I can have Nathaniel come by every day to handle your heavy chores and run errands." She turned to Rebecca, who was quivering with excitement. "Rebecca, you can sleep in my bed and I'll ask Clay – err – I mean – Mr. Long – to watch over you. Maybe he could bring Fred and Henrietta over to visit, so they won't think they've been forgotten." She grinned. "But when my four children are together, you mustn't let Nathaniel boss everyone around, Rebecca. He always tries to act like the man of the house when Bear is..."

Bobbi's face fell. She gave Jo a tight-lipped smile; the sparkle gone from her green eyes. "I started to say, whenever Bear is away from home. It's odd – he's been gone a while now, but sometimes I still forget."

Anna interrupted with a knock on Bobbi's door. The young man accompanying her reminded Lily of a young Superman, minus the costume – tall, with dark, unruly hair, blue eyes and a square jaw. But instead of a red cape, he wore a red cotton work shirt, brown wool pants with leather suspenders and heavy boots. His large, calloused hands looked permanently stained with black ash.

"Bobbi, I'd like to introduce you to Jack Stanley, the blacksmith I was telling you about," Anna said. Noticing Jo's puzzled expression, she added, "Jack is going to make a brace to support Bobbi's injured leg."

"Pleased to meet you all," Jack said.

Bobbi noticed he was having a hard time keeping his eyes off Rebecca. She gave her niece a sideways glance just in time to see her reward Jack's obvious interest with a shy smile.

"Aren't you rather young to be a blacksmith?" Jo asked.

"I'm eighteen," Jack replied. "My granddaddy opened one of the first blacksmith shops in these parts. My pop grew up working with him at the fire-pit and he raised me the same way." He puffed out his chest at Rebecca. "I've been smithing iron ever since I could lift a poker."

Rebecca dropped her gaze to the floor to hide her smile.

Bobbi was amused by the innocent flirtation, but she was anxious to discuss the brace. "Do you think you can make this?" She held out the diagram for his inspection.

Jack stepped forward and took the sketch. He studied it a moment and then nodded slowly, as if envisioning the project in his mind. "Iron would be too heavy, but if I used thin steel..." He pulled a pencil from behind his ear and made several additional marks on the sketch. "I can make this," he concluded. "And I'd enjoy the challenge. Business has been awfully slow, what with money being tight and motor cars starting to outnumber carriages. I think I could have it ready for fitting in a couple of days."

He glanced at Bobbi's leg; concealed beneath a blanket. "I'll need measurements," he said, producing a ball of thin twine and a pair of scissors from one of his pants pockets. He tied a single knot near the end of the twine and held it out to Anna and Jo. "I'll need your help, ladies."

"Tell us what you need," Anna said, reaching for the twine.

"See where I wrote down numbers on the sketch of her leg?" he asked, pointing to the number '1'. "Well, I need you to measure her leg right there by looping this string around her thigh. Cut the twine exactly where the end of the string meets the other side of the loop. Then put two knots in the twine and take the next measurement where I wrote the number '2', and so on. You understand?"

Anna nodded.

"Good. I'll wait outside. Let me know when you're finished." He flashed one more smile at Rebecca before stepping into the hall.

"I think the three of us can handle this," Bobbi said, giving Rebecca a wink. "Why don't you go keep Jack company?"

As the fog gathered to carry her away, Lily smiled, watching Rebecca skipping through the door. She floated in the clouds wondering, *"Could leg braces be the connection between Bobbi and me?"* she wondered. Her contemplation was broken by Bobbi's disembodied voice filtering through the thinning mist.

"I was finally allowed to go home – twelve months and three weeks after the accident. Alton and Anna drove me home and helped me settle in, while Rebecca scurried about, shooing the children outside."

When the mist cleared, Lily was back at the table in her hotel room, sitting with Bobbi and Margaret; her teacup in her hand as though she never left.

"Once I was comfortably situated in my bed, Alton told me he had an announcement to make. He and Anna were engaged to be married! Because I was the person who brought them together, Anna hoped I would stand up for them at their wedding." She smiled at Lily. "Standing up, by the way, was something I was able to do by the time I left the hospital, thanks to the brace Jack Stanley made for me. It was terribly heavy and awkward, and it rubbed sores on my thigh if I wore it too long, but it was wonderful to stand upright again."

"It's easy to take the freedom of movement for granted until it's taken from us." Margaret agreed. "You must have been grateful to have at least a portion of that gift returned to you. After all, what purpose is served by suffering more than one must?" She refilled Lily's cup with steaming tea.

Lily squirmed under Margaret's intense gaze, certain her comment wasn't aimed exclusively at Bobbi. She was relieved to see the gathering mist and closed her eyes as her hotel room disappeared from view.

Chapter Fifty

An instant later, Lily heard the clippity-clop sound of approaching horses. Her eyes blinked open to find herself standing on the porch of Bobbi's house. An old, horse-drawn buckboard wagon was pulling into the yard, with Jo on the front seat and Nathaniel at the reins.

Seated in her wheeled chair, Bobbi waved as Jo crossed the sandy yard and climbed the three wooden steps to the porch. She plopped into a straight-backed wicker chair next to Bobbi just as Rebecca came out of the house with two glasses of cool, sweet tea.

"Hello, Mama," Rebecca said. She set the glasses down on a wobbly wooden table between the two ladies. "I can't get over how pretty you look these days."

"Thank you, dear," Jo said, reflexively touching the left side of her face with her open palm.

The pleasantries ended when a loud squeal, followed by a crash, sent Rebecca racing back into the house to resolve the latest child-related catastrophe.

"I'll bet you're glad I'm taking my brood home today," Jo said, glancing after Rebecca. Realizing she was still touching her cheek, she pulled her hand away and studied her fingers. "You know, I find myself quite confused these days. I always believed what Papa said about God wanting him to mark me, to save me from becoming a seductress in my youth, like you. And when you had that awful accident, I thought God was punishing you for your sins."

Bobbi stared into her glass, uncertain what to say.

"But if that were true," Jo continued, "then why did God allow your face and mine to be healed? And why wasn't Lou punished for being so ungrateful when my husband took her in after our parents died or when she ran off the way she did? And why in the world would He allow poor Lucian, who never wavered from the church, to be struck down so miserably?" She sighed and shook her head. "It makes no sense." She knitted her eyebrows together. "Perhaps, God is testing Lucian's faith, like Job in the Bible."

Bobbi cleared her throat, trying to formulate a response.

"I think God finally decided to give Papa a taste of his own medicine."

Lily, Jo and Bobbi swiveled their heads in unison. Rebecca stood in the open doorway, her arms folded tightly across her chest, defiant.

"How dare you speak that way about your father!" Jo sputtered.

Rebecca pressed her lips together. She trembled, but stood her ground.

Bobbi, her eyes wide, interceded. "Come over here, Rebecca."

Rebecca hung her head to avoid her mother's incredulous stare and moved close to Bobbi, her arms still squeezed tight against her ribs.

"Rebecca, what makes you think God is punishing your father?" Bobbi asked in a gentle voice.

To Jo and Bobbi's astonishment, Rebecca crumpled to her knees, laid her head in Bobbi's lap and began to sob. Bobbi stroked her hair until she calmed down.

"Please tell us what's troubling you, Rebecca," Bobbi urged.

Rebecca sat on the porch floor in front of Bobbi, crossed her legs, and smoothed her long skirt until she caught her breath. Finally she lifted her chin. "It's true," she mumbled, still avoiding her mother's eyes. "Papa is an evil sinner."

Bobbi raised her eyebrows. "What makes you think that?"

"Uncle Bear came to see Papa right before he died," Rebecca said. "They didn't know I was hanging bedding on the clothesline next to the porch and could hear them talking. Uncle Bear told

Papa that bootlegging was getting too dangerous and he wanted to quit. He begged Papa for a job at the store. He promised he'd do the work of two men, but Papa refused. He said that if Uncle Bear stopped supplying him with good Canadian rye, he would see to it that he got arrested for bootlegging."

"Liar!" Jo jumped to her feet. She raised her hand to slap Rebecca, but Bobbi caught her wrist.

"Sit down, Jo. She's telling the truth." Bobbi said. "Bear told me about it. I didn't say anything because I didn't want to upset you."

She released Jo's wrist and the stunned woman sank back into her chair. Bobbi turned her attention back to Rebecca, gently wiping her tear-stained cheeks. "Your father was tempted by alcohol, but that doesn't make him a bad man, Rebecca. Remember, the Bible says that Jesus himself drank wine."

"Maybe so, but Jesus didn't beat his family every time he drank wine," Rebecca sneered. "And Jesus wasn't a fornicator, either."

Lily's jaw dropped as she watched Bobbi and Jo exchange shocked looks. Jo opened her mouth to speak but was at a loss for words.

Bobbi kept her voice low. "Rebecca, do you know what that word means?"

Rebecca nodded. "It's when a man puts a baby into a woman who isn't his lawful wife." She swallowed hard, her voice cracking. "Like Papa did to Aunt Lou."

"No!" cried Jo. "That's not true! He would never..." She cringed against the back of her chair, her hands pressed together against her nose and lips, as if in prayer. She glared at Rebecca.

"I'm sorry, Mama," Rebecca whimpered. "Papa made us swear we wouldn't tell, but you should know the truth. Do you remember when I complained that I was getting too big to sleep in the same bed with Sarah and Mary? Aunt Lou suggested I could share her bed, but Papa told me to stay put and quit my grumbling."

The color drained from Jo's face, suggesting to Lily that she remembered the discussion.

"Well, that night, after Mary accidentally pushed me out of our bed again, I decided to sneak into Aunt Lou's bed, even though I knew I shouldn't." Rebecca gulped as a tear trickled down her cheek. "When I opened the door to her room, I saw Papa squirming around on top of Aunt Lou." She rubbed her eyes, as if trying to erase the image of that awful sight. "Papa cursed and told me to come in and shut the door. He pulled down his nightshirt and sat on the edge of Aunt Lou's bed. He said he prayed about it and God granted him permission to take two wives like Jacob in the Bible, but it had to be a secret because if you found out, you might question God's decision and send him away, even if that meant all of us children would starve to death."

Rebecca cast her eyes down, unable to endure the looks of horror on the women's faces. "Papa said if I kept his secret, I could sleep with Aunt Lou except for whenever he wanted to be with her. Aunt Lou started crying and he smacked her – really hard – right across her face. He told her to keep her mouth shut or he would tell the pastor how she seduced him like one of Satan's whores." Rebecca dragged her sleeve across her wet face. "I'm sorry, Mama. I truly didn't understand what was happening until Aunt Lou..." Her voice broke off in hiccupping sobs.

Bobbi bent forward and patted Rebecca's back until she calmed down. Then she lifted her niece's chin and looked into her swollen eyes.

"You need to tell us all of it, Rebecca," Bobbi said. "What else happened to Lou?"

Rebecca snuffled and her lower lip trembled.

"Take a deep breath and blow it out slowly," Bobbi continued, stroking the girl's cheek. "Then finish it."

Rebecca took a deep breath and reached for the drink Bobbi offered. Finally, she began. "Mama, do you remember when we were supposed to go to that revival in Saint Petersburg last year?"

Jo didn't answer. She just stared at her lap, wringing her hands.

"Come on, Jo, let's peel all the layers off this festering boil right now," Bobbi said.

Jo nodded without lifting her eyes. "I remember," she whispered.

"Papa got sick at the last minute and decided that you and the little ones should stay home to take care of him, but that Aunt Lou and I should still go."

Ashen faced, Jo nodded again.

"Well, we took the train to Saint Petersburg, but we didn't go to the revival. Instead, we walked to an old house near the station. Aunt Lou told me I needed to help her be brave and then she knocked on the door three times. Before I could ask her why, a horrible man opened the door. He was skinny and filthy with a pockmarked face, and he smelled like whisky and cigars. He held out his hand and Aunt Lou gave him a small purse, filled with money. He counted it and then shoved the whole purse into his pocket. He told us to follow him into the kitchen." Rebecca closed her eyes. "It smelled like a butcher shop. He told Aunt Lou to take her clothes off and climb onto the table. Then he handed me a blood-stained sheet and told me to cover her with it and call-out when she ready."

Rebecca took another shuddering breath. "When Aunt Lou was lying naked under the sheet, the man came back. He offered her some whisky. When she told him drinking alcohol was a sin, he laughed like she was joking. He tied her legs and arms to four steel rings that were nailed to the corners of the table. After that, he put a wooden clothespin in her mouth and told her to bite down, keep her eyes fixed on the light hanging over the table, and hold still. Then he started poking between her legs with a long metal hook. I could tell he was hurting her really bad. She was crying and trying not to scream. I yelled at him to stop, but he told me to shut up and hold her hand until he was finished. It hurt her so bad that Aunt Lou fainted, but he kept going until she started bleeding."

Rebecca bit her lip.

"Then what happened," Bobbi asked.

"He said the baby was gone," she whispered. "And he said Aunt Lou was the last patient at this stop on his circuit. He untied her hands and feet and pried the four metal rings off the table. He put them into a doctor's bag, along with that awful hook. He told me to make Aunt Lou drink some water when she woke up and to be gone before morning. Then he just left us there." Rebecca gulped. "When we came home the next day, Aunt Lou said she felt sick and went straight to bed. She cried and cried, but at least Papa stayed away from her after that."

Jo slapped her hand over her mouth and bolted down the porch steps. She barely made it to the side of the house before she threw-up. Lily's heart broke for her. Although the circumstances were entirely different, Lily knew how it felt to have a spouse betray her trust.

Rebecca's voice drew her back to the scene. "I prayed Papa would die and be sent to hell for what he did to Aunt Lou, but God decided to just make him sick instead," she mumbled. "I know Mama's angry with me for not helping take care of Papa, but every time I see him in Aunt Lou's bed, I wish he was dead." She stared at the porch floor. "Aunt Bobbi, you must tell Mama you need my help to care for you and your children. If she makes me go home, I'm afraid I'll put a pillow over his face and send him to hell myself."

Just as Bobbi nodded her assent, the mist dropped over Lily, engulfing her. She closed her eyes and fell willingly into the void, grateful to leave this memory behind.

Chapter Fifty One

Lily woke in the hospital. The machine that automatically adjusted Grams' mattress was purring, doing its thing. The sun had set while she napped, and now the only light in the room other than the monitors, came through the open door.

She stretched and glanced at her leg brace, still thinking about Bobbi. *"I bet if bone transplants were available back in Bobbi's day, she would have agreed to the surgery in a heartbeat. Maybe she's trying to teach me to take advantage of new medical procedures like she did."* Lily sighed. *"It would be wonderful to walk without a brace and crutch again."*

The moment the thought crossed her mind, a wave of guilt washed over her, as if even considering surgery dishonored Dylan's memory. She struggled to her feet, limped to her grandmother's bedside and turned on the lamp. The old woman's breathing was growing raspier each day. Lily knew it wouldn't be much longer before she would be gone. She reached out and ran her hand over Grams' silky grey hair and across her hollow cheek. Then she stretched her body over the bed's side-rail and kissed her goodnight, hoping it wouldn't be the last time.

Just outside the door, Lily thought she heard someone softly calling her name. She glanced back, but there was no sound except for Grams' bed. She started down the corridor to the elevator, her metal crutch making a clicking sound with every step.

"Lily!"

This time, Lily was certain she heard her name. She turned and saw Mary Justus waving at her. She no longer thought of Mary as a heartless body snatcher, but still felt apprehensive watching her approach. She wanted Mary to prove that she was right – that Dylan wasn't brain dead at the scene of the accident, but then again, what good would it do? He was dead now and nothing was going to change that.

Lily waited for Mary to catch-up.

"I'm so glad you're still here," Mary said. "I have information for you."

"Information?" Lily was confused. "About Dylan – so soon?"

Mary nodded. "Why don't we go to the waiting room and talk?"

Lily glanced down the hall in the direction of the surgical waiting room – where just that morning she had watched two other parents come to grips with loss of their child. She didn't want to go back there. "I don't understand," she hedged. "I thought you said it would take a few days."

"I thought it would, but the hospital where you were treated stores their records digitally, so I just emailed the release form to them and they e-mailed Dylan's file back to me."

Lily nodded, her mouth suddenly dry.

"Why don't we go down the hall where we can talk privately?" Mary suggested for the second time.

"Not in there." Lily waved a hand in the direction of the waiting room.

Mary's brown eyes widened with comprehension. "I'm sorry – you're right. Let's go someplace else." She glanced at her watch. "Listen, it's almost 8:00. Have you had dinner yet?"

Lily's stomach rumbled in response. She put her hand over her midsection and forced a weak smile. "No, but apparently my stomach wants me to."

Mary smiled. "There's a restaurant one block over, called O'Keefe's. It's pretty noisy inside, but outside, there's a quiet café section where we can get a bite to eat and talk."

"I don't have a car."

"No problem; I'll drive," Mary said. "I'll go get my car and pick you up at the front door."

Lily hesitated. "I don't know..."

"Don't worry, they have great food." Mary said, already heading for the stairs. "I drive a silver Honda," she called over her shoulder.

The outdoor café turned out to be a pet-friendly patio and smoking lounge, located just outside the front door of the Irish pub. An eight-foot high, wrought-iron fence surrounded the area, separating it from the parking lot. Several planters were stationed just outside the fence, doing their best to disguise the fact that cars were parked only a few feet away from the outer row of tables. At the far end of the patio, a bulldog sat drooling at the feet of a middle-aged couple. He scrutinized each forkful of food as it moved from his masters' plates to their mouths, as if willing some of it to fall his way. A few tables over, a luckier Yorkie sat in a young blonde's lap, sharing her hamburger. Another table was occupied by two old men who were drinking beer and concentrating on a game of dominos.

The relaxed ambiance appealed to Lily.

Their waitress, a young, short-haired brunette, wearing a bright green tee-shirt with the O'Keefe's logo and tight blue jeans, delivered their two-for-one drinks and took their dinner orders – shepherd's pie for Lily, and fish tacos with sweet potato fries for Mary.

Lily watched the waitress walk back to the restaurant's entrance, envious of the youthful bounce in her stride. She picked up her merlot and shifted her gaze to Mary, studying her over the top of her glass.

Mary cleared her throat. "I want to tell you about something that happened to me several years ago, okay?"

Lily nodded, her curiosity aroused.

Mary took a swig of Killians from a frosted mug. "I started my medical career in trauma nursing, so I've seen my share of patients who arrived at the hospital too late, or too injured, to save. I was accustomed to the blood, the frantic attempts to play God, the anguished cries of loved ones when we failed... If you don't develop a thick skin in trauma nursing, well – you don't make it very long."

It was hard for Lily to imagine Mary Justus wearing scrubs in an emergency room, but she sat quietly, listening – just as she did while watching the spirits' memories.

"One night, there was a gang fight and some of the wounded boys were rushed to our trauma center. Unfortunately, my team was so busy working to save one of the boys, we didn't notice the fight wasn't over. One of the gang members burst through the door of the trauma center, his gun blasting."

Mary focused on the table, as if watching the scene play-out on its surface. "He took out our security guard first, and grabbed his gun. Then he started shooting every patient that wasn't a member of his own gang. When he appeared at the door to our trauma room, I saw him first – at least, I saw his guns first. Instinct kicked in and I threw myself across our patient. He was so young and defenseless – I wanted to protect him. I don't know what made me think a crazed gang-banger wouldn't shoot me, but I was wrong."

Mary took a long swig of beer and then set the almost empty glass near the edge of the table. "The rest of my story is going to sound truly bizarre, but I swear it's the truth, Lily."

Lily nodded, her lips pressed together.

Mary returned her nod. "I swear to God, I floated right out of my body and watched everything as if it were happening in slow motion. I felt no pain; no fear – I don't even think I was all that curious about what was happening to me. I watched as the police stormed in and overpowered the shooter. Then I watched my colleagues – my friends – roll me onto a gurney, strip my clothing and begin the standard trauma work-up for gunshot injuries. Just a few minutes before, I had been a part of that team – helping them perform the same procedures on the boy who was now lying dead on the gurney next to mine. I watched as the team assessed my wounds and rushed me to surgery while trying to stabilize my body. Three times, I watched my heart stop beating and my friends jolt my body back to life."

Lily gasped, momentarily breaking Mary's concentration. Her lips curved up slightly. "Don't look so worried. Obviously, the third time was a charm because I'm still here." She gave Lily a wink.

"While I was floating above the operating table, I remember being impressed that no one on my team took a break, even after everything they'd just been through. They just wouldn't stop trying to save my life. Then suddenly, I was standing right beside a surgical nurse named Kelly, who was – and still is – one of my best friends. Somehow I knew she could see me. I told her she was a dear friend and I thanked her for trying so hard to save me." Mary smiled and shook her head. "Kelly's face turned chalk-white and she dropped a pan of blood-soaked sponges right on the floor."

Mary wrapped her fingers through the handle of her two-for-one, second mug of beer, but she didn't pick it up. "The next thing I remember is waking up in the hospital three days later – in a *lot* of pain. They told me I had been shot twice and that I no longer possessed a spleen." Mary studied Lily for a moment. "Lily, I wanted to tell you what happened to me for two reasons. First of all, Kelly actually did see me standing next to her that day. At first, she tried to convince herself she only imagined it, but when I told her exactly what I had said and that I saw her drop the pan of sponges... well – we both knew it really happened. My soul separated from my body for a while and for some reason, she could still see me."

Mary took a sip of beer. "The second thing I want you to know is that I wasn't worried about what was happening to my body. It didn't hurt and I wasn't sad that it was so damaged. It felt perfectly normal to leave my body behind."

Lily considered telling Mary about the spirits at the Belleview Biltmore, but just then, the server arrived with their food.

"Sorry it took so long," the waitress chirped, serving Mary's fish tacos and fries. "We're getting slammed inside, so it's all-hands-on-deck." She turned and set Lily's shepherd's pie on the table. "Don't touch the plate – it's hot," she warned.

"Thanks." Peering at the steam pouring from the dish, Lily thought the obvious warning might qualify as an entry for Seth's book.

"Can I bring you ladies anything else?"

"I'd like a glass of water," Mary said.

"Sure. No problem," the waitress said, already turning away from their table.

"Now, getting back to my story," Mary said between bites of sweet potato fries, "I was cleared to return to work two months after I got shot, but I discovered I no longer possessed the tough-as-nails attitude you have to have in trauma nursing. As a matter of fact, every time I caught movement out of the corner of my eye, I jumped, and I suffered serious flashbacks whenever a patient was admitted with a gunshot wound."

"I can understand that," Lily said. "I still can't drive a car."

Mary nodded. She swallowed a bite of fish taco before continuing. "My co-workers tried to be supportive, but I was miserable. Then, a few months later, I was sitting by myself in the cafeteria, seriously considering requesting a transfer to dermatology, when I overheard a conversation between two women at the next table."

Recognizing the potential irony, Mary glanced around to make sure no one was eavesdropping. None of the other patio customers seemed to be paying any attention to them. Satisfied, she continued. "As I listened, I realized the husband of the younger woman had been in a nasty, bicycle verses truck accident and the older woman was talking to her about organ donation. I could tell she was having a hard time letting her husband go."

Lily shifted uncomfortably, wary of the direction Mary's story was taking.

"Suddenly, I realized I possessed a unique perspective that might comfort the poor woman. I walked over, introduced myself and told her about my encounter with death. I explained what it was like for my soul to float away from my body, and told her that if her husband had a similar experience when he died, then he didn't care about his body and it would be a shame if his organs were wasted."

Lily gasped. "But you lived! Maybe if the doctors had tried harder to save that woman's husband, he might have lived, too!"

Mary shook her head. "No, Lily – it doesn't work that way. Doctors try as hard as they can to save the lives of every single patient, but some people die, despite their most heroic efforts. Often, life support equipment is left on until it can be determined whether or not the individual is a registered OD – organ donor – or to see if the family would be willing to consent to organ donation, but that's not life... that's just machines keeping organs viable until they can be harvested. The person's soul is already gone. I'm certain of that."

Mary finished her fries, watching Lily and waiting for her to respond, but Lily just stared at her plate, poking at the shepherd's pie with her fork.

"Anyway," Mary continued, "the next day I put in for a transfer to the OD unit at the trauma center, and I've been working there ever since."

"Sad work," Lily mumbled.

"Yeah, but it also continually renews my faith in mankind. I mean, time and again, I see grief-stricken people find the strength to reach beyond their own pain to save the lives of strangers – it's inspiring."

Lily nodded without looking up.

Mary took a deep breath. "Lily, do you think it's possible that you talked with Dylan after the accident, the same way I talked to Kelly? You know, maybe his soul called to you – waking you up and giving you the strength to get the both of you out of that car?"

"I think it's possible that Dylan left his body for a few minutes right after the accident and then returned to it, just like you did," Lily admitted.

"But what if he was injured so badly that his spirit wasn't able to return to his body?"

Lily took a bite of food, filling her mouth as an excuse not to answer. After a moment, she shook her head in defiance.

"I reviewed Dylan's chart this afternoon, Lily," Mary continued in a low voice. "He suffered a severe skull fracture."

Tears filled Lily's eyes. "That doesn't prove anything. My skull was fractured, too. I recovered."

Mary wiped her mouth and pushed her plate aside. She reached across the table and took one of Lily's hands in her own. "I'm so sorry, Lily, but his head injury was much worse than yours. By the time the paramedics got to the scene, he was non-responsive and his pupils were fixed and dilated."

Lily dabbed her eyes with her napkin. "He was conscious after the accident. I'm sure of it. He talked to me."

"I'm afraid not, Lily." Mary shook her head. "He was gone."

Unbidden, the nagging question that always lurked in Lily's memories of the accident, resurfaced. *"If he was conscious, then why didn't Dylan try to get out of the car on his own?"* She had never been able to answer that question.

"Are you okay?" Mary asked.

"It's not fair," Lily whispered through clenched teeth.

Mary cleared her throat. "When I got shot, the bullets passed through my body and continued straight into the heart of the boy I was trying to protect, ending his young life. Death can be incredibly unfair and there's nothing we can do to change that."

When the waitress returned with two glasses of water, Mary released Bobbi's hand.

"Sorry it took so long, but..."

"It's okay – I know you're busy," Mary said.

"Thanks for understanding. Need anything else?" the waitress asked.

Mary shook her head and watched the girl veer toward another table. Then she turned back to Lily. "The point I was trying to make is that Dylan probably experienced some of the same things I did when I almost died."

"Like what?" Lily asked.

"Well, the moment I left my body, the pain was gone. I wasn't angry with myself for taking such an awful risk. I wasn't worried about whether or not I would live. I wasn't jealous of all the people who escaped getting shot. I wasn't even curious if I would survive or not – or what would come next, if I died. I simply existed outside of my body and that seemed perfectly normal. The empty shell lying on the table didn't matter to me any more than the hair that falls to the floor when I get a haircut. My only concerns were for the people I cared about – at first because they were in danger, and then because they were so scared and worried about saving me."

"So you think Dylan's spirit woke me up because he was worried about me?"

"I think that's exactly what happened, Lily. He was trying to save your life." Mary paused for a drink of water. "Over the last several years, I've talked to a lot of people who claim to have had out-of-body experiences when they were close to death. In every instance, the person reported being perfectly calm about leaving their body. The only concerns people reported had to do with leaving people behind – especially when their lives were in danger."

Lily pushed her half-finished meal aside and leaned forward. "Yes, but Mary – all of the people you talked to lived. You don't know what happens to those who actually die. You don't know how Dylan felt when he finally realized he was losing his life before he ever really got a chance to live it." Her voice hardened. "And most of all, you don't know whether or not he would have survived, if his doctors had cared about him the way your doctor-friends cared about you – if they would have tried harder to save him, instead of giving up."

"If I had suffered a blunt force trauma as severe as the one Dylan did, my friends couldn't have saved me, no matter how much they wanted to," Mary shot back. "Catastrophic damage of that magnitude is irreversible and once his brain was dead..."

Lily's shocked expression jolted Mary into an awkward silence.

"I'm so sorry. I didn't mean to..." Mary took another sip of water. "Listen, Lily – I don't pretend to have all the answers, but please believe this – Dylan's pain ceased the moment his soul left his body – and your decision to donate his organs allowed several other people's bodies to continue functioning. You saved their lives."

Lily's head was spinning. "It wasn't my decision and... I don't want to talk about this anymore." She raised her hand to catch the waitresses' attention and signaled for the check.

Chapter Fifty Two

The ride back to the Belleview Biltmore had been a quiet one, with Mary honoring Lily's request for time to think. They parted awkwardly at the hotel's entrance and then Lily hobbled through the massive lobby without pausing, barely noticing the happy guests clustered in small groups throughout the space. Once inside her suite, she hobbled to the nightstand and turned on the Tiffany-style lamp, but its warm glow didn't alter her dark mood. She shrugged on an old nightshirt and then limped to the bathroom.

She knew Mary was right. Dylan died in the accident. A part of her had known it all along. She had been adamant about him being alive at the scene because she didn't want to face the cold, hard truth. She pointed her toothbrush at her foamy-mouthed reflection in the gilt-framed, oval mirror, hanging above the porcelain sink. "It's all your fault," she hissed. "All of it. Not the paramedics. Not the doctors. Not Scott. You. You were driving the car that killed Dylan. Then you drove Scott away and now you've managed to destroy whatever chance you had with Seth. You ruin everything."

Suddenly, Lily felt a chill on the back of her neck. She spun around, instinctively preparing to defend herself from an intruder, but no one was there. She rinsed her mouth and turned out the bathroom light, still trying to shake the eerie feeling. In the first milliseconds of darkness, she heard a whisper in her ear.

"Good can sprout even from horrific events."

Lily flipped the light back on, but again, saw nothing. Shaken and covered with goosebumps, she pretended a calm she didn't feel and shut the light back off. "What's that supposed to mean?" She waited in silence for a full minute. "Besides, I thought ghosts – I mean spirits – could only talk to me while I'm sleeping," she mumbled.

After still more silence, she gave up, took off her leg brace and hopped to the side of the bed, feeling more alone than ever before.

When she reached over to turn off the bedside lamp, her cell phone caught her eye. She turned it on to call Scott.

"What could I possibly say," she mused, "Gee, Scott, I'm really sorry for all those times I insinuated it was your fault our son is dead. Turns out I was wrong. My bad." She stared at the phone. "It's way too late to apologize. Scott is finally moving on and after everything I've put him through, I *will not* mess up his chance for happiness with someone new. Besides, he would never answer his phone at time of night."

Lily had always loved the way Scott turned his phone off at 7:00 pm., insisting that evenings were for family and nothing at work was so important that it couldn't keep till morning. Giving into an impulse, she pressed his speed-dial number, closed her eyes and listened. "Hi there, you've reached the voice mail of Scott Thorne..."

"I am so, so sorry, Scott – for everything," she whispered, as his recorded voice requested that she leave her name, number and a brief message. She ended the call before the message beep, turned her phone back off, and reached for the lamp switch.

Lily hid her face in the comforter, tormented with guilt. Then she remembered what Mary said about Dylan's organs saving numerous lives. *"If Scott hadn't donated Dylan's organs, would his death have been any less painful? Did Dylan's spirit care what happened to his discarded body? Would he have been willing to give his eyes to someone like Seth?"* She contemplated these questions and more, until at last, sleep overtook her and the chilly mist carried her into the spirit realm.

Lily focused on the last memory Bobbi shared with her, grateful for the distraction. Rebecca had revealed that her father, Lucian, sexually abused her Aunt Lou and when she became pregnant, forced her to get an abortion.

When the fog dissipated, Bobbi was sitting at her kitchen table in her wheeled chair, cutting string beans. Across the small room, her sister stood with her hands on her hips, fussing at a coffee pot.

"Be patient, Jo – it just started perking a moment ago," Bobbi said. "Besides, you haven't answered my question. How are you coping with Lucian?"

Jo continued to stare at the uncooperative coffee pot. "I'm doing my best to care for him, even though I can barely stand to look at him. The pastor visits often, going on and on about how 'God tests the faith of good Christian men.' I have to bite my tongue to keep from telling him about Lucian's sins."

"Maybe you should tell him. Perhaps if he knew, he could help Lucian seek God's forgiveness."

"Lucian doesn't deserve God's forgiveness. Besides, old Pastor Phillips reasons like Father used to when it comes to women. He's more likely to blame Lou for being a temptress and seducing Lucian in a moment of weakness, than he is to lay the blame on one of his most generous parishioners." Jo sighed. "I can't allow Lou to suffer further humiliation and injustice at the hands of such wretched men."

"But don't you want him to pay for the evil things he's done?"

"I want to take him someplace dark and miserable, and leave him there to die alone – but I can't harm the father of my children. Besides, as long as I'm caring for Lucian, the manager at his bank agreed to release a small weekly allowance from his passbook savings account to purchase groceries and pay for necessities – as long as I provide him with a detailed accounting of how each dollar is spent, that is."

Jo rubbed her eyes and then re-crossed her arms. "I'll continue to care for Lucian as long as doing so means my children are fed, but I don't know what will happen if the money runs out or if he dies before Paul comes of age to take over the store."

"Perhaps..."

Without warning, the scene before Lily vanished and she fell backward, tumbling into the thick fog. Her heart was racing as she struggled to regain her equilibrium and sort out the voices coming from just beyond the mist.

"Is it really necessary for her to know all of this?"

Lily recognized Clay's irritated voice.

"Perhaps not all – but certainly some of it," Margaret replied.

"Then let me show her. Bobbi doesn't know the whole story anyway."

"I know most of it," Bobbi challenged.

"That's enough, you two," Margaret snapped, sounding like a frustrated babysitter at nap time. "Clay – get on with it. But try to remember – if this is going to work, she needs to understand everything."

Before Lily could form her confused thoughts into questions, she felt the dreamy sensation of falling in slow motion. When the mist cleared, she was standing with Clay and Nathaniel in a field of short grass, her head spinning. She took a deep breath and was surprised by the pungent smell of horses, mixed with the unmistakable odor of sea muck at low tide. She turned and saw the Belleview Biltmore looming in the distance and surmised they were visiting the hotel's stable on the bluff, overlooking the Intracoastal Waterway.

Clay was watching six-year-old Belle, seated in a child-sized pony cart, try to coax the pony to stop eating grass. "Pleeaasssee, pony!" she begged. "Let's go!" She wore a white lingerie lace dress, with a wide pink ribbon tied around the waist. A matching ribbon and bow valiantly attempted to hold her thick blonde, ringlet curls out of her face.

Clay chuckled at her efforts, but didn't step forward to intervene with the pony. Instead, he spoke to her brother. "You need to slow down Nate, my boy. Be like that pony. Enjoy what the world has to offer right at your feet. Don't be in a hurry to get all grown up. It's going to happen soon enough."

The pony gave Belle a sideways glance and pulled the cart a few steps, but stopped again as soon as he reached some longer grass.

"But I'm the man of the house," Nathaniel countered. "It's just not right for you to help out as much as you do while I do nothing at all."

"Going to school isn't nothing. Proper schooling will help you get a job that pays good wages so you can take care of your Mama and the other kids."

Clay glanced at the boy. He looked a lot like the picture of Bear he had seen in the wedding photograph that Bobbi kept on the fireplace mantle – tall for his age, broad shoulders, sandy-blond, wavy hair and hazel eyes. But Clay was certain Nate's impatience and determination didn't come from his father – those traits were all Bobbi.

"I've got plenty of time after school and on weekends," Nathaniel continued. "And Mr. Muldoon said he could use a boy with sharp eyes and ears."

"Frankie shouldn't have said anything without first talking to Bobbi... I mean, to your mother." Clay puckered his lips as if to whistle, and blew out a long, noisy breath. "You know she blames the booze business for your daddy's death. She'd worry herself sick, and she'd blame me if anything happened to you."

"Then let me do something else. I'm almost fifteen – almost a man." Nathaniel kicked at the dirt in exasperation.

Clay licked his lips and pinched his dark, thin moustache between his thumb and forefinger, thinking. "I'll tell you what. I'll have some logs delivered to your place and you can get some practice chopping them into firewood for your Mama's stove. Do you know how to handle an axe?"

"I can teach myself."

Clay snickered. "That's the attitude that earned a lot of men the nickname *Lefty*. I'll have the logs delivered and then show you how to wield an axe. Once you get the hang of it, I'll get Frankie to hire you to help chop wood for the hotel fireplaces – but only if you keep doing real good with your schooling. Do we have a deal?"

"Deal." Nathaniel smiled. He held his hand out and Clay shook it, pleased with the boy's firm grip.

"Pleeaassseeeee, pony!" Belle wailed from several yards away, interrupting their conversation. "Move your flea-bitten ass!"

Clay's mouth dropped open. He stared at the angelic child, hoping he had misheard her. Then he shifted his attention to glare down at Nathaniel.

Nathaniel shrugged. "I can't help it if she repeats everything she hears."

Chapter Fifty Three

Lily smiled as the fog engulfed her, but then her thoughts began to darken. *"What if another common denominator between me and Bobbi is the fact that we both lost young sons?"* Thankfully, before she could dwell on this possibility, the fog parted again.

Bobbi and Clay sipped iced tea in a rocking chairs on the hotel's veranda, while Nathaniel and Belle played on the lawn, using a pair of sticks to toss a thin wooden hoop back and forth. Bobbi's wheeled chair was parked at the bottom of the stairs. Since everyone was dressed in the same clothing as before, Lily deduced this was the same afternoon as the earlier memory.

"It's not that I'm ungrateful, Clay," Bobbi said. "And Lord knows I don't have the money to care for them. It's just that Max and Ed bring Fred and Henrietta over less often these days and I miss them." Her voice caught. "I'm afraid they'll forget who their real mother is."

"I can't say I'm all that surprised they're keeping close to home. Ed Winfield is hoping to run for Mayor of St. Petersburg, and I think it helps his image to be seen out and about with his wife and a couple of tykes. People are less likely to examine a fella's personal affairs when he appears to be an honest, hard-working family man."

"Are you implying he's not?"

"Well, let's just say that for an abolitionist, he sure buys a lot of hooch. I know most politicians think it's fine to support Prohibition while drinking ten times more than most regular folks, but I don't cotton to the brand of honesty that makes different rules for men, depending on the size of their wallet."

Bobbi nodded in agreement. "Speaking of money, Nathaniel tells me you're going to help him get work chopping wood for the hotel."

"Did he bother to tell you that I went out of my way to get him work that didn't involve using him as Frankie's lookout?"

"He did, actually." Bobbi smiled. "To thank you, I'd like to invite you over for dinner this Sunday. I'm making a big pot of chicken and dumplings, buttered cornbread, and an apple pie."

Clay twirled his black Fedora on his upturned forefinger and smiled. "Yes, ma'am, I'd like that. I'd like that very much."

As soon as the fog rolled in, Clay's voice said, "This day right here – this is when it started – her treating me like family and me thinking maybe that's what I wanted."

Snippets of memories began appearing at the edges of the mist, like video clips. Some featured Clay performing chores around Bobbi's house, while others showed him seated at the head of her dinner table – sometimes with Nathaniel, Belle and her, and sometimes with Bobbi and all four of her children.

"For a single fella," Clay continued, "I was becoming quite the family man. I took Belle to play at the Belleview Biltmore and I checked up on Nate." He chuckled at the memory snippet of Nathaniel returning soda bottles to collect the deposit money. "He didn't like me to give him money, so I took to dropping small change and empty pop bottles near where he chopped wood at the Belleview Biltmore."

"I'd drive to St. Petersburg to fetch Fred and Henrietta home for Sunday dinners and sometimes I took Bobbi and her whole family to the picture show. I got to where I ate more meals at her kitchen table than anywhere else. I was real comfortable." He paused. "But my job took me away a lot. I'd head out on the road or ride the rails wherever Butch – that's the fella who took over for George Applegate – needed me to haul shipments. As soon as I breathed in the freedom of the road, I'd relax and start wanting the trip to last forever. I loved both lives and hated the thought of giving either one of them up."

Lily floated in silence for a while before the fog finally parted. The overcast, winter night sky hid the stars and the moon, so the only light came from the glow of a few gas lamps along a walkway. It took her a moment to get her bearings and realize she was in a crushed-shell parking lot, just outside of the Belleview Biltmore. She couldn't put her finger on it, but something felt different about this memory.

She watched Clay lift Bobbi out of his car and into her wheeled chair, while shaking off the dizziness that frequently accompanied moving from one memory to another. Suddenly, she realized that she wasn't seeing this memory from a single perspective. She knew what both Bobbi *and* Clay were thinking and feeling.

"I detest this chair," Bobbi complained. "But I can't bend my knee to sit with my brace on, and I don't think I could stand up all evening."

"You know, most folks wouldn't mind relaxing while someone else did all the work of moving them from one place to another," Clay teased.

The white shell walkway crunched under the wheels as Clay pushed Bobbi's chair toward the hotel. When they reached the base of the wide, wooden staircase, leading to the entrance, Clay lifted Bobbi from her chair and carefully climbed the steps with her cradled in his arms. It took Lily a moment to remember that the Lobby Bar used to be the actual hotel lobby, and this was the main entrance.

While they waited for the bellman to pull the wheeled chair up the steps, Clay moved to the giant plate glass window. They peeked inside and saw Alton Farthing smiling at Anna, who was all aglow.

"Wasn't Anna a beautiful bride?" Bobbi asked as Clay deposited her back into her chair.

"Anna's a fine looking woman, but I reckon I can't tell brides apart," he said. "She looks just like the picture of you on your wedding day."

Bobbi laughed. "Of course we looked similar – we wore the same dress. It was the wedding gown Alton's mother wore when she married old Doc Farthing. He gave it to me when I married Bear, and it seemed only right that I return it to Anna."

Clay frowned and shook his head. "Women make no sense. Most of the time they worry another woman might show up wearing a dress that looks like theirs – but when it comes to their wedding day, they're happiest when they're wearing an old hand-me-down."

Bobbi grinned. "I hadn't thought of it that way. Folklore says the echo of a bride's joy stays in her dress, enhancing the bliss of the bride who wears it next."

Sharing a moment of male solidarity, Clay and the bellman shook their heads at the crazy female notion, but they knew better than to voice their opinions. Instead, the bellman opened the door and Clay pushed Bobbi's wheeled chair over the threshold, just in time to join the wedding party as they strolled down the main corridor to the elegant Tiffany Ballroom.

Lily had eyed the ballroom from the Promenade Corridor several times during her stay at the Belleview Biltmore, but never went inside. Now, floating alongside Clay and Bobbi, the magnificent room took her breath away. Tall, square white pillars stood like soldiers down both sides of the long hall. The length of each pillar was trimmed with decorative molding and finished at the top with wide, carved cornices and additional molding. The twenty-foot high, arched ceiling was a work of art worthy of royalty. The entire length of the coffered ceiling alternated back and forth, between double rows of rectangular Tiffany glass panels that were backlighted to show off their rich green and gold designs, and solid white ceiling panels, from which fabulous gold and crystal chandeliers were suspended. Beyond the pillars, both sides of the room and the far end featured enormous arched windows, interspersed with glass doors that provided both a pleasant sea breeze and access to wide verandas, which served as smoking parlors. Square tables, outfitted with fine white linen covers, graced the front half of the huge room, and a stage for the orchestra and an ample dancefloor filled the back section of the expanse.

Time began moving as if in fast-forward, as well-wishers toasted the newlyweds with spiced ice tea and dined on standing rib roast with fresh orange glaze, whipped potatoes, green beans, fruit and an assortment of warm breads, fresh from the ovens in the hotel's basement. A pianist played throughout the meal and then a small, formal orchestra joined him on the stage.

Time slowed down to normal speed when Alton and Anna rose to dance the first waltz, much to the approval of their guests, who began rising in pairs to join them on the dancefloor. Lily saw Bobbi's eyes well with tears, and sensed her mixed emotions – happiness for her friends and bittersweet memories of dancing with Bear.

When Clay noticed Bobbi growing melancholy, he pulled a silver flask from the inside pocket of his jacket and wordlessly poured a shot of sipping whisky into her tea. She smiled at him and raised her glass; clinking it against his before taking a drink.

Soon afterward, young Dr. Whiting came to say hello. "Isn't it wonderful that they both found love a second time?" he asked, pointing to Alton and Anna on the dancefloor.

"Not both," Bobbi corrected. "Anna lost a husband, but this is Alton's first marriage."

"His first marriage, yes – but he was desperately in love as a youth, and he said if the young lady had returned his affection, he wouldn't have stayed at Yale. How different things might have turned out for all of us, had he settled for becoming a small-town doctor, eh?"

Lily heard Bobbi's astonished thoughts as clearly as if she were speaking out loud. *"The only young woman in Alton's life back then was me. I loved him as a brother and assumed he felt a similar affection for me, but..."*

Bobbi took a drink, recalling that Alton made his decision to accept a position at Yale the same day she announced she was marrying Bear. "I believe it's fortunate for all concerned that Alton pursued his medical calling and saved his heart for a woman who is worthy of his love – Anna."

Dr. Whiting nodded amiably, but then their conversation was interrupted by a solemn-faced hotel clerk.

"Doctor, I'm sorry to intrude, but there's an emergency at the hospital in Tampa. They asked me to inform Dr. Farthing that his special surgical skills are urgently needed to help an injured child, but I hate to interrupt his wedding celebration..."

"Please say nothing to Dr. Farthing," insisted Dr. Whiting. "I'm a capable reconstruction surgeon. I'll go in his place. Can you arrange for a driver?"

"I'll try, sir, but at this hour, it might be difficult."

Clay interrupted, "You can drive my Stutz Bearcat." He held out a starter key. "It's parked just outside."

"Thank you, Mr. Long." Dr. Whiting's boyish anticipation at the prospect of driving such a fine automobile showed in his a brilliant smile. He disappeared through the doorway amid promises to be careful and return as soon as possible.

Bobbi turned to Clay. "What if he doesn't return before the reception concludes? Who will see me home?"

"If he doesn't return, you can just stay here for the night. It's a hotel, you know," Clay teased.

Bobbi's eyes widened. "You can't mean..."

"Don't worry," Clay said. "I wasn't suggesting we sully your reputation. I'll buy you a room of your own for the night. I'll bunk with Butch's crew."

Before Lily could decide if Bobbi was disappointed or relieved about this, time sped up again. She watched the newlyweds make their exit and the crowd of well-wishers go their separate ways in fast-forward motion. When Bobbi and Clay were the only remaining guests, time slowed again.

"My flask is empty," Clay said. "But we could move to the speakeasy and have a drink with Frankie while we're waiting for the Doc to return."

"Another drink and I'll be zozzled," Bobbi confessed. "Besides, I can't stay awake much longer."

"All right then, I'll get you a room. I'm a man of his word and besides," Clay winked at her, "I know better than to cross a witch."

Clay wheeled Bobbi's chair to the tall, mahogany registration desk in the lobby and rang the silver service bell. The desk clerk hurried from a small room that housed the post office, telegraph and telephone switchboard.

"Many decades from now, there will be a pool table in that room," she mused. *"And they'll build a new entrance, so this won't be the lobby anymore."* She patted the surface of the desk, admiring its intricate design. *"But don't worry – you'll make a marvelous cocktail lounge."*

"Do you mind if I ask why you want that particular room?" the clerk asked, drawing Lily back to the conversation.

"I stayed in that room years ago," Bobbi replied, smiling up at him. "My, um – uncle brought me here to watch the bicycle races."

Clay frowned, certain that wasn't the whole story. It reminded him that, although he spent a good deal of time with this complicated woman, he knew damn little about her. He shrugged. "Okeydokey. If you'd rather have a room instead of a suite, I'm not complaining."

Clay paid for the room and signed the register book.

"I'm alone, so I'll need the services of a maid to help me get settled into bed and to help me get up in the morning," Bobbi added.

"I was just about to suggest that," Clay said with a smirk. He knew Bobbi was making sure the desk clerk knew they weren't sleeping together. He twirled his Fedora on his forefinger. "She'll be needing a dressing gown, too. And if Dr. Whiting telephones, please tell him not to rush. He can bring my Stutz back in the morning."

The desk clerk scurried away to fulfill their last minute requests, leaving Clay and Bobbi alone.

"It wouldn't bother me to know that you stayed in that room with your husband," Clay said, still curious.

"How gracious of you." Bobbi watched him to squirm uncomfortably until she saw the maid returning at the elbow of the desk clerk; a folded nightgown in her hands. "Bear and I met here, and we often danced here, but we never slept here."

She smiled at Clay's relieved expression, wondering what he would think if he knew the real reason she wanted that specific room.

Chapter Fifty Four

When they left the front desk, Clay peppered Bobbi with questions about her weekend at the Belleview Biltmore with her Uncle Emmitt, as though he was amazed to learn she was once a child.

"That's enough for tonight," she said when they arrived at her room. "I'm tired."

"Good night, Bobbi. Maybe one day you'll trust me with your secrets."

She smiled. "Good night, Clay."

The elderly black maid proved to be strong and efficient, despite her willowy physique. She opened the bed and fluffed the pillows in a less than a minute.

"Folks call me Millie," she said while helping Bobbi out of her dress and into the nightgown. She hung Bobbi's dress in the closet and draped her slip and stockings over a high-backed chair. Then she helped Bobbi to the toilet.

"You've had experience nursing people, haven't you, Millie," Bobbi observed.

"Yes, ma'am. When I was a youngin', I helped my mammy take care of ole' Miss Grayson, God rest her soul," Millie replied. "She fell on some ice back home and broke her hip. It didn't heal-up right, so she moved to Florida and brung Mama and me along." She smiled. "Course that was a mighty long time ago."

Millie helped Bobbi sit on the side of the bed and brought her a glass of water. "Are you ready to lie back now?"

"No, thanks. I want to sit-up for a while."

Millie shifted from one foot to the other, uncertain. "You want me to come back in a little bit?"

"That won't be necessary. If you prop a pillow against the headboard and swing my legs up onto the bed, I can scoot myself back, and when I'm ready to sleep, I can scoot forward." Bobbi smiled. "I'll be fine until morning, but can you come back at seven to help get me up again?"

Millie nodded and followed Bobbi's instructions. Next, she pushed the night table against the bed and placed a glass of water, the lamp and a Bible within Bobbi's reach. With a final glance around the room, Millie edged toward the door. "I'll lock your door and leave the key at the front desk, but I'll be back right at seven," she said.

"Thank you, Millie. You've been a great help. Goodnight."

Millie nodded and slipped out.

Bobbi listened as the key turned in the lock and then Millie's footsteps faded away. She sighed, glad to finally be alone. Most of her childhood memories were tainted by the acts of her tyrannical father, but not the long weekend she spent here, frolicking at the bicycle races with Uncle Emmitt and meeting the spirit of Margaret Plant.

"Margaret, my old friend, do you still haunt the halls of the Belleview?" She hoped Margaret would appear if she stayed in the same room, but the whisky she drank made it difficult to stay awake. Finally, she gave up, and with a nostalgic sigh, sank into the goose down pillow and fell asleep.

As soon as Bobbi dozed off, the room began to chill. She pulled the covers tight around her neck and a moment later, she and Lily floated through the fog together.

When the mist cleared, Margaret was seated at the table in Bobbi's hotel room, her steaming teapot at the ready. Lily quickly realized she was only a spectator this time, watching Bobbi's memory of her own visit with Margaret's spirit.

"Am I dreaming?" Bobbi asked.

"No, my friend. I'm here with you," Margaret replied. "Complex matters crowd your mind these days, so I had to wait until you were at rest to make myself known to you."

"Was I dreaming when you came to visit me at the hospital – just after my husband died?" Bobbi asked.

"No, I was with you in that dark hour as well," Margaret said. She poured a cup of tea for Bobbi. "When you were hovering between life and death, your spirit left your body for a short time and we shared the space that exists between our two worlds."

"Until you told me to leave – to wake up," Bobbi reminded her.

"Because your life wasn't over."

"The best part was over. I stayed alive only to honor Bear's last wish – to care for our children."

"Hogwash," Margaret retorted. She picked up a silver spoon and stirred her tea with fervor. Then she rested the small spoon on the back edge of her rosebud-trimmed saucer and took a sip from the matching teacup. "Life is always good," she said. "You just need to stop grieving for what *was* and start appreciating what *is*."

Bobbi frowned. "I can't just suddenly stop grieving,"

"Yes, you can." Margaret replied. "You see, grief is like a tidal undertow. When a tragedy occurs, it's easy to be pulled under its control. Giving in to grief is fine for a while. It provides numbing comfort. But if left unchecked, grief will drag you down into ever darker depths of despair. It's up to you to decide whether you're going to drown in grief or fight your way back to the surface, take a breath of fresh air and start swimming again – feel the sun on your face – hear the birds sing – realize life can still bring you joy."

Bobbi hung her head. "I know I should appreciate that God spared my life, but I have too many woes that are beyond my control..."

Margaret eyed Bobbi curiously. "Other than a temporary separation from your husband, and an injured leg that appears to make everyone want to wait on you hand and foot, what have you got to complain about?"

Bobbi sat up straight, her eyes wide, startled by the rebuke. "My whole family is in disarray and I'm powerless to fix it."

"Powerless?" Margaret's skepticism was apparent.

"Yes, powerless!" Bobbi echoed, knitting her eyebrows together.

She told Margaret about Lucian's physically abusive relationship with Jo and his sexually abusive relationship with Lou, who had since run away, and how she had to give two of her children to her sister, Max, and accept charity from a bootlegger to eke out a living for the other two. She wound down her rant by detailing Jo's emotional and financial concerns since Lucian's stroke.

"Not only am I incapable of helping my family," Bobbi wailed. "I'm actually becoming even more of a burden to them. My leg is beginning to shrivel. Soon I won't be able to stand on it at all. I'll... be... bedridden..." She choked back a sob.

"I believe you had more gumption when you were younger." Margaret took a sip of tea.

Bobbi's jaw dropped. "And I see that you still find it easy to ignore reality," she snapped. She crossed her arms and narrowed her eyes, annoyed with Margaret's nonchalant attitude.

"Easy to ignore reality?" After a moment's pause, Margaret laughed. "Oh, I remember now. When we first met, I kept insisting that I was dreaming, didn't I? That seems so long ago..." She chuckled again. "Well, soon after we met, I realized that relationships in both worlds are temporary. Since then, I've learned to enjoy my existence in this realm, just as I did when I walked among the living."

"You don't grieve your losses?"

"I've learned to accept that no one person walks beside us throughout our entire eternal journey," Margaret said. "Relationships with our parents are replaced with those of friends, lovers, children and even enemies. But eventually these also fade away. Sometimes relationships disappear slowly, and we don't even notice until they're gone. Other times, they disappear without warning and cause dreadful pain. And sometimes, it is we who leave."

Margaret paused, watching as Bobbi relaxed her shoulders.

"Each of us continues our eternal journey, always walking forward and never back. Once I understood this important concept, I learned to accept my losses, welcome new relationships and enjoy others for as long as they walk with me."

"You make it sound easy, but it's not."

"It's not easy, but it is vital." Margaret settled her cup firmly in her saucer and poured herself a fresh cup of tea from the steaming pot.

Lily contemplated the concept while Margaret stirred three heaping teaspoons of sugar into her tea.

"Bobbi, when you were a child, do you remember watching waves break on the shore?"

Bobbi nodded.

"Did you notice that every time a wave breaks, ripples are created?"

Again, Bobbi nodded.

"Well, no one knows how far any single ripple will travel, or what change, if any, it might make to the vast sea. But every ripple has the potential of becoming a great wave. Likewise, every action you take creates ripples that affect other people, and some of those ripples may influence people in ways you cannot imagine."

"Like the way several small actions on our part helped raise enough money to build the hospital?"

"Yes – exactly like that," Margaret agreed.

"Margaret, do you suppose we'll learn the results of our actions when we get to Heaven?"

"Perhaps," she replied. "But for now, we must be content with simply knowing our actions do create ripples, and ripples can cause change. For my part, I strive to ensure that the ripples I create will have a positive influence on others." She paused and took a sip of tea. "So, would you like to figure out what ripples we can generate to help your sisters?"

"Okay, but we'll probably need to create a tidal wave to fix that mess!" Bobbi said, the corners of her mouth curving into a smile.

"There's the gumption you've been lacking!" Margaret clasped her hands together. "Now, I think taking control of Lucian's money will be the hardest part. Once that's done, the rest of the knots will be easier to untangle. So let's start by talking about Lucian's condition. Can he write and speak clearly enough to make himself understood?"

"He can't move his arms or legs, and his words don't come out right, but Jo can discern most of his needs from the various sounds he makes." Bobbi leaned toward Margaret, her curiosity piqued.

"Good. Now, remember what I always say – an intelligent woman with allies can accomplish anything. So, how many women can we count as loyal allies right now, and how many more can we bring into our trusted circle in short order?" Margaret asked.

Chapter Fifty Five

Lily wanted to stay and listen to Margaret's plan, but the fog descended rapidly, pulling her back into the thick bank of clouds. A moment later, she heard Bobbi's voice and as the mist fell, she rejoined the partially transparent trio at the table in her hotel room.

Without acknowledging the change of venue, Bobbi continued. "Before telling Jo what I was up to, I convinced Clay to use his charm to sweet-talk a young bank teller into sharing a few drinks with him at the Candlelight Speakeasy."

"You didn't talk me into anything. I volunteered," Clay interrupted.

Margaret clucked at him and he cowed like a scolded child.

"I suppose the *true* details of how I became involved in the plan don't matter," he said. "What's important is that once the bank teller had a little rum inside her, she was willing to tell me the amount of Lucian's rather substantial passbook balance. She also told me that Lucian paid the bank a monthly fee to keep a private strongbox locked in their vault, but she didn't know what he kept in it, and not even the bank president could access the box without Lucian's key..."

"... She also told him," Bobbi cut in, "that Agnes Pritchard had taken over accounting duties at Cabot's Mercantile following the death of her husband, Harold, the year before. Lucky for us, Lucian had sorely underestimated Agnes Pritchard – but I'm getting ahead of myself." She turned to Clay. "I know you're impatient, *Long Gone*, but I still think she needs to see the memory I was sharing with her earlier."

Clay grunted without conceding, as the fog carried Lily from the table. A moment later, she started falling through the cloud bank as though the bottom had disappeared. Her body jerked involuntarily and she flailed her arms, struggling to slow down. Then, as quickly as it started, the fall ebbed to a smooth stop. Lily landed on her feet with the grace of a cat. Unfortunately, her stomach still felt as though she had dropped fifty floors in an elevator. She bent at her waist, closed her eyes and gasped for air.

When at last she could focus, Lily discovered she was back in the little kitchen of Bobbi's home. Bobbi was sitting in her wheeled chair and Jo was standing by the stove, still fussing over the percolator.

"It seems God is determined to make my life a long, lonely tale of woe," Jo said.

"Jo, you're not alone. And even though your situation looks bad right now, you're not as powerless as you might think," Bobbi replied. "I've come to believe women can accomplish great things, as long as they stick together.

"Sounds like suffragette nonsense to me," Jo countered.

Bobbi cast a tolerant smile at her older sister. "Jo, I think we can recruit some allies who would be willing to help you take control of Lucian's store. But first, you must be certain that's what you want." She paused, studying her sister. "Running your household is one thing, Jo – but overseeing the Mercantile would drastically alter your life. You'd have to spend your days working at the store, and hire someone to help care for Lucian and the children."

"I don't understand. I mean, I'm better with arithmetic and bookkeeping than Lucian thinks I am, but he's the one with influence at the bank, not me."

"Battles aren't always won by the mighty. Remember it was David who brought down Goliath. It's been my experience that people in lowly positions often possess similar, hidden strengths." Bobbi locked eyes with Jo. "I must warn you, though – the caper necessary to bring down this particular giant will require both deception and risk."

Jo nodded. "As long as no one else gets hurt, I'm more than willing to participate in a ruse that would repay Lucian in kind for the pain and lies he brought into our marriage."

Bobbi clapped her hands. "Attagirl, Jo."

"Now if only this blasted coffee would finish perking," she grumbled.

As if taking Jo's complaint to heart, the pot's rhythmic perking stopped that instant.

"Look there," Bobbi teased. "Now that you've decided to stand up for yourself, even the coffee pot listens to you."

An envelope of mist engulfed Lily, carrying her away from this memory and directly into the next one. When the thick blanket of mist lifted, she took in the scene before her.

Jo and Bobbi were at Lucian's bedside. Jo clung nervously to Bobbi's left arm and Bobbi, in turn, clutched the handles of her crutches with white knuckles. At the foot of the bed, stood a prim woman who appeared to be the source of the sisters' distress. Middle-aged, she was dressed in a navy suit with wide, white lapels and a flared skirt, hemmed just below her knee. A matching bell-shaped cloche hid most of her short, grey hair, and she held a bouquet of flowers in her gloved hands.

The woman slid her round spectacles down her nose and stared at Lucian, a quizzical expression on her face. "But I don't understand," she said. "When Mr. Grant dropped off last night's deposit at the bank, the teller said Mr. Cabot was making remarkable progress. He sent me here today to assure Mr. Cabot that everything is running smoothly at the Mercantile under his management."

Jo cleared her throat and forced a smile. "My husband is doing much better, but his speech is still difficult for most folks to decipher. Fortunately, I'm able to translate for him."

Lily glanced at Lucian, who was making angry, guttural sounds at Jo. Even though his words were unintelligible, his fury was obvious by the daggers shooting from his eyes.

"What's that, dear Lucian?" Jo asked, struggling to maintain the cheerful charade.

She bent over her husband, pretending to listen intently. Then she straightened-up and faced the woman, the smile still plastered on her blushing face. "He says it is lovely of you to stop by, Agnes."

Jo rubbed her clammy palms against her skirt and widened her smile, unaware that the frozen grin, along with her red cheeks and wide eyes, made her look more like a deranged clown than a loving wife.

"He says he knows he's lucky to have such a competent person handling the books at the store and thanks you for your loyalty."

"Bull feathers. He said no such thing." Agnes Pritchard sniffed.

Jo's smile fell as she folded her arms tightly across her chest. Her voice quivered. "I... but... he certainly did..."

It was evident Agnes wasn't buying Jo's performance.

Jo hung her head and shook it slowly. "No, he didn't," she said. "I'm sorry for trying to fool you, Agnes. I pretended Lucian was speaking through me because gaining your cooperation is necessary if I'm going to take over the store. It was wrong..."

"You're darn tootin' it was wrong!" she scolded. Then her lips curved into a smile. "If you're going to succeed with this scheme, you're going to have to do a much better job with your acting. Lucian rarely speaks directly to me and never calls me by my name. He usually issues his orders through Mr. Grant – and even then, he refers to me only as 'Pritchard's widow.'"

Lily covered her mouth to keep from laughing at Jo and Bobbi's shocked expressions.

"Let me explain," Agnes said. "When my Harold became ill with stomach ulcers, he begged Lucian to hire an assistant bookkeeper, but Lucian refused. He was afraid another accountant would either foul my husband's double-bookkeeping system or reveal his secret accounts to the authorities."

Agnes scowled at Lucian. "When Harold's ulcers got worse, Lucian finally agreed to let me assist with the books. He knew my fear of criminal liability would motivate me to keep his secrets, just as it had motivated my husband, God rest his soul. Now that

Harold's dead, I'm the only person who understands the bookkeeping system at the Mercantile and..."

Lucian's snarls interrupted Agnes, growing so fierce that droplets of spittle sprayed from his mouth and drooled down his chin. He thrashed his head back and forth, as if shaking his brain would somehow allow him to wake from this nightmare and put these women back in their place.

The women stared at Lucian, terrified by his rage. But as he continued to flail helplessly, a sense of calm settled over the trio.

Agnes spotted an empty vase on the dresser. Turning her back on Lucian, she deposited the flowers she was carrying into it and began arranging them. "Mrs. Cabot, I accidentally overheard Lucian's telephone conversation when he made arrangements for your sister, Louise's, eh... medical procedure some time back. He told the person on the phone that his sister-in-law possessed loose morals, but I knew the truth. He was destroying evidence of his own depravity. Once, when he was drunk, he bragged to my husband and Mr. Grant, that all women living under his roof were his property, to bed as he pleased."

Jo and Bobbi gasped; then scowled at Lucian, who was making a host of new, but still unintelligible, sounds. Lily guessed he was trying to proclaim his innocence.

Agnes continued. "I'm ashamed to admit that I was too worried about my own well-being to speak up. Had I told my husband what I overheard, he might have risked his employment to intervene on Louise's behalf, and in these hard times..." She shook her head and turned around to face Jo and Bobbi. "Ever since that terrible day, I've been praying for the opportunity to help set things right. It appears God decided to grant my wish."

Lily glanced at Bobbi, Jo and Lucian. At first, all three were dumbstruck. Lucian found his voice first and let go a tirade of guttural noises. This time, Lily had no doubt that he was giving Agnes a piece of his mind.

"What's that, Mr. Cabot?" Agnes asked, batting her eyelashes. "Of course, I will. You can depend on me to let Mr. Grant know you're doing much better and that you asked me to help your good wife carry out your wishes." She smiled, pretending to listen to his next garbled rant. "Yes, you're absolutely right. She does need to learn all about the store's operations, as well as your secondary line of business – processing liquor shipments coming in from Canada and the Bahamas. I'll be sure to tell her all about how we're paid to repackage the bottles into mismarked crates and hide them in our storeroom until Mr. Capone's men can arrange to come and pick them up."

"Oh, Lucian," Jo moaned. Her knees buckled and she plopped down on the side of the bed. Her back slumped and she buried her face in her hands.

Lily felt sorry for Jo. Bobbi moved to comfort her sister, but suddenly, Jo stiffened her spine and slid her hands from her face; palms together, as if in prayer.

"Lucian, I thank God that you didn't die before you were able to change your sinful ways. I believe the Almighty has given you the opportunity to repent, and has burdened me with the task of helping you see the light."

Lucian thrashed his head back and forth, clearly disputing Jo's assessment of God's wishes.

"Dear Lucian, the more you resist, the harder the process of repenting will be on you," Jo purred, mimicking one of her late father's favorite admonitions. She picked up a thick towel and gently wiped Lucian's face.

Unwilling to concede, Lucian let loose a fresh assault of angry growls and then spat at his wife. Jo calmly covered his mouth and nose with the towel and pushed down hard, so he couldn't move his head. Lily, Bobbi and Agnes watched, their mouths hanging open, until Lucian's muffled screams subsided. The moment he quieted, Jo lifted the towel from his face. Lucian gasped for air, his eyed filled with terror.

"There, now, Lucian." Jo gave him a tender smile. "See how much better you feel when you cooperate with the process of repentance?"

Agnes raised her eyebrows, sensing an opportunity. "You know, Lucian only pays me a third of what he paid my husband to do my job. Do you think God would approve of raising my wages as a part of Lucian's atonement?"

Lily thought Lucian's eyes might pop out of his head if they got any bigger, but he didn't try to speak.

As the fog closed in around her, Lily heard Jo say, "I think God would definitely approve. I also believe God would want his family to be dressed in more pleasing fashions, but first we'll need to change a few things down at the bank and have to have a rather unpleasant meeting with Mr. Grant."

Lily laughed out loud as the mist surrounded her. She almost felt sorry for Lucian, who was about to learn what it was like to be helpless and at the mercy of others.

Chapter Fifty Six

Lily drifted through the clouds, happy that Jo was finally standing up to Lucian. When the fog lifted a few moments later, she and the two sisters were in Lucian's bedroom again, but nothing else about the scene resembled the last memory.

"What is going on?" Lily wondered.

The room was filled with light and crowded with people, but the biggest change was with Lucian himself. He was sitting-up in bed, wearing a clean and pressed nightshirt. His head lolled to the side and he had an odd, relaxed, expression on his face. Next to the bed, two small chairs had been placed on either side of a small table that held a chessboard, with a game in progress.

She recognized Dr. Alton Farthing and his wife, Nurse Anna. As Lily took deep breaths to settle her stomach, she identified the rest of the eclectic group. Just inside the door stood the blacksmith, Jack Stanley, and Rebecca, Jo's eldest daughter. Everyone in the room was studying Lucian.

"Should I slide him up a bit more on the board?" Jack asked, to no one in particular.

Jo looked at Lucian from a few different angles. "No, Jack – I think he looks fine. The pillows hide the supporting board perfectly and the fact that he slumps a bit is good, too. Lucian never was one to foster good posture. You're certain the ropes will hold him upright?"

"Yes, ma'am," replied Jack. "All that's left is to put this nightcap on him. The metal strip Rebecca sewed into it goes around his forehead and through the pillows behind him. Once I fasten the strip to the board, it'll keep his head from falling forward."

Jack and Rebecca went to work and in no time, Lucian's head was perfectly ensconced in the head-supporting nightcap.

Jo turned to Alton, wringing her hands. "You're confident his temper won't give us away?"

"I've administered just enough morphine to ease his concerns without putting him to sleep," the doctor replied. "He should remain congenial for the next hour or two, but after that, I can't say what he'll do."

As if to prove the doctor's point, Lucian, his facial expression the picture of cordiality, gurgled a few undecipherable noises.

"Thank you so much for helping us, Dr. Farthing," Jo said.

"It's Anna that you should be thanking. She's the one who convinced me this charade won't do additional harm to Lucian and was in the best interest of the entire family."

"I think you're just ducky for helping us, even if it's only because you were afraid I'd do it by myself if you didn't belly up to the bar," Anna teased. She raised-up onto her toes to kiss her husband's cheek.

Alton smiled down at her, yielding to her charms.

Bobbi clapped her hands together twice, drawing everyone's attention. "All right, then. I think everything is ready. Jack and Rebecca, perhaps it would be best if you two went downstairs to await the arrival of our guests." Then Bobbi maneuvered around the bed to the tall dresser in the corner. Her bad leg was visibly atrophied. She leaned on her crutches and swung her good leg forward while dragging the useless braced leg behind her.

Lily remembered that Bobbi told Margaret she would be confined to a wheeled chair soon. It was apparent that Bobbi had indeed *gotten her gumption back* and was fighting her prognosis as long as possible.

When she reached the dresser, Bobbi opened a carved box and pulled out a pipe and a small can of tobacco. She packed the pipe and reclosed the can. "Come here, Jo," she called.

"Put this in your breast pocket," she told her sister.

"Why on earth would I want to smell like that vile pipe?" Jo asked.

"Trust me," Bobbi said. "Lucian loves this smell." She tucked the pipe into Jo's pocket so that the end of it peeked out.

When they heard a knock on the front door, everyone froze until Lucian's gurgling noises brought them back to the present.

"Quickly now, everyone – get into place!" Bobbi whispered.

Jo went to the top of the stairs and called down. "Rebecca, dear, please answer the door for me. Your father is expecting Mr. Broomfield, from the bank."

Lily watched as Alton and Anna sat in the chairs on either side of the chessboard, and Bobbi took her place on the other side of the narrow bed, holding a nearly empty water glass. They all exchanged nervous glances when they heard the front door open and close. They could hear Rebecca's muffled voice, welcoming their guests, and then they heard heavy footfalls on the steps. Just as the visitors reached the top of the stairs, Bobbi took a deep breath and nodded at Alton Farthing.

"Ah, Lucian," said Alton, "You've got my king on the run again."

Lily's first impression of Mr. Broomfield was that he reminded her of the rotund character, Wimpy, from the Popeye cartoons. He was bald, with the exception of a tuft of hair just above his forehead. His bulbous nose and beady eyes appeared to be bunched too close together in the middle of his round face, and his walrus mustache covered his mouth. His brown wool suit fit as snugly as the metal band on a whisky barrel, and the buttons of his vest threatened to pop if he so much as coughed too hard. He held his bowler style hat in his stubby hands as he stepped into the room, with Agnes Pritchard trailing behind in his shadow.

Mr. Broomfield was clearly startled at finding the room full of people.

"Is that enough, Lucian?" Bobbi asked, pulling the nearly-empty water glass back from his lips. In reality, Jo had to use baby pap bottles to squeeze liquids and blended foods down Lucian's throat, so the glass was just a part of the act for Mr. Broomfield's benefit.

Lucian babbled nonsense in reply.

"Perhaps it would be better to wait until after dinner for a cola," Bobbi said, as if she understood his gibberish. Then she smiled and set the glass on a bedside tray, as if just noticing the new guests' arrival.

"Hello there, Walter," Alton greeted the newcomer. Half-rising from his chair, he extended his hand. "Good of you to stop by."

The plump man waddled forward, winded from walking up the flight of stairs. He shook hands with Alton and nodded to Anna. "Hello Doctor – Mrs. Farthing." Then he glanced at the chessboard, clearly perplexed.

Alton answered Bloomfield's unspoken question. "Lucian's condition has improved so much that we've been able to resume our weekly game of chess, as long as Anna moves the pieces for him. Do you play, Walter?"

Lucian interrupted with a string of garbled sounds.

"I didn't forget to make your move, Lucian," Anna said. "I was just waiting until you finished visiting with Mr. Bloomfield." She looked at the board and moved the black knight to D4. "It looks like he's pinned your king in the corner, dear. This game's all but over, I'm afraid."

Alton pretended to be surprised by the move and stared at the chessboard, contemplating his remaining moves. "Blast – not again!"

Lucian made a few gurgling sounds and everyone laughed. Alton turned to Bloomfield. "He's bragging. This is the third game in a row he's won. Would you like to challenge him to the next game?"

The bank president looked from one person to another. All of them seemed to be able to understand Lucian except him. "Uh – no thank you. Poker's my game, and truthfully, I need to get back to the bank. I was told that Lucian had some new directives for me, but given what I knew of his condition, I thought the message must be in error."

Lucian's babble increased in volume. Jo stepped around Alton and Anna to bend over her husband, pretending to listen very carefully. To Broomfield's amazement, Lucian smiled when his wife drew near and his eyes followed her, even after she straightened back up. This was more affection than Broomfield had ever witnessed Lucian demonstrate for Jo in the past, but given her improved looks, he wasn't surprised.

"As you can hear for yourself, Mr. Broomfield, Lucian is quite capable of speaking his mind," she said.

Bobbi, Alton, Anna, and even Agnes nodded their heads in agreement, as if they, too, had understood Lucian's ramblings.

"I couldn't... quite make out... what he said," Mr. Broomfield stuttered.

Jo nodded her head with empathy and squeezed Lucian's hand. "Don't fret, Mr. Bloomfield. It was difficult for all of us at first. I can repeat what Lucian says until you can make out his words on your own, if you like."

Bloomfield glanced at Dr. Farthing, who gave him a professional nod, as if concurring with Jo's suggestion.

"I must say, Mr. Cabot," Bloomfield said, "you appear more content here at home with your wife and friends than I've ever seen you before. If I didn't know better, I'd swear you were just lazing about rather than overcoming a serious illness."

Lily choked back a laugh. She knew Lucian wasn't smiling at Jo. He was smiling at his pipe and the scent of his favorite tobacco coming from her pocket. Still, Lucian emitted a few more pleasant gurgles in her direction.

"This ailment has caused my husband great distress, no doubt, but it's also given him a chance to reflect on his life," Jo said. "He understands that he's too weak to run the Mercantile – at least for a while." Jo gave Lucian a loving glance. "He's decided to entrust me with that responsibility, as well as his other business ventures and our personal finances."

Lucian began to babble a bit more strenuously, so Jo leaned over him again. Once more, the smell of his tobacco seemed to soothe the drugged man. Jo stood up and laughed. The others joined in, except Bloomfield.

"He said to tell you not to worry, Mr. Bloomfield – he'll be supervising my every move and reviewing Mrs. Pritchard's books,"

Jo said. "He said he might be a changed man, but he hasn't lost his mind."

"I brought the paperwork with me," said Agnes with a cough. "This gives Mrs. Cabot full access to Mr. Cabot's business and personal bank accounts, as well as his strong box."

Bloomfield eyed Agnes suspiciously. "His strongbox?"

Agnes nodded. "Yes, Mrs. Cabot is now aware of..." Agnes paused to glance around the room before sharing a knowing look with Bloomfield. "...of everything."

Bloomfield raised his bushy eyebrows, but accepted the stack of papers. He gave them a cursory review, and then handed them back to her. Lucian made a few unintelligible, worried sounds as Agnes drew near.

"Of course Anna can help you with your signature, Mr. Cabot." Agnes handed the forms and a fountain pen to Anna, who then pretended to guide Lucian's hand as he signed his name.

Afterward, Bloomfield affixed his signature and Alton and Agnes signed as witnesses.

Bloomfield glanced at this pocket watch and cleared his throat. "Lucian, it's good to see you getting along so well, but I must be getting back to the bank now." He tipped his hat at Jo. "Mrs. Cabot, please let me know if I can be of any assistance to you. You have Lucian's strongbox key, correct? I dare say, we're due for another transaction soon."

Jo nodded, hoping he couldn't tell she was lying.

Rebecca appeared in the open doorway. "I can see you to the door, Mr. Bloomfield," she said, giving him a shy smile.

Bloomfield eyed the young beauty and brushed his thick moustache away from his lecherous grin. "Why thank you, my dear." He glanced around the room. "Good day Lucian, Dr. Farthing – ladies..."

Rebecca turned and led the way back down the stairs, with Bloomfield following close behind, his eyes affixed to her swishing derriere. No one spoke until the front door closed and Rebecca and Jack came back upstairs. Jo plopped down on the side of Lucian's bed, her knees too weak to hold her up any longer. When at last she clapped her hands together and chuckled, it had a contagious effect.

The fog gathered and carried Lily from the memory just as everyone started laughing, hugging and patting one another on the back.

Chapter Fifty Seven

Lily was still laughing about what Bobbi and her allies accomplished, when the mist parted again. Bobbi was seated in her parlor when Rebecca Cabot and Jack Stanley arrived.

Jack, the gentle Superman look-alike, paused in the doorway, holding what looked like a new brace for Bobbi's leg. "Look at this new contraption Rebecca had me make for you, Mrs. Hamilton."

"First, let me explain, Aunt Bobbi," Rebecca said. "Doc Farthing told me your leg is getting thinner because you aren't using those muscles any more. He said it's called *atrophy*. Apparently, the only remedy is exercise."

Bobbi glanced at her injured leg. "But how can I exercise a leg that won't support any weight?"

"Hopefully, this new brace will help," Rebecca said, stepping behind Bobbi's wheeled chair. "Let's go try it on and see if my idea pans out."

In her bedroom, Jack lifted Bobbi from her chair as if she weighed no more than a porcelain doll and was equally fragile. He carefully laid her on the bed.

"Thank you, Jack," said Rebecca, gazing at the big man with adoration. "You can wait for us in the parlor."

Jack smiled and gave her a wink before leaving.

"*They're in love,*" Lily realized.

Rebecca cleared her throat, pushed Bobbi's dress up out of the way and began wrapping her leg with bunting. "I asked Jack to leave some room for muscle growth, so this lambs wool will keep the brace from rubbing. As your leg gets stronger, we'll use less of this."

"I still don't understand how I can strengthen a useless leg."

Rebecca held up the brace for Bobbi to examine, glowing with the pride at her invention. "Your new brace is also an exercise machine. You see, the brace you designed is like a tree trunk wrapped around your leg. It allows you to stand, but not sit."

Bobbi nodded, curious but confused.

"Well, a few weeks ago," Rebecca continued, "I was reading the story of King Arthur to the children, when Belle mentioned that your brace resembled a suit of armor. I thought about it and I realized that, like armor, it could be made to bend at the knee."

"But then it wouldn't brace my leg." Bobbi frowned, still confused.

"Ah, but with a few changes, it can do both things." Rebecca turned the steel brace over. "The secret is this locking hinge, here on the back. See how the steel rod fits through these metal loops?" she said, pointing to the hinge. "And these cotter pins fit through holes drilled in either end the rod, to keep it from sliding out. When the rod is in place, your brace will be as solid as it ever was."

Bobbi nodded. "And when they're removed?"

Rebecca pulled one of the cotter pins out and removed the iron rod. "Then the leg brace bends at the knee, and the front cuff turns upright on tiny hinges, just like a knight's armor." She demonstrated the device.

Bobbi's eyes lit up. "So I can sit or stand as I choose?"

"Yes." Rebecca beamed. "But there's more! When you're sitting, you can push a rope through this metal loop that's soldered to the front of the brace and use it to exercise your leg." She slid her finger through the front loop to demonstrate.

"Well, isn't that the cat's meow!" Bobbi clapped her hands. "Help me put it on and show me how it works."

Rebecca put the rod and cotter pin back into place, and then slipped the back half of the brace under Bobbi's injured leg. Next, she laid the front half on top of the leg and looped several leather belts through small metal wickets, spaced at regular intervals the entire length of the brace. She tightened and buckled each belt and then straightened Bobbi's dress.

"Okay, Aunt Bobbi," Rebecca said, trying to conceal her excitement. "I want Jack here, just in case, but with the rod in place, this brace should work just like your old one." She called Jack's name and a moment later, his bulk filled the doorway.

"Don't look so worried, you two," Bobbi said. "If I fall, it certainly won't be the first time."

Jack helped pull Bobbi to a standing position and Rebecca handed her the metal crutches. Much to the relief of all, the brace functioned perfectly. Even though Bobbi dragged her weak leg more than ever, she walked to the parlor.

"Would you like me to remove the iron bar so you can try sitting, Aunt Bobbi?"

"I'll try to do it myself," Bobbi said, "But perhaps Jack should stand in front of me, just in case I fall forward."

Lily realized she was holding her breath and exhaled. Although her brace was lighter and more efficient than Bobbi's, she was quite familiar with the helpless feeling of losing her balance and falling, unable to catch herself.

Bobbi put her weight on her good leg, reached around to the back of her braced knee, and pulled out a cotter pin and iron rod. She placed the items into Rebecca's nervous hand and, after a quick glance to make sure she was close enough; she slid her crutches forward and bent her good knee. It wasn't the most graceful recline, but she plopped into her wheeled chair.

"Hooray!" Rebecca and Jack cheered.

"This is a wonderful improvement," Bobbi murmured.

"And while you're sitting, you can exercise your leg like this." Rebecca pulled a length of braided leather rope from her pocket and pushed one end through a metal loop near Bobbi's ankle. Then she handed both ends to Bobbi. "Pull these toward you," she directed "but try to make your leg do as much of the lifting as possible."

When Bobbi pulled on the ends of the leather rope, her brace lifted off the ground, flexing her knee to a straight position.

"At first, your arms will have to do the lifting, but if this works the way I hope, you'll use your arms less and less as your leg gets stronger," Rebecca explained.

As Lily watched Bobbi struggle to lift her leg a second time, the thick mist descended over her, carrying her away from the memory.

Suddenly, Margaret's voice filtered in through the fog, catching Lily completely off-guard.

Chapter Fifty-Eight

"I've been a spirit for over a century and I thought I knew just about everything there was to know about this realm. But then you come along, and I discover I have much more to learn."

The mist lifted and Lily found herself sitting at the small, round table in her hotel room, across from Margaret Plant.

"Are you speaking to me?" Lily asked, casting an uncertain glance around the room.

"Of course, darlin'. I don't make a habit of conversing with myself."

"What can I possibly teach you about spirits?" Lily asked.

"I'm learning more about my world *because* of you, not *from* you," Margaret corrected. Two teacups with a rosebud motif and matching saucers appeared in front of her, along with a silver tea service. She poured two cups of tea and slid one over to Lily.

"Now, as I told you – my attempts to use tweening to communicate with your grandmother have been thwarted by a spirit who keeps distracting her with endless tales about her excursions around the world."

"Grams always did love listening to people talk about far-off places they visited," Lily said.

"Yes, yes..." Margaret waved a dismissive hand. "But as I watched your grandmother with that Sharon woman, I realized they weren't tweening – they had developed an actual connection."

"I thought dream connections only happened when a spirit was related to a person – or experienced a similar trauma."

"As did I," Margaret nodded, "but apparently, their mutual love of travel formed a bond between them. Now hush, please – chatter makes it difficult to maintain one's train of thought." She frowned.

Lily knew it was difficult for Margaret to absorb enough energy from her surroundings to maintain a connection with her, but she was too frustrated to stay quiet. "I'm sorry. I know you said I'll eventually understand what you spirits are trying to teach me, but I'm afraid Grams will be gone before..."

"If only you would listen," Margaret snapped, "I'm trying to tell you that I discovered a way to connect with your grandmother!"

Lily's mouth fell open. She fidgeted in her chair, choking back several new questions while Margaret stirred three teaspoons of sugar into her tea.

"Good thing spirits don't gain weight or get cavities," Lily thought, her impatience mounting.

When Margaret resumed her story, she spoke with the tone of a schoolmarm. "Normally, tweening is simply a form of entertainment – a chance to have engaging conversations with people whose spirits are still tethered to their bodies. The living usually believe they're dreaming, so tweening banter tends to flit from one subject to another," she said. "It's quite fascinating, but one rarely discovers a common passion."

Lily sighed, wishing Margaret would get to her point.

Margaret sniffed with indignation and took a sip of tea before continuing. "Whilst I was unsuccessfully attempting to insert myself into a tweening conversation with Sharon and your grandmother, Sharon started talking about a chalet on a hillside, just outside of Vienna – a chalet with which I, myself, am quite familiar. The moment I recognized the location, I was engulfed by Sharon's memory, along with your grandmother. The three of us watched visions of the chalet and surrounding countryside appear at the edge of the mist as though we were looking at Austria through windows. Immediately, I knew were watching Sharon's memories of that chalet. That's not tweening – that's a connection!"

"And that's unusual?" Lily asked.

"Quite. I wouldn't have thought it possible to develop a connection while tweening if I hadn't witnessed it with my own eyes. But it gave me an idea for developing a connection with your grandmother that didn't involve that pesky Sharon woman. While we were watching Sharon's memories of the chalet, I asked your grandmother if she thought her granddaughter, Lily, would have enjoyed visiting there. Of course, Sharon's memories disappeared the moment I spoke, so she's none too pleased with me – but it worked." Margaret didn't attempt to disguise the smug satisfaction she felt. "Finally, your grandmother gave me her full attention."

Lily gasped and pressed her hand over her mouth to keep from blurting out questions that might delay hearing the rest of Margaret's story.

"I didn't know if our connection would last and I wanted your grandmother to know she wasn't dreaming, so I told her that she's dying. I also told her you've been holding a vigil at her bedside in Morton Plant Hospital and that you're upset over your estranged relationship."

Lily's hands dropped to her lap, shocked by Margaret's blunt approach. "What did she say?" she whispered.

Margaret stared into her teacup. "I believe your grandmother is an exceptional woman," she began. "Many people are afraid of death, but she isn't. She understands that death is simply a transition – the next step in one's eternal journey."

Lily teared up. "But did you tell her..."

"Try to be patient, darlin'. I still have much to explain."

Biting her lower lip, Lily nodded.

"Each time I make a connection with a living being, the memories we share become a part of my own memory. For instance, I can recall that nightmare you had while we were connected."

Lily nodded to show Margaret she understood.

"Well, your grandmother shared some of her memories with me while we were connected, and now I remember those memories, the same way you can recall the memories we spirits have shared with you." She paused and stirred her tea. "Now, I'm not certain by any means – but I think there's a chance that I might be able share your grandmother's memories with you."

Excitement flashed in Lily's eyes.

Margaret held up her palms in a calming gesture. "Don't get your hopes up too much, Lily. This facet of the spirit realm is brand new to me and I'm not sure this is going to work."

When the mist swirled around her, Lily gave herself up to the fog, as she had done so many times since coming to stay at the Belleview Biltmore. But this time, anticipation made it difficult to relax. She was beginning to grow anxious by the time Margaret appeared in the mist at her side.

Margaret didn't acknowledge Lily, but instead, focused her attention on a point in the distance, like a child looking for pictures in the clouds. Lily trained her eyes on the same spot.

When an image finally started to form, it was like watching a fuzzy movie playing against the side of a soap bubble. At first, Lily worried her imagination was playing tricks on her, but as the picture cleared, she saw Grams and Gramps, seated at their old dining room table, sharing a cup of coffee and poring over a travelogue. Lily had forgotten they always preferred to share a single mug. Grams once told her the habit started because when they first married, they were so poor, they only owned one coffee cup, and in later years, they just liked the way sharing a cup encouraged them to sit closer together. After Gramps died, Grams never filled her coffee cup more than halfway. The precious memory tugged at Lily's heart.

Suddenly, the soap bubble image burst and was immediately replaced with another. This time, the memory featured Grams talking with Margaret. Both women had the semi-transparent appearance of spirits, which bothered Lily. It was a reminder that Grams' spirit wasn't going to be tied to her body much longer.

"It doesn't bother me to die," said Grams. "I've had a long life, filled with the love of a dear family on this side, and I have a devoted husband and daughter waiting for me on the other side. What more could I ask for?"

"I believe memories remain intact no matter where your eternal journey takes you," said Margaret. "And I also think the years of separation from your loved ones will feel like they passed by in the blink of an eye."

Grams nodded. "I hope so. And when their time finally comes to cross-over, I'll be waiting for Lily, Scott and Dylan. How wonderful it will be to hear all about their adventures and good works..."

The bubble popped, leaving Lily confused. Why was Grams talking as if Dylan was still alive? She stared into the mist, hoping another bubble would appear, but instead, the mist parted, returning her to the table with Margaret.

From the expression on her face, it was evident Margaret was quite pleased with herself, but Lily was rattled. The tea service reappeared and Margaret poured two steaming cups of tea, sliding one cup across to Lily. She picked up her cup and took a sip of tea. The calming effect of the hot liquid surprised Lily, given her dream-state. She took another drink and then wrapped both hands around the delicate, porcelain cup, trying to absorb its warmth.

"When I first met you," Margaret said, "I thought I could help you by explaining the spirit realm and providing guidance to Bobbi and Clay as they tried to help you learn some complicated lessons. But now that I've connected with your grandmother, I think I may possess other knowledge that will be valuable to you."

Lily blinked, growing uncomfortable. "I think Grams' memories are tainted by her dementia."

Margaret arched her eyebrows. "Your grandmother's memories are crystal clear," she said. "There is no dementia in the afterlife." She took a sip of tea, puckered her mouth and quickly set her cup down. She picked up a small, silver spoon and added the three teaspoons of sugar she had forgotten. After taking a more satisfying drink, she continued.

"Like yours, my childhood was a difficult one. I was born into wealth and prestige, but that all changed while I was still very young. My father died and my uncle took over the family estate, bringing us to ruin in short order. I feared I would always be destitute and full of woe, but then I discovered some important facts that changed my perspective. Like your grandmother, I learned that one can possess the wealth of Midas, but still be miserable. Conversely, one can own a single cup and be absolutely content. I discovered that my happiness in life was determined not by what others did to me, or did for me, but how I chose to respond to whatever happened."

Lily nodded, still puzzling over Grams' memories.

"I also learned to accept that all relationships come to an end – whether by choice, the death of another, or one's own death – and I realized that, regardless of their length, relationships added wonderful flavor to my life. Some brought joy to my heart, while others taught me valuable skills, and still others provided wisdom through painful lessons. Over time, I came to understand that when a relationship ends, I can choose to allow blissful memories, learned skills and wisdom to remain a part of my soul, while letting memories of discontent fade into the distance."

"But what if I'm the reason for most of her discontent?" Lily asked. "My needs kept Grams from pursuing her one goal in life – to travel with Gramps. And as if that wasn't bad enough, I abandoned her at the end of her life." Lily bowed her head. "Even if Grams has forgiven me, how can I forgive myself?"

"Darlin' girl, your grandmother's life has not yet ended, and far from abandoning her, you're here at her side." Margaret protested. "And what's this about you stopping her from traveling the world?"

Guilt churned like bile in the pit of Lily's stomach. "She and Gramps planned to take a trip around the world as soon as Gramps retired, but when my mom died, they got stuck with me. Gramps had to keep working to pay for my upbringing. They always planned big trips, but Gramps died before they had the chance to go anywhere. I didn't want to travel, so Grams and Dylan started planning journeys they'd take together after he grew up." Lily wiped away a tear. "But then he died, too..."

"You misunderstood them," Margaret said as the fog dropped like a curtain around Lily, carrying her back into the clouds.

As before, Margaret appeared in the mist right next to Lily, and an instant later, a memory bubble materialized before them. They stared at the bubble until a vision of Margaret and Grams came into focus. Even though the two women were semitransparent, Lily could see the sparkle in Grams' eyes and noticed she looked younger than she had in years.

"The only journey I'll take is the one that will carry me back to the arms of my loving husband," Grams said.

"I thought you longed to travel, Lois," Margaret said. "You seemed fascinated with Sharon's excursions."

Grams smiled. "When we were newlyweds, my husband and I relished Sunday afternoons. We spent them planning an impossibly long trek around the world that we could ill afford. At some point, planning trips became our hobby. We never talked about it, but we both realized that as long as our grand expedition was in the offing, the anticipation of our trip would never ebb. We never had to worry about language barriers, missed flights, lost luggage, illness or even bad weather. Instead, we spent countless, glorious hours learning about the wonders of the world and imagining ourselves successfully taking part in all sorts of activities – from climbing a mountain summit to learning to hula dance – and our adventures always played out perfectly. It was like writing an adventure story together."

"I always found travel thrilling," Margaret replied. "I enjoyed immersing myself in foreign cultures and discovering unusual art and delicacies, despite the inevitable ordeals I encountered along the way."

"To each his own, I suppose," Grams agreed. "My husband and I preferred armchair travel, but I believe my grandson, Dylan, is more like you. He wants to travel everywhere and experience everything."

When the memory bubble burst, the fog returned Lily to the little table to sort out her mixed emotions.

"You see?" Margaret said. "Your grandmother never wanted to travel and she isn't interested in staying in this realm. Therefore, your presence as a child, as well as the fact that spirits can only inhabit places they visited while they were living, are of absolutely no consequence."

"How can I believe any of that is true?" Lily cried. "Grams' memory isn't crystal clear – it's faulty." Her voice broke. "She doesn't even remember that Dylan died."

Before Margaret could respond, Lily's attention was drawn toward a loud noise in the distance. Instantly, her surroundings vanished and she plummeted downward through the clouds, as if she had stepped off a cliff.

Chapter Fifty Nine

Lily flailed her arms, trying to stop her free-fall, too terrified to scream. Her hands touched a solid surface and she grabbed at it with all her might. When she forced herself to open her eyes, the descent ended as abruptly as it had begun. It took a full second for her mind to register that she was in her hotel room bed, her hands desperately clutching to her mattress. She relaxed her fists and sat up; her heart still pounding. Only then did she realize someone was knocking on her door.

"Who is it?" she called, hoping her voice sounded calmer than she felt.

"Seth."

Lily's thoughts were as disheveled as her bed. Still trying to sort reality from dreams, she tried to recall the last time had spoken to Seth. She groaned. They had been kissing moments before she condemned him for being willing to accept corneal transplants to restore his sight. So much happened during the last day and a half that, for Lily, their fight on the porch swing felt like it had taken place long ago. She seriously doubted Seth felt the same way.

"Answer the door, Lily," he insisted. "We need to talk."

"Give me a minute," she called. Her mind raced, trying to concoct an excuse for her bizarre behavior.

The room was still freezing cold from the spirit's visit. Lily scooted to the end of the bed and tugged one of the hotel's plush complimentary robes over her goose-pimpled arms. Then she gingerly slipped

her brace onto her injured leg. Her body rejected surgically implanted steel rods, so her tibia wasn't healing properly. A long-bone
transplant was her best chance of avoiding amputation of her leg
below the knee, but she was repulsed at the thought of it.

*"It's not fair to expect Seth to understand my distain for trans-
plants,"* Lily reasoned, hobbling across the room. *"He didn't live
my nightmare. He just wants to regain his vision."* She glanced at
her watch. It was only seven o'clock – hours before they usually
met for breakfast. She braced herself for his indignant tirade and
opened the door.

Despite his anger, she couldn't help noticing that Seth was
gorgeous, from the top of his short-cropped blond hair, all the
way down to his tight-fitting jeans. His well-muscled arms were
folded across his chest, hiding the design on his black tee-shirt –
something about Harleys, no doubt. Feeling inappropriate for
ogling him, Lily focused her attention on his round, black glasses.

"It's barely daybreak," she mumbled.

"Yesterday I was on time," he replied. "You stood me up."

Lily hung her head. "I'm sorry – I really am."

"You know, Lily, I've worked damned hard to become Zen with
the world. But since meeting you, my head's all over the place.
I'm fascinated one minute and ready to put my fist through the
wall the next. I need to know. Are you intentionally trying to
drive me nuts or..."

"Come on in," Lily interrupted, "and I'll try to explain."

Seth blew out a breath. "I was expecting more resistance."

"Yeah, well... Listen. Are you up for a room-service breakfast?"

"That depends. Are you still ticked off at me for wanting to get
my sight back?"

"Not so much," Lily said, taking Seth's elbow. "And I want to
explain what that was all about."

Seth allowed her to pull him into the room. Lily felt goosebumps rise on his uncovered arms.

"Sorry it's so cold – the spirits zap the heat out of the room. I
think it has something to do with them using energy to recreate
their memories."

"No shit? That's wild."

"It should warm up pretty quick."

"No problem. Distract me. Describe your room."

Lily glanced around the spacious room and deduced he was talking about furniture placement, not the elegant Victorian décor. "Well, there's a messy, king-sized four-poster bed at your three o'clock," she began, "and a large dresser at your nine. Beyond that, at your twelve o'clock, is a round table with four chairs, where we can eat. It'll be great to sit there with a living person for a change."

Seth smirked. "What?"

"Never mind. You can wait for me over there or turn to your six and stand at the door of the bathroom while I get cleaned up."

"Your room lay-out's the same as mine, but I think I'll stick close to you. You know – in case more ghosts show up," he said, only half-joking.

While Lily sped through her morning routine, Seth pulled out his miniature tape recorder to share the latest additions to his collection of dumb warnings.

When he turned it on, Lily heard Seth's voice. "Yes, really… I'm writing a book. It's called 'Motorcycles are Dangerous and Other Dumb Warnings,' so I'm collecting as many of them as I can – um – dumb warnings, that is – not motorcycles."

A Tinkerbell giggle was the only response. Lily twitched, picturing a leggy blonde cheerleader. *Jealousy?* The emotion caught her by surprise.

"Okay then," chirped the energetic voice. "Like I said before – the label on my hairdryer says *'Do not use while sleeping.'* Seriously, how would that even be possible?" Just before the tape clicked off, she giggled again, and Seth laughed along with her.

Lily silently mocked the imaginary cheerleader in the bathroom mirror, tossing her long, auburn hair back with an exaggerated smile and puffed-out chest. She scowled and began vigorously brushing her teeth.

The next voice on the tape belonged to an elderly man. "Me and the wife eat TV dinners," he said, with a strong southern accent.

"And I swear to Jesus, one of them had a warnin' that we should heat it up before eatin' it." He chuffed. "I reckon you'd have to be some kind of serious stupid to try eatin' frozen fried chicken and mashed taters."

A female voice chimed in with the same accent. "That's true... that warnin' was on one of them dinners I got down at the Piggly Wiggly," she said. "But the dumbest one I ever saw was on a frozen cake I was fixin' to thaw out. I turned it over to see how long it would take, and there was this big old warnin', *'Do not turn cake box upside down.'* Now I'm no genius or nothin', but I figure a warnin' like that should be on the top side of the box – don't ya think?"

Lily laughed, the sound muffled by a mouthful of toothpaste. She washed her face and ran a brush through her hair as the taped recordings continued.

"I was giving my son some children's cough medicine," crackled another woman's voice, "and next to the recommended dosages, was the warning, *'Do not drive car or operate heavy machinery.'* Well, I told my six-year-old that taking my BMW out for a spin was a 'no-no', with or without cough medicine!"

Lily smiled as she slipped on a light, long-sleeved tee shirt and a long, gauzy skirt that covered her brace and orthopedic shoe.

Another woman's voice said, "A can of peanuts I bought had a warning printed in big, bold letters, right on the front label. It said, 'Warning – contains nuts.' I was all like – seriously?"

Seth shut off the tape player. "I think that's all the new ones I collected during the last couple of days," he said. "I'll have enough to finish my book pretty soon. If my surgery's a success, I'm going to put it all together while I'm at my folk's farm recuperating." Realizing he had accidentally broached the very topic of their fight, Seth shook his head. "I'm sorry..."

"Don't be," Lily replied. "Listen, I'm finished in here. Let's sit at the table. We can order breakfast and then talk about the elephant in the room."

Seth managed a weak smile and stepped aside. "Lead the way."

Once Seth was seated, Lily busied herself, placing their breakfast order and making coffee in the two-cup pot on the dresser.

By the time she sat down, the silence between them was deafening.

"Thanks for the coffee." Seth said. "Now, let's talk elephants."

"They're not just scars," Lily blurted. "It's Dylan's skin."

Chapter Sixty

Seth cocked his head to one side. "Excuse me?"

Lily took a deep breath. "I told you I flipped out when I learned about Dylan, remember?"

"Yeah." Seth nodded, his eyebrows knit with confusion.

"Well, a few days after that, a therapist was working on debriding the burns on my forearms, which is *unbelievably* painful. In some misguided attempt to console me, she started talking about how amazing it was that my body hadn't rejected the full-thickness skin grafts, since they hadn't come from my own body." Lily lifted her coffee cup and stared into the dark liquid for a moment before setting it back down without taking a drink. "Until then, I hadn't thought about where the ugly grafts had come from. I don't know why – I just didn't. Anyway, the therapist said she was convinced the transplants were thriving because Dylan loved me so much. The imbecile actually believed it would comfort me to know a part of my son was still with me."

Seth gasped. "Jesus. What did you do?"

In her mind's eye, Lily saw the scene unfolding in slow motion. The instant the meaning of the words sank in – that skin had been sliced from Dylan's body and attached to her own, she had begun screaming.

"I don't remember much after that. Scott said it took two orderlies and enough sedatives to knock out a bull elephant, to calm me down. When I finally woke up, my upper arms were tied

338

to the bedrails and a different therapist was doing the debriding." Lily hesitated, pressing her lips together. "Anyway, like I said, they aren't just scars."

"Holy shit, Lily – I don't know what to say. I mean, I can't imagine how awful that must have been."

"Yeah, well..." She pulled up her right sleeve and ran her fingers lightly over the red, puckered skin of her forearm. "They tell me the original skin grafts were either absorbed by my body or sloughed off as new skin grew, but I still think of it as Dylan's skin. Until yesterday, that thought kept me motivated to prove that mistakes the paramedics and doctors made were the real cause of his death." She pushed her sleeve down and picked up her mug.

"What changed yesterday?"

"I found out I was wrong." Lily took a sip of coffee to moisten her mouth before continuing. "In the police report, accident investigators speculated one of the falling logs smashed-in the rear window, killing Dylan."

"You thought the investigators were wrong?"

"I was positive they were," Lily said. "I clearly remembered Dylan waking me up after the accident. He shouted that we were in danger and had to get out of the car." Lily sniffed to stifle a sob. "But yesterday, an independent review of his medical records confirmed he was brain-dead immediately after the impact." She shook her head. "Maybe I imagined it... maybe it was his spirit, trying to save me – I just don't know anymore."

She didn't bother to wipe her silent tears. "The real irony is that I pulled Dylan's body from a burning car just so doctors could cut it into pieces. It was all for nothing."

Seth reached out to comfort Lily. When his hand touched her wet cheek, he slid from his chair onto his knees in front of her. He pulled her close and began rocking her like a child as she sobbed, her scarred arms pressed between their two bodies.

"Lily," he ventured, when her tears were finally spent, "I know losing Dylan broke your heart, but those scars are badges of honor. I mean, they're proof that you loved your son so much; you were willing to reach through fire to try to save his life."

She took halting breaths, as Seth continued to rock her back and forth, speaking gently into her ear.

"Because you pulled Dylan out of that car, your husband got to say goodbye to him – and a lot of other mothers did *not* have to say goodbye to their children that day."

He paused to let his words sink-in. "You need to stop thinking of death when you look at those scars and start thinking of life, Lily. Think of all the lives that were saved that might otherwise have been sacrificed if you hadn't pulled Dylan out of that fire."

Lily relaxed against Seth, thinking about everything he said as her breathing returning to normal.

"Room service!" a loud voice barked from the hallway.

An accompanying knock on the door shattered the tender moment. Lily bolted upright and dabbed her eyes to erase the evidence of her tears while Seth edged back into his chair.

"I'll be right there," Lily called, hoping her voice sounded steady.

She opened the door and directed the short Hispanic waiter to set the breakfast tray on the table. He lifted and replaced the various metal warming covers to confirm their order had been accurately filled and then, noticing Seth's white cane, he removed the plastic wrap from his water goblet.

"That's okay," Lily said, managing a smile. "I'll take care of all that." She signed the bill and saw him out; certain he had no idea that his arrival had been such an unwelcome interruption.

"Are you hungry?" Seth asked.

"Not particularly. It's too early."

"Okay, then – let's wait and eat after I show you what I do for a living." He stood and felt for his glass of water, then walked over to her bed. His confident strides reminded her that their hotel rooms had the same floor plan.

"I know what reflexology is... sort of," Lily said. "I don't need a foot massage."

"Be quiet and come over here," Seth directed. He placed the glass of water on the nightstand and then patted his hands on her mattress until he found a rumpled mountain of soft pillows near

.

the headboard. He dragged five of the six pillows to the middle of the mattress, forming a rectangle with its opening at the side of the bed, and dropped the last pillow on the floor. Next, he felt for the comforter and pulled it close.

He patted the mattress between the pillows. "Sit here," he commanded.

Something about Seth's tone told Lily that additional protests would be in vain, so she obliged. Seth dropped to the floor, put the pillow on his lap, and felt for Lily's legs. When his fingers encountered her long skirt, he lifted it and tucked it modestly just above her knees.

"Try to relax, Lily."

He slid his hands over her brace, trying to figure out how to release it. As Lily reached down to help him open the Velcro fasteners, a wave of shyness washed over her, reminding her of the night her teenaged-self helped an inexperienced boyfriend open her bra.

"Lay back between the pillows," Seth instructed. "Rest your head on the one at the top and your arms on the ones at your sides. Then cover your upper body with the comforter."

While Lily was busy making herself comfortable inside the pillow cocoon, Seth removed her socks and shoes and laid her bare feet on the pillow in his lap. Next, he pulled his cell phone and a miniature bottle of oil from small pouches on his belt and pressed a few buttons on the phone. When meditation music began to play, he set it aside and rubbed oil on each of her feet.

Lily relaxed as he gently massaged the warm oil between her toes and over her heels.

"Stress and toxins block the energy flow throughout your body," Seth explained in a soft voice. "I'm going to massage pressure points on your feet to work out those kinks. Most of this will feel great, but when I'm working to free a blocked point, it might feel like I'm pinching you."

"If you pinch me, I might kick you."

Seth chuckled. "Trust me. Once your energy is unblocked, your whole body will function better and you'll feel great."

"Yeah, right," Lily said. "No offense, but I don't understand how rubbing my feet will fix my body."

"When you take an aspirin for a headache, do you care how it works or are you just happy that it does?"

"Actually, I've always wondered how that works, too."

Seth sighed. "When you swallow an aspirin, it's absorbed by your bloodstream, which carries it to almost every cell in your body. Damaged cells create enzymes that send pain message chemicals to your brain. Aspirin sticks to those enzymes and stops them from producing the pain message chemicals for a while, while other stuff in your bloodstream works to repair or replace the damaged cells before the pain comes back. Think of reflexology as a means of improving the efficiency of your bloodstream by clearing out obstructions. Does that make sense to you?"

"I think so."

Seth carefully massaged each of Lily's toes; first on her right foot, then her left. She closed her eyes and occasionally moaned with pleasure.

"Specific pressure points on your feet correspond to organs in your body," Seth said, his voice almost hypnotic. "Most of the points on your toes and the insides of your feet are mirrored, while those on the outside of your feet are singular. For instance, toes on both of your feet correspond to your sinuses. They're clear, so I doubt you suffer from hay fever."

"No, I don't – but maybe you should keep massaging them for a while, just to be sure," Lily kidded.

For the next few minutes, Seth focused on Lily's right foot. Other than the peaceful spa music, the room was silent until Seth pressed on a pressure point that made Lily jump.

"Liver," he said, as he continued to rub on the tender spot. "Improving the flow of energy here will increase your body's ability to rid itself of waste."

"If you say so." Lily winced. "But I'm suddenly more concerned about an attack of hay-fever. Maybe you should rub my toes some more."

"Wimp."

Seth worked his way down to her heel and then massaged Lily's calf, taking care not to cause additional pain to the damaged section of her leg. When he finished, he laid her right foot gently on the pillow in his lap and picked up her left foot.

When she jerked, Seth nodded. "That's the duplicate point for your liver."

"If you cleared my liver blockage when you were working on my other foot, why does it still hurt?"

"Sorry, but toxins collect at pressure points on both feet," Seth explained.

When he began massaging the area around the ball of her left foot, Lily jumped again.

"This pressure point is for your heart," Seth said.

"I'll bet that's super-blocked," Lily replied with a choke in her voice.

Seth cocked his head. "Unfortunately, reflexology only works on your body, not your emotions."

"Too bad."

"I think that's enough for one day – except for this... "

Seth rubbed her toes, eliciting a grateful moan from Lily. Then he slid out from under the pillow on his lap, stood, and offered his hand to her, gently pulling her into a sitting position. He held out the glass of water from the nightstand. "Drink. Water will help flush away the toxins I dislodged."

Lily gulped the water, enjoying the cool sensation. "I'm sorry for falling apart earlier," she said.

"You don't have anything to apologize for." Seth tossed the pillows toward the head of the bed and then sat down next to her. "You're entitled to be emotional... you're losing your grandmother and confronting painful aspects of your past," he said, "and as if that's not enough, you're being haunted, for God's sake!"

"Yes, but on the bright side, a handsome man came to my hotel room to rub my feet," she teased.

Seth's lips hinted a smile as he slid an arm around her. "I have to hand it to you – you're pretty good at directing the conversation away from subjects you don't want to discuss." He placed his free hand against her cheek and pressed her head against his shoulder.

For an instant, Lily thought about pulling back. But Seth's broad chest, lightly scented with Obsession cologne, proved too enticing. She tilted her face up and brushed her lips against his chin—barely touching him with a light kiss.

It was all the encouragement Seth needed.

Chapter Sixty One

Seth proved amazingly agile and tender as he lifted Lily to the middle of the bed, taking care not to twist her injured leg. Once they were lying facing one another, Seth rested his head on his folded arm, while the fingers of his other hand skimmed back and forth along the curve of her hip.

Lily stared at him as lust, curiosity, guilt and apprehension challenged one another for possession of her mind and emotions. His touch felt incredible and his scent was intoxicating. Finally, she leaned forward to taste another kiss.

Seth responded with obvious desire, but when she broke away mid-kiss, he let her go and waited patiently for her to make the next move. Lily repeated her advance and retreat several times, until Seth's message was clear – if she wanted to stop at any point, he would comply – but he was also willing to take her as far as she wanted to go.

Each kiss left her feeling less inhibited than the one before until at last, her conscience was blissfully quiet. With thoughts of her tragic past and murky future subdued, Lily focused on the delicious, tingling sensations erupting over her skin wherever he touched and melted into the next kiss.

She slid her hands down Seth's chest to his waist and pulled his black tee-shirt up, revealing a portion of his tanned torso. "Take it off," she whispered.

Seth sat up, crossed his arms over his abdomen, grabbed both

sides of his shirt and pulled it over his head in one, smooth motion. He tossed it to the floor and then lay back down, locking his
fingers behind his head – a silent invitation for her to explore his
half-naked body at her leisure.

Lily's breath caught as her eyes drifted over him. He still wore
his small, round, black-lensed glasses and she made no attempt
to remove them. They served as a reminder that Seth couldn't see
her, adding a layer of privacy to this intimate encounter. She
traced the bridge of his narrow nose with her forefinger, letting it
drop off the tip to his smooth upper lip. She smiled when he
licked her finger with the tip of his tongue, but continued sliding
her finger down, over his full, lower lip and into the cleft at the
center of his square, clean-shaven chin.

She traced the outline of his Adam's apple into the gully of his
neck, where she could feel his strong heart beating. The tendons
on either side of his neck were stretched taut and his breathing
was ragged with anticipation. At his breastbone, she fanned out
her fingers, letting them dance over his well-defined pectoral
muscles, circling each nipple as she marveled over his tanned
chest.

Perhaps because Scott's patch of unruly, black hair was such a
sharp contrast to Seth's bare chest, her husband's image popped
into Lily's mind. She suffered a momentary pang of remorse, but
it subsided as she traced the muscle contours of Seth's six-pack
abs. Her eyes continued the journey down, following the trail of
dark, curly, blond hair that began just under his navel and disappeared into his low-riding jeans. She considered opening his belt
to free the hard bulge trapped inside, but held back.

"You. Are. Gorgeous," she whispered.

"So are you," he replied in a gravelly voice.

Lily started to protest that he had no way of knowing that, but
bit her tongue. Instead, she sat up and tugged her long-sleeved
blouse over her head. She flipped it onto the floor, ignoring her
scarred forearms, and retrieved the small, open bottle of oil Seth
had left on the nightstand. She sprinkled droplets over his chest
and abdomen, enjoying the way his body jerked when cool oil

landed on a particularly sensitive spot. Finally, she smoothed the beads of oil into an even coat and lowered her torso to rest against him.

When he felt her skin touch his, Seth moaned and licked his lips. He encircled her with his strong arms and caressed her back. His practiced hands made child's play of unhooking her bra, but then he paused with his fingers on her shoulder straps, waiting for her to make the next move. Lily lifted up just enough to allow him to slide the straps off and pull the lace barrier from between them. She watched him fling the garment to the floor before pancaking her naked breasts against his chest.

"Holy shit," he mumbled, as she slid her upper body in small circles over his oiled chest. "That feels incredible."

A small sigh escaped Lily's lips as Seth's nimble fingers explored the sides of her breasts and wandered over her naked shoulders and back. Her flexed instep pressed against the mattress, putting additional pressure on her injured leg, but she ignored it.

When she slid her hips over his, Seth cupped his hands under her bottom and pulled her tight against his erection, causing sharp pains to shoot up Lily's leg. She flinched and stifled a groan.

"What's wrong?" Seth asked, releasing his grip on her.

"I don't want to stop," she whimpered. "It's just that..."

Seth smacked his palm against his forehead. "It's just that your leg hurts like a son-of-a-bitch when you lay on your stomach. I'm sorry... I should have realized..." He gently rolled her onto her back and stood beside the bed.

Even though her leg felt better in this position, Lily flushed at the reminder of her unsexy, crippled status. She worried Seth was about to make an excuse to leave, but instead, he unsnapped a small, square pouch on his belt and removed a condom.

Mortification was instantly replaced with anticipation. "Holy cow," she managed to squeak, "That's quite the utility belt you've got there, Batman."

Seth chuckled. "Yeah, a buddy of mine made this belt for me. It's handy – and a lot cooler than a fanny-pack." He clasped the condom package between his teeth and kicked off his sandals. Then he unbuckled his belt and dropped his jeans, revealing a pair of sexy, black, boxer briefs. When he pulled the elastic waistband of his underwear down to tuck the condom out of the way until he needed it, he exposed a tan line so precise that it looked like someone had drawn a line around his waist, with bronzed skin on one side and marble white skin on the other.

Amused by the stark color difference, Lily was unable to suppress a giggle.

Seth tilted his head to the side, confused. "You know, that's not exactly the sound a guy wants to hear when he gets naked in front of a woman."

"There's nothing wrong," Lily assured him. "You look amazing. Your tan line just caught me off-guard, that's all. You know your upper body is tanned, but you're snow-white down to your thighs, right?" She patted the bed loudly enough for him to hear. "I'm sorry for laughing. Please come back."

Seth sat on the side of the bed, but hung his head. "I forgot all about tan lines," he said in a low voice.

"Don't worry about it. I don't have any tan whatsoever. My whole body is lighter than your whitest parts."

"It's not the tan line that bothers me. It's that I'm forgetting colors. I can remember what most things look like – you know, the size and shapes of stuff – but it's getting really hard to remember what things look like in color... even the stuff I've seen hundreds of times – like the mountains. I knew it was getting harder for me to imagine the colors of new stuff, but when you just mentioned tan lines, I realized that I'm starting to visualize everything in black and white." He paused. "Damn, I miss color."

Lily took a deep breath. She understood perfectly. Lately, every time she dreamed of Dylan, his face was imbedded in the bodies of strangers, making it difficult to remember what he really looked like. She took Seth's hand. "The shirt I was wearing has dark pink swirls on a cream-colored background. When I pulled it off and dropped it on the floor, it landed in a small, rounded heap, so it kind of looks like a bowl of raspberry sherbet and vanilla ice cream on the floor."

Seth turned his gaze to the floor, trying to picture the blouse as Lily described it. "Cool," he said. "Tell me more."

"Okay." She licked her lips. "The bra you exhibited such skill in removing, is shiny white satin, with narrow, pink lace trim at the top of each cup, and a tiny pink rosebud in between them. It landed right-side-up on top of your black tee-shirt, and the contrast reminds me of a painting on black velvet."

Seth nodded; a smile teasing the corners of his mouth.

"The only other articles of clothing I have on are a cream-colored gauze skirt with an elastic waist and plain white panties," Lily said. "If I would have known *this* was going to happen, I would have worn a matching bra and panty set, but... hey, now that I think about it, how is it that your clothes always match?"

"Easy. Almost everything I own is black, other than my jeans. But that's boring. Let's talk more about your colors." He slid his hand over Lily until his fingers touched her breast. "What about these?"

Lily sucked in her breath and eyed her body nervously. "My nipples?" She hesitated. "I guess they're pinkish-brown at the base and get pinker toward the tips."

"Keep going," Seth said, sliding his hand down over her belly.

"I already told you my skin is chalk-white – or alabaster, if you want to make it sound better. I have a few freckles on my cheeks, throat and shoulders, and if you look close, you can see tiny blue veins all over the place." She considered describing the bright pink scars on her arms, but decided against it. "You know my hair is dark auburn and," she paused. "Well, let's just say all the hair on my body is roughly the same color."

"Oh my God," Seth said, licking his lips. "A natural red-head, huh?" He lay down next to her and rained small kisses along her neck and chin until he found her mouth.

As soon as his tongue snaked with hers, Lily's passion reignited. She barely breathed as he cupped her breasts and lowered his head down to lick first one nipple and then the other. "Pink," he whispered to each one.

The touch of his lips was soft and his movements were slow and sensual. He continued to shower kisses on her skin, leisurely working his way down her belly, while whispering the word "alabaster," over and over again.

Seth's gentle foreplay was opposite from Scott's passionate style of love-making. The image of her husband's naked body popped into Lily's mind again, tempting her to compare the two men. Scott was handsome and well-proportioned, but his muscles weren't as defined as Seth's. But Scott's dark brown facial hair did give him a sexy five o'clock shadow...

A wave of guilt washed over her. *"What are you doing here? You're married!"*

Then she remembered the last time she called her husband, a woman had answered his phone and said he was in the shower. She banished him from her thoughts and focused on Seth, who was tugging at her skirt. She rolled onto one hip and then the other, letting him pull it off, along with her panties.

"Promise you'll tell me if any of this hurts," he implored, carefully sliding her thighs apart.

"Promise," she breathed.

He touched her as if she were made of tissue paper, gently parting her hair and sliding his fingers over the soft, wet flesh hidden beneath. "Tell me these colors," he said.

Lily gasped, grateful Seth couldn't see her face flush scarlet with embarrassment as she contemplated how to best describe her nether-region.

Seth blew warm air over her nub, reminding her that he was waiting for an answer.

She took a shaky breath. "I think it's sort of like the end of a sunset," she murmured. "You know – light pink with bluish-tinges at the outer edges, becoming darker shades of pink as you move inward, leading to a small circle of red at the center, and then disappearing into darkness."

"I like that image," he said. He lowered his head and began exploring her with his tongue.

Lost in a sea of sensations, Lily couldn't think or speak. She was torn between her desire to reach climax, and wanting to relish the tantalizing tension a little while longer.

Seth pulled his mouth back a few inches and rubbed her hyper-sensitized nub with the wetted tip of his forefinger as she squirmed with sexual anticipation. Then suddenly, he pinched it between his thumb and forefinger and licked it with the tip of his tongue, back and forth, as fast as he could.

Lily came so hard that she saw stars as her body convulsed; a mixture of erotic shocks and waves of pleasure.

Seth pressed two fingers firmly against her mound as she continued to twitch. "Great pulse," he noted, obviously pleased with his handiwork. He kissed his way back up her body to her breasts, where he lingered.

As her breathing began to slow, Lily's curiosity was piqued. "What did you mean, 'great pulse'?" she asked.

Seth scattered kisses as he moved up her throat, as if using his lips to search out the landmarks that would lead him back to her mouth. He gave her a light kiss on her lips before answering. "It's blind man's trick. Women can fake the sounds of an orgasm, but they can't fake the throbbing pulse of a real orgasm. Yours was great."

"I don't know about that, but it felt amazing." As Lily regained her senses, she felt Seth's long, hard penis pressed against her thigh. She slid her hand to the elastic waistband of his underwear, pulled it back and let it snap. "I think it's time to lose these," she said.

Seth didn't need further encouragement. He peeled off his last article of clothing, tore open the condom, and rolled it on with practiced ease.

Lily was suddenly anxious. *"Scott fits into my body perfectly. What if Seth doesn't? Maybe I should stop him. Wait. What if it's better?"*

Again, Seth sensed her unease. "If you don't want to do this, Lily – just say so."

"I do," she said, bringing her internal debate to an end. "It's just that this is the first time..." Lily bit her lip. *"If I tell him I haven't had sex with anyone but Scott in the last fifteen years, he might want to stop..."*

"Since your accident?" Seth asked, attempting to finish her thought for her.

"Uh... yeah," Lily lied.

He lay down beside her and stroked her inner thighs. As the last of her misgivings gave way to lust, Lily opened her legs for him. Seth eased first one, and then two of his fingers into her, moving them slowly until she twisted and pushed against his hand, wanting more. Finally, she reached down for his penis and gently tugged it toward her, craving an end to this exquisite torture.

Seth drew a sharp breath. Following her lead, he removed his fingers and positioned himself between her legs. But instead of plunging into her depths as she expected him to do, he entered her body slowly – inch by inch – until he had pressed himself into her as deep as her body would allow. Then he reversed the motion, pulling back until only the tip of his penis remained inside of her.

Unbidden, another comparison popped into Lily's mind. *"Scott did this sometimes. He'll go slow a few seconds and then speed up until he's banging me like a drum."* With growing confidence in her sexual prowess, she circled her hips, tightening her pelvic muscles as Seth reentered her depths – determined to enjoy the erotic sensation of slow sex while it lasted.

But instead of speeding-up his tempo, Seth continued to drive her wild with unhurried, purposeful movements until all at once, she tightened and a strangled cry escaped her lips. She bucked against him, as her body convulsed for the second time.

Without pulling out, Seth caught her hand and pressed her fingers between them, against the base of her clitoris. She felt it immediately – her own, wildly beating pulse. It only lasted a few seconds. As the aftershocks of her climax subsided, the pulse point disappeared.

Lily reached around to cup Seth's tight butt and pushed against him, burying his full length in her core. Seth moaned and started moving again. His movements were only slightly faster than before, but now, he buried himself deep inside her body with every stroke. Suddenly, he plunged into her, groaning with his final spasms of release. When he collapsed onto her, Lily felt a shiver run through him. She held him tight until his panting breaths began to slow.

"Sorry," he said, lifting the weight of his chest off hers. "I was hoping to hold out a little longer."

"Oh my God, Seth – what happened to your Spidy-senses?" she teased. "I'm completely satisfied."

He smiled and rolled over to her left side, scooting down far enough to rest his head against her breast. Lily relaxed, her fingers playing with his short, blond hair, enjoying the perfect moment.

Then her stomach growled.

Chapter Sixty Two

Seth chuckled. "I guess you're ready for that breakfast now," he said, already getting to his feet.

Lily watched as Seth felt his way to the table and picked up their room-service breakfast tray. She coached him, guiding his movements, until the tray was nestled in the center of the bed, between them. Even though the food had grown cold, they attacked it as though they hadn't eaten for days.

"Lily," Seth asked between bites, "have you thought about what you're going to do with your life after you settle your grandmother's affairs?"

"Not really... other than getting back to writing my blog."

"Yeah, but you can write anywhere," he said, popping a bite of a bagel into his mouth. A sly smile spread over his face. "Just think about how perfect life could be if you took to the road with me. We could sign-up for bike rides and events all over the country. Get to know great people. See amazing sights. And at the end of the ride each day, you could write your blog while I do my reflexology thing. Then we could enjoy the night – partying with the locals or just spending time together."

Lily tried to imagine what it would be like to live in Seth's world. She imagined herself perched on the back of a Harley, wearing a black leather jacket, clinging to Seth as though they were a single being. It was...

"Ridiculous," she said out loud.

Seth cocked his head to the side. "Why? Seriously – wouldn't you rather put this whole shit-storm behind you, instead of torturing yourself over a car accident for the rest of your life?"

The temporarily forgotten conversation with Mary Justus thundered back into Lily's thoughts. Tears welled in her eyes. "You don't understand. All this time I've been blaming doctors for Dylan's death – blaming Scott for giving them permission to kill our son... but last night, I learned he died at the scene of the accident. That means his death was my fault."

"It wasn't your fault. It was an accident." Seth pushed the breakfast tray to the foot of the bed and moved closer, pawing the air until his fingertips brushed her arm. He wrapped his arms around her. "There isn't anything you could have done to change the events of that night, Lily. I mean, your car was knocked from the road by an avalanche of trees, for God's sake."

"I could have done something differently..." she protested, her voice cracking.

"Like what? What exactly could you have done?" Seth demanded.

"I could have said 'to hell with the budget, let's fly to Florida' or 'let's stop for the night at a hotel.'" She burst into tears. "I shouldn't have volunteered to drive through the night."

"Nothing is gained by dwelling on *what ifs*, Lily. And besides, who's to say changing your plans would have kept Dylan alive? I mean, what if you *had* decided to fly and your plane crashed? What if you stopped at a hotel for the night and there was a fire? If he died like that, you'd probably beat yourself up for *not* driving through the night, certain *that* decision would have kept him safe."

Seth paused and tightened his arms around her. "You lost your son in a terrible accident, Lily. It's horrible and it's heartbreaking, but there's nothing you or anyone else could have done to prevent it. Period."

Lily wiped her cheeks, emotionally exhausted.

Seth kissed her hair. "You told me what caused the crash and you told me what happened afterward – but can you remember what was happening right *before* the accident?"

Lily shrugged her shoulders against him and closed her raw eyes. "I was driving and then suddenly I heard all these crashing sounds..."

"Stop. Go back a little further than that. You were driving. Was the radio on?"

Lily shifted, trying to recall the fuzzy memory. "I think so."

"Think harder, Lily. What song was playing?"

Lily concentrated, trying to shine light on the inky black memory. Slowly, a tune began to filter its way through her consciousness, bringing a thin smile to her lips. *'Good, good, good – good vibrations...'* "It was an old Beach Boys tune," she whispered. "I was singing..."

"Singing loudly?"

Lily pictured Scott in the reclined passenger seat, wearing no safety belt. He snored softly; his forearm flopped across his eyes. "No. Scott was sleeping, so I kept my voice down."

"Okay now, what about Dylan? What was he doing?"

Lily was startled. She had imagined many scenarios... what Dylan was thinking when he found himself in the upside-down car, surrounded with fire; what he was thinking when he realized they had given up on saving him and were going to harvest his organs. She had imagined how Dylan would have felt had the roles been reversed and he had been the one that lived. In her dreams, she often imagined him as a grown person – as a doctor – or a chef... a father... But for some reason, she never imagined what Dylan was thinking just *before* the accident.

"Can you see Dylan?" Seth prompted.

Lily squeezed her eyes shut even tighter. She took a deep breath and pictured herself glancing into the back seat. She nodded against Seth's bare chest, not wanting to shatter the precious vision with words. Dylan's head was resting comfortably against the cool window and his arms were wrapped around his favorite little pillow – the one he had slept with ever since he decided he was too old for a teddy bear. There was an angelic expression on his sleeping face – the slight smile that suggested he was enjoying a nice dream. The road was dark and the new pavement was smooth. If only she could stop time...

"Tell me, Lily."

"He was sleeping, like his father," she said, her voice cracking. "He was probably dreaming about the adventures he was going to have in Florida."

"Sounds nice," Seth replied.

Lily imagined the seconds ticking by in slow motion. When the logs crashed down around the car, the impact lifted the vehicle completely off the ground, as though she had driven over a stunt ramp. While they were in the air, one of those logs crashed into the rear passenger compartment, where Dylan slept. Maybe he had a second to dream he was flying before his brain was gone. Then again, maybe his adventurous soul didn't hit the ground with the car. Maybe it floated out of his broken body and just kept on flying. Lily pictured Dylan, floating free from the horrific scene and being drawn toward the warm, golden light of heaven, totally unconcerned with what was happening to his body in the real world beneath him.

She sniffed and let out a shuddering breath. "My son went to sleep dreaming of dolphins and woke up as an angel. He felt no pain."

Seth nodded and kissed the top of her head. "That's what I think, too. Now, do you really believe Dylan would want you to spend the rest of your life feeling guilty and miserable, or do you think he would want you to get on with your life?"

Lily opened her eyes, reluctantly letting go of the last tranquil memory of her happy family. "Dismissing guilt isn't that easy, Seth, but I'll try. And thanks. Between the foot rub, the sex and the counseling sessions, I really do feel a lot better than I have for a long time."

Seth grinned. "Good to hear. And I want you to think about my offer. If all goes according to plan with my surgery, I'll head back to my folk's farm in Idaho to recuperate and finish my book, but I should be ready to hit the road before too long, and I'd love for you to join me. I don't expect an answer today, but soon, okay?"

"I'll think about it," she said, "But right now I need to get cleaned up and head to the hospital. You're welcome to join me in the shower, but I have to warn you – I like it hot."

"Talk about your dumb warnings..."

Chapter Sixty Three

Lily and Seth had just finished getting dressed when there was a rap on the door.

"Housekeeping," Lily hissed in a whisper. "Damn it. I forgot to hang the *Do Not Disturb* sign on my door." She raised her voice and called, "Come back later, please."

"Mrs. Thorne, it's Mike from the front desk. A nurse at the hospital asked me to check on you. She's been trying to reach you."

Lily's heart dropped to her stomach with the realization that she had unplugged the desk phone when she was trying to avoid Seth's calls the night before last, and she had turned her cell off last night.

"Please, God, don't let Grams be dead," she prayed. *"Please don't let her have died alone while I was..."*

"Mrs. Thorne," Mike continued from the other side of the door, "the nurse said you should come quickly. Can we offer you a ride?"

Lily nodded; then realized he required a verbal response. "Yes. Thank you." She struggled to clear her thoughts. "I'll be right down."

She grabbed her cell phone from the nightstand and turned it on, cursing herself for shutting it off in the first place. "Come on, come on," she hissed, waiting for it to power up. "Finally!" She pressed the speed-dial for the hospital and asked for the nursing station. "This is Lilyanna Thorne, Lois Bloom's granddaughter. I understand you're trying to reach me?" She paused, listening. "Thank you. I'm on my way." She turned to Seth. "She's alive, but she had a bad night. I have to leave right now."

"Of course," Seth said. "Do you want me to go with you?"

"No, I need to go alone."

"Okay. I'll walk you to the shuttle."

"No thanks. I'll be fine. Let's part ways at the stairs, okay?"

She knew it was irrational, but she couldn't help worrying that everyone who saw them together would know they had been having sex while her precious Grams lay dying all alone.

Seth was more perceptive than she imagined. "Lily, I seriously doubt people are as judgmental as you think they are, but even if they were, who cares what strangers think?"

"I just don't need any more negative thoughts today," she said.

"All right then." Seth picked up his white cane, while Lily grabbed her purse and crutch. Together, they made their way down the steps at the end of the hall and stopped next to the narrow, old phone booths. Seth gave Lily a tight hug and a modest kiss on her cheek.

"Call me if you need to hear a friendly voice," he said. "I have a doctors' appointment this afternoon, but I'll be here most of the day."

"Thanks – I mean it." Lily hurried through the lobby and climbed into the waiting shuttle, her heart filled with worry and remorse. The short ride to the hospital felt twice as long as usual. She didn't even protest when Pete, the shuttle driver, called ahead to arrange for an attendant with a wheelchair to meet Lily at the door and rush her to Grams' room.

Her favorite nurse, Opal Sanders, was sitting with Grams when Lily arrived, quietly humming an old gospel hymn. When she spied Lily, her eyes lit up. She heaved her heavy body off the chair and patted Grams' hand tenderly – her plump, dark hand, a stark contrast to Grams' thin, pale one. "Looky-here, Miz Bloom – Lily's here. I knew you wouldn't leave without saying goodbye to her." She smiled at Lily. "She's been waiting for you."

"I'm so sorry for being late today... I was... I..." Lily sputtered, words failing her.

"Hush child. You're here now and that's all that counts," Opal said, stepping around the end of the bed to make room.

Lily gave the nurse a grateful smile, raised herself from the wheelchair, and hobbled to Grams' bedside. When she bent to kiss Grams on her cheek, tears sprang to her eyes. Her grand-mother looked far more dead than alive. Her tissue paper skin had taken on a deathly ashen pallor and appeared to be draped over her facial bones as if there was no flesh between the two. Her eyes were sunk into dark sockets. Oxygen tubes rested in her nostrils, and her mouth hung open – an empty void, surrounded by cracked lips. She wondered if Grams was upset with the hospi-tal staff for removing her dentures. She had always refused to be seen without her teeth – even by her own family.

"I'm here, Grams," she said, smoothing imaginary wrinkles from her grandmother's favorite afghan.

Lily was so intent on her grandmother's face that she scarcely noticed Opal signaling the wheelchair attendant to follow her out of the room. She glanced up in time to see the kindly nurse close the door. The action felt symbolic. "When one door closes –" she whispered.

She hoped another door would open for her grandmother, ushering her into paradise, but not just yet. She wasn't ready to say goodbye.

"I love you, Grams. I know it's time for you to go, but I can't imagine my world without you in it." Lily sat in the bedside chair and rested her head against her grandmother's frail hand, enjoy-ing the feel of Grams' fingertips against her cheek. Then, physically and emotionally exhausted from waking so early and spending the morning with Seth, she closed her eyes and let her thoughts wander.

Lily's earliest childhood memories flooded her mind in a brief, hellish collage. Although her mother loved her, she became so bent on chasing her dream of Broadway fame and fortune, that tiny Lily often suffered neglect and near the end, abuse. Just before her fifth birthday, Lily's mother dropped her off on Grams' front porch, telling Lily she would be safer there. She promised to be back in a few weeks, but she died of an accidental drug overdose three days later. For several months afterward, Lily suffered from nightmares about her mother and Roy – the drug dealer with a leather belt who was the last man in her mother's long parade of boyfriends. Back then, whenever Lily woke crying, Grams would sit by her bed and rest her hand against Lily's cheek until she fell back to sleep. Lily's heart ached with the knowledge that today would be the last time she would ever feel that symbol of loving comfort.

The fog descended moments after Lily closed her eyes, chilling the air as she floated into the mist. Almost immediately, she heard Margaret Plant's voice.

"It's harder for the living to let go than it is for the dying, because the living recognize that a noticeable presence will be missing from their lives henceforth. The departed, on the other hand – well, they usually begin a new adventure right away, so they don't look back any more than a snake shedding its skin."

The clouds parted to reveal Margaret, sitting at the familiar round table, stirring three teaspoons of sugar into a steaming cup of tea.

"Don't people want to keep living?" Lily asked.

"Not usually. When the lighted path beckons, most discard their old lives like an old coat that no longer fits. They're eager for the new coat that awaits them just beyond the light. A few do turn away from the light, preferring to hold onto their old, comfortable coat for a little while longer, and fewer still are like me – choosing to keep wearing that comfortable old coat for a long time. That's just the way it is." She blew across the surface of the hot, sweet tea and took a sip.

"For me," Margaret said, "life in this world remains interesting, and from time to time, even fascinating – as it has become with my connection to you."

Lily frowned. "Glad to hear my situation has provided entertainment for you."

Margaret ignored the sarcasm. "When we first met, I thought it would be interesting to guide the connection that had formed between you, Bobbi and Clay. I hoped that, after learning Bobbi's story – seeing the hardships she faced and all she was still able to accomplish, you'd learn to accept your loss, avail yourself of modern medicine, and finally decide to either forgive your husband or move on with another man."

Lily's eyes widened at the aloof description of her circumstances, but she said nothing.

"But my-oh-my," continued Margaret, "this connection turned out to be far more complex than I originally envisioned. Why, I never dreamed that establishing a tweening link with your grandmother would open new avenues of understanding about the spirit world."

"What could Grams teach you about the spirit realm?"

Margaret gently settled her teacup in its saucer. "Well, as you know, your grandmother and I formed a connection while we were tweening. I've never heard of that happening before. Normally, tweening is just an entertaining conversation between a spirit and someone near death – similar to a dream or fantasy. But a connection allows us to exchange actual memories, which is a horse of quite a different color."

"How so?"

"The living tend to alter their recollections of events in order to justify their actions, or to place themselves in a more influential or favorable light. However, once one becomes a spirit, memories are factual in every respect. None are forgotten, and none can be altered in any fashion. Some say absolute clarity of a spirit's memory is necessary in preparation for final judgment when one travels the lighted path... but I digress. Where was I?"

"You were telling me what you learned from Grams."

"Ah, yes." Margaret smiled as the fog enveloped Lily.

Before Lily had time to wonder what was happening, Margaret materialized next to her inside the cloud and a snippet of memory appeared on a bubble in front of them. Lily waited impatiently for the blurry image to come into focus, but when it did, her jaw dropped.

Grams was in her room at the nursing home, holding Dylan's old football phone to her ear. "I always said you could grow up to be anything you wanted," she cooed. "But I never dreamed you could be so many things all at once."

Lily was confused. *"Margaret said memories were supposed to be accurate, but Dylan died before Grams went to live in the nursing home. Maybe because she isn't a spirit yet, Grams' memories are still clouded,"* she thought.

She froze when she heard laughter. Dylan's laughter.

"I never thought of it that way, Grammy," Dylan's voice on the other end of the phone replied.

"That was Dylan's nickname for Grams." Lily struggled to make sense of the memory.

"All of them are connected, but they don't know it," Dylan continued. "One woman is a math whiz. I absorbed all of her knowledge, and suddenly, math became a piece of cake for the medical student. I'm pretty sure that guy knows I'm here, though. He tells people it's like a light switched on in his brain, but sometimes when he's alone, he talks to me. He calls me *'dude'* and he thanked me for helping him earn an early admission into medical school. And one of the moms is using what she's learning about medicine to make healthier food choices for our children... I mean, her children... no, I think I had it right the first time... they're our children now."

"I don't understand," Lily cried. "How is this possible?"

The moment she spoke, Lily dropped through the fog like a stone. She cursed herself for talking, wanting more than anything to return to the memory – to listen to Dylan's voice again, even if he was talking nonsense. She was pleasantly surprised to discover the fall didn't wake her up. Instead, she was back at the parlor table with Margaret – a much crankier Margaret.

"I explained how much concentration is required to share my memories, did I not?" Margaret snapped. "Well, it takes even more focus to show you the memories your grandmother shared with me."

"But that memory made no sense. I think Grams was hallucinating."

"Perhaps if you remained quiet, all would have become clear," Margaret replied, taking a sip of tea to calm herself. "Your grandmother's memories taught me about a new aspect of the spirit realm. I'm going to call it *'gifting.'*"

"Gifting?"

Chapter Sixty Four

"When a body dies, its tethered spirit is released from the living realm," Margaret explained. "It can choose to take the lighted path, or remain here in the spirit realm, where it can exist anywhere it went while it was alive."

Lily wrapped her cold hands around her steaming teacup, paying rapt attention.

"What I learned from your grandmother is that *gifting* – that is, giving a living piece of oneself to another living being – provides a released spirit with a remarkable third option."

"It's called organ donation," mumbled Lily, a knot growing in her stomach.

Margaret ignored the comment. "*Gifting* occurs when pieces are removed from a body *before* its spirit has been released. A spirit is attached to every part of its body, and that bond isn't broken just because the part was placed into another person. Therefore, when the spirit's tether to its own body is finally broken, it can choose to straddle the divide between the living world and the spirit realm by retaining its connection to the body part that was gifted to another.

"*Tethered? Gifting? Bonding?*" Lily grappled with the strange concepts, trying to understand.

Margaret puckered her lips thoughtfully. "Let's use my earlier analogy," she suggested. "I said a spirit could choose to shed its former life like an old coat and follow the lighted path, *or* it could step off the path and remain in the spirit realm, continuing to wear its comfortable old coat of a life. You understood that, right?"

Lily nodded.

"Well, when a spirit is connected to a body part that has been placed inside another person, the spirit could choose to share coats with that person or blend the two into one."

Margaret charged on without noticing the frown deepening on Lily's face.

"I haven't learned all there is to know about gifting yet, but I think when an individual, such as your son, gives living parts of himself to numerous people, he can opt to share *all* of their coats. Does that make sense?"

Lily fought a growing sense of unease. "Is Dylan's spirit tethered to his donated organs?"

"As long as a part of the spirit's body remains alive, the tether to the realm of the living isn't completely severed, but it wouldn't be strong enough to hold him against his will. If bonding with a recipient's spirit felt uncomfortable – like a coat that just didn't fit right, I'm certain he could sever the connection. And likewise, the recipient's own spirit could refuse to accept the connection. But if I'm right, your son has chosen to form bonds with quite a few living beings, all of whom welcome his presence. I think he moves between them, exchanging knowledge and sharing their adventures."

Lily tried to form her racing thoughts into words. "Dylan's spirit is inside all the people who received organ transplants from him?"

"Yes, I think so. You're one of those people. Don't you feel him with you sometimes?"

"I dreamed Dylan came to me in the hospital, just before I woke from my coma, but not since then. At least, not..." Lily's visions of Dylan transforming into a number of different people flashed through her mind.

"Perhaps he's too busy enjoying adventures elsewhere to spend time with you right now."

"Maybe he's not having grand adventures," Lily cried. "Did you ever think of that?"

"No, but I don't think like a living being anymore." Margaret took a sip of her tea. "Once I finally accepted that my tether to the living realm had been severed, I realized I was no longer subject to the desires and sorrows of that world. The spirit realm is fascinating – and full of adventures. Relationships are less confining and – unless I'm trying to help one of the living, time passes without consequence."

"But what if Dylan's experience has been different than yours?" Lily persisted. "What if he hates the spirit realm? Maybe he's been as miserable as I've been since he died."

"Every journey is bound to be different, but there's no reason to assume he's unhappy. After all, how long and how terribly we suffer adversities is largely up to us. Time spent mourning is better spent remembering how lucky we were to have shared love in the first place. Instead of spending our lives pining for what we've lost, we can choose to live our lives looking forward to the unknown, opening our hearts to whatever happiness might be found tucked into the folds of our future."

"That's easier said than done."

"Yes, but what's the point of living if you don't make the effort? And besides, good things can come from what was initially disguised as misfortune," said Margaret. She sipped her tea.

"For instance, I'm reminded of a time, long ago, when I journeyed to the seaside as the companion of a nervous acquaintance for a short holiday. We were both quite young and had been invited to join the festivities of her uncle's neighbor. Our five days at the seaside were to be filled with picnics, races, rides and other outdoor amusements. Unfortunately, stormy weather ruined those plans. The neighboring group cancelled its holiday, and so my associate and I were trapped inside her dreary old uncle's humble beach cottage for four solid days. We had no books, music or other persons to entertain us. We located one deck of playing cards, but the only game her uncle knew how to play was unfamiliar to us. To put an end to his complaining, we indulged him and learned to play poker. Later in life, my dear Henry and I whiled away many a pleasant evening together, playing that wonderful game – one I might never have learned to play, had rain not spoiled that holiday."

"But what good things can come from the death of a child?" Lily asked. "Dylan never got the chance to learn how to play poker... he never fell in love... or had adventures..."

A sudden tap on Grams' hospital room door plummeted Lily through the fog, landing her back in the chair by Grams' bed in a startling rush. Realizing her head still rested against Grams' fingers, she sat up.

"I'm sorry to interrupt you," said Opal, stepping into the room. "But the receptionist phoned up from the lobby with a message. I wrote it down for you."

She handed Lily a note and then bent over Lois Bloom to check her pulse. "According to the receptionist, the man who sent the message is quite handsome," she added.

Lily unfolded the note and read: *L – I don't want to intrude, but I'm here in the lobby if you need me. S –*

She felt a flush of warmth, moved by Seth's willingness to wait near her, in the event she needed comfort, without attempting to force his presence on her. She recalled his offer to travel the country on the back of his motorcycle. *"Perhaps it is time to move-on – to start living life looking forward, with no ties to my past."*

"There, now, Miz Bloom," Opal said, bringing an end to Lily's musings. "You're doing just fine." She patted the old woman's hand and turned her attention back to Lily. "Would you like to send a return message to the man in the lobby?"

"How is Grams doing? I mean... How long do you think...?"

"There's no way of knowing exactly when the Lord will call her home, but she seems to have rallied a bit since last night," Opal said. "That happens more often than not. Some folks call it a brain surge or a last spark. I like to think she's talking with angels, preparing for her journey to Heaven. How long it lasts is anyone's guess. Sometimes it's only a few hours, other times it lasts a day or more."

Lily thought about Margaret and wondered if she was tweening with Grams at this very moment. She considered telling Opal about the spirits, but decided against it. "Do you think there's time for me to go down to the lobby for a few minutes?"

"I think so. I'll send a pager downstairs with you, so if there's a change, we can buzz you. I'll go get one."

Lily was surprised at how swiftly and gracefully the big woman moved. She looked at her own injured leg and considered Margaret's admonition to avail herself of modern medicine. She had to admit, the idea was becoming more palatable, especially since she was considering spending a lot of time on a motorcycle.

Opal returned, holding what looked like a restaurant pager in her hand. "This slow flashing blue light tells you the pager's working. If there's any change in your grandmother's condition, we'll send a signal and the pager will start vibrating and a row of blue lights will start flashing all around the edges."

When a wheelchair escort appeared in the door, Lily glanced at Grams, uncertain.

"Everything will be fine," Opal assured her, pressing the pager into her hand. "Remember? I have a sense about these things."

Lily nodded and stood, pausing another moment at Grams bedside. She pressed the woman's withered hand to her cheek and then kissed it. "I'll be right back, Grams. I promise."

Lily was grateful the escort didn't try to start a conversation. As he wheeled her to the elevator, she sank into her thoughts. *"Dylan might be nearby. Grams might not have been hallucinating when she claimed he talked to her. I should tell Scott..."* When they reached the lobby, she shook her head, dismayed that her automatic impulse was to talk matters over with her husband.

She glanced around the lobby, searching for Seth, confident he would be easy to spot and not at all certain what she would say to him. Suddenly, her jaw dropped. As if walking straight out of her imagination, Scott was crossing the expanse, headed directly toward her.

Chapter Sixty Five

Lily stood up and let Scott wrap her in his arms without speaking. The long and comforting embrace reminded her how many memories they shared, both good and bad. For more than a minute they simply clung to one another, each feeding off the tender mercy of the other.

Then Lily remembered Seth's note. She pulled back and nonchalantly swiveled her head to search the room for him, uncomfortable about having to introduce the two men.

"I'm glad you came down, Lily," Scott said, nervously raking his fingers through his unruly black hair.

His voice was as smooth as milk chocolate, but he looked exhausted. His five o'clock shadow was becoming a full-fledged beard, and his brown eyes bore the tell-tale dark circles of sleeplessness.

"I'm serious about not wanting to intrude, but when the hospital called to say Grams was fading and they were having trouble reaching you, I couldn't stop myself from grabbing the first flight down. You shouldn't have to go through this alone, but if you want me to leave..." his voice trailed off.

Lily closed her eyes and she let out an audible sigh of relief. *"Stupid, stupid girl,"* she chided, *"Seth and Scott's names both start with the letter 'S'. The message was from Scott."*

With a mix of awkwardness and jealousy, Lily scanned the lobby again – this time looking for the woman who answered Scott's phone a few days before. "You came alone?" she asked, sounding more judgmental than she intended.

"Alone." Scott gazed at the floor. "I... she... it was over before it even got started, Lily. I'm sorry. I was pissed and lonely..."

"Don't forget how you and Seth spent the morning," Lily's conscience reminded her. Instantly contrite, she shook her head. "You have nothing to be sorry for, Scott. We need to talk this out, but not right now."

"Oh... God... of course not..." he stammered. "Is Grams still – hanging on?"

"Yeah. She rallied this morning, but they don't expect it to last long. I need to get back up there."

"I understand, but wait. I brought you something," he said. He knelt down and unzipped a black flight bag.

When he got to his feet, Lily stared openmouthed at Dylan's urn, resting in his big hands.

"I thought you might like to have him with you when it came time to say goodbye to Grams," he explained. "But if not, I can just keep him with me."

Lily's eyes brimmed with tears. "You thought right," she whispered. She took the small urn and clutched it to her breast. "Thank you."

The attendant helped her back into the wheelchair. "Do you want to say goodbye to Grams?" she asked, hoping he wouldn't. She didn't want to spend Grams' last moments making small talk, and she definitely didn't want to discuss infidelity or the spirit realm.

"If it's all the same to you, I'd rather remember her as she was the last time I saw her," he said.

Lily nodded, relieved. "That's probably best. They took her dentures."

Scott gave her a half-smile. "I'm surprised Grams didn't wake up to demand them back."

"Me too," Lily agreed.

"I can either wait here, or check into the hotel and come back the minute you call." He frowned. "That is, if your phone's working again."

"My phone is fine – I accidentally shut it off," she lied. "Go to the hotel. You look like you could use a nap. I'll call when it's over."

He bent down and kissed her cheek, pausing to breathe in her scent before pulling away.

When the attendant turned the chair around and backed into the elevator, Lily locked eyes with Scott until the doors closed, unable to ignore the butterflies in her stomach. She turned her gaze to the small, cobalt-blue urn, recalling the hallucination she experienced at the hospital, just after the accident – the one in which Dylan promised to stay away from the light – promised to wait for her. *"Is it possible that really happened? Has Dylan's spirit been here all this time?"*

The bell of the elevator brought Lily out of her reverie. In a fluid series of movements, the attendant rolled her to Grams' door, pressed down on the door latch with his elbow, bumped the door open with his backside, and pulled the chair into the room, all before Opal even had time to push herself up out of her chair.

"There, now – didn't I tell you she wasn't ready to go just yet?" As Opal lifted Grams' hand to check her pulse, the heart monitor slipped off her finger, triggering an alarm. Opal slid the monitor back into place and reset the machine to stop the beeping. "I'm sorry about that, Miz Bloom," she cooed, as if the comatose woman had been disturbed by the noise. "Lily, I was hoping you'd come back with a handsome visitor in tow, but..."

Lily gave Opal a good-natured wag of her finger and then hobbled to the window. She placed Dylan's urn on the sill, next to his football phone.

Opal raised her eyebrows, recognizing the urn for what it was. "I see you brought someone else instead."

"It's my son," Lily explained. "He and Grams were very close. My visitor thought his presence might comfort Grams as she crosses over."

"Okay then," Opal said, "we'll get out of here and give you some privacy. Press the call button if you need anything."

Lily slipped into the bedside chair as the door closed. "Grams, Dylan is here," she whispered. Resting her cheek against her grandmother's hand as if she never left, Lily closed her eyes and a moment later, drifted into the clouds with a sense of anticipation – certain she was about see her son again.

When the clouds parted to reveal Bobbi, her niece, and the blacksmith gathered around Bobbi's kitchen table, Lily felt a sting of disappointment. She tried to focus on the sketch the group was discussing.

"This modification," Rebecca said, "should help you strengthen your leg even more, Aunt Bobbi."

"This is a nifty idea," Jack said, studying the image. "Adding weights would work her muscles harder, no doubt. And I could fix it so they wouldn't fall off the ends... but what does Doc Farthing think about this new exercise contraption of yours?"

"He doesn't know about it," Bobbi admitted. "But I've discussed it with his wife, Anna. She's a good nurse and she said that as long as Aunt Bobbi promises to stop if the exercises cause her pain, she'll observe and testify that my reconstruction experiment is on the level." Rebecca replied.

"Are you sure you want to give this a go?" Jack asked Bobbi.

"I don't exactly have much to lose," she replied. "I know my dancing days are over, but if there's a chance I can get this leg walking again, then I'm game to try."

"Okay then, I'll go make the changes. Hopefully, we'll be able to give it a whirl this evening." He turned to Rebecca. "That is, if I'm still invited for a chicken dinner tonight."

"Are you planning to make an honest woman out of my niece anytime soon?" Bobbi teased. "She already cooks you supper more often than not."

"I wish I could," said Jack, glancing at Rebecca before casting his eyes to his boots. "But people don't have much use for a blacksmith these days, and I refuse to walk her down the middle aisle until I'm sure I can provide for her."

"Don't worry, Aunt Bobbi," Rebecca said. "I suspect Jack will be back in the berries before long."

"He's lucky to have an intelligent ally like you to in his corner," Bobbi observed.

Chapter Sixty Six

The fog surrounded Lily and tumbled her through its clouds for only a moment before it parted again.

"That's enough for today," said a woman's voice that Lily didn't recognize. "You don't want to overdo it."

Bobbi sat in a high-backed wooden chair, her face flushed. "You know I won't stop until I do a little more than I did yesterday," she replied.

Lily narrowed her eyes, trying to figure out what Bobbi and the woman were up to. An iron rod was pushed through two metal loops, soldered near the bottom of Bobbi's leg brace. Small round weights were fastened on both ends of the rod, like a dumbbell.

Bobbi lifted her leg, the brace, and attached dumbbell from the floor – her whole body trembling with the effort. Once her knee was straight, she counted to three and lowered it again. A satisfied smile spread across her face. "Thirty-seven. That's one more than yesterday," she said.

Her homely companion covered her smile with one hand while sliding her Coke bottle thick glasses up her nose with the other. She looked familiar, but Lily couldn't place her.

"Alright then," she said, "let's get you back into bed. Mr. Long hired me to nurse you until the children get home from school – not to work you into a frenzy. If he knew what we were up to, he'd skin me alive."

"I'll get into bed, but I'm taking the long way around."

"*Nurse!*" thought Lily. "*She worked at the hospital while Bobbi was a patient there.*"

The nurse removed the weights and brace, and massaged Bobbi's calf. "If your leg muscles get much bigger, we'll have to have the blacksmith make a bigger brace."

"Oh, no we won't, Ethel." Bobbi hoisted herself into a standing position. "Between Rebecca's device and your exercises, my leg supports more weight every day. Soon, I won't need a brace."

Bobbi leaned against the mattress with her elbows locked and began edging her way around the bed, taking small steps with her stiff leg.

The fog rolled in and right back out again, making Lily's stomach flip. Lily recognized Bobbi's bedroom in the new memory, but this time she heard voices and laughter on the other side of the door. She focused on the conversation with closed eyes, hoping to ease her queasiness.

"Lucky for me Belle didn't know what an uncle was," Clay joked, "or she would have ruined my plan to spring her from that quarantine clinic."

"I did too know," Belle retorted indignantly. "I just figured since they were making me call the nun at the clinic 'sister', it was okay to call you 'uncle.'"

Lily smiled and opened her eyes as warm laughter erupted in the next room. Bobbi, dressed in a striking knee-length black dress with long sleeves, tucked her brace under one arm. She took a deep breath and turned the handle of the bedroom door. She walked with a heavy limp and her leg had healed with a noticeable bow in it, but her pride was evident. When she stepped into the room, everyone stopped hanging popcorn on the scrawny Christmas tree and stared in amazement.

"Merry Christmas!" she exclaimed. "This is the surprise I promised you. Thanks to Rebecca, Ethel and Jack, I'll never have to sit in another wheeled chair or wear this brace again! And that's not all. Cricket agreed to rehire me at the clothing factory."

Clay, Nathaniel, and Belle stood frozen in place, while Rebecca, grinning from ear to ear, stepped forward to take the brace from her aunt's outstretched hands.

"We may have created the mechanical device," Rebecca said, "but it was you and Ethel who did all the hard work to strengthen your leg enough to walk."

"This is from Rebecca and me," Jack chimed in. He presented her with a four-footed, steel cane – its shaft engraved with delicate vines. "Merry Christmas!"

Ethel smiled, momentarily forgetting to hide her crooked teeth behind her hand. "You've been a wonderful patient, Mrs. Hamilton."

Nathaniel and Belle finally recovered from the shock of their mother's dramatic entrance and ran to her, kissing her cheeks and hugging her tight. Bobbi returned their affection and then locked eyes with Clay.

Clay smiled and shook his head. "I always knew you were a witch, but you never fail to stupefy me with your powers." He strode across the small room and held the crook of his arm out to her. "And now, unless you have more magic tricks to show us, I'd be honored to escort you to the Christmas shindig. I can hardly wait to see the look on everyone's faces when you walk through the door."

A few minutes later, Lily floated alongside Bobbi as she climbed the stairs to the main entrance of the Belleview Biltmore, aided only by her new cane. Nathaniel gave a loud cheer when she reached the veranda, and Clay, Belle, Rebecca, Jack and Ethel joined in.

Lily envied Bobbi, wishing she could be rid of her own brace, but when the doors to the grand hotel opened all such thoughts vanished – replaced with childlike wonder.

The entire lobby was decked with holiday trimmings. A huge Christmas tree stood in the middle of the space, decorated with oranges, glass balls, and brightly colored ribbon bows. The lower half of the tree held cookies, candy canes and small paper cone ornaments, filled with nuts and candy for the children. Handrails were wrapped with pine garlands, and plates of gingerbread cookies decorated the tables. Vases filled with red roses, holly and cinnamon sticks had been strategically placed at both ends of the registration desk and on either side of the box-spiral staircases, filling the entire room with a perfectly delicious scent. The ambiance was made complete by two violinists seated in the corner, playing holiday music.

Anna and Alton Farthing, along with Bobbi's sister, Jo and Agnes Pritchard, sat in the lobby listening to the music, awaiting the arrival of the rest of their party before joining the Christmas festivities in the ballroom. Anna was aware of Bobbi's surprise, but when Alton spotted her walking with only the aid of a cane, he rose from his chair, his jaw dropping. Anna laughed with delight and clapped her hands, drawing the attention of the others.

"Well, I must say," Bobbi teased, hugging each person in turn, "your flabbergasted expressions make all those hours of exercise worthwhile."

Anna tugged on her husband's coattail, drawing him from his stupor. "Alton, dear," she said. "I think several of your colleagues might like to meet with Rebecca and Jack about making therapy devices for their own patients – and perhaps now they'll stop laughing at Ethel's exercise remedies."

"As well they should," Alton replied, still in awe of the recovery he had deemed impossible.

After hearty congratulations were exchanged, Clay and Bobbi led the others down the Promenade toward the Christmas gala.

"You know I don't mind taking care of you and the children," Clay said. "I wish you weren't so hell-bent on going back to work in that sewing factory."

"Clay, you are a dear man, but..."

Bobbi stumbled on a pine cone that had dropped unnoticed from one of the garlands above. Lily, forgetting she was just watching one of Bobbi's memories, instinctively reached out to catch her at the exact same instant as Clay.

Lily dropped through the clouds in a rush, confused by the growing sound of an alarm. It took a moment for her to recall where she was and to recognize the loud beeping sound of Grams' heart monitor.

Chapter Sixty Seven

"Grams – no!" Lily cried. *"You can't be gone yet... not without saying goodbye..."*

Then she noticed the heart monitor had slipped off Grams' finger. *"I must have knocked it off when I tried to catch Bobbi,"* she thought. With trembling hands, she pushed the monitor back into place and held her breath until the flat green line on the screen above the bed displayed Grams' heartbeat.

"Do you need assistance?" The woman's voice, barely audible above the beeping, came from a speaker located on the side rail of Grams' bed.

"I accidentally knocked the heart monitor off Grams' finger." Lily's voice sounded as shaky as she felt. "I put it back on, but the alarm didn't stop."

"I'll send someone to check it," the woman replied.

Seconds later, Opal scurried into the room and reset the monitor.

"I'm sorry..." Lily began.

"Hush, child. This wasn't your fault. I should have taped it on the last time this happened."

Opal pulled a roll of tape and a pair of scissors from the drawer in the nightstand. "Some nurses use so much tape; you'd swear they own stock in the company that makes the stuff. But it hurts when we pull it off, so I sometimes make the mistake of using too little."

She cut a short piece of tape and carefully wrapped it around the heart sensor and Grams' thin knuckle. "That should hold it. I'm sorry you got a scare. Can I bring you a cup of coffee or tea?"

"Tea, please – with sugar," Lily murmured, surprising herself. She usually drank black coffee.

"I like my tea the same way," Opal said. "I'll bring you a blanket, too. This room is freezing."

Lily's gaze followed Opal as she exited the room. *"The world would be a better place if more people acted like her,"* she thought.

"Like stones tossed into water, actions create ripples," a disembodied voice whispered, "And those ripples can change lives and fates in ways you can't imagine."

Goosebumps covered Lily's body in an instant. She shot a glance at the speaker on Gram's bed, already knowing the voice hadn't originated there.

"Margaret?" There was no answer, but Lily was sure she hadn't imagined the voice. "Grams probably changed a million lives for the better," she said, trying to calm herself. "She sure had a positive influence on me. But I doubt she knows that, given the way I've acted this last year."

"I'd bet dollars to doughnuts Miz Bloom believes you're just about perfect."

Startled, Lily whipped her head around and saw Opal reentering the room.

"She's probably proud as punch for having a hand in raising-up such a fine woman as you."

Opal handed Lily a paper cup of tea and spread a warm blanket over her shivering shoulders.

Lily forgot about spirits for a moment, and sighed. "That feels wonderful – nice and toasty."

Opal nodded. "Straight from the blanket warmer. I've noticed the temperature in this room tends to drop when a patient..." She checked herself. "When the door is closed for a long time."

Lily was certain Opal had almost said, 'when a patient is dying'. She watched silently as the nurse hovered over Grams, checking her pulse. A grim expression crossed Opal's face, but it vanished a moment later.

"I keep forgetting to ask you, Lily – is your friend still collecting silly instructions for his book?"

"Dumb warnings, you mean? Yes he is. Did you find one?"

"A few days ago, I mentioned it to the staff and they made a game out of it. We're keeping a list on the bulletin board behind the nurse's station." She pulled a folded sheet of paper from her pocket. "I made a copy for you – but if you're not in the mood to look at it right now, I understand."

Lily set her tea on the window ledge, unfolded the paper and read the first item to herself. *'Found on a child's Superman costume: Warning – wearing of this garment does not enable you to fly.'* She snickered. "That's great. I know my friend will love it. " She scanned the list and chuckled again, "This one from the Midol label is priceless: *'Do not use if you have an enlarged prostate.'*"

"Anyone who needs that warning is very confused." A toothy grin spread across Opal's face. "My favorite is the one from the package of fish hooks. *'Warning – hooks are sharp.'*"

"These are all great," Lily said, refolding the paper. "I can't thank you enough."

"It's me who should be thanking you. We keep an eye out for things to make us smile around here and this list is working wonders."

Opal glanced at Grams. "Miz Bloom's chart says we're to call Hubbell Funeral Home in Belleair Bluffs when the time comes. Is that right?"

"Yeah," Lily replied. "They handled Gramps' service."

Opal gave her a nod and walked to the door. "Well, I best be getting back to work now."

"She doesn't have long, does she?"

"No. I'm sorry, Lily."

Lily bit her lip as tears welled in her eyes. When the door closed behind Opal, she started to reach for her cup of tea, but her eye caught sight of the urn. She picked it up and carefully removed the lid, revealing the ashes inside. "Hi, sweet boy," she whispered. "It's Mom. I'm here with Grams. She's coming your way soon, and I'm counting on you to take care of her, okay?"

She laid the open urn on the window sill next to the old football phone and touched her first two fingers to the surface of the course ashes. Then she turned back to Grams and rubbed the light film of ash into her withered palm.

"Maybe that will help you find one another." Lily rested her head against Grams and closed her eyes. It took a while for the fog to overtake her, but eventually, she drifted into the spirit realm.

In the nearby mist, Margaret was talking with a young woman. Lily gasped with the realization that it was as if she were watching one of Grams' old photographs come to life. She called out and waved, but Margaret and Grams couldn't hear her.

A dazzling light appeared in the distance, intensifying to the point that Lily had to squint her eyes and watch through her lashes. Margaret and Grams continued their discussion, but the illumination was beginning to distract Grams. Lily didn't know if the radiant spectacle moved toward the women, or if it was the other way around, but the distance between them was definitely shrinking.

Lily's eyes were fixed on the light, so she didn't notice the spirit of a man floating toward Grams until he was at her side. Startled, Lily watched as he hugged her and then kissed Margaret's hand. He looked vaguely familiar, but Lily couldn't place him. He and Grams separated from Margaret, floating closer to the mesmerizing glow. The light seemed to defy physical description. One moment, it appeared to resemble a doorway, and the next, it looked like a path – then a pool, then a snowflake, then a star, and so on. It was golden, but also glittery white, pink pearlescent, an iridescent shimmer of silver, and a kaleidoscope of color.

Grams and the man moved toward the light, which danced before them, drawing them even closer. Suddenly, Lily noticed the man was changing form, just like the light. Grams smiled, not the least bit bothered as he shape-shifted from an Indian man into a middle-aged black woman, then a freckle-faced teenage boy, a Caucasian woman with her hair twisted into a tight, dishwater blonde bun, and so on.

"Are these spirits from Grams past, who have come to greet her?" Lily wondered.

The spirit, now a pale, thin man with olive skin, hugged Grams as the shimmering light licked her back. While they were embracing, the being morphed again – this time, into a young boy with black hair.

Lily's breath caught in her throat. *"Turn around,"* she silently begged. *"Please let me see your face."*

The boy stepped back from Grams as the glowing beam of light began showering her with millions of tiny, brilliant stars. The sparkling waterfall reminded Lily of fireworks. Grams glanced over her shoulder into the depths of the luminous pool and smiled with delight at whatever she saw there. She waved to Margaret in the distance, blew a kiss to the boy, and then stepped onto the path, becoming one with the illumination.

The light had appeared in an instant, and it vanished the same way.

The boy turned around, giving Lily a momentary glimpse of Dylan's smile before she plunged through the clouds. Waked by the shrill beep of the heart monitor, she bolted upright, tears streaming down her face. Even without checking, she knew the sensor was still taped to Grams finger. The monitor was functioning properly this time.

Grams was gone.

Chapter Sixty Eight

Opal appeared at the doorway and swiftly crossed the room to silence the alarm. She glanced first at Lily and then at Grams before pushing the call button on the bedrail. "Page Dr. Chen to room 4544 –Code Blue DNR," she said.

"Heart stopped but do not resuscitate, right?" Lily squeaked, feeling numb.

Opal nodded, confirming what Lily already knew. Grams heart would never beat again. "I'm sorry, Lily. Then she patted Grams' lifeless hand. "It's all right, Miz Bloom. You can rest in peace now."

"I watched her go into the light," Lily said. "I know it sounds crazy, but it was beautiful. She looked younger and happier than I've ever seen her. And I saw my son, too."

"I knew there would be loved ones there to welcome Miz Bloom home," Opal said, indicating she believed Lily's story.

Lily, still confused about many details of her vision, was relieved their conversation was interrupted by the arrival of a young, female doctor.

Opal handed Grams' chart to the nervous-looking doctor, prompting her to action.

"Ah, yes," she said, with an Asian accent that made it obvious that English was not her first language and perhaps not even her second. She turned to Lily. "I Docta Chen. We are so sowy to you. I examine now. You to stay or to go – is okay."

"I'll stay," Lily replied.

The doctor nodded and lifted Grams' limp arm, comparing the name on the hospital band to that on the chart. Satisfied she had the right patient, she pushed Grams' afghan away and bent close to her ear. "Messus Bwoom," she called. She shook Grams' shoulder and then patted her cheek, watching for any signs of life. Next she listened for a heartbeat and then she felt for a carotid pulse. Then she shined a light in Grams' dull, vacant eyes. Finally, she looked at the clock. "Time of dett is fie fitty seven pm," she said.

Dr. Chen shifted her attention back to Lily. "Dis was expected dett, so no awe-topsy unless you request to have one."

"No, an autopsy will not be necessary," Lily said, shaking her head.

Dr. Chen scribbled a few notes in the chart, signed it, and then returned it to Opal. "You have question?" she asked Lily.

Lily shook her head.

"Okay, so I go put chart for Docta Weston to sign. You stay for goodbye if you want. We again so sowy for the loss of your loved person."

Dr. Chen reached out her hand and Lily automatically took it, although the action of shaking hands at the foot of Grams' corpse added to the already surreal ambiance. Then, with something between a nod of her head and a bow, Dr. Chen turned and left.

"Lily, is there anyone we can call for you?" Opal asked. "I hate to leave you all alone."

"Thanks, Opal, but I'll be fine. I don't plan to stay long. I just need to make a couple phone calls."

"Alright then, I'll arrange for a transportation gurney. And don't worry. I'll make sure Miz Bloom's nice outfit goes with her to the funeral parlor."

Once she was alone, Lily studied the lifeless form with its drooping, toothless mouth. Even if she hadn't watched her grandmother travel into the light, she would have known Grams' spirit left this world. She sagged back in her chair, thinking about the lighted path and what she had witnessed.

"What were you and Margaret talking about before you crossed over?" she wondered. *"Who were those people? Why didn't Dylan*

go into the light? Where is he now?" She closed her eyes, hoping for answers, but no fog came forth to claim her. She squeezed her eyes tighter shut, but still, no mist appeared.

Lily felt lonelier than she had ever been before. Finally, she reached for her phone and called Scott.

"It's over. Grams is gone."

Telling Scott – saying the words out loud – made Grams' death *real.* Lily sucked in a trembling breath, fighting back sobs.

"I'll be right there," Scott said.

Lily didn't argue. She needed his strength and stability, at least for a little while. She idly wondered if Scott and Seth would get along. *"Oh my God... Seth!"* She felt guilty he hadn't crossed her mind until now. She dialed his number and repeated, "Grams is gone."

"Oh, Christ... I'm sorry, Lily," he said. "I know this sucks. What do you need me to do?"

"Nothing," Lily replied. "My hus... Scott is here. I didn't ask him to come, but since he did – and because he loved Grams, too, I think it would be better if the two of us handled her arrangements."

There was a strained pause before Seth spoke. "Okay. I understand. Call me if you want to talk."

"I don't think you do understand, Seth. I'm seriously thinking about taking you up on your offer to hit the road together, but that's in the future. Grams is part of my past, and Scott's is the only person who shares those memories."

"You don't have to explain yourself to me, Lily. Just promise you'll let me know if you need me, okay?"

"I will. Can we meet for breakfast?" Lily asked.

"Really? Sure – in your suite?"

Lily blushed, remembering how they spent the morning. "Given the circumstances, I think the restaurant would be more appropriate," she said.

"Jesus, Lily – I didn't – I mean... shit. I wasn't s-suggesting..." Seth stammered. "I just thought you might need a massage – a professional massage, that is. Goddamn-it – none of this is coming out right."

"It's okay, Seth. I know your intentions are honorable. I just think I'd be more comfortable eating at the restaurant while Scott is here."

"He's staying with you?" Seth's tone was uneasy.

"No, but he is staying at the same hotel."

"Oh – okay." His voice relaxed. "I understand. Will he be joining us?"

"Not a chance." Voices down the hall caught Lily's attention. "I have to go now, Seth. I'll meet you at our table tomorrow morning at ten thirty."

She barely ended the call before Scott was at Grams' door. He was clean-shaven and his thick, black hair was brushed back in a neat wave. Despite the circumstances, Lily couldn't help noticing the way his navy blue polo shirt, tucked into pressed kakis, accentuated his strong arms and the 'V' of his torso.

She struggled to her feet. "How did you get here so fast?" she asked, limping toward him.

"I was already pulling into the parking lot when you called."

Scott crossed the room and swooped her into a protective embrace before casting his eyes toward Grams' bed. "Aw, Grams," he said, slowly shaking his head. "I'm going to really miss you, sweet lady."

He released his grip on Lily and together, they moved closer to the bed.

"Good God," Scott said. "She's nothing but skin and bones. Poor thing." He brushed the back of his hand against Grams' hollow cheek in a loving caress. "Still, I think she looks kind of peaceful."

Lily wanted to tell Scott about watching Grams cross over, but the topic of ghosts had been a sore subject since the accident. "I bet she found Gramps right away," she said instead. "The two of them are probably already sharing a cup of coffee and planning new adventures."

Scott nodded, his lips turning up in a half-smile at the thought.

A few minutes later, Opal and two aides returned with a gurney. Lily and Scott waited in the hall while they prepared Grams for transport and stripped her bed. Then they exchanged places so Lily and Scott could say a final goodbye.

Scott bent and kissed Grams' forehead. "It's goodbye for now, Grams, but please don't forget that I'm counting on you to look after Dylan until we get up there. I love you." With glistening eyes, he brushed her cheek and then turned to Lily. "I'll wait outside while you say goodbye," he said.

Lily nodded and gazed down at her grandmother. She tried to focus on happy memories, like the winter Grams took her to North Carolina to see snow for her eighth birthday. She smiled, remembering Grams patiently explaining why she couldn't take icicles back to Florida as souvenirs.

"I'll always treasure my memories of you, Grams. I don't know what would have become of me if you hadn't taken me in. I love you so much. I hope you can visit my dreams sometimes, but even if you can't, I'll think of you often and try to live a life that would make you proud." Lily swiped at her tears and kissed her grandmother's forehead for the last time. "Goodbye, Grams."

When she opened the door, Scott stepped inside and held his arms out to her. She sighed. Slipping into his warm embrace felt like coming home.

They moved aside to give the team room to maneuver the gurney. Lily turned toward the window, not wanting to watch them wheel Grams away.

She gulped at the sight of Dylan's open urn. "Scott, would you mind grabbing the cardboard box out of the closet? I want to pack up these pictures and get out of here."

"Sure." Scott glanced at photos lining the window sill and then turned to retrieve the box. "Are those from her room at Bay Manor?"

"Yeah," she replied, covertly closing the urn. "You were right about personal things making the room feel homier."

"I bet Grams knew they were here."

Lily picked up football phone. "You never know."

Chapter Sixty Nine

If circumstances were different, the task might have been pleasant – reminiscing as they wrapped photographs in tissue paper and packed them into the box.

"Remember this?" Scott said with a grin, holding up the photo of Grams 80th birthday cake, all ablaze with candles. "The camera flashed just as the fire alarm went off."

Lily laughed, but then blushed, recalling that when she went to the nursing home to choose these pictures, Seth had gone with her. She caught her breath at the erotic memory of how his fingertips caressed her facial features, creating a picture of her in his mind. *"What if the face he imagined is better than my real one?"* She worried. *"What if he gets his eyesight back and is disappointed?"*

"Don't be sad, Lily," Scott said, misunderstanding her expression. "These pictures show Grams led a long, full life."

Lily nodded, embarrassed by her inappropriate thoughts. "Check out this one," she joked, hoping to change the subject. "Me at thirteen – all arms and legs with teeth too big for my mouth."

"Yeah, but everything came together real nice when you grew up," he teased.

For an instant, their eyes sparkled with sweet, intimate familiarity, but then the awful memories of the last few years surfaced, rebuilding the wall between them.

"Can you fold her afghan?" Lily asked, pretending the intimate exchange hadn't occurred. She packed Dylan's ashes and the old football phone into the box and closed the lid.

Scott laid the folded afghan on top of the packing box, picked it up, and walked toward the door without comment. Lily blew out a long breath, leaned on her crutch, and followed him.

Opal was waiting in the hall with a wheelchair. "I figured I'd take Lily down myself," she explained. "It'll give us a chance to say goodbye."

The group rode the elevator down in somber silence.

"You two take it easy while I go get the car," Scott said, obviously attempting to give them privacy.

Once he was out of earshot, Opal raised an eyebrow at Lily. "It's none of my business, but I hope you know that man is still in love with you."

"I'm afraid our marriage is too broken to be mended," Lily said. "He's probably just being kind for Grams' sake."

"A marriage isn't like Humpty Dumpty, you know... it can always be put back together if both parties want it badly enough."

Lily caught her breath Opal's choice of words, immediately recalling Nurse Anna's advice to Bobbi. *"Focus on fixing one crack at a time,"* she thought. *"Could that be what the spirits are trying to teach me?"*

"Now, about Miz Bloom," Opal continued, abruptly changing the subject. She handed Lily a business card for Hubble's Funeral Home. "Tomorrow, you need to call these folks to finalize her arrangements."

"Thanks." Lily bit her lip.

"I know this is hard, but try to remember that vision you had of your son leading Miz Bloom through the gates of Heaven. The part of her that's still in this world is just the baggage she didn't need for that flight to paradise."

"That's not exactly what I saw," Lily thought, recalling the vision. *"Dylan didn't go into the light."* Even so, she gave Opal a thin-lipped smile of gratitude.

Opal patted her shoulder. "Looks like your ride is here," she said, pushing the wheelchair through the automatic doors. She helped Lily to her feet and smiled. "I'll miss you, Lily. Take care of yourself, now, you hear?"

"Thanks for everything, Opal." Lily hugged the stout woman. "I don't think I could've gotten through this without you. I'll never forget you – not in a hundred lifetimes."

A knot formed in Lily's stomach as they drove away, realization finally sinking in that Grams was gone. When they got to the Belleview Biltmore, Scott left the car with the valet and walked her to her suite.

"Where do you want this box?" he asked from the doorway.

Lily cast a nervous glance into the suite before answering. She breathed a sigh of relief. The room had been serviced. All traces of breakfast for two in the middle of the bed were gone. She pointed in the general direction of the windows. "Anywhere over there."

Scott nodded and put the box down. "Listen, I haven't had anything to eat today. Do you think we could talk about Grams' arrangements over dinner?"

"I'm not very hungry, but I should eat something. The café down the hall is excellent."

"Or we could order room service," Scott suggested.

Lily felt an uncomfortable wave of déjà vu wash over her. "I'd rather eat outside on the patio." She picked up a notepad and pen from the nightstand and hobbled into the hallway, hoping he hadn't picked up on her discomfort.

The balding server had twinkling blue eyes and the rotund physique of a man who clearly enjoyed sampling the restaurant's menu on a frequent basis. Lily and Scott accepted his recommendation and ordered the chef's special– chicken parmesan, served over pasta with red sauce, paired with a raspberry pinot noir from Oregon.

With a few practiced turns of an old-school corkscrew, the server pulled the cork and offered it to Scott, who declined the gesture with a polite wave of his hand. He poured a sample and watched as Scott swirled the glass, sniffed the bouquet and then took a sip.

"Excellent," Scott said.

The server smiled, poured two glasses and left to check on his other tables.

"I chose Hubble Funeral Home," Lily said, once they were alone.

"Cremation?"

"Yeah, you remember – she always wanted her ashes scattered in the Gulf of Mexico with Gramps. I thought we'd have a small memorial service and then charter a boat at Clearwater Beach." She hesitated. "What day of the week is this?"

"Monday."

"Right. Okay, I'll call the funeral home in the morning. Hopefully they'll be able to meet with us tomorrow afternoon."

Scott nodded. "Have you already written a draft obituary?"

"No, but I think we should keep it simple. After all, she outlived practically everybody. I'm not sure anyone's left to mourn her but us."

"Yeah, but we should still post it in the Tampa Bay Times, as well as the Belleair Bee and Belleair Living magazine."

"I suppose."

The combination of tasty food, good wine and exhaustion relaxed Lily's inhibitions. When the conversation lulled, she decided to tell Scott about authorizing another review of Dylan's medical records.

"I really believed the results would be different this time," she said. "But she reached the same conclusion as the others."

"That Dylan was brain dead before he reached the hospital?"

"Yeah. I think I can accept that now, but only because I've learned so much about..." Lily searched Scott's eyes, trying to read his thoughts. "Never mind. If I tell you, you'll probably think I've gone down the rabbit hole again."

Scott frowned. "Try me. You never know. I might surprise you."

"What if I told you this hotel is haunted by spirits that are helping me understand some things?"

"Like what?"

She told him about Margaret and her connection with Grams.

"She helped me understand that Grams was satisfied with her life. And when Grams crossed into the light, Margaret was there and she shared the experience with me. It was beautiful, but strange."

"Strange?"

"Yeah." Lily paused. "I mean, a lot of people were there to meet Grams at the entrance to the light, but it was like one person kept morphing into the next and I didn't recognize anyone except — well, except the last one."

"The last one was Dylan?"

Lily nodded. "I thought he would cross over with her, but he didn't. He just disappeared into the clouds."

"You mean he like, floated up into Heaven?"

Now it was Lily's turn to frown. "No – just the thick fog that always..."

"*Always*? This happens a lot?"

"Yes." Lily narrowed her eyes. "I know you don't believe any of this. So what's with all the questions?"

Scott shrugged. "I told a friend about the hallucinations you had after the accident. She said tons of people swear they've had similar experiences. Some claim they saw dead loved ones, but others say they met strangers, like this Margaret you mentioned. One theory is that people tap into higher brain functions while they're unconscious, but only a few people remember what they saw when they wake up."

"But that doesn't explain how I know things about people I've never met in real life, like Margaret Plant."

"Wait a minute. The Margaret you've been talking about is Margaret *Plant*? In that case, maybe your higher brain functions are recalling facts you learned as a kid but thought you forgot, and mixing them with stuff you imagine." Scott shook his head. "You know what? It doesn't matter whether it's ghosts or dreams or higher brain functions. What's important is that it's helping you come to grips with what happened."

Lily nodded, although she was certain the spirits at the Belleview Biltmore were not a product of her imagination. "I'm impressed someone got you to open your mind to new possibilities. Who is she?"

Scott flushed. "Just a friend."

Lily didn't press the issue. She was certain it was the same woman who had answered his phone while he was in the shower, but she didn't want to hear about Scott's lover any more than she wanted to tell him about Seth.

"As long as we're talking about far-fetched possibilities," she ventured. "Do you think it's possible that Dylan's spirit is still tied to the people who received his organs?"

"I don't see how a person's flesh could be connected to their soul," he said. "But I'm glad you brought up that topic." He cleared his throat. "I know you said you didn't want to read their letters, but I brought them with me anyway. I think you might find comfort in knowing how much good came from – you know..."

"You brought their letters to Florida?" she asked, her mouth suddenly dry.

"Yeah. They're in my room. I can bring them to you after dinner."

"Thanks," she said. "I think I'm finally ready to look at them."

Lily was startled by her reaction, but was certain it had something to do with finally accepting the fact that Dylan could not have been saved. They walked back to her room holding hands – a comfortable habit from happier times. He unlocked her door, and then left her to retrieve the letters from his room.

"Want to come in?" she asked when he returned with the small bundle.

"No thanks," he said. "You've been through a lot and need some rest. Call me in the morning after you talk to the funeral home." He started to turn away, but hesitated. "Listen, Lily. After we've honored Grams with the farewell she deserves, we need to talk."

"About what?" Lily asked.

"About this."

Scott stepped close, wrapped an arm around her waist and pressed his lips to hers, cradling the back of her head in the open palm of his other hand. His soft lips melted into hers as he probed her mouth with his tongue, reminding her of his fiery passion.

He stopped as abruptly as he had begun, leaving Lily stunned and breathless.

"Goodnight, Lilyanna."

Chapter Seventy

Lily stood in her doorway watching Scott walk down the corridor, too astonished to speak. Finally she regained her senses enough to close her door. *"What the hell is going on?"* she wondered, still dazed. *"Are men attracted to emotional wrecks or something?"*

Too exhausted to read the letters, she dropped them on the round table, got ready for bed and crawled under the comforter. But the moment she closed her eyes, thoughts of Grams, Seth, Scott and Dylan began clamoring for her attention. When the fog finally descended, she sighed gratefully and drifted into the haze.

As the mist began to dissipate, she heard a gruff voice say, "I give Herbert his walkin' papers yesterday."

When rows of sewing machines came into view, Lily recognized the weakly-lit sweatshop where Bobbi worked before her accident. The lanky shop foreman's thin, gray hair, handlebar moustache and attire were typical of a 1920s businessman – white dress shirt, black vest, and wide-legged pants. His language and mannerisms, on the other hand, revealed a lifetime of working on a cattle ranch. Even his nickname came from his habit of clucking out of the corner of his mouth at people, as though they were cattle.

"Good riddance, I say," Bobbi replied. "You're well rid of that character, Cricket. He had a bad habit of forcing his attention on the girls – married or not."

"Yep, the last thing I need is somebody's husband showin' up here, raising a ruckus." He ran a hand through his frizzy hair. "I swear, a day don't go by that I don't suffer woeful regret about lettin' my wife nag me into workin' for her pappy. If ever a cow-poke got out of hand, I could put things right with one snap of a bullwhip. But you can't wrangle city-folk that away."

"I don't suppose so." Bobbi smiled at the thought.

"Yeah, well... When you was workin' here afore, you always had a way of keepin' peace in the herd, so to speak, which got me to thinkin'... how about I hire you on instead of a new floor boss? I'd be willin' to pay you two dollars a day to watch over the gals, in addition to a penny per piece for everything you sew."

"Whoa there, Cricket." Bobbi's eyebrows knitted with concern. "I happen to know you paid Herbert six dollars a day – he bragged about it."

Cricket drew back in surprise. "You don't expect me to pay you a man's wages, do you, Bobbi?"

Bobbi glared at him a moment, but then conceded with a shake of her head. "I suppose not. But could you make it three dollars a day? You know I have children to feed."

"I suppose that's fair," Cricket said, shaking her hand to seal the deal. "O'course, for that kind of money, I'll expect you to learn the new gals how to work fast and sew ram-rod straight seams... and keep their minds from wanderin' off. That's when they make foolish mistakes that waste thread and material."

"All right. When do I start?"

"First thing in the morning, I reckon."

"Thanks, Cricket." She gave him a wink. "You try to hide it, but you have a swell heart."

"Says you. Now get a wiggle on out of here, before I change my mind."

Lily was bristling about the blatant income inequality as the fog swept over her, but she before had time to dwell on the mat-ter, the clouds parted again. She concentrated on the fireplace in the corner of the room where she and Bobbi stood, waiting for her dizziness to pass. She thought she recognized the dark, rich-ly-grained walnut mantle and pale yellow tiles trimming the firebox. One glance through the open door confirmed her hunch.

This was the Magnolia Room at the Belleview Biltmore – a small parlor, located near the west end of the Promenade corridor.

Lily gazed around the room, admiring a semicircle of wing-back chairs near the fireplace, upholstered in aqua blue satin and trimmed with gold embroidery. A magnificent walnut sideboard filled the far wall, adorned with mirrors and intricate carvings, reminiscent of the Orient.

Bobbi beamed as Clay entered the parlor with her four children in tow. Once they were seated, a servant poured glasses of iced tea and then exited.

"Before we begin our celebratory dinner, I have an announce-ment," Bobbi said, grinning. "My new job pays well enough that Fred and Henrietta can finally return home to live."

Nathaniel whooped and Belle jumped to her feet, rushing to hug her brother and sister. Fred and Henrietta, however, weren't pleased with the news.

"Must we return, Mama?" Fred asked. "Mother and Father said we are welcome to live with them as long as we please. And with only two children to provide for, your income might afford Nate and Belle better – um, opportunities."

Henrietta nodded in agreement. "Father says our school – the Hampshire Academy – is where all the best families educate their children."

Bobbi's hand trembled as she set her glass down on a small rose-wood table. "When did you start calling Uncle Ed and Auntie Max *Mother* and *Father*?" she asked, clasping her hands in her lap.

Henrietta shot an accusing glare at Fred. "I told you Mama wouldn't like that."

Fred looked down, as if suddenly fascinated by the pattern on the Oriental rug. "Father assured us that taking his name would garner more respect from our classmates – and he was right. In our society, family names matter." When he glanced up at Bobbi, her wounded expression shamed him. "We wouldn't call them Mama and Papa," he added feebly.

A tear rolled down Henrietta's cheek. "I'm sorry, Mama. I'd miss St. Petersburg and my school friends, but I'll come back here, if that's what you want."

Bobbi closed her eyes, fighting back tears. Fred and Henrietta had spent more than two years of their young, impressionable lives on her sister's elegant estate, forming parental bonds and socializing with other prominent families. Demanding they return home to the cottage would generate resentment and misery. Like it or not, Fred and Henrietta belonged to her sister now.

She took a deep breath and reopened her eyes. "Calm yourselves, children. If you want to continue living with your auntie and uncle, I won't interfere. I'm grateful they take such good care of you, and I know they can provide far better opportunities for your success than I ever could."

"Bull feathers," Clay boomed. "That jingle-brained politician your sister married believes that his money makes him better than other folks. If you don't hurry and bring your kids home, their thinking will get completely zozzled."

Grateful tears welled in Bobbi's eyes as she gave Clay a tender smile. "I appreciate your concern more than you know, Clay, but I must do what I think is best for my children's future."

She turned her attention to Fred and Henrietta. "You both have good hearts, but Mr. Long is right. Money can turn your heads unless you remain humble. That's why I want you to always remember that Auntie Max picked you two because your auburn hair looks like hers and mine, while Nathaniel and Belle are blond, like Papa. Had your hair colors been reversed, they would be living a grand lifestyle instead of you."

Fred, looking sheepish, idly ran a hand through his red waves.

"Therefore, once you both become established," Bobbi continued, "it will be your responsibility to introduce Nathaniel and Belle to your associates and help each of them procure good situations, just as they would have done for you."

Bobbi paused, letting the weight of her words sink in. Then she smiled. "Now, no more wet blankets. This is a celebration!"

Clay raised his glass, glowing with admiration. "Here's to you, Bobbi," he said. "I hope your boss has enough sense to avoid your temper and respect your magic."

"Especially since he's only paying me half of what he paid a man to do the job," Bobbi teased.

"Mama, if you're doing the same job, why aren't you paid alike?" asked Henrietta.

"That's a good question." Bobbi eyed her children. "After I prove a woman can do the job, maybe you can help me campaign for a higher wage."

Henrietta's eyes narrowed, considering the challenge.

As the fog descended, Lily heard Clay laugh out loud. "Come along, Bobbi. Let's have our dinner. You've put quite enough revolutionary ideas in their young minds for one night."

The next time the mist parted, Lily barely recognized the garment factory. Several new light fixtures were suspended from the ceiling and the ladies were gathered in small circles, chatting and exchanging fabric.

"Okay, ladies," Bobbi announced, ringing a bell. "Swap time is over. Let's get to work."

She walked around the vast room, switching on several radios. As jazz music began to fill the air, the women tucked small bits of cloth out of sight and set their sewing machines whirling into action.

Bobbi's sewing machine was turned around to face the room, much like a teacher's desk. As she sat down, Cricket sauntered over with a man she didn't recognize.

Cricket smiled at her. "Bobbi, this here is Harold Schultz, the man I just done hired to manage the cutting room. I was tellin' him how you use music and trading games to get the gals to work harder, but he thinks..."

"I wouldn't expect a woman to understand," Harold interrupted with a demeaning tone in his voice, "but giving the company's fine cloth scraps to your workers isn't good business. They may be sewing faster, but they're also carrying the profits right out the door."

"It's nice to meet you, Harold," Bobbi said, ignoring his remarks. "We used to distribute those scraps of material to the seamstresses to clean and oil their equipment, test newly threaded machines and so on. The trouble was they weren't cleaning or testing their machines very well. They didn't want to ruin good fabric scraps that they could use at home."

Cricket held up a dirty rag. "When sewing machines git bogged down with sticky old oil and lint, they break. Stops production and I have to pay a mechanic to fix 'em. Bobbi lets the gals bring rags from home to clean their machines, in trade for the scraps of good material we'd been givin' 'em to use."

"Before the bell rings to start the day, I put fabric scraps on their machines, just like we've always done, but now they collect and trade those scraps to make clothing and quilts for their families." Lily nodded at the room, now buzzing with activity. "They clean their machines better, which equals fewer repairs. Plus, the seamstresses work harder."

Harold remained skeptical. "The same result could have been accomplished by making the workers return their rags at the end of each day. If they had nothing to gain, they might have used the scraps of fabric to clean the machines properly," he said.

"But why waste good fabric? And what about their temperament?" Bobbi asked.

"There's the problem." Harold sighed, making no effort to hide his contempt. "Women operate under the delusion that workers' contentment matters. Men understand that achieving superior performance is simply a matter of close observation and fear of dismissal – which is why the key to good *man*-agment is the *man*."

Bobbi bit her lip. "If you're confident your methods are superior to mine, then I'd like to propose a wager."

Cricket clucked, enjoying the debate. "What'd ya have in mind there, Bobbi?"

"I propose that we count the number of completed pieces each day for a week. If more pieces are cut and pinned than are sewn each day, you win. However, if the seamstresses are kept waiting for cut and pinned pieces to sew, we win the day. At the end of the week, we'll know whose method of management is superior."

"Agreed," Harold proclaimed, already turning to go back upstairs to the cutting room.

"Hold on, there," called Cricket. "One more rule. If this bet results in a bunch of wasted fabric from cutting mistakes or crooked seams that have to be ripped-out and re-sewn, then your own jobs will be on the line. Is that clear?"

Bobbi and Harold both agreed as the fog drifted in, pulling a reluctant Lily from the memory.

"But who won?" Lily said without thinking. As soon as she spoke out loud, she fell through the clouds and woke in her bed. "Damn it," she mumbled.

She sat up, too wide awake to hope for sleep. "Come on, Margaret. Can't you help me out here?"

Lily turned on the bedside lamp and stared at the round table, trying to 'will' Margaret to appear. Then the bundle of letters caught her eye. She hopped across the frigid room, snatched them up, and carried them back to her warm bed. There, she spread them out and scrutinized each one.

Forwarded by the Organ Procurement Organization, there were no return addresses and no postage marks – just the words 'To the Family and Friends of My Donor,' handwritten on each envelope. Some were written carefully on expensive stationary and others were scrawled on plain white envelopes.

"They're all grateful Dylan died." Unable to bear this thought, Lily tossed the stack of letters back on the table, but one of the envelopes fell to the floor, spilling its contents. Tempted, she retrieved the letter and carefully unfolded the single page.

Dearest Family and Friends of My Donor – How odd that salutation sounds, even as I write it. I wish I knew your names, but they won't tell me. Please be assured that I am acutely aware that on the day my life was saved, your hearts were broken. I promise to appreciate every breath I take with these lungs – the precious gift I received as a result of your tragedy. I plan to dedicate the rest of my life to inspiring students to reach for the stars, secretly hoping they will acquire some knowledge or skill that will benefit you, your loved ones, and perhaps all of mankind, one day. That might sound like a lofty goal for a mathematics instructor, but I hope it's one that will prove worthy of your tremendous gift. Thankfully yours always, M

"Dylan saved the life of a math teacher," Lily murmured, feeling a peculiar sense of pride that her son had possessed ideal organ donor qualifications – a tall, athletic body and type 'O' blood.

She read the letter twice more; then folded it and carefully slid it back into the envelope. She stared at the plain, white envelope. The recipient of Dylan's lungs was no longer a vile, abstract concept – some greedy vulture, standing in line before her dying son, waiting for his precious organs to be served-up. She was a person who appreciated the cost of the gift she received. Comforted, Lily opened the next letter, and then the next.

She discovered Dylan's pancreas saved the life of a young mother who had suffered from diabetes since childhood, and who had risked her life to give birth to two children. Thanks to Dylan, she hoped to watch them grow up and have children of their own.

A letter from a young boy's mother explained how his intestinal transplant meant that her child, who had suffered from short-gut syndrome, had been given a second chance at life. She said he was learning to play baseball, and doing quite well.

Dylan's liver saved a Jamaican baker whose large family had almost lost hope. Some of his tendons helped a young musician recover the use of his legs, after his own tendons were destroyed by tumors. One kidney saved a chef and the other saved a medical student. Dylan's heart had gone to a young scientist who hoped his work in the field of genetics might one day identify the cause of sickle cell anemia. His corneas returned sight to a soldier who had been blinded in combat.

Lily refolded the last letter, tucked it into its envelope and laid it gently on top of the stack. *"And Dylan's skin covered my burns and helped saved my arms,"* she thought, tumbling back into bed.

She pulled the afghan up to her chin and tried to picture the people who had written the letters, now unable to separate Dylan's death from their lives. *"Where is Dylan's spirit? Could he form connections with some his recipients and if he did, what memories would he share with them?"* she wondered.

She fell asleep and drifted into the clouds of the spirit realm, with no concept of time. Finally, the mist fell away, bringing her out of her stupor. She floated into a chair at the little table, across from Margaret.

"That aspect of the spirit world is new to me, too," Margaret said, nonchalantly stirring sugar into her tea. "But I must say – I thought you would have grasped the lesson Bobbi and Clay are trying to teach you by now."

Chapter Seventy One

Lily's temper flared. "In the past couple of weeks, I've discovered there's a whole spirit realm that I never knew existed. I also learned that I was wrong about what caused my son's death. And I lost my grandmother. And I'm thinking about starting a new life with a man I scarcely know. And my husband, who I thought was planning to divorce me, just kissed me. And I'm worried that all the people whose lives my son saved might be keeping his spirit trapped in this world. Exactly when have I had time to figure out lessons from my dreams?"

"Calm down, darlin'," Margaret said, sliding a cup of tea across the table to Lily. "That red hair of yours is getting the best of you."

Lily glared at her. "Tomorrow, I'm planning Grams' memorial service, and once that's over, I'm leaving. So maybe you could slip me a few answers."

"Taking a step back sometimes helps one understand how several memories are revealed to teach one lesson."

Without thinking, Lily scooped three teaspoons of sugar into her tea and stirred briskly. "Can't you just tell me what I'm supposed to learn?"

"Bobbi and Clay's stories are not mine to tell, but I can say the memories they've shown you are all connected. When Bobbi made that wager with my stepson, Morton, she never imagined how far the ripples from that action would travel. The hospital she helped build changed the course of many lives, including her own."

"You mean, because she helped build the hospital, it was there to save her life when she needed it," Lily said.

"That's right." Margaret smiled. "And because Bobbi married Bear Hamilton, Alton Farthing moved his broken heart to Connecticut, where he acquired the skills necessary to give her the miracle she needed after the accident. And because Alton returned to help her, he was able to hone his skills in the art of facial reconstruction, while mentoring a multitude of other doctors. And because of his training, those doctors were able to help her sister, Jo, and countless others..."

"Ripples that began with a single bet kept going, affecting change," Lily murmured. "They're still going. Morton Plant Hospital has become a massive complex, changing lives every day."

Margaret winked in response. "And ripples from Bobbi's accident had other effects, too," Margaret said. "For instance, they changed Clay Long's path in life, making him a better man."

"I don't know about making me a better man,"

Startled, Lily whirled around and found Clay Long sitting next to her at the little table. Her heart was pounding, but Clay continued speaking as though he had been there all along.

"... but I guess there's no arguing with the fact that she changed my life," he said. "And of course, if she and I had gotten hitched, then maybe..."

Bobbi suddenly materialized at the table, interrupting his thought. "Lots of other things happened, too," she said. "Important things that affected the lives of scores of people, including my sisters."

Lily barely had time to register Bobbi's presence before the curtain of fog dropped over her, whisking her from the table and into the mist. She began to hear Jo's voice in the distance and strained to listen.

"Whatever will I do?" Jo wailed. "Walter Broomfield called from the bank. He said Lucian can choose not to participate in *special transactions* going forward, he must complete the one that was supposed to take place just before he had his stroke. Mr. Broomfield warned me that backing out might not be good for his health – or mine."

As the mist lifted, Lily saw that Bobbi was having coffee in Jo's parlor – the same room where Lucian had suffered his stroke the year before. "It's been so long, I thought he'd forgotten about that shady business."

"Me too, but Mr. Broomfield said I should bring Lucian's strongbox key to the bank at eleven o'clock tonight," Jo continued. "He thinks I have the key, but I have no idea where Lucian keeps it, nor do I have any idea what's in the strongbox or what I'm supposed to do with it – and what happens if everyone realizes how sick Lucian really is?"

"One obstacle at a time, Jo," Bobbie replied. "The key has to be hidden among Lucian's personal things. "Come on, I'll help you search."

Lily floated next to Bobbi as she climbed Jo's stairs, noticing that Bobbi's injured leg had healed to the point that she only required a cane for balance. Lily felt a pang of envy, wishing she could be rid of her own brace.

As soon as the sisters entered Lucian's room, he began to snarl and make rude noises. Physically, he had become a shadow of his former self, but his malicious disposition remained intact.

"There, now, Lucian. I know it's hard for you, but do try to keep your mouth shut for just a few minutes, won't you dear?" Jo said. "We *women* are trying to have an intelligent discussion and can't be bothered with your pathetic sword-rattling nonsense right now."

Lily almost laughed out loud as Jo turned her back on Lucian, clearly continuing to get even for years of demeaning treatment at his hands. "I've already searched the chifferobe and the drawers in the tallboy, but found nothing."

Bobbi noticed a smug look of satisfaction shining in Lucian's eyes, but didn't let on. "I think I know where the key is hidden," she said.

Jo's eyes widened. "Truly?"

"Yes," Bobbi replied. "Because Lucian maintained such a tyrannical rule over this household, no one dared touch his personal things, making one of them a perfect hiding place for the key. It's a shame he never considered the possibility of becoming a helpless invalid."

Bobbi kept watching Lucian out of the corner of her eye. When she started to move away from the chifferobe, she thought his smug pretense faded slightly. She was certain his eyes narrowed as she approached the tallboy. When she reached for the Delftware tobacco jar sitting atop the chest of drawers, Lucian hurled a string of guttural noises at her that, although unintelligible, were obviously obscenities.

Certain the only reason Lucian would be so upset was if the key was hidden inside the jar, Bobbi smiled. "Jo, please hand me a dish so I can dump this tobacco out." She continued to watch Lucian as she lifted the sculpted lid off the jar, admired its intricate blue and white design, and then set it aside. However, when she started to tip the tobacco out, she noticed Lucian's gaze had not followed the jar, but instead, remained riveted on the lid.

"Why thank you, Lucian," Bobbi said. "I might have overlooked that." She set the tobacco canister down, and turned the lid over in her hand. On the inside was a small, rectangle opening, in which rested a humidor moisture capsule. It was held in place by a tab, which rotated on a tiny spindle. She pushed the tab to the side with her thumb and lifted out the capsule, exposing the key beneath.

With a triumphant whoop, she held the key up for Jo's inspection, barely noticing Lucian's fresh tirade of furious gibberish. "One problem solved," she said. "Now we need the help of a trusted crook."

The fog rolled over Lily, carrying her away from the memory, but it parted again almost immediately, revealing a moonless night outside the Cabot Mercantile.

"Shove over, Bobbi. I'll drive," Clay said, climbing into the already crowded cab of the pickup truck. "Agnes says that once the deal is done, we'll have to go somewhere to pick up a shipment of liquor."

"That's right," said Agnes. "Lucian would always hide it in the storeroom until someone else came for it."

"What do you suppose is in Lucian's strongbox?" Bobbi asked.

Jo shook her head. "I have no idea."

Clay frowned. "You birds are going to have to open the box and try to figure out what they expect you to do without letting on that Lucian didn't tell you anything. But don't worry – I'll be there watching out for you." He patted his chest, alluding to the holstered pistol under his jacket.

Lily's heart pounded as the truck pulled up in front of the bank. The window shades were pulled down and a *closed* sign hung in the dark window, but Jo knocked on the door anyway. "What should we do if no one answers the door?" she whispered.

Bobbi, Clay, and Agnes shrugged in unison.

Just then, the window shade moved – almost imperceptibly. "Get out of the street, you bunch of saps," a harsh voice hissed. "Go 'round to the alley door before you get us all pinched!"

Feeling foolish, the group did as they were told, looking over their shoulders to make sure no one witnessed them ducking around the side of the building. As soon as they made their way to the bank's back door, it cracked open and they were ushered inside. The inky interior added another layer of terror to the illicit rendezvous, until Walter Broomfield shut the door and struck a match to light a short-wicked candle.

"This way," he grunted in the same, harsh whisper. They followed him to the vault. Once they all stepped inside, he pulled the outer door closed and lit a hurricane lamp, located on a square counting table at the center of the vault

"We don't want the cops to notice a light and come snooping – that could land all of us in the poky," he said, reverting to his normal, bank president's voice.

He walked to the large strongbox in the corner of the dimly lit vault and then turned expectantly to Jo.

"Mr. Broomfield," Jo began, "Lucian told me what I'm supposed to do, but I'm so nervous that I can't remember."

Broomfield sniffed. "Do you have the key?"

Jo nodded, producing it from an otherwise empty drawstring bag. It twinkled in the lamp light.

"Good. You just have to make an even exchange for their cash, less your service fee."

"Ah, yes. My service fee," Jo repeated. "How much was that again?"

Mr. Broomfield took a deep, exasperated breath, rolling his eyes at Clay. "This is exactly why I don't like doing business with women. They can't remember the simplest instructions." He shook his head. "You keep a ten percent service fee. It's Lucian's reward for..."

A faint rap on the back door sent shivers through Lily's spine. From the expressions on Bobbi, Jo and Agnes' faces, she was certain they felt the exact same way, but if Clay was scared, he concealed all traces of it.

Broomfield lowered the lamp to a dull glow and relit his candle. "Wait here," he said, leaving them alone while he went to guide the others inside.

Less than a minute later, two men followed Broomfield back into the vault. They stood motionless until he raised the flame of the lantern enough that they could see. Both men wore black suits with white shirts and black ties, and both wore black fedoras, but their physical characteristics were almost comically dissimilar. The tall, thin one dropped back into the shadows of the vault, just as Clay had done, where he could discreetly observe the proceedings. Lily was certain he carried a concealed gun, and she prayed neither he nor Clay would have cause to draw their weapons.

"Three dames and their daddy?" the short, broad-shouldered man sneered. "Are you sure about this, Broomfield?"

"They're all right. I told you, remember? Lucian's laid-up. This is his wife, her crippled sister and his bookkeeper. Their friend over there works for Butch's crew at the Belleview Biltmore."

The man surveyed each of them, as if assessing the threat level. Finally he nodded to his tall associate. "All right. Let's get on with it." He tossed a leather bag onto the table. "That's a lot of dough, doll face – twenty large."

Lily shivered, certain these men had killed before and would do so again if provoked. She watched as Jo knelt by the strongbox and put her trembling fingers to work, turning the key in the lock. Everyone breathed a sigh of relief when it clicked open and Jo raised the heavy lid of the strongbox.

Then they gasped.

Stacks of banknotes lined one side of the box and small gold bars and coins lined the other side.

The short man whistled, instinctively casing the vault. "Ain't that a sight for sore eyes. Does your old man own a gold mine or something?" He exchanged a knowing look with the tall man in the shadows.

Fortunately, Broomfield hurried to make sure the men knew he was both well-informed and well-connected. "Lucian used to exchange as much cash for gold as possible in his regular business dealings, because it's easier to hide gold from the IRS. Once he collected enough gold to provide a profitable transaction, he'd let me know and I'd place a call to the Chicago Outfit."

Broomfield shot a glance over his shoulder at the trio of women, who stood clutching one another, certain they were about to be killed for the contents of the strongbox.

"This time," he continued, "I got a call straight from Scarface, promising his *personal* protection if I could help him hide some cash from the revenuers. That's when I remembered Lucian had been ready for a transaction when he took ill."

He turned and held his hand out to Jo, as if inviting her to dance, but the trio of women remained frozen in place.

"It's okay, ladies," Broomfield coaxed. "*No one* is stupid enough to mess with people under the protection of Scarface." He pulled the cash from the black bag and placed it into even stacks. "Mrs. Pritchard, if you wouldn't mind..."

Everyone stared as Agnes crept to the table and counted the cash. "Exactly twenty thousand dollars," she confirmed.

Broomfield nodded and then helped Jo assemble the equivalent amount in pressed gold bars and coins, less her cut, on the opposite side of the table. He also took a large gold coin for himself.

"Bank fees, you know," he chuckled. He stacked the cash into the strongbox for Jo and then stood to help the short man pack up the gold. Jo stooped down to close and relock the box.

Bobbi cleared her throat to draw everyone's attention. "Excuse me, but aren't we supposed to buy some liquor? I thought Lucian said..."

"We must conclude one deal before starting the next," Broomfield said, stacking the last of the gold bars into the leather bag. "It prevents confusion. And besides, you don't buy the liquor. The agreement is that you retrieve the shipment and watch over it until someone is sent to collect it."

The stocky man buckled the leather bag and then pulled a thick money clip from his jacket pocket. He peeled off $100 for Broomfield and $200 for Jo. "Here's the address," he said, handing her a note. "A couple of our men are there waiting for you." He tipped his hat to the ladies, hefted the leather bag, nodded in Clay's general direction and then exited the vault, with the tall man trailing behind like a shadow.

Lily shuddered as the mist carried her from the memory, adrenalin still coursing through her veins. *"The only thing that kept those two from killing everyone and robbing the bank was their fear of a man who was even more ruthless than they were."*

The mist suddenly evaporated, leaving Lily gulping air, in an attempt to calm her churning stomach.

"This is the last of it," Clay said, placing a wooden crate in a stack with several others, each marked with a picture of a fish and the words "Lancaster's Fish Oil." He had removed his Fedora and jacket and rolled up his shirt sleeves, but still wore his shoulder holster.

"Tomorrow evening, someone will come pick it up from us," Agnes said, glancing at the stacks of crates over Clay's shoulder. "That's the way it always happens – liquor comes in one day; out the next."

Lily realized this must be the storeroom of the Cabot Mercantile.

Bobbi sidled over to Clay and gave him a peck on the cheek. "Thank you so much for doing this, Long Gone," she said, "I don't know what we would have done without you."

Clay smiled down at her. "Can I offer you a ride home, Witch?"

"Not just yet," Jo interrupted. "I need to show you something." She reached into the deep pocket of her skirt and pulled out a thick stack of cash. "I took it while I was relocking the strongbox. I don't think it's stealing – not exactly, anyway. I mean, the money belongs to Lucian and I'm legally in charge of his accounts, right?"

"Goodness, Jo – that's a huge head of cabbage," Bobbi marveled, gaping. "What are you going to do with it?"

"Well, ever since I learned about Lou and her doctor friend offering aid to mistreated women up there in New York, I've wanted to help," Jo replied. "And, considering what he did to her, Lucian owes her this and more."

A sudden buzzing sound in Lily's ear distracted her. When she turned to see what was making the annoying racket, she plummeted through the clouds as though she had stepped off a cliff.

Chapter Seventy Two

Lily whirled her arms, trying to stop from plunging further into the abyss. With her senses still in hyper-drive from Bobbi's last few memories, it took a moment for her to remember she was dreaming.

She woke with a start and threw her arm out towards the nightstand to slap the buzzing alarm clock into silence. Then she reclosed her eyes and allowed her thoughts to drift, reliving Bobbi's latest adventure.

Until she remembered that Grams was dead.

Her heart, which had been racing with adrenalin only moments before, suddenly felt like a lead weight in her chest. She sat up and clutched a pillow against her breast, trying to recall Grams' blissful expression as she disappeared into the light. Then she picked up the hotel phone and dialed the number on the business card Opal had given her.

"This is the best way," she murmured. "Pull off the Band-Aid."

The woman answered the phone after only one ring. "Good morning," she said; her voice warm and friendly. "You've reached Hubble Funeral Home. This is Christine. How can I help you?"

"*Say it. Make it official.*" Lily cleared her throat. "My grandmother passed away yesterday." Tears filled her eyes, spilling over onto her cheeks as she took a shaky breath.

"I'm so sorry. Is this Lilyanna Thorne?" she asked.

Lily wanted to ask how the woman knew that, but only managed to utter "Yes" before her voice cracked.

413

"Your grandmother, Lois Bloom, arrived yesterday. I promise we'll take good care of her, and we'll do everything we can to help you through this, too."

"Okay," Lily said with a sob.

"I understand you're already in town. Would you like to meet with our staff this morning?"

"Would this afternoon be okay instead?" Lily squeaked.

Lily made an appointment for one o'clock that afternoon, mumbled a stiff goodbye and hung up. Then she hobbled over to the box of Grams' memorabilia and picked up her afghan. As she draped it around her shoulders, she caught a whiff of Chanel No 5, the only perfume Grams' ever wore. She buried her nose in the blanket and inhaled, but the faded scent was too fickle to satisfy her longing. She unlocked her hotel room safe and retrieved the ancient Chanel No 5 powder box that Grams, who had never been one to throw things away, used in place of a jewelry box. Lily lifted the lid and breathed in the nostalgic aroma while probing the contents with her forefinger.

To her delight, she found a small travel-size bottle of the perfume amongst the modest jewelry collection. She removed it, along with a delicate gold necklace with a rose pendant and matching earrings. Reluctantly, she returned the powder box to the safe and placed the selected items into a zippered pocket of her purse. Still consumed with thoughts of Grams, she checked the time, only to realize she was running late.

"Before I meet Seth at the café, I need to call Scott about the funeral arrangements." She picked up her cell phone and pressed Scott's speed dial number. She didn't remember he kissed her until the first ring.

He answered on the second ring.

Lily fought the childish urge to hang up. "I, um, was calling to let you know I made a one o'clock appointment at Hubbell – if you still want to go."

Scott made a half-coughing sound – the one he made when he was trying not to overreact. "Of course I want to be there – unless you've changed your mind and don't want me there because of – last night."

"I do want you there. Very much. But I – we – need to focus our attention on Grams for now, okay?"

"I understand. No problem. Listen – since we don't have to be there until one, do you want to grab some breakfast?"

"I'm sorry, but I already made plans for breakfast," she replied, hoping he wouldn't ask for details. "Why don't we meet in the lobby at say, quarter till one?"

The pause before his reply was brief, but spoke volumes. "Oo-kay," he said, drawing the word out. "Actually, that's good," he continued unconvincingly. "I can call the office and take care of a few things. I'll pull the rental car around to the front and meet you in the lobby at twelve forty-five."

"Sounds like a plan," Lily said, still feeling awkward.

"Love you," he said, using their traditional sign-off.

"Love you, too."

When she stepped into the shower, vivid images of Seth from the day before – wet, soapy and ripped – pushed all other thoughts from Lily's mind. He had washed her hair. Then she washed his entire body, asking him questions about each little scar, just as he had done with her earlier that morning.

In doing so, she learned an apple farm in Idaho was a more dangerous place to grow up than she might have imagined, what with tractors, tree trimming and roughhousing with three brothers. She also discovered he was the middle child and more like his mild-tempered, inquisitive mother than his rowdy, old-fashioned father. He practiced meditation and yoga, but never felt more alive than when flying down an open road on a motor-cycle. His parent's love and support was unconditional, even when he decided to study massage therapy and live the life of a motorcycle gypsy. He said they were looking forward to his be-ing home for a few months, but once he recuperated from surgery, they understood he would return to his adventurous life on the road.

"If Dylan had lived to manhood, what adventures would he have had?" Lily wondered. *"What stories would he have shared when a woman asked about his scars? What would he have told her about*

his parents?" She turned off the water, heartbroken that her little boy never got the chance to live out his story.

She dressed in a dark pantsuit and made her way to the Terrace Café. Instead of sitting at their usual table, she found Seth standing at the entrance, waiting for her. When he heard the clicking sound of her crutch, he strode to her and took her into his arms.

Lily melted against him, but then pulled back, suddenly afraid that Scott might be having breakfast, too. A quick scan of the room put her mind at ease.

"How are you holding up?" Seth asked.

"Weaving between emotions like they're gates on a downhill ski run," she replied, relaxing. "One moment things are surreal, the next I'm devastated, then I'm relieved – followed immediately by an overwhelming sense of guilt and loneliness... Other than that, I guess I'm doing okay."

"Sounds about right. When my favorite grandma died, it hit me like a ton of bricks. And I know yours was more of a mom than a grandmother, so it's got to be way worse for you."

A young, beautiful couple walked by, eyeing them with curiosity – as though they were exhibits on display. Lily shrank back, feeling ugly and damaged. "Let's go sit down, all right?"

"Sure – I'll bet your leg's bothering you."

"Sometimes your blindness is a blessing," Lily thought.

They settled at their table and placed their orders before resuming their conversation. Lily told him about her appointment at the funeral home, but decided not to mention Scott or the letters from Dylan's organ recipients.

"My day is going to suck after breakfast," Lily said, "so I need you to cheer me up as much as possible while it lasts."

"Damn – I left my stand-up routine in my room," Seth wisecracked.

"Oh – I just remembered something." Lily reached for her purse. "The staff at Morton Plant found some dumb warnings for your book."

"No shit? That's great!"

"Do you have your recorder handy?"

Seth held the tape recorder while Lily read the list. "You know, I'm not sure if these next two are exactly warnings, but apparently, on a package containing a tricycle, there was a disclaimer: *'Child Not Included.'* And on a three-inch newspaper ad for three hundred dollar tire, there was one that read: *'Tire Pictured Is Not Actual Size.'"*

Seth laughed. "Those are absolutely dumb warnings."

"Okay, well here's the last one," Lily said. "It's from a tag on a swim suit: *'Do not wear in sunlight.'"*

"Or what?" Seth grinned.

Lily chuckled. "Is your mom going to help you finish your book?"

"Yeah, but I'm hoping I can see well enough to take over after the first week or so. Hopefully, I'll publish it before I hit the road."

"Then what?"

"Volume two, probably. I mean, dumb warnings keep turning up everywhere, right? While I was waiting for you, I was talking with some nice old guy who said that while he was in the Army Air Corps during World War II, all the claymore mines came with the warning: *'Point explosive side toward enemies.'"* He cocked his head to the side. "Hey, that could be my next title – *Weapons are Dangerous and Other Dumb Warnings.* Instead the motorcycles, I could use pictures of bombs and shit."

"Doesn't sound very Zen."

"You have a point there. How about racecars?"

All too soon, breakfast came to an end and Seth walked Lily back to her room.

"You want to get together for dinner?" he asked. "I have a few lab tests this afternoon, but I think I can pull together some funny stuff to cheer you up by tonight."

"I think I'll want to be alone, but thanks," Lily said, giving him a kiss. "Breakfast tomorrow?"

"You got it," he replied. "I guess I'll spend the evening listening to more of Randy the bartender's stories about this hotel." His expression changed, becoming serious. "Lily, you'd tell me if you need something more from me, right? I'm still learning to read your signals."

"You're doing fine. I'm sure things will get better after Grams' memorial service."

"Don't worry. I'll be right by your side. You can lean on me as much as you need to."

Even though he meant to comfort her, Lily suddenly felt like she had two dates for the same event. "Thanks," she said, giving him a final peck on the cheek. "See you in the morning, Seth."

Chapter Seventy Three

By the time Lily limped to the lobby, Scott was already there, impeccably dressed in grey slacks and sport coat over a black shirt. He helped her into the rental car; his touch wordlessly sharing her grief.

"Do you know how to get there?" she asked.

"It's the same place we used for Gramps' service, right?" he asked.

"Yes." Lily couldn't put her finger on it, but there was something comforting about the fact that Scott remembered that. They shared so much history.

"Did you get any sleep?" he asked.

"Some." She paused. "I read the letters."

Scott shot a surprised glance at her. "You did?"

"Yeah. I know I said I never wanted to, but reading their stories was actually kind of nice."

Scott nodded. "I thought so, too."

A few minutes later, he pulled the car into the parking lot of the Hubbell Funeral Home. Except for the hearse, parked in the shade of the carport, the parking lot was empty. Four stately white columns marked the corners of a broad, covered portico, leading to the double-door entrance. On either side of the entry, the funeral home's long, white walls were symmetrically punctuated with large blue arches, painted to look like windows, and modest landscaping extended a few feet from the well-maintained building.

Lily stared at the funeral parlor, overwhelmed by a sense of déjà vu. *"Gramps died years ago, but it feels like it was yesterday."*

"Do you need a minute?" Scott asked.

"No. I'm okay," she said, opening the car door.

They linked arms and crossed the parking lot together, adding to the surreal sense of repetition. A dark-haired man greeted them when they stepped inside the well-appointed lobby. His fitted grey suit, white shirt and light blue necktie, complemented his medium build and his eyeglasses framed compassionate brown eyes.

"I'm Kenneth Hodge, one of the directors here," he said, extending his hand first to Scott and then to Lily. "Please call me Ken."

"Scott and Lily Thorne," Scott replied. "Lois Bloom is – was – Lily's grandmother."

"Of course. We're sorry for your loss. If you'll follow me, we can discuss the details of the service and I'll do my best to answer any questions you might have."

Ken led the way to a small conference room with a dark walnut, oval table. Scott pulled out a chair for Lily, while Ken opened a bottle of cold water for each of them.

"I know this is a sad time for you," Ken said, "but we'll do our best to make sure your grandmother's memorial service honors her while comforting those who mourn her passing. We want to make this experience more about remembering Mrs. Bloom and less about handling all the legal issues involved, so we'll coordinate with the hospital and governmental agencies to make sure nothing gets overlooked."

Lily nodded, feeling numb and robotic.

"Now, because we handled your grandfather's service and your grandmother made most of her arrangements in advance, we were able to complete the majority of the paperwork in advance. Once you review the information for accuracy, we'll process the death certificate and make as many copies as you need to resolve insurance and estate issues."

Lily nodded again. *"It sounds so impersonal. The business end of dying,"* she thought.

"I understand that you plan to honor Mrs. Bloom's wish to be cremated and have her ashes scattered in the same body of water where her husband's ashes were laid to rest, correct?" Ken asked, interrupting her thoughts.

"Yes," Lily confirmed.

"And you wanted us to arrange for a boat and captain to take you out?"

Lily nodded.

"No problem – we'll come back to that. I think you already know that we're required by law to wait for forty eight hours before performing a cremation, but what we do in the meantime depends on whether or not you want to have a viewing and memorial service for your grandmother before the cremation."

When Lily looked uncertain, Ken continued. "If you prefer not to have your grandmother's body prepared for public viewing, you could have a private viewing today and then hold a memorial service after the cremation – or you could choose to have no memorial service at all. It's totally up to you."

Lily took a sip of water to wet her dry mouth. "I'd like to see her one last time, but not at the memorial service. Scott and I will most likely be the only two people in attendance, and we need to get back to St. Louis, so..."

"I understand. We can schedule her memorial service for Friday and arrange to have Captain Mike take you out on his boat, the Dreamcatcher, to scatter her ashes right afterward. We recorded the latitude and longitude where your grandfather's ashes were laid to rest, so the captain can take you to the same location."

Lily smiled with gratitude at the unexpected level of detail. "Now I know why Grams chose you guys to handle her arrangements. You've thought of everything."

"Well, we try," Ken said. "Lily, I'd like to suggest using a biodegradable salt urn for the ceremony. It looks like marble, but it would sink to the bottom intact and then slowly dissolve, releasing your grandmother's ashes over time, rather than scattering them in the wind."

Lily had a vivid memory of how wind gusts had made it difficult to maintain the dignity of her grandfather's ash-scattering ceremony. "That sounds perfect," she said without hesitation.

"Good. I'll advise our staff to prepare Mrs. Bloom for a private visitation, while we work out the rest of the details of her service." Ken said.

Lily nodded. She unzipped her purse and retrieved the jewelry and perfume. "These are for Grams," she said, placing the items on the table.

Scott covered her hand with his. "Grams can be cremated wearing her dentures, but no metal jewelry."

"That's correct, but we can place her wedding band inside the urn on top of her ashes, if you like," Ken added.

"But she hated going anywhere without jewelry," Lily protested.

"It's all right, Lily," Scott said. He reached into his jacket pocket, pulled out a small jewelry box. "I had an organic necklace and earrings made for her." He opened the box to reveal a small, white, delicately carved, wooden cross, hanging from a navy ribbon, and matching earrings that attached with adhesive.

Lily's jaw dropped at the unexpected gesture.

"What a nice gift," Ken said. He pushed a button on the table and a moment later, a woman appeared in the doorway. "Christine, this perfume and jewelry are for Mrs. Bloom," he said, handing her the items. "Please make preparations for a brief, private visit in the small parlor and let me know when they're complete. Thanks."

Ken turned his attention back to Lily. "If you have some pictures you'd like to share as a part of your grandmother's memorial service, we can scan them into a video for you. We find that pictures depicting happy moments help mourners focus on celebrating life rather than loss.

Before Lily could tell him about the framed pictures in her hotel room, Scott removed a disk from his jacket pocket.

"Here," he said, holding out the CD. This has a lot of our favorite pictures of Grams on it – there's even a few from her childhood."

Lily gaped openmouthed, looking as though she wouldn't have been any more surprised, had he pulled an otter from his pocket.

"When you told me she wasn't going to make it, I went through our photo albums," he explained. "I thought it would be a good idea to scan some of them so we could make a gallery picture board, like we did for Gramps." He turned to Ken. "But a video would be even better."

Speechless, Lily took his hand and squeezed it. Scott gave her a self-conscious half-smile in return. Understanding slammed through Lily's consciousness like a thunderbolt. *"I've been so self-absorbed that I forgot Scott would be grieving about Grams, too. He must have spent hours choosing photos to honor her life."*

She didn't realize tears were rolling down her cheeks until Ken handed her a tissue.

By the time Christine tapped on the door, they had coordinated with Pastor McIntyre at St. Paul's, selected a salt urn, written Grams' obituary, chosen the music, and ordered flowers.

"We're ready," she said.

Ken responded with a nod and then returned his attention to Lily. "I think that should just about do it. Do you have any remaining questions or concerns?"

Lily shook her head. "I don't." She looked at Scott, expecting him to concur.

"Actually, I do have one more request," Scott said, avoiding Lily's stare. "I haven't talked this over with Lily, but I'd like to scatter a small portion of our son Dylan's ashes with Grams'. They used to plan big adventures together, so if we scatter their ashes together, they could sort of – you know, travel together."

"I like that idea," Lily agreed. She gave Scott a tender smile.

Ken held his fingers up, about five inches apart. "Tiny keepsake salt urns are usually used by people who want to scatter their loved one's ashes at several different favorite locations, but I think one would work perfectly for what you're planning. If you bring your son's remains to us before the service, we can transfer some of his ashes into a keepsake urn that matches your grandmother's design. Is there anything else we can do for you?"

Both Lily and Scott shook their heads.

"Okay, then." Ken stood, motioning toward the door. "If you follow me, I'll take you to your grandmother."

As they entered the small parlor, Lily caught her breath. She knew the casket was just fabric-coated cardboard, but it looked elegant, and Grams had a peaceful expression on her gentle, time-worn face that death had not stolen from her. Dressed in her navy suit and small pillbox hat, she looked as though she might have been taking a quick nap before church. The cross necklace and earrings were perfect accents. When the fragrance of Chanel No. 5 wafted up from the casket, Lily smiled. It was the perfect last image of Grams.

Chapter Seventy Four

After the visitation, Ken provided a package of information about the memorial service, including directions to Captain Mike's boat slip in the Clearwater Beach Marina and navigational coordinates to Gramps' resting place in the Gulf of Mexico, before escorting them to the door.

Once they were in the car, Scott turned to Lily. "I think I'm going to head over to Clearwater Beach to see where the *Dreamcatcher* is docked, and then grab a bite and catch the sunset. Want to go with me?"

"Sure," Lily replied, attempting to sound cheerful. "Why don't we try someplace new, though?"

Scott clenched his jaw. "I want to go to Frenchy's Rockaway Grill and sit out on the veranda overlooking the beach."

Lily didn't respond. There was no use arguing with Scott when he put his foot down, but she knew Frenchy's would bring back painful memories of watching Dylan play in the sand – never suspecting how soon he would be gone.

"If you don't want to go, it's alright," Scott said, as if reading her mind. "I'll drive you back to the hotel and head over alone."

"It's fine. I just thought it might be nice to try something new," Lily lied.

They drove in silence, but not even Lily was immune to the stunning view from the top of the Memorial Causeway Bridge. A wide variety of sailboats and motorboats dotted the sparkling greenish-blue water far below, while a few bicyclists and pedestrians made use of the sidewalks that ran the length of the bridge, next to the traffic lanes. Here and there, people paused in sightseeing nooks, designed to allow visitors to catch their breath or photograph the Intracoastal Waterway without blocking the sidewalk. Once across the bridge, they continued down the palm-lined causeway, while pedestrians and bicyclists veered off onto a paved path, close to the water's edge.

Lily decided to break their silence. "I hear the Clearwater Aquarium plans to move over to the mainland."

"That's what happens, Lily. Things change."

She pressed her lips together, ignoring Scott's *not so subtle* reference about her refusing to move on. When he stopped at the main entrance of the restaurant to drop her off, her only comment was, "Busy."

He replied, "Yep. As usual," and then drove off in search of a parking spot.

Happy, sunbaked tourists moved out of her way as she limped up the short ramp to where a brunette beauty queen, dressed in a tight tank top and tiny shorts sat on a barstool, taking reservations. Lily added her name to the girl's waiting list and then shuffled over to the covered walkway that separated the tiki bar from the white, sugar-sand beach and also served as a waiting area for the restaurant.

She plopped down on one of the wood benches that lined the whimsical, blue and pink wooden railing and glanced around. The entire natural wood plank walkway was protected from the weather by a bright yellow awning and people of all ages, shapes and sizes filled the space, laughing, chatting, and drinking.

Longing to be one of them again, she turned her head away from the crowd. "*Could I really just leave my past behind me and start over with Seth?*" she wondered. She watched a young family come off the beach, stopping to rinse sand from their feet and beach toys, before heading for the nearby parking lot.

Then she saw Scott, walking on the sidewalk next to the showers. He had removed his jacket, but still looked overdressed for the current Rockaway crowd. She knew that would bother him, and smiled when he started rolling up his shirt sleeves as he approached the restaurant's entrance. He spotted her and smiled back, his boyish grin unchanged over time.

"Did you sign us up for a table on the deck?" he asked from the other side of the railing.

"I told her it didn't matter – whichever opened up first," Lily said.

"It matters when we're only an hour from sunset," he replied. "I'll tell the hostess we'll wait for an outer rail table."

When Scott sauntered up the entrance ramp, the beauty queen smiled and sat up straighter, admiring his casual male-model appearance. She tossed her wavy hair over her shoulder, trying hard to make it look as though thrusting her chest forward in the process of changing their reservation wasn't intentional.

Lily was amused by the obvious flirtation until she remembered that Scott planned to file divorce papers following the funeral. Even though she had been contemplating a new life with Seth only moments before, her heart ached at the thought of Scott belonging to anyone else.

At the tiki bar, a couple of bikini-clad college girls made room for Scott to lean in and catch the bartender's attention. While he waited for his order, he chatted with the girls, garnering him steely-eyed stares from a couple of football-types hovering near-by. Lily couldn't tell if they were the girls' dates or if they were just hopeful suitors, but either way, they looked relieved when Scott left the bar with two glasses of red wine.

"Pinot Noir," he said, handing her a glass.

"Thanks. For a few minutes there, I thought I was going to lose my dinner date."

Scott looked at her, puzzled.

She laughed. "Come on... the hostess? Those girls at the bar?"

He turned around, visually retracing his steps. "I think your imagination is a lot better than my reality."

Lily smirked and shook her head at his humble demeanor. Then she raised her glass and took a sip of wine. It tasted good.

Very good. She leaned her back against the rough wood railing and closed her eyes, allowing the essence of the beach to wash over her. The cacophony of fifty conversations intertwined with jukebox music still wasn't loud enough to drown-out the sound of screeching seagulls in the lapping surf. The gentle breeze carried the salty scent of the water to her, while simultaneously tugging at her loose curls of auburn hair, encouraging them to take flight. The familiar, relaxing ambiance reminded her of the days when the world was still her oyster.

"Lily, party of two; Lily, party of two" a girl's voice called over the scratchy speaker. Lily's eyes flew open, catching Scott observing her. He looked away before she could interpret the complex emotions she saw in his dark brown eyes.

She stood and hobbled after the beckoning server, weaving between rows of round, plastic umbrella tables, until they reached one located next to the rail, overlooking the beach and surf. She pretended not to notice that the server was holding a white plastic chair out for her, instead choosing the seat that put her back to the beach.

Scott took the chair the server had intended for Lily and smiled at the young woman. "This is a perfect table – uh, what's your name?"

"I'm Amy," she said, handing him a menu. "Do you need a few minutes to decide?"

"That would be great, Amy. Thanks."

Scott didn't look up from his menu until Amy returned with an open order pad.

"Want to split a fried calamari appetizer?" Lily asked.

Scott shrugged with indifference.

"I'll take that as a 'yes'," she said, wondering what happened to sour his mood. "And I'll also have a bowl of She-Crab soup and a half-order of peel-and-eat shrimp."

"And you?" Amy asked Scott.

"I'm going with the Four Kings – grouper, shrimp, scallops and a crab cake, cooked Cajun style."

"Good choice," Amy commented. "How are you guys doing on your drinks? Can I bring you another..."

"Pinot Noir. And yes you may," Scott replied, without consulting Lily.

Lily held up her half-full glass. "Not for me," she said. She shifted her gaze to the tiki bar and watched as a growing number of tourists staked out territory for optimal sunset viewing.

A few minutes later, Amy returned with Scott's wine and the calamari. He tilted his first drink back and then traded his empty glass for the full one. Their strained silence continued as they nibbled on the appetizer, but eventually, the sound of the surf had a calming effect on Scott.

"Man, this is a great beach," he said. "What was it that Dylan used to call it?"

"The bestest beach," Lily replied quietly, without looking. "Oh, look. Here comes our food," she said, ending the exchange.

After Amy served their meals, Lily tried another topic. "It was wonderful of you to make that CD of Grams' pictures. And the cross was just perfect."

"Thanks. You know, I always thought losing someone you love would be easier to handle if it was an old person, but I guess that's not the way it works." He swirled his wine, watching the dark red liquid glisten in the light of the low sun. "I'm glad we're having a proper memorial service for her – paying tribute to her life and saying goodbye before we scatter her ashes."

"I agree."

Scott took a drink. "It's what we should have done for Dylan," he muttered. "I mean, at first it made sense to postpone his service because of your injuries. But we never rescheduled it. Lately I've been wondering if maybe the reason we haven't been able to move on is because we never really said goodbye."

"I am moving on," Lily protested, dipping a shrimp into cocktail sauce.

"Oh really?" Scott spoke softly. "Do you think I don't know why you picked that chair? You can't even sit and have dinner facing the beach where Dylan used to play."

He took a slug of wine and then held his nearly empty glass up above his head, trying to catch Amy's eye. She gave him a thumbs-up from several tables away, recognizing the request for another re-fill.

Lily froze. *"He's right. How can I move forward if I can't make peace with the past?"*

"I'm sorry, Lily. I know you're going through a lot right now. That's why I didn't want to get into this until after Grams' memorial service." Scott took a deep breath, studying her face. "You know I hate living in our house by myself. You also know I tried finding someone new. What you don't seem to know is that you're the love of my life."

Tears welled in Lily's eyes.

Amy, noticing they were having a serious conversation, quietly exchanged Scott's empty wine glass for a full one and slipped away without a word. Scott shifted his gaze to his wine glass and began rolling the stem back and forth in his fingers while he framed his thoughts.

"Time is slipping by, Lily. Grams turned ninety one this year. Gramps didn't live quite as long, but he still got seventy two years. Dylan had the least amount of time – just thirteen short years… but they were good years… filled with wonderful memories. I don't know how much time I get and I don't want to waste any more of it."

Lily tensed, a lump in her throat, waiting for him to make his point.

Scott took a sip of wine and set the glass down before meeting her eyes. "I made a huge mistake letting you move out without a fight, and if there's one chance in a million that we can put our marriage back together, I want to take it. But here's the thing… whether or not we can fix things between us, Dylan's life deserves to be remembered and celebrated."

"Remembering hurts too much."

"Damn it, Lily, I feel cheated that we didn't get to watch Dylan grow up, too. But you know what? Now that Grams is gone, no one else in the whole world cares about his memory, except us." He shoved his fingers through his hair in frustration. "We should do what Ken suggested – focus on the memories instead of the loss. When we drive over to Clearwater Beach, we should remember the old drawbridge and how, when Dylan was little, he believed mermaids told the bridge go up and down by smacking their tails on the water. We should laugh, thinking about how he watched for those mermaids every time we got stuck in traffic, waiting for the bridge to close."

Lily gulped. "Sometimes he swore he saw them."

"Yeah, he did. And remember how excited he got when the Pirate Ship blasted the cannon at sundown? And how much he loved eating at Post Pizza after playing miniature golf... and how he loved summer camp at the Aquarium? That's why I wanted to sit out here. I wanted to remember all those times we toasted the sunset while watching Dylan play in the sand."

Lily cast a glance over her shoulder at the sun, sinking toward the water as Mother Nature painted the skyline with majestic swirls of red, orange, yellow, purple, and lilac. She pictured Dylan playing on the beach, but the thought of his abandoned pail and shovel still broke her heart. "I don't know if I can."

"Okay, here's the deal. We won't discuss this again until after Grams' memorial service. But then you need to decide. If you don't think we can put Dylan's death behind us, I'll let you go. But if you decide to give us a second chance, I'll do my best to make you happy for as long as we live – just like I promised when we got married."

Lily closed her eyes. Scott had whispered those words in her ear during the first dance at their wedding reception. She felt the warm glow of his love as the music played in her memory. But then Seth appeared in her imagination, holding his hand out, offering to be her next dance partner.

She gulped hard. *"What in the hell am I going to do?"*

Chapter Seventy Five

Even though it was relatively early when they returned from the beach, Lily was glad to crawl into bed and turn out the light. Emotionally drained, she drifted off to sleep, looking forward to escaping into the fog and the spirit realm beyond.

Instead, she tossed and turned as her old nightmare returned – the accident unfolding in meticulous detail, as it had so many times before. She heard Dylan's voice calling, *"Wake up, Mom!"* and experienced the excruciating pain of climbing through the broken windshield and reaching through fire to pull him to safety. She felt her head connect with the rock as they fell to the ground and rolled down an incline away from the burning car. Then she felt nothing – just the peaceful illusion that she had saved her beautiful boy.

This was the part of the nightmare she dreaded the most. The part just before the lie was revealed – drifting between life and death, believing her sacrifice, no matter how great, was worth it because Dylan was safe. It was like the slow *click, click, click* of a roller coaster climbing to an impossibly high peak, followed by the drop into her new, horrifying reality.

Suddenly, a macabre doctor would appear in her nightmare and begin carving up Dylan's body like a Thanksgiving turkey, gleefully serving his parts to a long line of equally ghoulish dinner guests. Lily would be forced to watch helplessly, until the only thing left on the table was Dylan's ashes, captured for eternity within a small, blue urn.

But when the doctor appeared in tonight's nightmare, he seemed sad as he methodically attended to his task of filling little white coolers with red crosses on them for the line of people who filed by. And each person who received a cooler thanked Dylan for saving their lives before fading away.

When they were all gone and Lily was left alone with the urn that held Dylan's ashes, she picked it up and cradled it against her heart. "Your father gave his permission because he knew you would have wanted to save as many lives as you could. He didn't know you'd be trapped…"

Just then, a man in a long white coat appeared next to her. He had Dylan's face, but spoke with a strong Boston accent. "Tha's no science to sah-pot the hypothesis that a spirit khan be trapped hee-are or anywhere else. And fah-thermore…"

The fog descended abruptly, carrying Lily into the folds of the spirit realm. By the time the mist opened into a memory, she was dizzy and had to close her eyes to regain her equilibrium.

"Bobbi, I've been thinking. It's high time we got married."

Lily's eyes flew open in surprise and she gaped at Clay and Bobbi. They were standing on the winding crushed shell path in the south garden of the Belleview Biltmore.

Bobbi rested her weight against her cane. "You're a swell fella, Clay. But you're a gambler and a wanderer. You'd be miserable, rooted to one spot."

"I won't deny being fond of riding the rails and playing cards with fellas I meet along the way. It keeps life interesting. But I always come back, don't I?"

Bobbi licked her lips. "You mean the world to me, Clay, but I still love Bear – God rest his soul."

"Of course you love him." Clay frowned. "He's the father of your children. But I know you love me, too."

Bobbi shifted her gaze to the shell path; her emotions divided.

As if he was reading her thoughts, Clay continued. "You have a big heart, Bobbi. There's enough room in there for the both of us." The right corner of his mouth twitching into a half smile. "Come on. Marry me."

He held his arms out for her, but Bobbi shook her head.

"I do care for you, Clay – a great deal. Perhaps I even love you, as you claim I do. But if I ever remarry, it will be to someone I know I can depend on to be here for me and my children, day in and day out."

Clay drew back, a wounded look in his eyes. "At the risk of sounding like I'm polishing my own brass buttons, I think I take pretty good care of you and your kids."

"Yes – of course, you do. You've been a real ace from the start, but..."

"But what?"

"Bear didn't just die. He was murdered. And you already escaped one swim in cement shoes. How long do you think your luck can hold out? Every time you leave, I'm terrified I'll never see you again. I can't..." Bobbi bit her lip.

Neither of them spoke for a long moment.

"Listen, Bobbi. No man knows when the good Lord's gonna call for him, or what he'll be doing when that call comes. But if getting out of the booze business is what it takes for you to accept me as your husband, then I'll quit and go to work at your sister's mercantile, cash money be damned."

"I can't ask you to do that. The life of a merchant would be dull as a rusty axe for someone with your wanderlust. And I couldn't stand knowing you were making yourself miserable just to please me."

"You didn't ask me to do it – it was my idea. Besides, maybe I'd like coming home every night. And maybe I'd still feel like a hero every time I brought you a box of groceries. Did you ever think of that?"

"Oh, Clay – even if that were true, you deserve someone who...," Bobbi's voice cracked. She took a deep breath and started again. "I've always heard that a loving husband sees his wife as the young, beautiful girl he first met, no matter how old she gets."

"Yeah, well, dames tend to have a lot of goofy ideas about what men think. So what?"

"It's just that when we met, I was so – damaged. I can't help but think you'll always see me as a helpless, wretched woman in need of rescue."

Clay's laughter caught Bobbi off-guard.

"Helpless? You?" He chuckled again. "When we first met, I thought you were a witch with the power to haunt me from beyond the grave if I didn't do your bidding!"

"But I don't possess any real powers," Bobbi said, taken aback. "You would have discovered that pretty quickly if I had died."

"Not dying was one of the first things you did to convince me that you *do* possess amazing powers," Clay replied. "And ever since then, I've watched you use those powers to change the lives of everyone around you for the better, including me. Why even when we're apart, I can hear you nagging me to do the right thing."

Bobbi started to protest, but Clay cupped her chin, closing her mouth as he raised her lips to his.

Lily thought this was Clay's memory, but suddenly she wasn't sure. She could still sense his emotions, but now she felt Bobbi's excitement, too.

Clay's moustache tickled at first, but as his warm, soft lips pressed harder against hers, a shiver raced all the way down to Bobbi's toes. His hand slid from her chin to cradle the back of her head, while his other arm encircled her waist, pulling her closer for a second kiss. She melted into his embrace, her cane falling to the ground unheeded.

Finally, Clay pulled back and gazed at her, his hand still pressed against the small of her back. "Marry me, Bobbi," he repeated in a raspy whisper.

Lily could tell Bobbi wanted to accept Clay's proposal, but she held back.

"Please – I need time to collect myself and think."

"Absolutely," Clay said, dropping his hand. "I have to oversee rail shipments to New York and Canada this week, anyhow." He smiled, lifting her chin again. "While I'm gone, you can make a list of all the changes you expect me to make before you'll take me as your husband."

Bobbi returned his smile. "That might take more than a week."

"I'll wait as long as it takes, Bobbi."

Clay saw another couple approaching on the path, so he bent down and retrieved Bobbi's cane.

"Did you say you'll be in New York next week?" she inquired, changing both the mood and the subject.

"Yes. And before you ask, I'll be happy to check-up on your sister, Lou," Clay teased.

As the clouds engulfed Lily, carrying her away from the memory, she heard Clay's voice waft through the mist. "If she had made up her mind right then and there to take a chance on me, things might have turned out differently."

In the distance, Lily heard a conversation between Clay and Bobbi escalate into an argument, but try as she might, she couldn't make out any words. The fog lifted as Margaret's strong voice intervened.

"Stop this nonsense immediately," Margaret demanded. "You can't possibly hope to help someone resolve an issue that you have yet to settle between yourselves! Time runs short. Let's make the most of this connection, shall we?"

Lily was able to peer through the clearing mist just in time to watch Clay's spirit fade from the small round table, where he had been sitting between Margaret and Bobbi. Lily floated into her seat, puzzled by the spectacle.

"Spirits don't always agree about which memories will be of most help to the living," Margaret said, reaching across the table to pour Lily a cup of steaming hot tea. "Clay is annoyed because we disagree about the best way to make the most of the short time we have together."

Lily pressed her lips together in a thin line, wondering how *any* of their memories were supposed to help her, but she remained silent as the fog gathered around her, carrying her into the folds of the mist.

When the clouds cleared this time, the surroundings were unfamiliar to Lily. A middle-aged caregiver stood behind a rocking chair, brushing the hair of an exceptionally old woman. Next to them was a single bed, covered with in ivory lace bedspread, and a nightstand that held several framed photographs. On the opposite wall, a large window cast sunbeams over the tops of two high-backed, upholstered chairs and a small table. The third wall was filled with bookcases.

Lily examined an old wedding photograph sitting on one of the shelves and then spun around, mouth gaping, finally recognizing Bobbi's green eyes shining within the withered face.

"Which one of your children is visiting today?" the caregiver asked.

"My middle child – Henrietta. She lives in New York, but Stetson University invited her to return to present a lecture on her career as a civil rights attorney."

"You know, I participated in a civil rights march when I was a girl." She finished brushing Bobbi's hair and handed her a mirror. "But then I met Ralph. I didn't have time for all that nonsense after we got married."

"All four of my children graduated from college," Bobbi boasted. "One earned a master's in business, two have law degrees, and my youngest is a doctor."

"Goodness," the woman said. "How in the world did you pay for college for four children? Didn't you tell me you were seriously injured and widowed while they were young?"

"Yes, but I had a lot of help. A dear friend helped my eldest son earn a scholarship to Yale – his alma mater – by advising the admissions board that Nathaniel's late father had been a well-published business efficiency expert." She smiled, waving a hand toward the bookshelf. "He knew full-well I was the one who wrote all those books."

Bobbi smoothed down her wavy, silver hair. "My sister and her husband, Senator Winfield, paid for Fred and Henrietta's law degrees. By the time Belle was ready for college, the other three children were working and they all helped her pay for medical school."

"That's amazing."

"I suppose," Bobbi replied. "But it was really just a matter of encouraging them to keep moving forward. After all, every big wave starts out as a little ripple, right?"

Lily considered the struggles Bobbi faced throughout her life. Time and time again, her perseverance provided an excellent example for her family and friends to follow. *"You never know how far a ripple will travel,"* she thought as the mist gathered around her, pulling her from the memory.

Chapter Seventy Six

When Lily opened her eyes, it took a moment to clear her head and remember where she was. She wanted to stay in bed and collect her thoughts, but one glance at the clock on her nightstand put an end to such notions. She was supposed to meet Seth for breakfast in twenty minutes.

She took a quick shower, left her hair down and dressed in a black, long-sleeved blouse and white, wide-legged palazzo slacks that hid her brace. *"You know, if you're going to live life on the back of a motorcycle, you're going to need to do something about that leg,"* she thought.

Seth was already seated at their table when she arrived, still trying to imagine wrapping her arms around him with her chest pressed against his back; leaving her entire past in the rearview mirror. The image was inviting.

"I love your scent and that little click, click of your crutch that lets me know you're almost here," Seth teased as Lily took her seat.

"Listen, I have great news," he said, still beaming. "All of my test results came back great, so my surgery is scheduled for Friday morning."

"That's, um... great," Lily said. "Really. I'm happy for you."

"You don't sound happy."

"I am – truly, I am. It's just that Grams' memorial service is on Friday."

Seth's smile fell. "No way – I thought that would be on Saturday. I mean, I haven't been to that many funerals, but I thought they were always on Saturday or Sunday." He paused. "I guess I could try to reschedule my surgery for Monday..."

"Nonsense," Lily interrupted, relieved that she wouldn't have to divide her time between Seth and Scott throughout Grams' service. "You can't change something that important in order to sit through a short memorial service for someone you've never even met. I'll be fine – really. But what about you? Will you have to stay in the hospital for a few days?"

"No – corneal transplants are done on an outpatient basis. I'm supposed to stay in town for one night, just to make sure there are no problems, but that's all. I was planning to stay through the weekend, so I could be here for you, and then catch a flight back to Idaho on Monday."

"Wow!" Lily was incredulous. "You'll have your vision back Friday afternoon?"

Seth laughed. "Not exactly. My eyes will have to remain covered until I get home. An ophthalmologist near my folks' farm will coordinate with my surgeon to oversee my recovery. It could take as little as a week or as long as few months before I can see clearly."

"That long?"

"Yeah, apparently I have to teach my brain how to use my eyes again. Hopefully it'll come right back to me, like riding a bike – pun intended."

"I'm sure you'll be fine in no time," Lily said.

"I hope you're right. I'm also hoping you'll come with me when I hit the road again. I'm serious about that, Lily. I want you to ride with me."

"Will you feel the same way when you get your eyesight back?" Lily wondered. "I just might do that," she said, trying to ignore her inner negativity.

"Wait and see – once you feel the thrill of tearing down an open road on a smooth-riding Harley, you'll never want to do anything else."

Lily gulped, suddenly realizing that every time she imagined herself perched behind Seth on his Harley, the motorcycle wasn't moving. *"Okay, genius. How is this supposed to work, given your pathetic fear of traffic accidents?"*

Before she had time to contemplate this new wrinkle in her future, her phone beeped.

"Whoa, I hardly ever get text messages anymore." She pulled the phone from her pocket, trying not to think about Dylan.

"It's from Scott – 911," Lily murmured. "He wouldn't do that unless it's something serious. Can you excuse me for a minute?"

"Sure, no problem. I hope everything's okay."

Lily hobbled into the lounge across the corridor from the restaurant and dropped onto a red, circular sofa with a high tufted-back. She dialed Scott, hoping he sent the message by accident.

"Lily, I'm sorry to bother you, but I've been monitoring your blog this morning and you have a serious situation on your hands."

"My blog?" Lily repeated, confused.

"Yes. Some woman in your chat room says she's contemplating suicide and has questions. A couple of assholes are egging her on, telling her to do it. The situation is escalating. You need to take control of this before something bad happens."

"She probably isn't serious, Scott. Some people post suicide threats just to get attention."

"I don't think she's faking, Lily. She seems really depressed."

"Does she have a terminal illness?"

"No. That's the thing. She's perfectly healthy. She says her daughter died, and now she doesn't want to live anymore."

Lily felt a chill run up her spine.

"My Wi-Fi connection only works in my room," Scott continued. "Can you come up and take a look?"

"Okay, I'll be up in a few minutes," she said, casting a wistful glance in Seth's direction. She took a deep breath and headed over to let him know he'd be eating alone this morning.

"How in the world can I help this woman?" Lily moaned as the elevator doors closed.

Her knees turn to jelly when an eerie voice whispered, "A mother who knows for a *fact* that her child's spirit lives on beyond death could be a great comfort to one still in the throes of grief."

"Margaret?" Lily squeaked, trying not to hyperventilate. "Is that you?"

The elevator doors reopened and a young mother stepped in with two children and an armload of pool toys, ending the ethereal conversation.

Lily scrolled to the top of Scott's computer screen and skimmed through the comments a second time, allowing the seriousness of the situation sink in. The woman was still on-line, as were the two jerks who were encouraging her to take her life immediately.

"Sickos," she mumbled, quickly taking administrative control of her site. She blocked the malicious duo's access and deleted their previous comments, leaving only the woman's cries for help. Lily surmised the woman's daughter overdosed on prescription drugs, found in her medicine cabinet.

Lily placed her fingers on the keyboard, hoping to engage the woman before she broke off her connection: *There is no worse guilt than that of a mother who feels responsible for the death of her child. It wraps around you like a vine until you can't breathe. I know. I've been where you are.*

Anonymous: *Then you understand why I can't go on.*

Lily: *Why do you think this was your fault?*

Anonymous: *The pain pills my doctor prescribed following surgery upset my stomach, so he prescribed something else. I didn't like those either, but I didn't throw either prescription out because I didn't want to be wasteful. WASTEFUL! I am so stupid! If I had flushed them down the toilet, Rachel would still be alive.*

Lily learned the war widow's name was Barbara and that she had never suspected her only child and her friends were experimenting with prescription drugs. When Rachel blacked-out one afternoon, her friends went home, assuming she would 'sleep it off'. By the time Barbara returned home from work, her sixteen-year-old daughter's life was over.

Three hours later, Lily was finally able to coax the distraught mother into opening up and sharing some happier memories of Rachel – the first step in trying to change her mind about suicide.

Lily: *Guilt is a heavy burden, but if you die, who will be left to care for Rachel's beloved cat? Who will comfort her friends to keep this tragedy from ruining their lives, too? Who will warn other parents about the dangers lurking in their medicine cabinets and help prevent this from happening to other children? You must live, Barbara. It's the only way to honor your daughter's memory.*

Chapter Seventy Seven

By the time Lily talked Barbara into seeking help for her grief, her neck and shoulders ached from hunching over Scott's laptop. But her heart felt stronger than it had for a long time.

"You did great," Scott said. "I'm proud of you, Lily. You really helped that woman. I think you might have even saved her life." He gave the computer a wary glance. "Maybe you should stick around a while to see if she comes back."

"Maybe." Lily rolled her shoulders, trying to relieve the stiffness. "I should post some contact information for grief counselors, too."

Scott moved behind her and began massaging her shoulders.

"Mmmmm, that's nice," she moaned, mentally comparing his massage technique to Seth's. *"He might not be eliminating toxins, but damn, that feels good."*

"It's the least I can do," he replied. "Hey, are you hungry? I never ate breakfast and now it's way past lunchtime. I could order room service."

"Yeah, I'm starving," Lily replied. "I was just about to have breakfast with – um, *when* I got your text." Lily picked up the room service menu, but thoughts of Seth made it difficult to concentrate. *"He's probably freaking out, wondering where I am,"* she thought. *"But how am I going call him with Scott right here?"*

"I'm going to have the Cuban sandwich with fries and a beer," Scott decided, reading over her shoulder.

"Me too, but with fresh fruit instead of fries," Lily said, closing the menu.

"I don't know why I decided to check your blog today," Scott said, picking up the phone to place their order, "but I'm sure glad that I did."

"Me, too," Lily whispered. Then another thought occurred to her. *"What would have happened to Barbara if I had been on a motorcycle ride in the middle of God knows where, with no internet connection?"* She shook her head to clear it. "I'm going to step out onto the balcony and make a couple calls while we're waiting for our food."

Pretending not to notice Scott's wounded expression, Lily added a half-truth. "I'm calling Mary – a transplant coordinator I know. She probably has a lot of contact information for grief counselors." She nodded toward the laptop. "Could you keep an eye on my site while I get some fresh air?"

Scott smiled, reassured. "Sure, no problem."

Lily stepped outside and closed the door behind her. She took a deep breath, admiring the Intracoastal Waterway on the horizon and the breathtaking gardens, four stories below. The sparkling blue swimming pool was a tempting distraction, so she moved to the far end of the balcony. There, she spotted a small cluster of people enjoying a game of croquet. In the distance, golfers played on a perfectly manicured course, beneath a blue sky dotted with white puffy clouds.

Lily sighed with envy and dialed Seth's number. Although disappointed, he understood her situation and agreed she should stay and help Barbara. Next, she called Mary who, as it turned out, really did have contact information for several helplines and grief counselors.

When she came back inside, Scott barely glanced up from the computer. "Lily, check this out. Barbara hasn't been back, but apparently, a few people were monitoring your chat with her, and after you signed off, they started adding their own comments. Some of them must have forwarded the link to your blog, because so far about twenty people have responded and every time I refresh the page, there are more comments."

Lily's jaw dropped.

"They *love* you!" Scott continued. "They're asking for your advice on other stuff, too," I wouldn't say your blog's gone viral, but you're definitely drawing some attention. It's like *Dear Abby* for people who've lost a child."

"Oh my God," Lily thought, switching seats with Scott. *"I created a ripple!"* She scanned the questions, and then set to work, responding to every single person, offering advice or consolation. Scott acted as her sounding board and also redesigned the home page to highlight the grief counseling contact information.

"I can't type anymore," she finally said, flexing her stiff fingers. "I'm signing off."

"I agree," Scott said. "That's plenty for one day."

She peered out at the balcony, surprised to discover they had missed the sunset.

"Listen, Lily – if you don't have any plans," Scott said, "the Moody Blues are playing at the Capitol Theater tonight. I bought two tickets hoping..."

Lily screwed up her face in disbelief. "The Moody Blues are playing at the old movie theater? Times must be hard."

Scott laughed. "They overhauled the place. It's a first-class venue these days." He cocked his head at the door. "Come on. You look great and it would do you good to get out of here for a while."

"It would be nice to see the theater," Lily agreed, doubting the accuracy of the compliment. "Besides, if I went back to my room, I'd probably just worry about Barbara all night."

Much of the Mediterranean theater's historic 1921 ambiance had been preserved, but it was far grander in both scale and amenities than the cinema of Lily's youth.

"I can't believe this is the same place," she exclaimed.

"I know," Scott said. "The bar's packed, but if you want a drink, we can try to squeeze in."

"I can't handle crowds," Lily reminded him, tapping her brace with her crutch. She nodded toward the ushers; guarding the interior theater doors. "Let's see if they'll let us take a peek inside."

The ushers were polite, but refused to break the rules by opening the theater doors before show time.

"Aw, come on," Lily pleaded. "I've been coming to this theater since I was a little kid."

"She tried to sneak in back then, too," a man's voice called from behind them.

Lily turned, instantly recognizing the tall, silver-haired man who had come up behind her. "Steve Fowler," she beamed. "It's been ages! And Molly..." She hugged the brunette woman standing at his side. "It's great to see you." Still smiling, she turned to Scott. "Steve is the architect who remodeled Grams' house when I was fifteen. He caught me trying to sneak into an R-rated movie, but he didn't snitch."

They laughed at the memory.

"Can you guys believe this is the old Capitol Theater?" Lily asked, changing the subject. "Isn't it gorgeous?"

Steve Fowler grinned. "I think so. But it's my design, so I might be biased."

"You did this?" Lily gushed. "It's fantastic! Hey, can you take us in for a tour?"

"Probably not this minute," he said, "but I could show you the VIP lounge."

"Even better!" she declared.

The foursome settled into high-backed chairs beneath a colorful tiffany-style chandelier and ordered drinks.

"I haven't seen your grandmother recently," Molly said. "How is she?"

Lily shook her head, but was unable to speak.

"Unfortunately, we just lost her," Scott said, coming to her rescue. "Her memorial service is this Friday."

"Oh, no!" Molly exclaimed, taking Lily's hand. "I'm so sorry, Lily. She was a wonderful person."

"Thanks," Lily mumbled. "They tell me she didn't suffer..."

"I'm glad for that," Steve said, "But it still hurts to lose some-one you love."

Just then, the lights flashed, indicating it was time for the audience to take its seats.

"I guess we better go in," Scott said. "I got our tickets at the last minute, so they're way up in the balcony."

"Why don't you join us?" Molly said. "The couple who were supposed to be our guests had to cancel at the last minute – sick kids."

"Seriously?" Scott asked. "We'd love that! I'd be happy to pay you for our tickets."

"Nonsense," Steve replied. "It's a balcony box, so the seats would go to waste otherwise."

The good company, spectacular venue and prestigious seating enhanced the amazing concert. Lulled by the music, Lily didn't mind when Scott wrapped his arm around her shoulders. She rested her head against his chest and listened to the band play "Nights in White Satin," pondering the lyrics. *"Just what the truth is, I can't say any more..."*

Lily was sorry to see the performance come to an end, but had to admit she was exhausted from the day's events. She barely remembered the short drive back to the Belleview Biltmore or Scott walking her to her room.

"I'm glad you came tonight," Scott said, gazing down at her with soft, brown eyes. "It was like old times. I miss you, Lilyanna."

"I had a wonderful time, too." Lily unlocked her door and stepped inside, fighting the urge to kiss him. Confused, she changed the subject. "Hey, would you mind if I used your computer to check my blog again tomorrow afternoon?"

"No problem." He paused, his dark eyes losing some of their sparkle. "I suppose you have plans for breakfast again."

Lily nodded, tormented by mixed emotions. "Thanks again for a wonderful evening," she said. "I'll call you tomorrow." She closed the door.

When she crawled into bed, her mind was still racing with thoughts about the future, considering first a life with Scott, and then one with Seth. Lily tossed and turned until she finally drifted off to sleep, unaware of the fog settling over her.

"No good ever comes from juggling multiple suitors," Margaret admonished.

Chapter Seventy Eight

"I'm not juggling *multiple* suitors," Lily protested, floating into her chair at the familiar table. "Just two."

Margaret raised an eyebrow and slid a steaming cup of tea across the table. "That's still one too many, darlin'," she clucked. "You know, there's no sweeter sound than two lovebirds singing together on a perch. But any time you put a third bird in the cage, they stop singing and start fighting. It never stops until you take one bird out."

"But how can I choose?" asked Lily. "One minute I'm sure I want a new life with Seth and the next minute, I want Scott back."

"You don't have a choice. You're already married," Margaret said.

"Oh, horse feathers!" Bobbi declared.

Lily whirled around, unnerved by Bobbi's abrupt arrival.

"She's a Catholic. You're not. You're young and beautiful and you *can* choose."

"Beauty and age are of no significance over the span of eternity," Margaret retorted. "Beauty lasts only a few years, and a spirit can appear to be any age she achieved during her lifetime."

"That's true," Bobbi agreed. "But it's irrelevant to the living."

"All right then – life is more enjoyable with a husband who shares your memories," Margaret countered. "And memories are the only possession you take with you on your eternal journey."

Lily frowned. "I'd like to forget a lot of my memories."

"Nonsense." Margaret replied. "From what I've observed, only a few of your memories are tragic. The problem is that you allow yourself to dwell on them."

"*Allow* myself?" Lily mocked.

"Well, whatever you do, don't lollygag," Bobbi advised. "Spirits recall every single moment of their lives in crystal clarity. We can't alter, rationalize or forget a single moment, good or bad..." She bit her lip. "So it's much more difficult to make such a choice here."

Lily's eyes went wide, recognizing another connection. "Wait a minute, Bobbi. You faced a similar dilemma, didn't you? To make new memories with Clay or wait to be reunited with Bear. Why didn't you choose?"

Bobbi pressed her lips together and vanished without another word.

"I don't understand," Lily moaned. "Why did she leave?"

Clay's spirit materialized next to Margaret, startling Lily yet again. "You guys should really consider wearing bells around your necks," she muttered.

Clay ignored the dig and spoke directly to Margaret. "I should show her what happened."

Margaret studied Clay for a moment and then conceded with a single nod of her head.

An instant later, the fog engulfed Lily. She drifted aimlessly for several minutes, consumed with curiosity, until at last Clay's voice began to filter through the clouds.

"You know, I loved hauling boxcars of rum from the Belleview Biltmore to Canada. Sometimes me and my men would take a route through Chicago, and other times, we'd head up the east coast to drop off shipments of the hooch in New York along the way. On the return trip, we'd usually stop and sell some of the Canadian whisky that had replaced the rum in our boxcar. Speakeasy owners and politicians lined up to buy top-shelf booze, and most folks were smart enough not to steal from Scarface, so business usually ran as smooth as melted butter."

Scenes of Clay riding in a boxcar appeared at the edge of the mist. When he wasn't playing cards with his crew, he sat near the open door, watching the scenery roll by. At stops along the route, he often joined poker games in smoke-filled speakeasies and apparently did quite well. However, Lily sensed he was happiest when the train was in motion.

"We usually handled our business right there in the boxcar," he said. "And afterwards, me and the other fellas took turns – some guarded the remaining shipment while the rest blew off steam in town. It was the perfect life. Well, except that I was usually away for two weeks at a stretch and I didn't get much time off between liquor runs."

At the edge of the mist, scenery started sliding by in a rapid cornucopia of sights, sounds, and smells – picturesque rolling hills, woods, cow pastures, lakes, bridges, small towns, big cities, blue skies and stormy weather, as well as vehicles and people of all sizes, shapes and colors.

"If Bobbi agreed to marry me when I got back, this would be my last run. I was determined to enjoy every minute of it," Clay murmured as a field of wild flowers drifted by. "On the first leg of the trip, we were scheduled to stop in New York City overnight. I planned to spend the evening at the Cotton Club – but first I promise to check up on Bobbi's sister, Lou-Lou and her doctor-husband."

The pleasant scenery faded away.

"If you ask me, Lou's marriage was just for show. I think the doc was a fancy dandy – you know – the kind of fella who's goofy for other men? But Lou didn't want a real man anyway, so it worked out all right. The two of them spent most of their time – and all the money they could raise, trying to help ill-treated women."

When the mist cleared, Lily shook off a wave of nausea to bring the scene into focus. She was certain this was New York City, but not the New York City she knew. The streets near the train station were filled with an eclectic assortment of cars, trollies, delivery trucks and horse-drawn wagons, along with the pungent, intermingled smells of food, animals, people and gasoline. Most buildings were five stories or less, but a few taller ones hinted at the city's future skyline.

Lily floated next to Clay as he turned onto a narrow brick alley. Unappealing brownstone apartment buildings flanked both sides of the road, blocking the late-day sun. Clay took in his surroundings, instinctively patting the holstered gun, hidden under his jacket.

He stopped near the end of the deserted alley and struck a match against the wall to light a thin cigar. He took a few puffs, casually searching the shadows until he was convinced he was alone. Then he dropped the cigar, ground it under the toe of his black, wing-tipped shoe, and began retracing his steps.

He stopped at a shabby, oak door with no house number and knocked three times. Lily glanced up just in time to see a woman's face appear and then disappear from a small window on the second floor. She wondered if they were about to enter a secret speakeasy, but instead, Lou opened the door.

"Hurry – get inside," she whispered, stealing a quick peek down the alley.

Like Bobbi and Jo, Lou's auburn hair was thick and wavy, but hers was coiled in a messy bun at the base of her neck. She wore a loose-fitting black dress and no make-up, but she couldn't conceal her beauty.

The moment Clay stepped in, she re-bolted the door.

"Hello, Lou-Lou," he said, shifting his weight from one foot to the other.

Lou clasped her hands behind her back. "Hello, Clay," she murmured. "It's good of you to come."

The brief, awkward exchange revealed that neither of them had forgotten the desperate actions Lou had taken a few years before when, unbeknownst to Clay, she was attempting to escape her brother-in-law's sexual abuse.

"This is from Jo," Clay said, pulling a thin envelope from his pocket. "She said to let you know she wishes it could be more, but these are hard times."

"Please tell her we appreciate every nickel." A momentary smile lit her face. "Last month we helped two women find jobs and safe places for them and their children to live."

"You're a good woman, Lou-Lou," Clay said. "You deserve a better life than this. I wish I had known..." He paused; surprised by a small rubber ball bouncing down the stairs, a few feet from where they stood. His eyes darted to a young child sitting on the landing, watching him.

Lily understood why Clay's heart skipped a beat. The girl's blonde ringlet curls were identical to Belle's, but the entire left side of this child's face was bruised and one eye was black and swollen shut.

"It's a boot-print," Lou explained. "Her father was trying to kick her mother and she got in the way. A kindly flat-foot discovered the two of them hiding in the park and brought them here. They can't stay, though. I'm sure the boozehound's already searching for them and we can't risk him finding out about this house."

"Where can I find the bastard?" Clay growled, reaching for his gun.

Lou put her hand on Clay's forearm and shook her head. "There are hundreds of men out there, worse than this one and funds are tight. They want to go home to Richmond, but all we can do for now is provide them with a warm meal and a safe bed for the night."

"That's not enough," Clay hissed. "He might kill them the next time."

Lou nodded. "He might. But you can't save everyone, Long Gone. You've already done more than most. Now, go on home and take care of my sisters."

Clay clenched his jaw, but gave her a curt nod to acknowledge he understood her position.

Lou opened the door just enough to let him out and then closed it again, taking care not to draw any more attention to the brownstone than absolutely necessary.

He wandered in the general direction of the Cotton Club, but he couldn't shake the image of the battered child from his thoughts. He paused in front of a familiar, weather-beaten church, took off his Fedora and stepped inside. There in the annex, stood a frail clergyman, who looked as shabby as the church itself.

"Hello, Pastor," Clay said. "How much does it cost for the wicked to help save the innocent today?"

"Twenty dollars," the clergyman replied, pointing to a polished collection plate.

"The price has gone up since I was here last."

The pastor bowed his head. "So has the number of needy parishioners."

"Fair enough," Clay said. He dropped the cash into the collection plate and then followed the pastor past the rows of pews to the cleric's office.

"Sacramental wine and whisky are available inside, in exchange for additional offerings," the pastor advised. Then he knocked three times and a huge black man, armed with a double-barrel shotgun, opened the door.

"God be with you," the clergyman said as he turned away. "And if He is, remember to give thanks in the collection plate on your way out."

As Clay took his seat at the high-stakes poker table, the fog settled around Lily, pulling her from the memory. She floated in the clouds, wondering if Jesus would approve of drinking and gambling in church if it benefited the poor. She also wondered how any of this affected Bobbi's decision to marry Clay.

Dawn was breaking by the time the fog lifted once more. Clay stood in front of Lou's brownstone, holding a small suitcase. He knocked three times. When he saw the curtain open upstairs, he saluted Lou, but before she had time to come down and open the door, he turned and walked away, whistling the tune "London Bridges."

He stopped on Fifth Avenue to purchase a ring for Bobbi and then returned to the rail yard, where he bought a bag of fried dough for his crew. He and his men were finishing their breakfast in the boxcar, when they heard a high-pitched male voice call out.

"Yoo-hoo!" the man cried, waving a handkerchief to get Clay's attention. "Over here!"

Clay and his crew watched slack-jawed as a slight man approached the train, wearing white pants with a matching vest over a blue shirt, and a puffy yellow scarf around his neck, in place of a tie. He sashayed a few steps closer, trying to avoid mud puddles.

"Mr. Long – please come with me, won't you? We all want to thank you before the train leaves the station!"

"Are you Lou's – uh..." He couldn't bring himself to call this man a husband. "You're the doctor, right? Marion?" Clay asked, stalling. "Tell Lou she can thank me by coming to Florida to visit her sisters this winter."

"It's not Lou – I mean, Lou's up there, too, but it's Ruth and her daughter who want to thank you for the train tickets and things." Marion waved his handkerchief in the direction of the rail station platform. "Please, hurry!"

A few of Clay's men chuckled.

"Are you sure you spent the *whole* night playing cards there, Clay?" one of them teased. "Sounds like you spent a good part of your evening doing somethin' else altogether!"

Clay flushed and jumped to the ground. "Get the car ready to roll," he barked, waving his Fedora at them. "I'll be right back."

"Look real close before you kiss any of 'em, Clay," another man jeered, "you had a lot to drink last night, and they might all look like this one in the daylight!"

Marion, apparently used to such insults, ignored the men and hurried toward the platform, waving his handkerchief at the ladies. Ruth and the little girl were leaning out the window, waving goodbye. Ruth gushed tearful thanks for the tickets, clothes and traveling money, but most of her words were drowned out by the earsplitting whistle, signaling the train's departure. Clay kissed her outstretched hand and winked at the little girl as the train pulled away from the platform.

"Don't thank me," he shouted above the din. "I just put the matter into God's hands." He turned to Lou. "And then God put aces over kings into mine. Now, if I don't skedaddle, I'll still be standing here when my own train pulls out!"

He started to give Lou a hug goodbye, but thought better of it. Instead, he took off his hat, bowed and kissed her hand, earning smiles from both Lou and Marion.

Much to the amusement of his crew, by the time Clay raced back across the rail yard, the boxcar was moving slowly down the track. He rolled inside, got to his feet and stood in the doorway to give Lou one last exaggerated bow, before reaching out to slide the heavy metal door closed.

He didn't hear the crack of the rifle or Lou's strangled screams as he fell to the ground.

Chapter Seventy Nine

Lily struggled to understand what was happening. She could see Clay, but she could also hear his thoughts. He suffered no pain as he crumpled to the ground; just the odd sensation of lying on the dirt and gravel, watching the bottom of the boxcar roll by as the train pulled away from him. At first, he wondered if he had tripped and fallen, but when he saw his crew raise their guns and close the boxcar to protect the shipment, he knew something more sinister had happened. He tried to focus.

From within a cacophony of sights and sounds, he saw a dark-haired, heavyset man, unshaved and dressed in filthy coveralls, aiming a double barrel shotgun at him. The man's face was contorted with rage, but all Clay felt was curiosity. He had no idea who the maniac was, let alone why someone was intent on killing him.

Above the cries of bystanders and the screech of steel wheels on iron tracks, Clay heard someone yell, "Put that gun down, in the name of the law. I'm not gonna' warn you again, mister!"

Ruth's train was disappearing in the distance, but the gunman turned and took aim at it anyway. Before he could empty his second barrel, a short blast of automatic gunfire rang out and he fell, dead.

Lily was in shock. Although the entire incident lasted less than a minute, the scene played out as if in slow motion. Marion and Lou sprinted over to Clay and dropped down on either side of him. Marion's flamboyant demeanor was gone, even before he tore away Clay's shirt to assess his injuries. But when he saw the hole in Clay's chest, a look of helpless dread filled his eyes. He gave Lou a shake of his head before pressing his hands against the wound.

Clay was still baffled. He tried to think; to pull the man's face from his shady past, but it was no use. "Who – is – he?" he asked, gasping for breath.

"That monster was Ruth's husband," Lou sobbed. She gently lifted Clay's head into her lap. "He must have been hunting for her. He was a crazy, jealous son-of-a-bitch. He probably saw her saying goodbye to you." Lou burst into tears. "I'm sorry, Clay. I'm so very, very sorry..."

"Don't cry, Lou-Lou," Clay took a deep, rattling breath. "I deserved to get shot – lots of other times." He tried to chuckle at his joke, but coughed and then stiffened, as an agonizing wave of pain washed over him.

Lou wiped his wet forehead with her lace handkerchief. "Hold on, Clay. You wait and see. You'll be fine."

"You don't believe that – any more than I do," Clay said. "It's damn bad luck, though – just when I finally have reasons to live." He coughed and blood bubbled out of his mouth.

Lou turned his head to the side enough to let the blood trickle down his cheek. He struggled to draw another breath. "Tell Bobbi – I'll be waiting for her – on the other side." Clay coughed-up more blood and shuddered. "Tell her," he gasped, his voice growing weaker. "I – love – my witch."

"I promise." Lou whispered. "And I'll make sure she knows you died a hero."

Clay laughed and let out a final, rattling breath. As his gaze faded to a vacant stare, his pained expression relaxed into one of peaceful calm. His spirit, hovering above his body, was visible only to Lily.

Marion slipped off his white vest, laid it on the ground, and helped Lou gently move Clay's head from her lap. Then he closed Clay's eyes and covered his face with his beloved Fedora, shielding him from the prying eyes of gawking onlookers, clustered on the train platform.

As Lou offered a heartfelt prayer for Clay's soul, the fog dropped over the scene, carrying tearful Lily into its folds.

"Death is a sad affair." As the haze dispersed, Margaret materialized at the table, holding her trusty teapot. "No matter how strong our faith, a part of us still believes the departed would have preferred a longer life on Earth, over the perfect bliss of Heaven."

Lily sniffled, wiping her eyes. "But it's true, isn't it?" she asked. "I mean, you, Bobbi and Clay all chose to stay in this realm."

Margaret filled two teacups. "There are scores of reasons for postponing the next step in one's eternal journey. I think I stayed mostly out of curiosity. On the other hand, I suspect Clay did so because he worries the path won't take him and Bobbi to the same destination."

"Why is he worried?" Lily asked. "He has nothing to fear from judgment day. He was killed because he tried to save a woman and her child, for goodness sake."

"Ah, but you only witnessed memories from the tail end of his life," Margaret observed. "And, while I'm certain the Almighty takes notice of how a person spends his last minutes on Earth, I would imagine the bulk of His judgment is focused on how the person spent the previous *years* of his life."

Lily nodded, paying rapt attention. "So you think Clay's good deeds don't outweigh his bad ones?"

"While I was alive, I endeavored to help people in need. I continue to do so here in the spirit realm. Perhaps if I do enough good deeds, the next step in my eternal journey will be even more pleasing than my current existence. But..."

Margaret shifted her glance to her lap and smoothed her skirt.

"But, what?" Lily asked, leaning forward in her chair.

"Throughout my life, I also made a practice of gleaning information from people through deception and gossip. Sometimes I even plied men with liquor to encourage them to speak more freely. And I used the knowledge I collected to my advantage – however and whenever it suited me."

"But you used some of the knowledge you gained to do good things – like when you helped Bobbi solicit donations to build the hospital."

Margaret looked up and gave Lily a half-smile before shaking her head. "That's the rub of it. We'll never know if Bobbi might've succeeded in raising the money without making threats. Years ago, I began to think about Judgement Day and decided to start avoiding gossip as part of my self-imposed penance. Now I try to keep everyone's counsel and let them tell their own stories."

Lily frowned. "So you're saying there's something wrong with Clay, but you can't tell me because that would be gossip?"

"That's not at all what I meant!" Margret blew out a breath in exasperation. "I'm saying Clay committed countless sins before Bobbi and her children came into his life. He turned his life around, but he didn't live nearly long enough to make amends for a lifetime of wickedness and he knows that. Therefore, he continues to atone for his sins by staying in this realm and helping people. Unfortunately, his plan traps Bobbi here, too."

"But he loves Bobbi. I'm sure of it."

"Yes, he does," Margaret agreed. "And she loves him, too. And because he died when he did, their love story remains full of hope and possibilities. Had he lived, they would have inevitably discovered that their desires are so different, only one of them could ever be happy in their marriage. Clay was born filled with wanderlust, yet he was willing to give up traveling in order to make Bobbi happy. And now Bobbi has sacrificed her yearnings for the same reason."

Lily's eyes widened as an idea occurred to her. "Is that the reason they fight all the time? Bobbi wants to travel the lighted path, but Clay needs to stay in this realm?"

Margaret didn't answer, but Lily was certain that she was right. "Do they know it can't work out?"

"No," Margaret replied, with a shake her head. "They have to come to that conclusion on their own – and they will, in time. In the meantime, perhaps their dilemma can guide others." Margaret took a drink of tea.

"How..."

Before Lily could finish her question, she dropped through the fog.

Chapter Eighty

A combination of two noises jolted Lily awake in the dark hotel room. One was her alarm clock. She rolled over and shut it off before her fuzzy brain could identify the other sound – her vibrating cell phone. Panic swelled as she grabbed for the phone; her only thought: *"The hospital's calling about Grams!"*

She choked out the word "Hello" before remembering that Grams was no longer at the hospital. An icy wave of sorrow washed over her pounding heart.

"Lily?" Scott repeated. "Are you okay?"

She sucked in a deep breath and blew it out again. "I'm fine – I was still sleeping and the phone startled me, that's all."

"Damn, I'm sorry," he said. "Go back to sleep. Just call me as soon as you wake up, okay?"

"No... it's alright. The alarm just went off anyway." She double-checked the clock to confirm it was 8:00.

It was.

"What's up?" She rubbed her eyes with her free hand, flipped back the covers and hopped over to the window. Shivering in the cold, she pulled back the room-darkening curtains and winced as bright sunshine filled the room.

"I think you're going to want to see this. The traffic on your blog quadrupled since yesterday – and people have started a bunch of new discussions."

"So what's the problem?"

461

"I guess having an open forum blog hasn't been an issue in the past." He paused. "But the new discussion topics don't fit the content of your website. They're all related to deaths of kids – and not from terminal illness. Still, I figured you wouldn't want me to delete anything until you had a chance to read them. Besides, everyone's asking for your advice."

"People are asking for my advice?" She felt unsteady and grabbed the back of the desk chair for support.

"Are you still there?"

"I'm... still... here..." Lily stammered. "But I can't... me being able to help Barbara was a fluke. What if something horrible happened because I gave someone bad advice?"

"What if something horrible happened because you didn't try?" Scott countered.

"Point taken." She sighed. "Let me grab a shower and then I'll come up and take a look – but no promises."

"Are you hungry?" he asked. "I can order room service."

Guilt bubbled up, threatening to overwhelm Lily's already heightened emotions. *"Seth!"* She had been looking forward to breakfast with him. *"I'll have to tell Scott about him pretty soon."*

"I'll eat later," she said, trying to sound calmer than she felt.

"Okay. No problem," Scott replied; a tinge of disappointment in his voice.

Lily ended the call and dialed Seth. "Hi, there. Listen – I'm sorry, but I have to do something this morning, so I'm going to be a little late for our date."

"I understand," Seth said. "You probably have a million details to work out before your grandmother's memorial service tomorrow. Can I help? Maybe drive you somewhere or help arrange flowers?"

"What?" Still distracted, Lily didn't catch the humor of his absurd offers.

"I'm sorry – bad joke," he apologized. "I was trying to lighten your mood. But seriously, I can hang out with you if you need a shoulder to lean on."

"Sorry, I'm a bit preoccupied." She puckered her face, trying to decide if it would be worse to let Seth think she was handling issues for the memorial, or tell him that she was going to her husband's room to borrow his laptop. She opted for the truth without specific details.

"Actually, it's not about Grams. I need to put out a few more fires on my blog. That issue I was working on yesterday seems to have spawned more pleas for help and I need to make sure none of them are too serious. It shouldn't take too long. I can meet you at eleven."

"They stop serving breakfast at eleven," Seth reminded her, "but I guess we can have lunch."

"Oh, I forgot. Listen, why don't you just go on and..."

"No – I'll wait for you. But man, I can hardly wait to get you unplugged and on the road. Believe me – once you feel the wind blowing through your hair, you'll relax and forget all your troubles – and everyone else's, too. I'm telling you, you're going to love it!"

Lily laughed. "So you keep saying." She hobbled to the bathroom. "Listen, I've got to run. The faster I get started, the sooner I'll be finished."

Twenty minutes later, she was showered, dressed and wearing light make-up. She studied her reflection in the bathroom's oval antique mirror. *"Why do you care how you look?"* she wondered. She stepped into the hallway, ignoring another annoying thought, *"And why are you wearing the cologne Scott likes?"*

When Scott opened the door and gave her one of his devastatingly sexy smiles, Lily felt her cheeks blush. Fortunately, he didn't seem to notice.

"You're not going to believe how many people are posting on your site," he announced. "Go on and have a seat while I pour us some coffee."

Lily noticed he had pulled an extra chair over to the desk, so they could sit side by side in front of the screen. *"After all we've been through together, how can the thought of sitting close to my husband in a hotel room make me so nervous?"* She sank into the nearest chair and focused her attention on the computer screen.

As soon as she began to read, all other thoughts vanished from her mind.

"Black, right?" Scott called from the opposite side of the room.

"Actually, I take sugar these days" she said absentmindedly.

He started to say something, but thought better of it. He carried the coffees and a couple sugar packets to the desk.

"Thanks," Lily said, pulling her eyes from the screen long enough to stir sugar into her cup. "How much of this have you read?"

"Not much. I started reading the new comments in the Barbara discussion, but when I saw how many people were posting new topics of discussion that had nothing to do with terminally ill people, I decided my time would be better spent changing the protocols on your website. From now on, if someone tries to start a new discussion, it will go into an unpublished folder until you approve the topic."

Lily grinned. "Thanks! I forgot how handy you can be."

"I live to serve. I can also delete all the discussions that went live on your blog before I reset the protocols, but I wanted to wait for your approval."

"Thanks again." She took a sip of her coffee and wrinkled her nose, wishing it was tea. She sighed and turned her attention back to the computer screen without noticing that Scott hesitated and then sat on the side of the bed instead of taking the seat next to her.

Lily skimmed through dozens of comments, posted by people who joined the on-line discussion with Barbara after she had signed off last night. Most encouraged Barbara not to give up. A few people shared their own stories of loss and offered suggestions for dealing with grief.

Lily wanted to respond to several of the comments, but first, she decided to scan the rather substantial list of new discussion subjects that popped up overnight. Almost immediately, the subject heading on one discussion jumped out at her: *My Dead Son Still Visits.*

Lily clicked the mouse to open the discussion, which had been started by a woman using the pseudonym: *CallMeCrazy.* Her post read: *My son, Paul, was an Army medic who died six years ago.*

People think I'm crazy, but I know that only his body is gone. His ghost frequently visits my dreams. He talks about wounded soldiers at the VA Hospital where he died. Sometimes he encourages soldiers to wake up from their comas. Other times, he just keeps them company until they go to Heaven.

The comments below the woman's post astounded Lily; partly because there were so many of them, but more so, because they were all from people claiming to have experienced similar dream encounters with the dead.

Scott interrupted her contemplation. "So, do you want me to delete the discussions that aren't related to terminal illness?"

"Come over here. You've got to read this!" Lily insisted.

Scott walked over to the desk, eyed the empty chair for a long moment, and then dropped into it. "Okay. What's got you so riled up?"

Lily was so focused on the comments that she didn't notice how close they were sitting. Excited, she flipped her wavy auburn hair over her shoulder and turned the computer slightly, so they could both read the screen. She scrolled to the top of *Call Me Crazy's* post and pointed. "Start here," she said.

"Whoa," Scott muttered a few moments later. "She sounds like..."

"I know," Lily interrupted. "And wait till you read the comments."

Scott returned his attention to the computer screen.

Lily's mind was racing. *"We can't all be crazy."*

"I'm a slower reader than you," Scott reminded her. "It's going to take me a few minutes to read all of these."

Suddenly, Lily remembered she was supposed to be meeting Seth at the restaurant. "Oh my gosh, what time is it?" she blurted.

Distracted, Scott pointed at the clock.

"Eleven. Damn it, I'm late." She struggled to her feet.

"Wait. You're leaving? Now? What about..." Scott waved his hand at the screen; clearly confused and frustrated.

"No. I'm staying," she said, avoiding eye contact. "I just need to make a call." She opened the door and stepped out on the balcony.

The bright white sun in the pale blue sky forced her to squint as she closed the door behind her. She glanced at the gardens and pool below, trying to organize her thoughts. Then she pulled her cell phone from her pocket and dialed Seth's number.

"Hello?"

"I'm so sorry, Seth, but..." Lily began.

"Oh, no," he moaned. "You're cancelling, aren't you?"

"Yeah. I'm sorry," she repeated. "My blog exploded overnight and I just can't get away until I clean it up and respond to some of the comments."

"I get it," Seth said. "Your blog is important and I guess you can't be expected to change your work habits overnight. I'll make you deal... if you promise to meet me for dinner, I won't even make you feel guilty for standing me up."

"It's a deal. Thanks for understanding, Seth."

"No problem. Can you meet me at the bar at seven? My surgery is tomorrow, so I'm not allowed to eat or drink anything after midnight."

Lily grimaced, ashamed for forgetting that tomorrow was an important day for both of them. "Seven it is!" she replied, trying to sound cheerful. "What time is your surgery tomorrow?"

"Not until noon, but you'll be tied up with your grandmother's memorial service all day, right?"

"Yeah," Lily said, swallowing the lump that formed in her throat each time she was reminded that Grams was gone. "But for now, I'm trying to keep my focus on getting this blog mess under control."

After they said their goodbyes and hung up, Lily called Mary and brought her up to speed about her blog.

"As an Organ Donor Coordinator, I'll bet you've heard a lot of similar stories from mothers who lost children."

"Not really," Mary said. "ODCs encourage people to seek grief counseling and we offer contact information, but that's about it. We don't usually stay in contact."

"But you had a near-death experience – and you said you believed Dylan's spirit visited me the night of the accident..."

"Yes, but I keep my private and professional lives separate. As an ODC, I only address the physical aspects of brain-death and the benefits of organ donation," Mary said. "Personally, I love the idea of an on-line chat room for women who communicate with their children's ghosts. You know, most grief counselors say ghosts are a symptom of depression, and that they usually disappear as a person works through the stages of grief. You might be able to help a lot of people who don't believe that."

Lily frowned. "Like I told Scott – I can't hand out advice. I don't have any professional training. What if..."

"I didn't mean to imply you should offer therapy," Mary assured her. "I just think women who believe they've seen their child's ghost would be comforted to know they're not alone – or crazy."

"I guess so," Lily agreed, deciding not to reveal that she also saw spirits regularly at the Belleview Biltmore Hotel and Morton Plant Hospital.

"Give it some thought," Mary said. "In the meantime, I'll check out your blog."

"Were you talking with your nurse friend again?" Scott asked when she stepped back inside.

Lily hesitated but then nodded, feeling guilty about letting Scott assume she had only made one phone call. "She thinks I might be able to help some of these women by telling them – you know – how I saw Dylan."

"You know I believe our son is with God, but I can't deny that a lot of these posts sound similar to your dreams about Dylan. Maybe some grieving women have more realistic dreams than others..."

"Or maybe some spirits really can visit dreams," Lily snapped.

Scott shifted his eyes to the computer screen and changed the subject. "Well, anyway... if you leave these discussions open on your *Way to Go* site, you'll probably lose followers and advertisers." He cleared his throat. "If you want me to, I can set up a second blog, move these discussions, and design a link to take interested people to your new site."

"*He thinks I'm totally wrong, but he's still willing to help me,*" Lily marveled.

For the next hour, Lily watched her new blog, *Ghost Dreams,* take shape. Then she ordered cheeseburgers from room service and began responding to posts. Traffic to the new site increased throughout the day, as people joined conversations, voicing delight that Lily could relate to their paranormal experiences. Some women hadn't seen ghosts, but simply wanted to commiserate with people who had suffered similar tragedies. Lily was amazed at how often the information Margaret taught her about the spirit realm helped her provide answers and comfort to people.

Lily was beginning to tire when she read a post from a woman who had lost a son in a helicopter crash: *My husband and I agreed to purchase Charlie's flying lessons as a high school graduation gift. Our son loved flying, but I'm deathly afraid of heights and hated every minute of it. When Charlie decided to drop out of college and earn a living giving helicopter tours, I should have stopped him. He was good with numbers. If he had become an accountant, he would still be alive today. Instead, he's gone and I'm just another broken-hearted mother who, like Barbara, wishes she had acted while there was still time.*

Lily reread the entry several times. The story nagged at her. Why? Then all at once, she understood.

"*Flying terrorized her,*" she thought. "*No matter how much her son loved flying, she couldn't change that about herself. And no matter how much Seth loves riding motorcycles, I would hate it.*"

Speeding down a road with the wind whipping through his hair might be heaven for Seth, but Lily knew she would always worry that an accident was lurking just ahead, and be terrified of falling logs each time they rode under an overpass.

"*And Seth would be as miserable trying to live in one place as I would be living on the road,*" she realized.

Despite the lump in her throat, Lily decided that when she said goodbye to Seth after dinner, it would be forever.

"Are you okay?" Scott asked, peering at her over the top of the novel he was reading.

Lily smiled at him. He looked comfortable, reclined against a stack of pillows on the bed.

"Getting tired," she replied.

It was the truth – even if it wasn't the *whole* truth. She glanced at the clock, flexed her fingers and then began to typing: *Dear Broken-Hearted Mother – I know the loss of your son is unbelievably hard to accept, but ask yourself – would it really have been better to watch him sitting in a cramped office somewhere, year after year, staring longingly out the window, wishing more than anything that he could fly? By letting him to chase his dreams, you gave your son more joy than he would have known living decades in someone else's dream.*

Lily locked her fingers together and stretched her arms. "That's it for the day," she said. She stood and stretched her back. "I'm meeting a friend for dinner and then I'm going to bed."

Scott closed his book and swung his legs over the side of the bed. "Yeah, tomorrow is going to be rough." He stood and walked her to the door. His slight limp reminded Lily that his leg was broken in three places the night of the accident. He paused and rubbed his five o'clock shadow, the way he always did when he had something on his mind. "Will your friend be coming tomorrow?" he asked, dropping his gaze to the carpet.

Lily flushed, certain Scott knew that her friend was a man. "No," she said. "We're parting ways tonight."

Scott didn't push for details. "Okay then," he said. "Do you want to meet in the lobby at noon?"

"Let's meet at eleven," she said. "There's a little restaurant nearby, where we can get breakfast."

He looked up, surprised. "Sounds good."

"And thanks again for all your computer wizardry today." She leaned in for a quick hug and then left.

"No problem," Seth called after her. "Love you!"

"Love you, too," she responded over her shoulder. Even though she didn't look back, she knew he was smiling. She pressed her lips together, knowing her goodbye to Seth wouldn't be nearly so pleasant.

Chapter Eighty One

"Have a drink with me to celebrate," Seth said, the moment Lily joined him at the bar.

"What are we celebrating?" Lily asked, trying not to think about how this evening was going to end.

"I've collected enough dumb warnings to finish my book," Seth said with a grin. "Want to hear the last three?"

"Absolutely," she said, turning to the petite, twenties-something, brunette bartender. "I'll have a margarita on rocks with a sugar rim instead of salt."

"Regular or top shelf tequila?"

"Top shelf," Seth answered for her. "This is a special occasion!"

Lily smiled as Seth pulled the familiar miniature tape recorder from its pouch on his custom-made utility belt and queued the tape. "Come and listen," she urged the bartender. "These are usually pretty funny."

The first voice on the tape was that of a young woman. "The warning label on one of my curling irons says, '*Do Not Use Internally.*' When I first read that, you know, I didn't understand what they meant. Then I got it and – eewww! That's gross, you know? It makes me wonder who decided *that* warning was necessary!"

"Eeewwwww!" Lily's exaggerated imitation of the girl's voice made Seth and the bartender laugh.

The next voice on the tape was that of a soft spoken young man. "I decided to rent an apartment for my last year of college and learn to cook. Well, a couple weeks ago, I decided to fry some frozen hash-brown potatoes. But one line of the cooking directions warned me to keep the skillet covered at all times, and the next line warned me to stir the hash-browns frequently. Now, how was I supposed to do both things? I wound up burning the hell out of them and throwing the whole damn mess in the trash – including the skillet."

"Sounds like something my ex-boyfriend would do!" the bartender murmured, leaning forward to hear the final interview.

The next voice reminded Lily of an old biddy who used to belong to Grams' bridge club. Her shrill voice used to carry through Lily's closed bedroom door.

"I was cleaning my microwave a few weeks ago," the woman yelled into the microphone, "when I noticed a warning sticker on the inside of the door that I just could not believe! It read: *'Caution – Do not put live animals inside.'* My sister told me they had to start putting that warning on microwaves because people kept trying to microwave their pets to dry them off. Can you believe that? I mean, what kind of idiot would do that?"

The bartender wailed dramatically, "I always wondered what became of my grandma's cat. Poor Fluffy!"

Seth laughed out loud, nearly spilling his beer as he clicked the tape recorder off.

"So, you write books?" she asked.

"Actually, this is my first book. I started it before I lost my sight. I'm having surgery to restore my vision tomorrow, so I'll finally be able to finish it."

"Cool beans," the bartender said. "You know, I read a dumb warning last week. Would you like to hear it?"

"You bet!" Seth pushed the record button on his miniature tape recorder.

"There was a huge sticker on the glass of the bar's new blender that said *'Warning: do not to touch spinning blades'* – as if someone would be stupid enough to think that a machine that pulverizes ice cubes in seconds, would be perfectly safe for fingers." She rolled her eyes at Lily.

"Good one," Seth replied, clicking off the tape recorder. "As a matter of fact, that might make it into my book!"

"I want a copy," the bartender pleaded.

"No problem," Seth joked. "I'll drop one off the next time I ride through town."

Lily's chuckle was tinged with sadness. *"I'm gonna miss you so much."*

Her contemplation was broken when a rowdy group of nearly a dozen men, ascended the stairs and elbowed their way to the opposite end of the bar.

"Oh, goody," muttered the bartender. "Those guys are here for a plumbing convention. They've been downstairs shooting pool in St. Andrews since before I started my shift. Now that they're good and drunk, I guess they decided to move their party up here. Lucky me. Do you guys want another round before I go wait on them?"

"No, thanks," Seth said, raising his voice to be heard. "I think this is our cue to head out."

"I don't blame you a bit," she replied. "Should I add these drinks to your room tab?"

He reached into his left jeans pocket and pulled out a bill. "Yes, please, but this is for you." He slid a twenty dollar bill in the direction of her voice.

"He keeps different denominations in specific pockets," Lily said, noticing the girl's curiosity.

"Quit giving away my secrets!" Seth protested.

"Oh yeah, I forgot," Lily teased, winking at the bartender. "I meant to say, Seth's fingers are so sensitive, he can feel the shape of Andrew Jackson's head."

"That's better," Seth said with a wry smile.

The bartender's laugh was cut short when a burly man with buzz-cut gray hair smacked his open palm on the bar. "Barkeep! Jägermeister shots for all my friends!"

"Make mine Jack Daniels," yelled one of the men over the commotion.

A thunderous and vulgar debate immediately ensued over which liquor was the better choice for *real* men.

"Good luck," Seth shouted to the bartender.

"Thanks!" She gave Lily a parting smile and then turned her attention to the unruly crowd.

"Can you lead the way?" Seth asked. "It's hard for me to keep my bearings straight when there's so much noise."

"Sure, but that won't be a problem much longer," Lily reminded him.

"That's right!" he grinned. "Pretty soon, I'll be able to lead you around. Better yet, I'll be able to drive you around!"

Lily pressed her lips together, not wanting to spoil the moment. "Did you reserve a table?" she asked.

"I was going to, but the hostess said we didn't need one for the patio tables."

Lily leaned on her crutch and placed her other hand on Seth's arm. She cast an annoyed glance at the raucous men, but they were too busy trying to drink shots while balancing quarters on their noses to notice.

Once they were seated at a quiet corner table and had placed their dinner order, Lily described the illuminated landscape and the full moon, shining on the water in the distance.

"You know, describing things for you has turned me into a more observant person."

"I won't miss being blind one bit," Seth said. "But I must admit, losing my sight changed me for the better."

"How so?"

"Well, I learned to appreciate all of my senses more – especially my hearing and sense of touch. And I stopped smoking and started working out."

"You used to smoke?" Lily asked, amazed.

"Yep, and to be honest, I probably wouldn't have quit except that I kept burning myself – and I was worried I'd set fire to my folk's house." He laughed.

"Well, I hope you don't start-up again after your surgery."

"Not a chance. Smoking dries out your eyes and I won't take healthy eyes for granted ever again. You'll see."

Lily shifted uncomfortably, reluctant to talk about the future.

"Oh look, here comes the waitress with our drinks," she said, happy for the distraction.

"I would look, but..." Seth pointed at his dark, round glasses and grinned.

"There's another change – after tomorrow, no more blind jokes," she quipped.

The plump waitress skillfully spun the tray from her shoulder and balanced it on her open palm while using her other hand to serve their drinks. "A sugar-rimmed margarita on the rocks," she said with a southern accent. She placed the drink on the table in front of Lily. "And a Newcastle Ale," she continued. "Would you like a frosted mug?"

"No, thanks," Seth replied. "I was a bottle baby and never broke the habit." He shot a broad smile in her direction.

The waitress giggled, but then noticed Seth's dark round glasses and the folded white cane on the table. She hesitated, suddenly nervous.

Sensing her unease, Seth held out his hand. "You can just hand me the bottle."

Relieved, the waitress touched the bottle to Seth's palm and he wrapped his fingers around it.

"What's your name, pretty lady?" he asked, smiling in her direction.

"Kaitlin, or Kate for short," she gushed, flustered.

"Well, thank you, Kate for short," Seth said in a smooth, sexy voice.

"Your burger should be up in just a few minutes," Kate said, without taking her eyes off of him.

Lily watched the interaction, amused at how quickly the waitress was falling for Seth's charm. She felt better, knowing he would never lack for female company. After Kate left, he returned his attention to her.

"You're awfully quiet tonight, Lily. Are you thinking about your grandmother, or is something else bothering you?"

"It's something else." Lily took a deep breath.

"Talk to me."

"Well," Lily began, "I kept trying to imagine myself on the back of your motorcycle, flying down an open road with the roar of the engine filling my ears, and..."

"You're gonna love it!" Seth grinned.

"No, Seth – I won't," Lily said. "Even *thinking* about it terrifies me."

"What?" Seth's smile fell away. "Motorcycles aren't scary, Lily. You'll see."

Lily ran her finger over the sugar rim of her margarita, watching the white granules disappear into the light green liquid. She thought about what Margaret had said and steeled her resolve. "I just can't do it," she insisted.

"Sure you can. Once you get used to it, you'll relax and..."

"I'd *never* be able to relax because, you know what, Seth? It's not a dumb warning – motorcycles *are* dangerous. *Extremely* dangerous."

"That's one of the reasons riding them makes you feel so alive, Lily." Seth slumped in his chair, shaking his head. "I don't want to miss a fantastic life on the road just because there's a chance something bad might – or might not – happen out there."

"But I'm a homebody, Seth." Tears welled in her aqua blue eyes. "I'd be miserable living on the road. Travel never appealed to me, and ever since the accident, I absolutely *dread* it. You'd be having a blast, but I'd either be worrying about crashing or wanting to go home."

"Well, I'd be miserable staying in one place – I learned that working on my family's farm."

"I know," Lily said, lowering her voice to almost a whisper. "I want you to live the life that you love, Seth. I really do. I just can't live it with you."

"What does that mean?"

"Our relationship changed my life, Seth. A part of my heart will be yours forever – no matter what."

"Wait a minute." Seth's voice cracked. "Are you – saying goodbye to me, Lily?"

"Yes," Lily gulped. "It's what's best for both of us."

"Bullshit," Seth growled, folding his arms across his chest. "I can't believe you're willing to give up on us without even trying."

"Trying what?" Lily countered. "The lives we want to live are so different that only one of us would be happy if we stayed together. Remember that line from 'Fiddler on the Roof' – *A bird may love a fish, but where would they build a home together?* Well, that's us."

"Maybe, but I don't want to lose you," Seth said.

"You won't. Margaret says our memories remain with us throughout eternity. I'd rather savor memories of a short, perfect relationship with you, than to have memories of a longer relationship that ended badly."

Seth nodded. "I guess that makes sense. But can we at least put off saying goodbye until I can see? I want to know what you really look like."

"I thought about that, but honestly, I'd rather not change the picture of me that you created in your imagination. You made love to that image of me, so that's how I want you to remember me."

"My mysterious, gorgeous redhead?"

"Something like that. And I'll remember you as a sexy Zen master who, despite being blind, could see into my soul. I don't think either of us could improve on those images, do you?"

Seth blew out a breath. "I know you're right, but damn it, Lily – I was really looking forward to a future with you and this hurts like hell." He slowly moved his open hand across the table until he found his bottle of ale and then took a long drink.

Lily stifled a sob.

"Why don't we pretend this isn't our last date?" Seth suggested. "I'd rather just eat and laugh and share secrets like we always do and then kiss goodnight. Tomorrow we'll both be too busy to think about ourselves too much, and a couple days from now, this might not feel like such a huge kick in the gut."

"That sounds perfect," Lily said, picking up her margarita glass. "And it's exactly what I'd expect a sexy Zen master to recommend after looking into my soul."

Chapter Eighty Two

Lily and Seth clung to one another outside her hotel room door. She was reluctant to let go, but resisted the great temptation to invite him inside.

"Seth," she murmured against his neck. "We could never recreate the magic of our first time together, so let's not risk spoiling those perfect memories, okay? Let's just say goodbye out here."

He pulled back just far enough to lift her chin and kiss her one last time. "No goodbyes," he whispered, letting his fingers glide over her face – *seeing* her one last time.

"Okay," she whispered back. "Just know that I'll think of you every time I hear a motorcycle – and I'm going to buy a copy of your book and treasure it for the rest of my life."

"You'll always be in my dreams, Lily. And if you ever change your mind..." his voice trailed off. They both knew she wouldn't.

He slid his forefinger down her cheek, wiping away a silent tear. Then he stepped back and forced a grin. "Eternity is a long time, Lily. We're bound to run into each other eventually, so – I'll see you later!" Without another word, he turned and walked away.

"See ya!" she called after him. She stepped inside her room and stood there for a long time, her forehead pressed against the closed door, her moist palm still on the doorknob. "Let go," she murmured. "It's the right thing to do for both of us."

Lily let her tears fall as she got ready for bed and pulled the comforter up around her neck. She was still trying to press every moment she spent with Seth into her memory when the clouds gathered around her, carrying her back into the realm of the spirits.

Despite being dizzy when the fog dissipated, Lily recognized the garment factory where Bobbi worked.

"The textile mill that Harold went up to Virginia to oversee just unionized," Cricket told Bobbi. "He wrote to warn me – says the unionizers are headed south. He reckons they'll barrel right over me, seein' as I'm already so soft on my workers."

"I'm of the opinion that if he treated his workers better, they might not have felt the need to unionize," Bobbi replied, glancing around the sewing room, where all the seamstresses were hard at work.

Cricket nodded. "When I took over this here business from my wife's father, I wouldn't have believed that, but you've got the women sewing faster and better than ever."

"You draw more flies with honey than vinegar, Cricket. Once women hear about a good place to work, they line up asking for jobs, and work harder to keep them. And because we promoted Sarah to oversee the shirtwaist cutting room and Alice to supervise the pinners, everyone knows that excellent work can lead to advancement."

"My other section supervisors could learn a thing or two from you if they weren't so proud. But to most men, a woman's ideas on better bossin' are as welcome as farts in church."

Bobbi puckered her brow in thought. "You know, a wise lady once told me that an intelligent woman with allies can accomplish anything. Suppose I wrote down my methods in an instruction pamphlet, and then you told all the other managers it was written by some famous authority on garment factory operations..."

Cricket grinned. "They'll be willin' to listen, because they'd figure any expert was a man."

Bobbi nodded. "And as my first ally, you'd buy enough instruction pamphlets to make it worth my while, right?"

The clouds dropped over Lily, carrying her away from the memory, as Bobbi's voice filtered through the mist.

"I wrote a series of guides about effective labor management in the manufacturing industry, using the penname, Barrett Hamilton. The guides became quite popular, earning me – the supposed widow of the author – a tidy sum. For the most part, my allies kept mum about my secret, but there were a few notable exceptions."

As the mist began to dissipate, Lily floated into her seat at the small, round table, between Margaret, attired in a blue satin dress with a high, lacy collar and puffy mutton-chop sleeves, and Bobbi, wearing a sleeveless emerald slip-dress that matched her green eyes.

"Morton Plant was always fond of me," Bobbi continued, as though they were still floating in the mist. "He used to brag to his associates that I was as shrewd as any man he'd ever met. So when a few big cheeses read my manuals while wintering at the Belleview, they saw through the dodge and knew I was the authoress. The Fords invited me down to St. Andrews Pub for a bull session. It turns out they shared my opinion on labor management – that better wages, shorter work weeks and safer working conditions would increase worker's production and fuel a stronger economy. After they made the changes we discussed, their factory became so successful, it set the standard for the rest of the nation."

"Henry Ford's forty-hour work week," Lily nodded, astonished.

"Bobbi inspired many people throughout her life," Margaret said, giving Bobbi a warm smile.

"Not right after my accident," Bobbi demurred. "For months, I was angry at God for letting me get hurt so badly and for taking my husband from me. And I was angry with Bear for dying and leaving me alone to take care of our children – and with Alton Farthing for refusing to let me give up. "

Bobbi glanced at Margaret and smiled. "But then our friend here reminded me that my actions, good or bad, would create ripples that could affect the course of my eternal journey. I noticed Alton's actions were inspiring those around him, and made up my mind to do likewise. When I began walking without a brace, Alton invested in Rebecca's and Jack's new medical appliance business and encouraged Ethel – the little nurse who helped me strengthen my muscles – open her own physical restoration shop. That trio proceeded to help hundreds of injured people. Heaven only knows how many ripples they created!"

Bobbi started to take a sip from her teacup, but before it touched her lips, another thought sprang to mind. "And after growing up surrounded by successful women, my children joined the fight for equal pay. They've helped countless women acquire jobs that were once denied to them and get paid on equal footing with men. Of course there's always more work to be done..."

Suddenly Clay appeared, looking magnificent in a black three piece suit with thin white pin stripes, a white linen shirt, black silk tie, and his ever-present Fedora. Twin peaks of a starched white handkerchief poked out of his jacket pocket and his dark brown mustache was sculpted into a thin line.

"He looks just like Clark Gable," Lily thought.

"Hello, ladies," he said, removing his hat and gliding into the remaining chair. Margaret reached for her teapot, but stopped when she saw him pull a silver flask from his inside coat pocket.

"You can't talk about ripples without including Anna," Bobbi said, scarcely acknowledging his arrival.

"Yeah," Clay agreed. "After witnessing Bobbi's miraculous re-covery, she and the other nurses never gave up on another patient. There's no telling how many folks lived on account of that." He grinned at Bobbi. "Some of them even fell in love."

"That's true." Bobbi gave Clay a teasing smile. "Alton and Anna met at my bedside – and so did my niece, Rebecca and her husband, Jack."

"And who else?" Clay asked, obviously wanting her to admit she had fallen in love with him.

Bobbi wrinkled her brow, as if thinking hard. "Oh, that's right – James Mumper and Amy fell in love while she was living in my home, caring for Belle and Nathaniel."

Bobbi winked at Clay and began listing other ripples that re-sulted from her accident.

"Alton Farthing became one of the first surgeons to work from photographs during facial reconstruction," she said. "And he trained over a hundred doctors before he finally retired."

"What about your sisters?" Clay asked. "Jo gave Lucian his come-up-in's, and..."

"And Lou used some of his money to help other victims of abuse," Bobbi agreed, finishing his thought.

"And your kids learnt to face the world head-on."

Lily felt as though she was watching a tennis match, turning her head back and forth between Bobbi and Clay.

"And all four of them graduated from college and married well," Bobbi added, sitting up straighter.

"And they spent their lives trying to improve the world," Clay added, turning to Lily. "Belle and her husband were doctors who volunteered at a free clinic."

"And Henrietta became a litigating attorney," Bobbi added. "Her goal was to become the first woman partner at her firm. She didn't live long enough to accomplish that feat, but one of the young women she mentored took up the challenge and succeeded." Bobbi smiled. "And Nathaniel attended Yale as the son of the late Barrett Hamilton, an esteemed labor management consultant and author."

Clay chuckled. "No one at Yale found out that Bobbi wrote those books until Nathaniel told them. Everyone just assumed he got his knack for business from his father."

Bobbi bit her lower lip and shook her head, recalling the ruse. "Nathaniel became a successful labor negotiator, and years later, he was asked to deliver a commencement address to a graduating class at Yale. Can you imagine everyone's surprise when he told them the story of how his mother was forced to write under his father's name in order to establish and maintain credibility?"

"He made Bobbi stand up and take a bow," Clay said, beaming with pride. "The whole crowd applauded."

Lily smiled, envisioning the scene.

"And my younger son, Fred," Bobbi continued, "spent his career as a legislator in Tallahassee, fighting to improve education and working conditions for everyone in Florida."

Suddenly, Bobbi's eyes glistened with tears. "Excuse me, Lily," she said, dabbing the tears with a lace handkerchief. "My children are all gone now, and talking about them sometimes reminds me how much I miss them." She sniffed. "But I wanted you to know that loads of good things happened *because* Bear and I had that terrible accident."

Margaret nodded. "Time and time again, I've witnessed positive outcomes arise from even the most tragic sets of circumstances."

"One of these days I'll be reunited with my family and we'll celebrate all that we accomplished," Bobbi said, her voice still tinged with sadness.

Clay slipped out of his chair and took Bobbi's elbow, pulling her up and into a tight embrace. "You've waited long enough." He lifted her chin and gave her a light kiss. "It's high time you go and join the children."

"You're ready to move on?" Bobbi asked, her eyes widening.

"No." He shook his head slowly, giving her a crooked smile. "I'm afraid I'm more like Margaret – content to remain in this realm. But I know this isn't where you want to be and you've grown weary of waiting for me to feel the lure of the lighted path."

"But I can't leave you alone, Clay. Not after all you've done for me and my family. Not after you gave your life for us!"

"Nonsense. I was an unattached wanderer most of my life, remember? I'll get by just fine."

"But... what about..." she stammered.

"You and me?" Clay asked. "Don't you worry your pretty head about that. I'll cross over soon, and when I do, we'll sort everything out. For now, it's enough to know we love one another."

Bobbi looked over her shoulder at Margaret, who was still seated at the table. "What should I do?"

Margaret floated to her feet. "I'll miss you, my precious girl, but I think Clay's right. It's time for you to continue your eternal journey."

Bobbi paused for a long moment before she murmured in Clay's ear, "Okay, I'll go ahead – but don't forget – the children and I will be waiting for you to join us!"

She swiveled her head toward Lily. "Don't waste any more time, Lily. You only live a short while, but the memories you create will last forever. Make good ones."

Lily nodded, unable to swallow the lump in her throat.

"Goodbye, dear Margaret," Bobbi continued. "Try to keep our scallywag out of trouble until he crosses over, won't you?"

Margaret smiled. "I'll do my best."

She turned back to Clay, her green eyes reflecting a mix of excitement and regret. "I know you'd rather not watch me take the lighted path, so I guess this is goodbye for now, Long Gone."

Clay bent forward and kissed her forehead. "Goodbye, Witch."

He continued to hold her until she faded from his arms.

"I always suspected you possessed a spark of gallantry, Clay," Margaret quipped.

Clay opened his eyes, a sad smile on his face. "Do you think she believed me?"

"Does it matter?" Margaret asked.

"Wait. You lied?" asked Lily, confused.

Clay bowed his head. "When you told that motorcycle fella that you couldn't live the traveling life that he craves, I realized I couldn't keep pretending that Bobbi was happy living a similar life with me. If she stayed in this realm much longer, it would ruin her love for me. But I doubt we'd be any happier on other side of the lighted path – at least not until I make amends for some bad things I've done. Watching what you did gave me the courage to set Bobbi free, even if it means never seeing her again. Thank you for that."

"I never thought I'd see the day..." Margaret shook her head. "It seems you've changed more than I ever thought possible, Clay." She gave him a tender smile. "You never know – you might be ready to take that lighted path sooner than you think!"

Clay tipped his hat to Lily and Margaret and then vanished.

"He let her go because he loves her," Lily whispered.

"Yes – which truly amazes me. Clay has always been afraid he'd lose Bobbi to her late husband if she took the lighted path alone. So what you just witnessed was something of a miracle – Clay Long behaving selflessly. And because you were partly responsible for him making that noble decision, you now understand that it's possible for the ripples you create to have an effect on spirits in this realm as well as the living. That might help explain how..."

Beep, Beep, Beep, Beep....

Chapter Eighty Three

Lily's head whirled toward the sound, knowing what was about to happen, but unable to prevent it. "No!" she cried as she fell through the clouds and awoke back in her hotel room bed. "Damn it!"

She slammed her hand down on the alarm clock and, hoping to rejoin Margaret, closed her eyes. Then she remembered that Grams' memorial service was today.

"Whatever Margaret was about to say will have to wait," she decided.

She arranged her thick auburn hair into a loose French braid down her back, the way Grams had always liked it best, and tied a small black ribbon bow at the bottom. Then she got dressed and stood in front of the mirror. The jacket of her black suit, a last-minute purchase, was more form-fitting than she would have preferred, but the skirt flared at mid-thigh and covered the majority of her brace. She tugged on the scooped neckline of her white blouse. *"A bit low, but not too bad,"* she observed. She decided to wear Grams' golden rose earrings and pendent, happy to still have them in her possession.

Determined not to wear her orthopedic shoes for the service, she slipped on a pair of new black leather pumps. *"They don't hurt too bad,"* she thought. *"At least not yet."*

Just as she finished dressing, her cell phone rang. She hoped it wasn't Seth. Last night's visit in the spirit realm convinced her that saying goodbye to him had been the right thing to do, and she had no desire to rehash the issue this morning.

She glanced at the caller ID and breathed a sigh of relief as she answered. "Good morning, Scott."

"You doing okay?" he asked.

Lily recalled the way Grams looked as she stepped onto the lighted path – so young and carefree. "Yeah, I'm good," she said. "I miss Grams, but I know she's happy to be reunited with Gramps."

"I'm sure she is. Listen, we don't need to be there for a couple hours, so I thought you might like to come up and check your blogs before breakfast."

"Yes, I would," Lily replied without hesitation. Not only was she was happy for the distraction, but the last few days reminded her that it was easier to forget her troubles when she was trying to help other people.

When Scott opened his door a few minutes later, his jaw dropped open.

"Yeah...you still clean up pretty good, too," she joked, grinning.

"I don't mean to stare..." Scott licked his lips and stepped aside to let her in. "But damn – you look amazing."

Lily limped across the room to his computer, wishing she didn't have to rely on a crutch to walk. She recalled how happy Bobbi was when she got rid of her brace and suddenly realized she wanted the same thing. "I've decided to have transplant surgery to repair my leg," she said, as she sat down.

"Seriously?" Scott clapped his hands together. "That's fantastic, Lilyanna!"

Lily smiled without looking up, opting not to tell Scott that she made her decision only seconds before. She turned her attention to the computer screen. "Do you know if any of these posts need to be addressed immediately?"

Scott rubbed his hand over his mouth and chin before answering – his method of clearing his thoughts. "There's a lot of traffic on your new site, but I don't think any of the posts qualify as emergencies."

Lily scanned the new posts and agreed with Scott's assessment. Then she sighed, distracted by thoughts of Grams' upcoming memorial service.

Scott accurately sensed the shift in her mood. "Do you want to get out of here for a while? Maybe go down to the hotel restaurant for a bite to eat?" he asked.

She knew Seth was at the hospital, but didn't want to risk having the waiter in the Terrace Cafe ask the whereabouts of her *regular* breakfast partner.

"Food sounds good, but let's go someplace else, okay?"

Once they were settled at a corner table in the Wildflower Café awaiting their blueberry Belgian waffles, scrambled eggs and bacon, Lily absentmindedly stirred sugar into a cup of tea, thinking about Grams.

"I spent most of last night reading your blog," Scott announced, breaking the silence.

Lily flushed, embarrassed. Scott never read her *Way to Go* blog. It was for strangers. Her confidence in total anonymity allowed her to open-up and write exactly what she felt. It never occurred to her that things might be different with her new *Ghost Children* blog.

"Why did you do that?" she demanded. "That's private."

Scott raised his eyebrows, but kept his calm. "No it's not. It's the exact opposite of private. Your blog is open to anyone with Internet access."

Lily gulped and shook her head. She knew her argument wasn't logical but she still felt violated – as if he had read her personal diary. "That's different. Nobody out there *knows* me."

"I'm sorry if I upset you, Lilianna," he said, keeping his voice low. "But I'm not sorry I read what you had to say. I've been trying to get a handle on what you've been going through for three years now and I think I learned more about it in one night than I have in all that time."

Lily's mind raced, trying to remember exactly what she had written, but it was of no use. She had tried to answer as many of the posts as she could in just a few hours and now they were all tangled together in her mind. Finally, she shrugged. "So what do you think you learned?"

"Well, for one thing, I learned that it's a lot more common for a grieving mother to believe she has seen her departed child than I thought it was. I'm sorry for brushing off your claims about seeing Dylan."

Lily kept her eyes glued to the paper napkin in her lap, twisting its edge, but she gave Scott a single stiff nod of her head to acknowledge she was listening.

"Do you remember the post from the woman who blames herself for her son's death in a drive-by shooting? She had given him an ultimatum – reenroll in college or move out. He moved out. She was certain he wouldn't have been sitting on the front steps of his friend's house, if she hadn't done that. You told her you understood how she felt because you blame yourself for your son's death, too."

Lily gulped, recalling the post. "I also told her to try to focus on happier memories with her son."

"Yeah, you did," Scott said. "But that's not the point. The point is that she's no more to blame for her son's death than you are for Dylan's."

"But Dylan's death *is* my fault," she said. "I was driving. That makes me responsible." She shrugged. "It's progress, actually. At least I finally accepted the fact that he couldn't be saved and stopped blaming you and the doctors for letting him die." She gave him a weak smile, but didn't meet his eyes. "Why don't you hate me for all the times I accused you of not doing enough to save him?"

"Lily, the accident wasn't your fault. And I know that because I investigated every single aspect of that night, trying to prove to you who really *was* to blame."

She listened without looking up, still twisting the napkin in her lap.

"At first," Scott continued, "I tried to blame the logging company. But then I discovered their safety record was spotless before that night. When one of their trucks broke down at a remote site, a brand new manager was worried about missing a delivery deadline his first week on the job, so he made the decision to overload one truck. He didn't think he was taking that much of a risk. The poor guy had no idea Mother Nature would decide to suddenly drop a blanket of fog over the road, thicker than anyone could remember ever seeing in that area before. And of course, he couldn't know the driver would jackknife the truck while trying to swerve to avoid a stalled car." He paused, watching her.

"Please look at me, Lily," he pleaded.

Reluctantly, she raised her gaze to meet his – her lips pressed into a thin line.

"Do you know the odds of that truck tipping over when it swerved?" Scott asked. "Or the odds that the logs would break free when it happened? Or that it would take place on an overpass, just when our car was passing by on the road below? How likely do you think it is that falling logs would hit the road and bounce *so precisely* that one would come through the window and hit Dylan while another knocked off the passenger door, threw me out, and still another pushed our car off the road, out of sight?" He shook his head. "Christ, it's mind-boggling to think that so many random, astronomically long-shot odds hit at one time to make things play out exactly the way they did." He blew out a long breath. "It was a freak accident, Lily. It wasn't anybody's fault."

Lily stared at him, barely breathing. "Then why do I feel so guilty?" she whispered.

Scott's big brown eyes filled with sadness. "I guess, for the same reason I feel guilty for being asleep. You know, while I was investigating, I talked to the manager who made the decision to overload the truck, the truck driver, the cops and firemen who responded to the accident, and even the driver of the car that stalled on the overpass. Every single person I talked to feels guilty about the role they played in that damned accident. We all have our own lists of things we wish we had done differently. But the truth is, none of us could have stopped that accident from happening – or saved Dylan."

Lily recalled something similar that Seth had said. "And if we had done things differently and the accident still happened, we'd all be certain that whatever changes we made caused it to happen."

Scott nodded. "Yes, I believe we would."

They sat quietly for a few minutes, lost in thought.

"I'll grieve for Dylan the rest of my life," Scott said, his voice breaking, "But the bigger tragedy – for me, anyway – will be if I also lose my marriage because of that accident."

"How could you possibly still want me after everything I've put you through?" Lily moaned.

Scott shook his head as if he hadn't heard her correctly. "I fell in love with you long before we ever *thought* about having a child. Sure, I have a million great memories of us as a family, but I have a million more of the time we shared before Dylan was born. And I believe that, despite the fact we'll always miss our son, the two of us can still make new, happy memories together."

"You sound like Margaret Plant. She always says that memories are precious because you can relive them whenever you choose, and people are never truly gone as long as they're remembered. Plus, she says memories are the only thing you get to take with you when you leave this world."

"I don't know who she is, but I think she's right."

Lily knew that if their marriage was to have any chance of mending, she had to reveal everything she knew about the spirit realm. And Scott would have to believe her.

"Margaret is one of the spirits I connected with the Belleview Biltmore Hotel," she said in a matter-of-fact tone, as if the notion that spirits haunted the old hotel was a well-known fact. "She and a couple of other spirits have been teaching me some important lessons during my stay there."

Scott furrowed his eyebrows with concern.

"I'm not crazy, Scott. And I don't think the women on my blog are crazy, either," she said. "I believe we share a unique bond – each of us has seen the spirit of our departed children, and some of us have connected with other spirits as well. I think that maybe my experiences with Dylan allowed my subconscious to be more receptive to these other spirits."

Scott gave her a partly quizzical and partly should-I-call-the-guys-in-white-coats look. "Do you see any spirits right now?" He glanced nervously around the café.

Lily smiled. "No. I only connect with them at the hotel, and even then, it's almost always while I'm sleeping."

"Aren't those called dreams?"

"No." Lily shook her head patiently. "Connecting with spirits is quite different from dreaming. Over the last few days, I've come to think of people who have communicated with spirits as being members of an exclusive club. We're sort of like astronauts who have walked in space. No matter how hard they try to describe what it feels like to be weightless and tethered to a spacecraft far above Earth, the only people who can truly understand what it's like are other astronauts who've had the same experience."

Scott glanced over her shoulder at the server, who was carrying a tray to their table. "Here's our food," he said.

Lily understood his comment was a signal for her to stop talking about spirits while the waitress was within earshot, and she obliged. Scott commented on the beautiful presentation of their breakfast, and Lily agreed by nodding her head.

The server smiled. "And it tastes even better than it looks," she said, glancing at their near-empty cups. "I'll be right back to warm up your coffee and I'll bring more hot water for your tea. Do you need anything else?"

After they assured her they didn't, the server turned and scurried away.

Lily nibbled on a blueberry waffle while watching Scott gulp down his scrambled eggs and bacon, as though it was his first meal in days. She recalled that he and Dylan shared that trait. No matter what was going on in their respective worlds, it never seemed to affect their appetite for breakfast. Her mind flashed back to one Sunday morning, when they were anxiously waiting to hear if Dylan had made the Little League Majors team. To her amazement, the two of them wolfed down fifteen pancakes and almost as many slices of bacon.

She smiled with the realization that, for the first time since his death, a fond memory of Dylan wasn't overshadowed by the pain of loss. *"Maybe there's hope for me yet,"* she thought.

"I think I get what you mean," Scott said between bites, bringing Lily back to the present, "You know – about sharing a connection with people who believe they've seen ghosts. But..."

"But what?" Lily said, trying to keep the defensive edge from her voice.

"Well, are you sure you want death to be such a big part of your life, Lily?"

"Hmm." She cocked her head, thinking about everything she learned during the past few weeks. "I guess I don't look at it that way. I see both of my blogs as opportunities to create positive ripples in people's lives."

"What's a ripple?" Scott asked.

"The basic concept is that every action we take – big or small – that affects another person, creates a positive or a negative ripple."

"Like when you throw a rock into a pond and ripples fan out on all sides?"

"Sort of, but bigger... think of waves," Lily said. "If the actions we take influence other actions, a ripple can roll on forever, creating thousands of other ripples along the way. In terms of my blogs, every post I write has the potential to create a ripple in the life of every person who reads it."

"And they might take actions that create ripples for other people?"

"Yep." Lily grinned. "Hopefully, some of the ripples I create will help people through their grief – or at least let them know they have an ally who understands what they're going through and shares their belief that a realm of spirits exists between life and the lighted path – and that our eternal journeys continue beyond the light."

"Sounds fascinating," Scott marveled. "You know, I can't believe how much you've – I don't know – *blossomed* in the past couple of weeks. You seem to have gained a sense of purpose that you didn't have before."

"Thanks," she said. "I've learned a lot from spirits who shared some of their memories with me. I can tell you more about them later, but today should be all about Grams."

"Okay, but before we change the subject, I want to say one more thing. I think it's wonderful that you've found a purpose that's worthy of your time and dedication, and I hope you know that I'll help you any way I can. But I want you to promise me that you'll make more time to enjoy life from now on – you know, smell the roses and all that...."

The rumble of thunder surprised the pair, drawing their attention to the gray clouds outside café window.

"Man, that came out of nowhere," Scott said, eyeing the sky. "We better get going." He raised a hand to signal the server to bring their check.

Lily continued staring out the window, considering how the change in the weather was a simile for life in general. *"Life is unpredictable,"* she mused. *"You never know when you'll encounter rough weather or how long it will last. All you can do is enjoy the sun when it shines and hope you're lucky enough to have someone who wants to be with you, no matter what. Someone who will remind you to smell the roses."*

She returned her gaze to Scott, knowing in that instant that he wasn't just her past. He was her present and, if she was lucky, her future as well.

Chapter Eighty Four

By the time they reached Hubble Funeral Home, the first few drops of rain were beginning to fall. Two men in black suits stood under the portico; each holding a large, black umbrella.

Scott recognized the funeral director, Ken Hodge, and raised his hand in half-wave, half-salute greeting. Ken nodded and signaled Scott to pull under the covered carport.

"I guess if there isn't a need for the hearse, they park it out of sight," he said, absently turning the car into the oversized parking space.

The moment Scott put the car in park and shut off the engine, Ken was at Lily's door, opening it for her and offering his hand.

"It's good to see you, Mr. and Mrs. Thorne," he said. "I apologize for not scheduling some private family time before everyone else arrived, but I was under the impression that you weren't expecting any guests to attend Mrs. Bloom's service."

Lily and Scott exchanged looks of surprise.

"We didn't," Lily confirmed, "Other than Pastor Dave, of course."

"It appears several of your grandmother's friends read her obituary and came to pay their last respects." Ken said.

He held his umbrella over Lily's head as they walked toward the front entrance, even though the rain was little more than a drizzle.

"We reserved a loveseat at the front of the parlor for you and your husband and added additional seating to accommodate the other guests," Ken continued.

The second man held the door open and took Ken's umbrella in one, well-rehearsed move, so that Ken didn't have to take his hand from Lily's elbow as they entered the lobby, with Scott following right behind them. He guided Lily to the small guest book, standing open on a wall-mounted shelf, along with a framed picture of Grams and an agenda for the memorial service. Lily froze, staring at Grams' picture.

Ken seemed to understand her reaction. Lily guessed it probably wasn't the first time he'd seen it. "Take your time, Mrs. Thorne," he said. "Would you like me to ask the other guests to retire to the lobby for a few minutes, to give you a moment alone with your grandmother?"

"No. Don't do that," Lily managed to mumble. "We'll be fine."

She tore her eyes from Grams' kindly face to look at Scott. His expression confirmed that he had just realized the same thing she had – all that was left of Grams were her ashes and once they walked into the parlor, they could never again pretend otherwise.

"Would you like Pastor Dave to accompany you inside?" Ken asked.

Lily shook her head, leaning on her crutch more heavily than usual.

Scott stepped closer and took her arm. "We can manage," he said.

Ken nodded and led the way to the small parlor. It was the same room where they had said goodbye to Grams before her cremation, a fact which Lily found both comforting and sad. She tried to focus on the memory of Grams' peaceful expression and glanced around the room, trying to avoid looking at the altar, on which rested the urn containing Grams' ashes.

More than a dozen mourners were seated in the parlor. With the exception of Pastor Dave and Nurse Opal from the hospital, Lily knew none of them. Ken escorted them to the front of the room and removed a *Reserved* sign from a small couch. Lily sat, concentrating on the subdued floral pattern of the upholstered loveseat, still reluctant to look at the altar.

"Would you like me to begin the photo memorial now?" Ken asked, pointing to a television monitor.

Lily felt the eyes of both men upon her, waiting for a decision. She nodded; words failing her. Ken turned to exit and Scott sat down next to her.

"The altar looks nice, Lily," he said. "I like that Dylan's little urn is there with Grams'."

Lily forced herself to look at the elegant display. The tall, mahogany altar was covered with white lace and although the urns were made of salt, they had the appearance of fine, cream and rust-colored marble. Dylan's miniature urn sat directly in front of Grams' larger one. Pillars on either side of the altar held large baskets, overflowing with some of Grams' favorite flowers – pink and white stargazer lilies, white roses and purple orchids. Silk fichus trees provided background greenery.

"Grams always seemed larger than life to me," Lily mused. "It doesn't seem possible that she could fit inside that urn."

"The most important part of her isn't in there," Scott replied. "Her spirit is with Gramps, your mom, and Dylan."

Lily cringed, her thoughts involuntarily returning to the memory of watching Grams take the lighted path – and Dylan waving goodbye from the spirit realm. *"Why didn't he go with her?"* she wondered for the hundredth time. *"Is he still tethered to this realm because parts of his body are still living inside other people?"* She wanted to discuss it with Scott, but now was definitely not the right time for that revelation.

"Let's go on up to the podium," she said, putting the issue out of her mind.

Scott nodded and helped her to her feet. At the altar, he kneeled on the low, padded bench, closed his eyes and prayed, while Lily read the small placard next to the urns.

Lois Ann Fleming-Bloom – "Grams"
Beloved Wife, Mother, Grandmother, & Great Grandmother
No longer by our side, but forever in our hearts

And

Dylan Jacob Thorne
Precious Child
A beautiful soul, taken from this world much too soon

When the room filled with the soft sound of classical music, Lily and Scott looked up at the large monitor. The display read:

Lois Ann Fleming-Bloom
1934 – 2013

"Those we love don't go away.
They walk beside us every day.
Unseen, unheard, but always near.
Still loved, still missed and very dear."
...Unknown

Scott stood and helped Lily back to the loveseat to watch the video presentation. Beautiful local landscape shots gave way to photos of Grams enjoying family and friends. The photographs weren't in chronological order, keeping the focus off the aging process.

"What's this?" an elderly woman asked from behind her.

Lily's ears pricked up. She had noticed several elderly people sitting together in the row directly behind the loveseat. She eavesdropped, hoping to determine how they knew Grams.

"They're pictures from Lois's life," another woman replied. "See? That's her at the beach with her family. Now, hush."

"Do you suppose they'll show pictures of her adopted grand-kids?" the first woman asked, refusing to be quiet.

"I don't think so," the other woman said, lowering her voice even further. "I don't think her family approved of them."

Lily bit her lip, resisting the temptation to turn around and ask what in the world they were talking about.

"Well, I can't blame them. It's unseemly – adopting grown..."

A loud clap of thunder seemed to shake the building as the midday storm erupted, full force.

"That was a close one," a man's voice commented.

"Yes, it was, Marty," the second woman agreed amiably. Then she hissed, "See there, Thelma? God himself is telling you to be quiet and show some respect. This is a funeral, for goodness sake, not a gossip party."

"Oh, hush yourself, Maureen," Thelma retorted. "And besides, it's not a funeral, smarty pants. Funerals have caskets. This is a *memorial service.*"

Scott, oblivious to the conversation, squeezed Lily's hand. She looked at the screen, just in time to see a photo taken at her wedding reception. Grams and Scott were dancing a Jitterbug together and grinning, ear to ear.

Lily smiled, recalling how excited Grams had been to help her choose her wedding gown and plan the event. How many times over the years, had her relationship with Grams helped ease their mutual sense of loss – Grams mourning her lost daughter and her, missing her mother? Now, only Lily was left to mourn them both.

Chapter Eighty Five

Scott had done a wonderful job collecting photographs that portrayed Grams as a woman who had lived a full and happy life. By the time the presentation ended, Lily's eyes were clouded with bittersweet tears.

Pastor Dave stepped in front of the loveseat and took Lily's hand between his own. "Your grandmother was one of my favorite parishioners," he said, "and even though I'm happy to know she's with Jesus now, I'll miss her dearly." He let go of Lily and reached out to shake Scott's hand, holding it for an extra moment. "I hope you know how much joy your family brought into Lois's life."

Scott's jaw trembled and tears filled his eyes as Pastor Dave released his hand, patted him on the shoulder, and then walked to the podium, a few steps away. He led the mourners in prayer and then gave a service filled with hope, humor and compassion for the pain her loved ones were suffering. Then he asked everyone to sing along with a recording of *Amazing Grace*, performed by Susan Boyle. The small crowd started out strong, but their voices dropped off after the first stanza, with everyone preferring to listen to Boyle's version. When the hymn was over, Pastor Dave thanked everyone for coming and closed the memorial service with a blessing.

He stepped from behind the podium and asked Scott and Lily to join him at the front of the room to receive condolences. The memorial video played a second time, as people filed by. Lily felt numb, but she tried to listen to what each person had to say and thank them for coming. In addition to a few ladies from Grams' church and a representative from her bridge club, Lily was pleasantly surprised to meet several residents from Bay Manor nursing home.

As the formal procession dwindled, small clusters of people milled about, trying to decide whether to make a dash for their cars in the rain or wait in the parlor until it subsided. Lily and Scott moved toward the small couch, but stopped when Lily noticed Nurse Opal approaching. She stepped forward to shake the stout woman's hand, but Opal ignored the formal gesture and embraced Lily within her thick, protective arms. Lily crumpled against her, letting go of the tears she had been holding back without even realizing she was doing so.

"It's all right, sweet child," Opal cooed into her ear. "Miz Bloom is at peace now. I'm able to sense these things, remember?"

"Yes, I do," Lily sniffled, collecting herself. She pulled back and dabbed her face with a tissue. "And you always seem to know how to make me feel better." She gave the nurse another hug before turning to Scott, who had observed the emotional interaction.

"Scott, you remember Opal. She walked us out of Morton Plant Hospital the day Grams..." She paused, still unable to say Grams *died*, even now.

Scott smiled and shook her hand. "Of course, I remember. It was kind of you to come."

"Opal is the nicest, most skilled nurse you could ever hope to meet," Lily gushed.

"You're a nurse?" a woman asked from behind them.

Lily turned around in surprise, recognizing Thelma's voice from earlier.

"Look how swollen my fingers are," Thelma said, holding out her chubby digits in Opal's direction. "I know it's not normal, but the doctor at Bay Manor says I shouldn't worry. What do you think?"

"I'm a nurse, not a doctor," Opal replied, without the least bit of sarcasm. "But if your doctor says not to worry, you can probably rest easy. Fingers swell for many reasons, but you might want to watch your salt intake." She pointed at a large bag of potato chips poking out of Thelma's satchel-sized purse.

Thelma frowned and mumbled "Thank you," before resuming her self-examination, holding her fingers up, first this way and then that way.

Opal turned back to Lily and winked, pretending not to notice that another woman in the group had begun fidgeting with a bandage on her arm. "I best be getting back to the hospital," she said in a low voice, "before these folks ask me to set-up a free clinic in the lobby."

They embraced once more, all smiles now. "I'll never forget you, Opal," Lily whispered. "Not for as long as I live. Thank you for everything you did for me, and most of all, bless you for being so kind to Grams."

"It was my pleasure," Opal replied. "And I'm also glad to see you're trying to put things right with that handsome man of yours. I have a good feeling about you two – I can sense these things, you know."

Lily chuckled, relieved that Scott had moved out of earshot to mingle with other guests.

"You have a fine laugh, Lily," Opal said, turning to leave. "I hope you'll start using it more often."

A tall, thin, silver-haired man in his late-sixties stepped next to Lily, as if the receiving line had moved to this new location, and he was next in line.

"My name's Marty," he said, biting his lower lip. "I knew your grandmother at Bay Manor. She was a good woman."

"I'm from Bay Manor, too," Thelma called out. "I'd stand up, but my knees are shot. Are you..."

"Thelma, wait your turn," Maureen scolded. "Marty's talking." She turned to the thin man and softened her voice. "Go on, Marty."

Marty gulped, making it obvious he had already said just about everything he had planned to say.

"Marty is a wonderful mechanic," Maureen gushed. "He wired up that computer you donated to the Manor, all by himself, and he knows how to work it, too. Why, he turns on the World Wide Web channel every day and reads all the local obituaries."

"Among other things," Marty added sheepishly.

"When Marty told us Lois passed," Maureen continued, "we had Frank drive us here on the bus."

"Frank usually drives us to lunch on Fridays," Thelma grumbled. "We'd be at the Cozy Corner Restaurant if Maureen hadn't commandeered the damn bus."

"I did no such thing," Maureen insisted. "We voted to come here before lunch, and majority rules." She gave Thelma an insincere smile. "Now, be polite. This is a funeral, for goodness sake."

"It's a memorial service," Thelma shot back. "And I was just trying to explain that I don't usually eat chips, so that's not what's wrong with my fingers. I only brought them so I wouldn't starve to death before lunch."

Lily glanced at the rotund woman and decided the danger of her starving to death for lack of a timely lunch was rather remote. "Well, I'm glad you came," she said. "It's good to know Grams had such thoughtful friends."

"I liked Lois," Maureen said. "And I enjoyed the pictures of her life they showed on that big TV. When she was young, she looked just like Lucille Ball... or maybe Katharine Hepburn."

"Lucille Ball and Katharine Hepburn didn't look anything alike, and neither actress resembled Grams," Lily thought, smiling indulgently.

Thelma scoffed and turned to a petite woman in a prim black suit, seated on her opposite side. "Well I, for one, wanted to see some pictures of the grandchildren Lois' adopted," she said. "She talked about them all the time."

"Maybe her adopted family will hold their own memorial," the tiny woman shouted – her booming voice a sharp contrast to her elfin stature.

"Flo – turn on your hearing aids!" Maureen called. She turned to Lily and lowered her voice. "Flo's just about stone deaf without her hearing aids," she apologized, "Unfortunately, she turns them off when her ears get tired and forgets to turn them back on."

Lily nodded, confused by their comments.

"Maybe they aren't welcome," Thelma told Flo, who was fussing with her hearing aids. "After all, one's a negro cook, one's a piano player, who's probably as queer as Liberace, and..."

"You're supposed to say *black* – not *negro*, and say *gay* instead of *queer*," Flo corrected, speaking at a more reasonable volume. "And besides, why wouldn't the medical student or the math teacher be welcome? They're respectable."

"Hush!" Maureen warned. "If you two can't be nice, go wait in the bus."

"What's wrong with talking?" Thelma demanded.

"I don't understand," Lily said, her knees suddenly weak. "What adopted grandchildren? Scott and I are Grams' only living family." She sat on the couch, her mind racing.

"See what you've done?" Maureen reprimanded the two women. "Now she's upset!" She sat down next to Lily. "Don't you mind those old busybodies, honey," she said. "Unfortunately, it's hard for us old folks to know what's real and what's not sometimes." She patted Lily's hand. "Lois must have been imagining things."

"Maureen," Marty said, resting his hand her shoulder; his voice gentle. "The rain stopped, so Frank can drive us over the Cozy Corner now. You're so good at getting everyone organized. Can you please get everyone back on the bus?"

The old man's touch put a smile on Maureen's face. "Of course I will, Marty," she said, resting her cheek against his weathered hand before accepting his help to her feet.

"It was nice meeting you," she said, shaking Lily's hand. "I'll miss Lois, but I'm sure we'll all be together in Heaven one day."

Lily gave her a warm smile. "Thank you, Maureen."

Maureen turned and began clucking to the others like a mother hen, rounding up her chicks. "Come on, Thelma. You too, Flo. The faster you move, the sooner we'll be having lunch!"

Marty watched until Maureen and the other two women were out of earshot and then he rubbed his chin. "Lily, your grandmother liked to work jigsaw puzzles in activity room at Bay Manor. That's where I set-up the computer, so I reckon I talked to

her more often than most folks. She told me her grandson introduced her to some of his friends. He said they were like family to
him, so she decided to call them her adopted grandchildren."

"But Dylan couldn't have introduced her to anyone. He died
before Grams went to live at Bay Manor," Lily reasoned.

"Yeah, I know. But I didn't say anything because, even if she
was a little delusional, Lois loved her family and never doubted
they loved her back – including you. That's what's really important." He paused, studying Lily for a long moment. "Lois knew
her time was about up, you know. She told me she enjoyed a
good, long life and was ready to join her husband." He rubbed his
chin again. "And having a stroke in your sleep – well, that's not a
bad way to go."

The corners of Marty's mouth turned up when he spied
Maureen waving from the doorway. "Speaking of going, I best be
on my way," he said.

"Thanks for coming – and for telling me about Grams," Lily
said, shaking his hand. "It was very kind of you."

"I hope you don't take offense," he said, winking a gray eye at
her. "But I had an ulterior motive for coming today. I wanted everybody to be all dressed up when I propose to Maureen at lunch."

"No offense taken," Lily said. "I'm sure Grams would love that
you two are getting married."

Marty nodded and then walked across the small parlor to say
goodbye to Scott and Pastor Dave. While the three men chatted,
Lily hobbled back to the altar.

She gazed at the two urns, her thoughts racing. *"Did Dylan's
spirit visit you, Grams? Did other spirits haunt you, too?"*

"How are you holding up, Lily?" Scott asked, suddenly at her
side.

Lily jumped.

"I'm sorry," he said, automatically sliding his arm around her waist,
as he had done for so many years. "I didn't mean to startle you."

"That's okay," she replied, enjoying the comfort of his touch.

Scott nodded, studying the altar display as if committing it to
memory. "Ken's ready to transport the urns and flowers to the

boat dock. He said we can head over whenever we're ready, but that old guy, Marty, had a good idea. He suggested we postpone the ash scattering ceremony a few hours, so we could enjoy the sunset on the water as we lay the ashes to rest." Scott chuckled. "He said the romantic ride back to shore would be a bonus."

"I don't know about the romantic part, but I like the idea of the having the ceremony at sunset. Do you think the captain would mind waiting?"

Scott checked his watch. "I'll ask Ken to find out. How should we kill the two hours till sunset?"

"We could go someplace and have a drink. Or two. Or three."

Scott raised his eyebrows; questioning.

Lily hesitated. "I have a lot more to tell you about the spirits of the Belleview Biltmore, and about Dylan." She bit her lower lip. *"Our marriage can't be fixed unless he believes me. But it would be better to know that sooner than later"*

She felt him tightened his grip on her waist.

"I've had a couple weeks to come to grips with all of this, Scott, but since I'll be dumping it on you all at once, you may need some help from Jack Daniels."

Scott let out a deep breath through pursed lips and nodded. "Okay, then. Let me talk to Ken and see what we can work out." He turned on his heel and headed for the lobby.

Chapter Eighty Six

After Captain Mike agreed to delay their scheduled departure by two hours, Scott and Lily drove to the Pier House 60 Hotel and took the elevator up to Jimmy's Crow's Nest – an open deck bar on the tenth floor, overlooking Clearwater Beach. The rain had chased off the afternoon crowd, but the clearing skies suggested a beautiful sunset was forthcoming, and the staff was busy drying chairs in preparation for the throng that would, no doubt, arrive shortly to watch the nightly spectacle. As Scott and Lily made their way to a corner table, one of the bartenders eyed them curiously.

"I don't think we look like their typical customers," Lily said, glancing at the bar, where a few regulars sat, attired in tee-shirts, baggy shorts and flip flops.

"Probably not," Scott agreed.

The table was shaded by a large, orange umbrella. Scott pulled a chair out for Lily while admiring the view – blue-green waves lapping up on the white sugar sand beach. He slipped off his suit jacket and rolled up his shirt sleeves before sitting.

Lily watched him, fascinated. He was able to blend in so effortlessly. She leaned her crutch against an empty chair at their table and frowned at her black suit, without noticing a bartender had sauntered over to take their order.

"Welcome to Jimmy's," he said with a friendly smile. "You folks here for the sunset?"

"Afraid not," Lily replied. "We'll be going out on the *Dreamcatcher* at sunset to scatter my grandmother's ashes."

The bartender dropped his smile. "Sorry for your loss," he said. "But it's cool you're doing that. I figure a person can't help but rest in peace out there – it's so beautiful."

Lily cast a glance at the horizon. "I agree," she said.

He gave her a nod to acknowledge their kindred spirit and then refocused on his job. "My name's Jeff," he said. "What can I bring you guys to drink?"

Scott pulled out his credit card to open a tab, and ordered a glass of chardonnay for Lily and a Jack and Coke for himself. Lily shifted uneasily in the plastic chair. Despite the shade and sea-breeze, her jacket was much too warm. Once Jeff returned to the bar, she took a deep breath and shrugged it off, amused that Scott was watching wide-eyed, as she folded it and laid it on the chair, next to her crutch.

She gave him a thin-lipped smile. "My friend, Mary – the ODC – told me that Dylan's organs saved the lives of seven people, drastically improved the lives of two others, and helped save my arms. She also said that every single one of his recipients was a six to ten-point match, which means they probably didn't suffer complications and only required low doses of anti-rejection medications."

Scott swallowed hard and sat back in his chair, trying to erase the stunned expression from his face. "Lilyanna, I'm not so sure you started at the beginning," he said.

"No, I guess I didn't," Lily agreed. "But I wanted you to know that I've changed my mind about your decision to donate Dylan's organs. It was the right thing to do. The spirits at the Belleview Biltmore helped me understand that, Scott."

Jeff arrived with their drinks, suspending their conversation. He was obviously startled by the sight of Lily's scarred forearms, but said nothing. "Sunset's still a ways off," he observed. "Would you guys like something to eat? We only have a small menu, but what we offer is tasty."

Scott's ears pricked up at the mention of food. "Yeah, I guess we should eat something," he said.

Lily looked over at Jeff, catching him staring at her arms.

"Burned in a car accident," she said, automatically dropping her hands into her lap. "Long time ago."

"Yeah, well –" he said, shifting his gaze to her face. "I wouldn't worry about it if I were you. You're still one of the prettiest ladies I've ever seen."

"Here, here," Scott concurred, raising his drink to toast the observation.

"Wow, Jeff... way to earn a bigger tip," she joked.

Both men chuckled, putting Lily at ease. Jeff took their order for chicken quesadillas and then left them alone again.

"I can't believe how relaxed you are, Lily," Scott said. "Maybe you should tell me more about those ghosts."

She obliged, telling him about when she first arrived at the Belleview Biltmore and her initial journeys into the spirit realm.

"To be honest, at first, I thought I was losing it again," she confessed. "But it was such a relief to sleep without nightmares, I didn't care." She shook her head. "Then Sss...some people told me that lots of people claim to have had paranormal experiences at the hotel."

Scott nodded, listening intently. Lily breathed a sigh of relief that she hadn't accidentally said Seth's name and continued. She explained how she had Dylan's medical records reviewed, and that spirits began sharing their memories with her, to help her understand that even when horrible things happen, there's a chance something good can come out of it.

"So that's why you wanted to start a new blog?" Scott asked. "To create something good?"

Lily nodded. "But even though I understand so much more than I did before, I still have a ton of questions."

She hesitated, knowing the one thought that had comforted Scott all this time was his certainty that Dylan was with Gramps in Heaven.

"No more holding back," she reminded herself. *"Tell him everything."* She took a drink to wet her dry mouth and then blurted, "When Dylan's spirit visited me in the hospital right after the accident, I made him promise not to go into the light because I wanted

him to live, and I think he listened to me. But now I'm afraid his spirit might be stuck between worlds."

Scott stared at her, stirring the ice in his glass with his cocktail straw. "What does that mean?"

Lily explained about watching Grams step onto the lighted path and how several people, including Dylan, had been there to bid her farewell, but they didn't go with her into the light. Scott listened without saying a word.

"And I don't know if these things are connected," she continued, "But on the drive over here, I recalled a memory Margaret showed me of Grams at Bay Manor, talking to Dylan on his old football phone. Then I remembered a nurse there telling me Grams insisted on keeping that phone next to her bed because she used it to talk to her grandson."

"You think Dylan's ghost talked to her on the phone and told her he's stuck here? I don't think God would let that happen to an innocent little boy."

Lily shook her head. "No, that's not what I mean. Well, not exactly. The nurse thought Dylan was still alive – that he had received an early admission to medical school. And today, at the memorial service, her friends from Bay Manor kept referring to Grams' *adopted* grandchildren. At first, that made me sad. I thought Grams had been hallucinating near the end. But they said one of them was a medical student, another was a math teacher, and another was a chef."

Lily waited a few seconds to see if Scott would make the same connection she had made.

"A math teacher?" he repeated. "You mean..."

She nodded. "You didn't tell Grams about the letters from Dylan's organ recipients, did you?"

Scott shook his head. "No. I figured that would piss you off, since you refused to read them."

"Well, what are the odds that every one of Grams' so-called adopted grandchildren would match the recipient's occupations? And there's more," she said.

"More?" Scott leaned forward.

"In some of my nightmares, Dylan's body morphs into different people and today, I realized their physical descriptions matched my dreams, too – like a Jamaican woman and a man in a chef's hat. I wish I would have read the letters a long time ago. I'm sure I would have made the connection a lot sooner."

"But you said the people who received Dylan's organs were good matches? Why would they all be dead?"

Lily shook her head. "I don't know. That confuses me, too."

Their lunch arrived while they were both lost in thought. Scott ordered another drink, but Lily passed, having barely touched her wine. They ate in silence for several minutes.

"Lilyanna, I don't know what's happening," Scott said. "But I just can't bring myself to believe that none of Dylan's organ recipients are still alive." He saw Jeff approaching with his fresh drink and drained his glass.

"Me neither," Lily said.

"Can I bring you anything else?" Jeff asked.

"No thanks – just the bill," Scott replied.

Once Jeff left, Lily said, "You know, Margaret said something about Dylan's spirit sharing the lives of the people who received his organs. And in the memory I told you about – you know, when Grams was talking to Dylan on the football phone – well, he told her that he and the recipients were all connected, but most of them didn't realize it."

"I have absolutely no idea what that means."

"What if Dylan's spirit shares their lives while they're awake and then they dream about each other's lives when they're asleep – kind of the same way Margaret, Bobbi and Clay have been pulling me into the spirit realm to share their memories? And maybe Grams thought she was talking to Dylan on the phone, but really he was visiting her dreams."

"And he told Grams about the recipients?" Scott asked.

Lily nodded. "That would explain how Grams knew about them, right?"

Scott's dark five o'clock shadow was beginning to appear on his chin and he rubbed it, as if the stubbly whiskers helped him concentrate. "Didn't you say some people came to say goodbye to Grams, but they didn't go with her?"

"Yeah – only Grams went into the light."

"Well, maybe Dylan pulled them into the spirit realm to introduce them to her before she entered Heaven."

"Maybe so," Lily said. "I hadn't thought of that. But even if we're right, it wouldn't explain why he stayed behind." She nibbled on a quesadilla. "Unless he won't go into the light because he promised me he wouldn't... or maybe he's tethered to this realm as long as any of his body parts are still alive."

Laughter erupted at a table nearby, startling Lily. She glanced around and was surprised to see that most of the tables on the large deck were now occupied, even though sunset was still about an hour away.

"I guess we better get going," Scott said, absently popping the last bite of quesadilla into his mouth. He raised his hand to catch Jeff's attention.

Jeff made his way to their table right away and wasted no time processing their bill. He jerked a thumb toward the Gulf. "The water's calm. Should be nice out there tonight." He picked up the signed check. "You guys take care," he said.

Lily slipped into her jacket and took hold of her crutch. "Thanks," she said.

"And come back some time to enjoy the sunset, okay?"

"Sure thing," Scott smiled. "After all, this is the bestest beach around."

Chapter Eighty Seven

Lily stood on the wooden walkway of the pier, watching brown pelicans float on the emerald green water between the boats, and breathing in the salty air – trying to ignore the slightly fishy odor that permeated the marina.

"The Dreamcatcher is a nice boat, but it sure isn't designed to be boarded by a woman who needs a crutch to support a bum leg," Lily thought, studying the sleek, white, twenty-six foot Sea Ray.

She didn't argue when Scott scooped her up and passed her down to silver-haired Captain Mike, who then deposited her on one of two club chairs that were bolted to the deck, their backs to the helm.

The moment Scott jumped in and took the chair next to hers, Captain Mike started the engine and plugged the coordinates into his navigation system. Meanwhile, his dark-haired deckhand untied the boat and stepped onto the bow. Based on the similarity of their stocky builds and bushy goatees, Lily guessed the younger man was Captain Mike's son.

The boat pulled away from the marina, barely creating a wake in the glassy water. Lily breathed in the thick, salty air, still mingled with the smell of rain. The younger man stored the ropes and then joined Captain Mike at the helm as the Dreamcatcher wound her way through the channel markers and out into the open water. Once there, they picked up speed.

Depending upon weather conditions and depth, the water in this part of the Gulf of Mexico could appear anywhere from greyish-green to deep cerulean blue. Tonight, conditions favored the bluer shades. The sun was just beginning to set; still too bright to watch, but the nearby sky and remaining clouds were starting to reflect hues of yellow and orange.

Captain Mike pointed to a pod of bottle-nosed dolphins racing alongside the boat. As if bent on entertaining them, the dolphins dropped back and began darting in and out of the wake.

"Dylan would have loved this," Lily mused, feeling the familiar ache in her heart. Even though Margaret had said spirits could leave this realm whenever they chose to, she continued to worry. *"What if the rules are different for organ donors? What if Dylan's tethered to his donated organs as long as the recipients are alive? What if he's miserable being stuck in the spirit realm?"*

All at once, the Dreamcatcher slowed, dipping her bow until she leveled off. Captain Mike sent his deckhand below to retrieve the items from the funeral parlor. Lily turned and watched as he carefully lifted the baskets through the narrow opening and carried them to the port-side bench seat, so the wind wouldn't blow the flowers away. On his second trip, the deckhand climbed the narrow steps with Grams' urn cradled against his chest like a football and Dylan's clutched in his opposite hand. He gently placed both urns between the flower baskets.

"We'll keep circling your coordinates," Captain Mike announced, dropping down to an idle and steering the boat in a lazy counterclockwise pattern. "So take your time."

After confirming they needed no further assistance, the deckhand retreated to the helm with the Captain to allow Lily and Scott some privacy.

Lily stared out at the water. She and Scott had been newlyweds when they helped Grams scatter Gramps' ashes. *"It sure doesn't feel like that was almost two decades ago,"* she thought.

Scott helped her to her feet and kept his hand on her elbow until she had a solid grip on the side of the boat.

"I want to save two of the roses," she said.

Scott nodded. He selected two of the finest white roses and laid them aside.

Lily sighed. It was nice not having to explain things to Scott. He knew she wanted to press them – one for Grams and one for Dylan – just like she had done with the one she had saved from Gramps' memorial service.

They began tossing the pink stargazers, white roses and purple orchids into the center of the water circle, one at a time, until only the two roses remained.

"Do you want to say something before we lay them to rest?" Scott asked.

Lily froze. *"Oh my God, I forgot to write a eulogy"* She shook her head with self-loathing. "I can't. Can you please speak for both of us?"

Scott was surprised, but nodded his assent. He rested Grams urn on the ledge of the boat, watching the water as the Dreamcatcher slowly circled the flowers.

"Wait," Lily said. "I want to scatter a handful of ash by hand – in case it takes a while for the urn to melt. I mean... I don't want to keep Grams away from Gramps one minute longer than necessary."

Scott carefully opened Grams' urn and held it while Lily reached in and withdrew a handful of ashes. Then he scooped out a small handful for himself and reclosed the lid.

"Grams," he began, his gaze shifting from the ashes in his hand to the sky.

Lily looked up, too. The sun was ringed in bright yellow, and shades of light orange were beginning to fill the horizon. Further from the sun, the sky and clouds were turning various shades of violet – the edges of the clouds still backlit with gold light.

"I don't know much about Heaven or the spirit world that Lily talks about. But I'm certain about a few things. For instance, I know that wherever the most wonderful people get to go when they die – well, that's where you are. And I'm positive that you and Gramps will be reunited for all eternity because you've earned that blessing. We thank you for all the love you gave us. Thanks for raising Lilyanna to be a great person, a wonderful wife and the best mother a kid could ever ask for."

"Now, about Dylan." He paused and bit his lower lip. "I don't pretend to understand why he was taken from us. Maybe I'll find out one of these days, but for now... well... I like to think he's in Heaven with you and Gramps, but Lily's not so sure about that. She's worried about him, so I guess we have a favor to ask of you. If you could please figure out a way to put her mind at ease, we'd be forever grateful." He took a deep breath. "Well, I guess this is goodbye for now, Grams. Please know that Lily and I will miss you and we will love you until the end of time."

Scott reached over the side of the boat and opened his fist. Next, he held Lily's waist as she stretched over the side to release her handful of Grams' ashes. Scott kept his arm around her as they watched the ashes swirl in the water and began to sink among the beautiful flowers into the deep blue water.

Then Scott lowered Grams' urn over the edge of the boat until it touched the water. The moment he released it, the urn sank out of sight.

Lily opened Dylan's tiny urn and poured a few ashes into her open palm before resealing it and handing it to Scott.

He clutched the urn in his fist and closed his eyes. "Son," he said, his voice breaking, "I miss you – every single day – but I'm grateful, too – grateful that I got to be your dad while you were here." He raked his free hand over his jaw without opening his eyes. "I just hope –" He sniffed, "you know – how much I..." He gulped back a sob, unable to continue.

"Dylan," Lily said, leaning against Scott. "Wherever you are, if you're unhappy, please don't be afraid to go into the light. Grams and Gramps are there. Think of the grand adventures you could have with them, exploring the universe. Your dad and I are only sad because we miss you. But we know we'll see you again one glorious day. Until then, never forget how much we love you."

Lily reached over the side of the Dreamcatcher and opened her hand, letting the water steal the ashes from her grasp. Then Scott lowered Dylan's urn to the surface of the water and let it go.

Lily grabbed the two white roses and dipped the blossoms into the water so that when she pressed them, they would retain a sense of this moment.

She and Scott clung to one another, watching the water as the boat continued to circle, as if herding the flowers within. Then Captain Mike shut off the engine and they drifted away from the coordinates until the flowers seemed to merge into the sunset.

As the sun began to set, it cast a brilliant yellow stripe across the surface of the water. *"There you go, Dylan,"* Lily thought. *"When you're ready to take the lighted path, just look west at sunset and it will be right there waiting for you."*

The boat continued to drift as they watched the sky turn a brilliant red-orange over the calm water. Finally the sun sank out of sight, leaving only streaks of purple and pink on the horizon. Lily sank onto the bench, still clutching the two white roses. Scott sat down next to her, wrapping his arm around her. Then he signaled to Captain Mike, who started the engine and turned the boat for shore.

Back at the dock, they disembarked and bid farewell. As they trudged back to the car, Lily had a hard time getting her *land legs* back. She wished she had changed shoes before going on the boat. Her crutch wobbled, and Scott caught her around her waist. She wrapped her free arm around him for support, but even after she regained her balance, they held onto one another, enjoying the familiar closeness.

On the drive back to the hotel, Lily's thoughts drifted to Seth. She tried to imagine how excited he was to have his sight back. *"He's probably flirting with his nurses already,"* she thought, a smile fleeting across her lips. She was pleased to discover that she was happy for him and at peace with herself for setting him free. She turned her attention to Grams and felt the same peaceful calm. Her only disquieting thoughts were of Dylan, trapped between worlds, but the ceremony had even lessened those concerns.

Scott pulled up in front of the grand entrance of the Belleview Biltmore and handed his key to the valet. He grabbed a bag from the back seat and then joined Lily, just as the doorman swung the huge glass door open for them.

The lobby was alive with people celebrating Friday night. They weaved their way through the crowd and past the grand piano, where the elegantly dressed couple was again entertaining people with a sing-along. Lily couldn't resist searching the faces of the crowd for Seth.

"Of course he isn't there," she chastised, *"He just had surgery, for God's sake."* She pictured him flying down an open road on his Harley – first alone and then with another woman clutching onto him. She waited for a pang of regret to stab at her heart, but none came. She was happy to be with Scott tonight.

She glanced down the wide, arched Promenade Corridor, certain the Lobby Bar was packed. "I'd like to get a drink," she said, "but I don't feel like dealing with the crowd."

"Good," Scott said, holding up the bag. "I was hoping you wouldn't make me drink this bottle of wine by myself."

She laughed, despite her somber mood. "My place or yours?" she asked.

"Yours. I thought we could re-read the recipient letters and see if we can figure out how Grams knew so much about those people."

At the top of the stairs, Scott took Lily's key and unlocked the door. She hobbled straight to the bed and sat down to remove the painful shoes from her throbbing feet. Just then, her cell phone rang on the nightstand, out of reach.

"Please don't be Seth," she thought, watching as Scott unplugged it from the charger and handed it to her.

Chapter Eighty Eight

Lily breathed a sigh of relief. "Hi, Mary," she said. Aware that Scott was listening, but could only hear her end of the conversation, she continued. "Thanks, but there's no need to apologize for not attending. I knew you had to work." She held her phone to her ear with her shoulder, and pulled off her shoes while Scott fetched two glasses and opened the bottle of Merlot.

She rotated her ankles and flexed her grateful toes, while giving Mary a short synopsis of what Grams' friends had said after the memorial. Then she listened for a while, adding only an occasional 'un-huh'.

"Okay. Scott's here with me. I didn't tell him yet, but I will. I'll let you know if we figure it out. Talk to you soon." Lily hung up.

"Tell me what?" Scott asked.

"I told you Mary's an organ donor coordinator, right?"

Scott nodded.

"Well, she read my new blog and she said she's heard lots of similar stories from people she's worked with over the years. She agrees there might be a connection between Dylan's donated organs and the mystery of Grams' *other* grandchildren, but she was as surprised to learn about them as we were."

Scott offered her a glass of wine.

"Hold that thought," she said. "I need to get out of this suit first."

She hobbled to the bathroom, but only closed the door part way. As she changed into a long, blue silk nightgown and unwound the

French braid from her hair, Lily told Scott about Mary's near-death experience. She emerged from the bathroom just as she finished the story.

Scott's jaw dropped at the sight of her long, wavy, auburn hair and unintentionally seductive attire, but said nothing. He refilled his glass and took a big gulp of wine, trying not to stare.

Lily was too engrossed in the mystery to notice Scott's behavior. She retrieved the recipient letters and writing supplies from the desk, and then took a seat at the table. "I figured we could make a list of all the known recipients and everything we can figure out about them from their letters and compare that information with what the people from Bay Manor said and the images I've seen in my dreams."

She took a sip of wine. "Umm – good stuff," she commented, searching through the pile of letters. She selected a letter that was written on blue stationary with a palm tree on the corner. "This one is from the woman who said she supports her family by baking authentic Jamaican pastries."

Scott nodded, focusing his attention on the letter. "Yeah, she received a liver transplant."

"Well, the Bay Manor crowd seemed to think one of Grams' adopted grandchildren was a black woman, and it's not much of a stretch to assume a Jamaican baker would be black."

"And you told me Dylan appeared in the body of a black woman in one of your dreams."

Lily nodded. "And a black woman with a red bandana tied around her hair was with the group that said goodbye to Grams just before she took the lighted path. Weird, huh?"

Scott reached for the next letter, while Lily wrote down the Jamaican woman's information. After reviewing all of the letters, they found that every recipient matched the description of someone Lily dreamed about, or had been seen in the memory of Grams' final farewell, or had been described by the residents of Bay Manor:

1. Jamaican baker – Liver (cancer)
2. Math teacher – lungs (Cystic fibrosis)

> *3. Young Mother of two – pancreas (Diabetes)*
> *4. Musician – tendons (Tumors in legs)*
> *5. Chef – one kidney (Lupus)*
> *6. Medical student – one kidney (Kidney disease)*
> *7. Scientist – heart, heart valves & veins/arteries (Viral infection)*
> *8. Soldier – corneas (Blinded in combat)*
> *9. Child – Bowel (Short-gut birth defect)*

"This is amazing," Lily said. "And not only because the list matches my dreams, Grams'– um – phone calls, and the memory I watched of her last farewell. Think about it – this list is a perfect match for what Mary told me – Dylan saved the lives of seven people and gave two more a chance to live a more full life. Three, if you count me."

"I can't believe every one of them wrote letters," Scott said. "I mean, what are the odds?"

"Maybe Dylan encouraged them to write." Lily paused. "You've thought a lot about them, haven't you?"

"Yeah, but never like this. Their letters helped convince me I did the right thing. Especially when you…"

"When I blamed you for letting him die?" Lily finished his sentence for him. "I'm so sorry. I know that hurt you."

Scott poured the last of the wine into their glasses. "It's not your fault. I should have believed you, but when you started talking about seeing Dylan's ghost, I got scared. The psychiatrist was sure you were hallucinating because of your injuries and I was terrified I was going to lose you, too. I tried so hard to get you back to normal that I wound up pushing you away."

"And I was so sure that Dylan was still alive after the accident that I couldn't consider any other possibility for what I had seen."

"But I never stopped loving you, Lilyanna. Not even when you told me to move on. I couldn't stop thinking about our life together – couldn't stop talking about you. Even when someone pointed out what I was doing, I couldn't stop. I didn't want to stop."

Lily was tired of rehashing their mistakes. "I never stopped loving you, either," she said.

She didn't anticipate the effect those simple words would have on Scott. Tears filled his brown eyes. "I tried to move on, but then I realized that I didn't want to live without you." He coughed, trying to hide his emotions.

Lily reached out to comfort him, covering his big hand with her small one.

Then, as if they were of one mind, they stood and wrapped their arms around one another. For the first time since the accident, Lily didn't think about all they had lost, or about her scars, or her injured leg, or what had become of their little boy's spirit. Her only thought was how good her husband's body felt next to hers.

Almost subconsciously, they moved backward until they reached the bed. Lily allowed him to lay her down and kiss her. In that instant, she remembered how good they were together. Their passion erupted as if they were discovering each other's bodies for the very first time.

Scott reined kisses over her face and neck, his stubbly beard scratching her – creating an erotic burn on her skin. He slid the silk spaghetti strap off her shoulder and moved his hungry mouth down to her breasts. Every nerve in her body stood on end and when the warmth of his tongue circled her nipple, it sent jolts of pleasure throughout her entire body.

She threw her head back and moaned, arching her back—turning to offer her other breast to him. He seized it with one hand, while pulling the other strap of her nightgown from her shoulder. Then he pushed himself up onto his knees and tugged her gown down, exposing her belly. He fumbled with the top buttons on his shirt before giving up and yanking it over his head with most of the buttons still fastened. He stood long enough to drop his pants, but an instant later, he was lying next to her again. His hand glided across her belly and over her hip. He cupped a cheek of her butt and pulled her pelvis tight against his own.

It was all so familiar and yet so strange. Lily's body responded to him instinctively, with no thought to the fact that she was still wearing her leg brace or that her silk nightgown was bunched up like a sash around her hips.

She didn't make him wait for what he obviously desired. She parted her legs and reached down to take his stiff, thick penis in her hand. Scott groaned at her touch, moving with her as she placed him in position between her wet thighs, her hips moving in a circle, aching for the feel of him.

She yelped as he entered her with one mighty thrust. She had forgotten how incredibly powerful he was and how good it felt to be taken.

"Yes... yes...oh, god...yes!" she panted, as he plunged himself deep inside of her, over and over again. He raised himself into a push-up position above her, building momentum with each driving strike.

Lily held her breath, her locked arms pushing against the headboard, her body writhing – knowing ecstasy was just a heartbeat away. Her pelvic muscles tightened around him with anticipation as he moved in and out, faster and deeper.

Finally she cried out... the electric shocks of orgasm riveting throughout the length of her body as she jerked beneath him. She felt for her orgasm pulse and for the briefest moment, thought of Seth.

Her sensual climax was too powerful for Scott to ignore. He let out a single groan of sweet torture, before giving in to his own release. His whole body shuddered and he collapsed onto her, shivers running through him like aftershocks following an earthquake.

They clung together as their moans turned to satisfied whimpers. Then he slid to her side just enough to take his weight off of her. They lay together for a long time, lost in private thoughts and emotions.

Suddenly, Lily felt Scott's chest heave and she realized he was sobbing, although he was trying to hide that fact from her. To her surprise, she discovered that she was crying, too.

She didn't understand the sudden outpouring of emotion, but guessed it had something to do with acknowledging the great loss they had suffered and recognizing the strength inherent in their rekindled love.

Neither tried to pull away or stop the tears, but eventually the long-pent-up feelings were fully released, and they fell asleep, still clinging to one another.

The chilly fog descended, causing gooseflesh to rise up on Lily's skin, still wet with sweat, sex and tears. Without waking, she spooned herself against Scott and pulled the down comforter over them both.

Chapter Eighty Nine

Lily tumbled into the mist all akimbo. After stabilizing herself in the clouds, she wondered, *"What must Margaret think of me sleeping with Scott just a few days after sleeping with Seth?"*

"I believe you will discover over time, that it was wise to choose your husband over a dalliance with a traveling man," Margaret replied as the mist began to clear. "A good marriage eases the burdens of life and increases the joy of pleasant moments tenfold."

A moment later, red-faced Lily found herself at the familiar round table, facing Margaret. "I suppose I should tell Scott about Seth," she said.

"For what purpose?" Margaret asked, reaching for a steaming teapot that materialized only an instant before. "You put an end to your tryst, did you not?"

Lily nodded.

"Then save your confessions for your priest. Your husband can neither undo the affair nor absolve you of your sin. And remember what you've learned about memories. If he discovers your infidelity, he'll be forced to carry that hurtful memory for all eternity, whereas if you keep the traveling man a secret, the memory of him will always provide you with a source of private bliss."

Margaret slid a cup of tea to Lily.

Lily nodded, knowing she was right. "I'm going to miss you, Margaret. We leave tomorrow, so this will probably be my last visit to the spirit realm."

Margaret picked up her teaspoon and gave her tea a brisk stir. "I doubt that. No one lives forever, my dear."

"Good point! Still, I want to thank you for helping me find comfort in Grams' passing," Lily said. "I only wish I could find the same sort of peace with Dylan."

Margaret knitted her eyebrows together. "But I thought you finally agreed that gifting life was a good thing."

"It is, but I'm afraid Dylan is paying a steep price for the lives he saved. I know you said he can take the lighted path whenever he chooses, but I believe his spirit got tethered to his recipients and now they're all stuck here until they all die."

"Whatever gave you that idea?" Margaret asked, her eyes wide with surprise.

"Because we watched the spirits of some of the recipients bid farewell to Grams', but none of them could take the lighted path except her."

"I forgot how little you know about the spirit realm," Margaret said, shaking her head. "Trust me. The only spirit you saw was Dylan, and the only reason he's still here is because he prefers to stay."

"But I saw them – the Jamaican woman, the doctor..."

"Don't you remember? I told you spirits can change their appearance at will."

"You said spirits can appear to be any age they reached during their lifetime," Lily clarified.

"That's right," Margaret replied.

"I don't understand. Dylan died when he was thirteen years old. How can appear as a grown doctor?"

"If *all* of Dylan died at the age of thirteen, he couldn't. But the parts of him that he gifted remain alive, therefore, he continues to age. And because his spirit merged with those he gifted, he can change his appearance to look like any one of them."

Lily clasped her hand to her mouth, understanding sinking in.

"Before your grandmother took the lighted path," Margaret continued, "I believe he changed his appearance over and over as an introduction of sorts. I suspect he had been able to establish a connection that allowed him to talk to your grandmother as she slept, but manifesting images in her dreams was beyond his capabilities."

"You mean," Lily stammered, "you know... that when she was talking to him... on that old football phone...Dylan was actually visiting her dreams?"

"Yes. And I believe he was trying to explain what was happening to him by changing his appearance when he visited your dreams, but you didn't understand."

"So, Dylan's a part of both the spirit realm *and* the living world?"

"Yes," Margaret replied, taking a sip of tea. "I think I've pieced most of it together from your grandmother's memories. Dylan died before becoming set in his ways, so his spirit was comfortable sharing an existence with several different hosts. And, in addition to the obvious medical miracles these people received from your son, his spirit prompted other changes in their lives. Depending on how open each person was to hosting Dylan's spirit, his influence could be subtle –a person might acquire a taste for one of his favorite foods or begin to appreciate his taste in music. Other times, his influence could be quite strong. He's actually able to share the knowledge he gains from one person with a few of the others."

"Dylan told Grams he shared the math professor's knowledge with the medical student."

Margaret nodded, smiling.

"I made him promise not to go into the light." Lily's lower lip trembled. "He agreed to wait for me. I've been terrified that he's trapped and miserable because I made him promise."

"I believe that postponing the lighted path for a short while has allowed him to embark on a truly unique and magnificent journey," Margaret replied. "He's experiencing life through the eyes of many people during the day, and visiting their dreams to whatever extent they welcome his connection."

"You think he'll stay here as long as any of the recipients are alive?"

"When you're ready to continue your eternal journey, I'm certain he'll be there waiting to take the lighted path with you," Margaret said, spooning sugar into a fresh cup of tea. "And until that day comes, you should follow his example and not waste another minute of your life."

"Thank you, Margaret – for everything," Lily said, her mind swimming with possibilities. "And to think, I was so angry with Scott for donating Dylan's organs..."

Suddenly, Lily remembered Scott was asleep in her hotel bed. *"Wait until I tell him about this!"* she thought. But the instant she whirled her head in his direction, she plummeted through the clouds.

Chapter Ninety

"Wake up!" Lily's mind screamed, as she plummeted through the fog. She forced herself to draw a huge breath and an instant later, she awoke – her heart racing and her eyes bright with excitement.

It was still dark and Scott was sleeping peacefully, but she knew it would be impossible to fall back to sleep. She sat up and glanced at the clock on the nightstand – four in the morning.

Thoughts raced through her head. *"What would Scott say if I woke him up to tell him what I just learned? What is Dylan doing right now?"*

She glanced at the clock again. Only seven minutes had passed. She feared she would burst if she had to wait much longer. *"Anticipation is overrated,"* she pondered, recalling that she always opted to use plastic squeeze bottles instead of waiting for bottled catsup to plop onto her burger like the advertisements suggested she should.

"Scott. Wake up!" she whispered urgently, promising herself that if a single whisper didn't wake him, she would let him sleep. "I have so much to tell you!" she added.

Scott snapped awake – alarmed at first, and then confused. He sat up and turned on the bedside lamp. "What's wrong? What time is it?"

"Nothing's wrong," Lily assured him, grinning. "As a matter of fact, things might be better than I ever imagined!"

"That's good," he said, bewildered. "But can we talk under the covers? It's freezing in here."

"It gets cold when spirits visit," she explained.

They snuggled under the down comforter, facing one another, each of them with one arm folded under their heads like an extra pillow and the other arm draped loosely over the other's waist. Lily's mind flashed back to when Dylan was a baby. How many times had they waked in the middle of the night to care for him and then stayed up, chatting for hours, even though they knew they should be sleeping?

"Dylan's spirit is happy," she blurted.

She explained what Margaret had said about Dylan's spirit merging with his recipients. Scott listened. He believed her. She could see it in his eyes.

"Oh, how I've missed this part of you – my friend and confidant," she realized.

"Wait a minute," Scott said. "If Dylan's spirit can go wherever he went when he was alive, then doesn't that mean he'll also be able to go anywhere that the recipients of his organs go throughout their lives? I mean, won't he get to be a part of their families and share their adventures?"

Stunned, Lily let this concept sink in. "I think you're right!" She thought about the wildly diverse group of people who received Dylan's organs. A wide grin spread over her lips. "Because Dylan's spirit lives within each of them, he'll feel their hugs. He'll learn everything they learn. He'll travel with them, and he'll be able to return to visit every place they traveled," she murmured. "He'll experience more love and adventure than anyone could ever hope for in a single lifetime!"

Scott nodded. "And he can also go everywhere he went while he was alive, right?"

"Yes... he can go everywhere he went while he was alive, plus anywhere that his remains are laid to rest. That's why scattering a part of his ashes with Grams was such a great idea."

"Then why would we want to keep any part of him in a dark little urn? I mean, why don't we scatter his ashes all around the world?"

Lily's rush of adrenalin came to a screeching halt at the thought of traveling. She shook her head. "Scott, I know most people love the idea of traveling, but I've come to realize that I associate travel with all the bad things that have happened in my life. While I was living with my mother, we moved all the time – and every move meant losing friends, my babysitter and any sense of belonging. Our moves also usually involved a new boyfriend and as you know, those guys..." she paused, reflecting on the neglect and abuse that accompanied most of her earliest memories. "I found a home with Grams and Gramps. I didn't even want to go away to college – I attended USF. When you took that job in St Louis, all I ever wanted to do is come back down to Florida. And then, of course, we were traveling when..."

"I know," Scott said. "Forget it. It was a dumb idea. And there's nothing wrong with being a homebody. As a matter of fact, I've been thinking... if you still want to move back to FL, we can do that. I mean, I can do my job from pretty much anywhere these days and we still own Grams' house..."

"I'd love that!" Lily exclaimed.

Scott smiled. "And if you're happier, maybe Dylan will visit your dreams more often... maybe he'll tell you what it's like to swim with dolphins in the wild."

Lily smiled and glanced over her shoulder to the window, admiring the glow of the morning sky. "Look at that – we've talked the night away again."

"Yeah. I guess we'd better get going or we'll miss our flight." He chuckled. "I can't believe I have to do the walk of shame back to my room at my age. Let's never sleep in separate hotel rooms again, okay?"

"Never – I promise." Lily whispered. "Listen, I've done most of my packing already. Let me grab a quick shower and I'll walk back to your room with you."

Scott sighed. "That would be great. I'll make us some coffee while I'm waiting."

Lily bit her lower lip. "Make mine tea – with sugar."

A short time later, juggling luggage and laughing like newly-weds, they left.

As the door closed, Margaret appeared. "I know you're here, Long Gone. You've been here all morning."

Clay materialized. "I reckon some folks are meant to be together for the long haul – and some aren't," he lamented.

"No one knows what lies ahead on your eternal journey," Margaret reminded him. "Maybe you'll find your true love just around the next corner. And until then, you can enjoy the thrill of the hunt."

"Maybe so," Clay said.

"Now, come along," Margaret said, taking his arm. "I just saw a young lady at the registration desk who's all alone... and I know for a fact, she's supposed to be here on her honeymoon."

Clay ran his fingers across the brim of his Fedora and smiled. "You don't say..."

Epilogue

Lily lay in her bed at Morton Plant Hospital, a small collection of memorabilia on her bedside table – an old football phone, a pile of letters, an old photo of her family, a book, and four dried roses. She smiled at the good-looking Indian surgeon, who had just stopped by to see if she had any final questions about the heart surgery that she was scheduled to undergo in the morning.

"I wish you would have come to see me sooner, Mrs. Thorne," he said as he closed her chart and prepared to leave, "But I think you'll feel much better after the valve replacement."

She reached out to him and he took her hand, cradling it within his skilled grip. They had liked one another from the instant they first met. Of course, he didn't know why she sought him out when she was diagnosed with her heart condition.

"Thank you, son," she said with a warm smile. He seemed to like it when she called him that. She wondered if he could feel her connection to Dylan. She wanted to ask after his family – his beautiful wife, Pari, and their children – the twins, Arjun and Anika, but she bit her tongue. He wouldn't understand. Not even if she told him she knew he had earned an early admittance to medical school or dug through the pile of letters on her nightstand to show him the thank-you letter he had written to the family of his organ donor so many years ago. It was too much to expect anyone to understand about *gifting* and dream connections with the spirit world.

He smiled back at her. "I want you to eat a good lunch, Mrs. Thorne. I'm afraid you'll have to skip dinner – nothing by mouth after six tonight."

"I have a taste for deep-dish, pepperoni pizza, but this hospital won't serve it to heart patients," she lamented.

He laughed. "Ah... my favorite meal. I lived on it throughout medical school."

She wanted to tell him pizza was Dylan's favorite meal, too. And she wanted to tell him that, while she would definitely see him again one day, it would not be tomorrow. But she didn't say any of those things, either.

Instead, she smiled and gently squeezed his hand. "You're a good man, Dr. Hingorani. I'm so happy to have met you. Have pizza for dinner in my honor, won't you?"

He grinned and laid her hand gently on the bed. "It would be my pleasure. Now get some rest, good lady. You have a big day tomorrow."

Lily smiled as he walked away. *"You have no idea,"* she thought.

A young volunteer stopped by her room as Lily was finishing her turkey and vegetables. Lily guessed the tall, thin girl with spiky purple hair was still in her teens. She had the look of someone who was trying to act more cheerful than she felt.

"Can I do anything for you?" she asked from the doorway.

Lily squinted her eyes, trying to make out the girl's nametag. "It's no use. I can't read your name without my glasses," she said.

The girl glanced down at the badge hanging from a lanyard around her neck. "It's not your eyes – this stupid badge always flips around backwards. She stepped into the room and came closer to Lily's bed. My name's Symone with a 'y'" she said. "I guess my Mom thought spelling Simone with an 'i' would have been too *normal*."

Lily smiled. "My mom named me Lilyanna Rose Bloom, so I understand. Mothers can be unintentionally cruel."

Symone smiled, obviously amused that an old woman was still irritated about the name her mother chose. "Did people always pronounce it like *Lily and a rose bloom*?"

Lily nodded. "Yeah – kids used to tell me I better get more sun. Or they'd ask me if I needed a drink of water. And I made it worse by marrying a man named Thorne."

"Nuh-uh. You didn't!"

"Oh, yes I did," Lily said.

The girl's smile was genuine now. Would you like me to turn on your TV for you?" she asked.

Lily wrinkled her nose. "I'm not a big fan of the TV. I'd rather chat, unless you're too busy."

The girl glanced at the open door. "No, it's a really slow afternoon and besides, the head nurse doesn't like me much. She thinks I'm weird, and I think she's got a stick up..." she censored herself and shrugged.

"Pull up a chair," Lily suggested. "Maybe you can read to me a while."

Symone rolled a comfortable-looking recliner next to the bed and picked up the only book she saw. "*Motorcycles are Dangerous & Other Dumb Warnings* by Seth Lyons" she read. "Sounds interesting."

Lily closed her eyes, thinking back decades, wondering what had become of Seth. "Could you read the dedication on the inside cover?" she asked.

"*This book is dedicated to the incredible redhead I've never seen, but always dream about.*" Symone read. "How could he dream about someone he never saw?" she pondered.

"He was blind at the time," Lily replied.

"Wait a minute – did your hair used to be red?"

"Technically, it was auburn."

"I think that story might be more interesting than this book," Symone said.

"Perhaps," Lily said, chuckling "It's all I have to remember him by and I wanted to make sure I had a connection to each of the most important people in my life, just in case. You know – to make it easier for them to find me when it's time to cross over – but that's not what I wanted you to read. I have a laptop computer here," Lily poked at the computer, half hidden by her blanket. "I was hoping to check my blogs, but I'm just so tired ..."

"You're a blogger?" Symone said, surprised. "What do you blog about?"

"Death and the afterlife."

"Nuh-uh. No kidding? You write about ghosts and stuff?"

Lily smiled. "Here," she pushed the computer toward the girl. "Power it up. I have two sites. One is called, *Way to Go,* which encourages people with terminal illnesses to make the most of their remaining life, and the other is called *Ghost Dreams.* That one is dedicated to people who have lost a child. I help them understand that they are not alone and that life never ends – some just take the next step on their eternal journey sooner than others."

"Which site do you want to check first?" Symone asked as she turned on the computer.

They finished faster than Lily anticipated. Several women from the group of allies she developed over the years had volunteered to help keep her blogs going in her absence and they were doing a wonderful job. She hoped they would continue the blog well into the future, but she was determined not to worry about such things anymore. "Thanks," she told Symone. "I did my best to create positive ripples and now it will be up to everyone else to make sure they keep going."

"What's a ripple?" Symone asked, her interest piqued.

"It means doing something positive for someone else, with the hope that your initial gesture will cause more good things to happen. For instance, I helped a woman deal with the loss of her child a few years ago and then she decided to start a group to match mothers who had lost children together with children who had lost mothers. Neither person can hope to replace the person they lost, but they can help fill the void in both lives."

"That's cool," Symone said. "Sort of like the Big Brother program, only for moms."

"Exactly," Lily said. "I also started an on-line group for people who are willing to scatter ashes for people who can't do it themselves for one reason or another. For instance, if someone wants a portion of their child's ashes scattered in the Gulf of Mexico, but they can't afford the trip, they can contact me. If I can, I volunteer to scatter the ashes on the water at sunset and send the parents a picture of the setting. That can be very comforting to someone who believes a spirit can travel anywhere its ashes are scattered."

"What's so comforting about that?" Symone asked; a tinge of sarcasm in her tone. "They don't even know if you really dropped their kid's ashes into the Gulf."

"Hand me that stack of letters, won't you?" Lily asked.

Lily riffled through the stack and pulled out a letter. Even that small effort tired her out.

"People don't volunteer to scatter a child's ashes unless they plan to honor that sacred trust. Here," she said to the girl, "read this one."

Symone took the letter and read out loud:

Lily & Scott – We rode on horseback with our guide to the top of a mountain ridge, just outside Colorado Springs. The enclosed picture is looking over the ridge where we scattered Dylan's ashes. It was breathtakingly beautiful there, with white capped mountains in the distance, dozens of tall trees, and a bright green meadow far below, leading to a canyon in the distance, where wild horses sometimes run. We believe Dylan is going to love visiting this place. Best regards, Tina & Craig."

When she finished reading, Symone gazed at the enclosed picture.

"Dylan was my thirteen-year-old son. He's been gone a long time now, but I'd like to think he loved visiting that spot in Colorado. I have pictures from many other places that are just as wonderful, including the Bahamas, the Australian Outback, an Alaskan glacier, a redwood forest, a waterfall in Belize, a rain forest in Puerto Rico, along a watering hole in Africa, and my favorite, even though I don't have a picture of it – outer space. When I am reunited with my son, I hope to hear all about his fascinating adventures in these places, as well as those he had with the families he joined through organ donation. I'm certain my sweet Dylan led quite an audacious life after he died..."

Symone stared at Lily, not sure if she was rambling nonsense. "Reunited? Like after you die?"

Lily nodded and rested her cheek against her fist. "Life has been good, but it has lasted long enough. I'm ready to take the lighted path with my son and see what adventures lay ahead on our eternal journey."

"Someone told me the light is like the entrance to a circle. It absorbs a person's energy into a giant cloud, mixing souls together and spitting them back out as new life – kind of like recycling, only with people. I don't know, though – I kind of like to think it's like one those ripples you were talking about. It just goes on and on. Do you think it's like that?" She paused, tucking the letter and photograph back into the worn envelope and placing the stack of letters back on the nightstand.

When she turned around, she noticed Lily's head drooped at an odd angle. "Mrs. Thorne? Are you okay Mrs. Thorne? Mrs. Thorne!" She hit the nurses' call button.

Lily didn't hear Symone's questions or the panic in her voice as she called for help. She slipped into a deeper sleep than she had ever known, her mind searching for the fog, eager to float into the mist once more.

"Margaret – are you here?" she called in her thoughts. Finally she began to float, but there was no fog. She looked around, curious and saw her withered old body far beneath her. A doctor she didn't recognize was listening to her heart, a grave expression on his face.

"Let me go," she whispered, as if the doctor could hear her. "See the DNR on my file?" Looking at her grey-haired, withered body from this perspective made her happy she had thought to sign a *Do Not Resuscitate* order.

"Mom?"

Lily spun around, thrilled to behold Dylan, her raven-haired thirteen year old child, looking exactly as she remembered him.

"I've been waiting for you, Mom," he said, coming closer. "Just like I promised I would."

"Oh my beautiful boy, Dylan." She reached out and touched his cheek; then hugged him to her. "Tell me, did it work? Were you able to have the adventures your Dad and I hoped you might?"

Dylan grinned. "You bet it worked. I know you were sad because you thought my life was so short, but I've had more adventures than I could ever have hoped to live in one lifetime, and my life was ten times more important than I ever dreamed."

Lily pulled back, placing one hand on his shoulder and letting the other comb through his wavy hair. "Did you travel to all the places where we scattered your ashes?"

"Yeah, I did. And I influenced some of my hosts to go to a few of those places, too. Like Jairam – you know, Dr. Hingorani." Dylan smiled. "It was so cool of you to find him, by the way. How did you do that?"

"Every so often, a vision of you would come to me in my dreams. I saw Dr. Hingorani's name tag in one of them."

Dylan gave her another grin. "I wish I could have visited you more often, but I was pulled from one of my hosts bodies to another all the time. It was sort of like when I was pulled toward the light when I first left my body. I spent most of my time with whichever host was living life to its fullest at that moment."

"You mean you stayed with whoever was having the best adventure?" Lily asked.

"Sometimes it was an adventure, like the time I convinced Jairam to go to Africa and work with *Doctors Without Borders* for few months. I kept visiting his dreams, showing him the part of Africa where my ashes were scattered until he finally wanted to go." Dylan chuckled. "His family couldn't understand his sudden urge to travel, but it was good for us. We did heart surgeries on kids who would have died otherwise and he'll always be a better doctor because of the experience."

Lily glanced down at her old body for a moment, but it no longer held any interest for her. She turned back to Dylan. "Where else did you go?"

"It's like I said, I was drawn from host to host by exciting moments," he said. "When a person is really living life, it emits powerful bursts of energy that draws me to it like a moth to a flame, whether the person was living a real life adventure, like when we were in Africa, or something way less dangerous – like teaching one of our kids to read a book, or playing a song that no one has ever heard before, or even creating the perfect bolognaise sauce."

"You're a lot smarter than the boy I knew and loved," Lily teased.

"Yeah, I guess so. But then again, when you knew me, I wasn't the mother of eight children and the father of four more. And I wasn't a mathematics professor, a scientist, a baker, chef, or musician."

"Or a doctor," Lily added.

"Yeah. And I didn't know what it was like to be a person of color, or to live with the knowledge that I'd killed someone that I didn't know, fighting a battle that I still don't understand."

"Oh, my poor boy," Lily cooed, suddenly sad for him.

"No, Mom – you've got it all wrong. I was able to take the knowledge I got from one person and give it to the next, so we all became better people. I helped all of them understand what life is like for both men and women, for wealthy and the poor, in good times and in bad times, and how to make the most of whatever they had to make the world a better place. You know Nelson, the guy who got my heart? Well, he hasn't wasted a single moment of the second chance at life he got from me. He's tall and skinny and as white a guy as I've ever seen, but he's working to find a cure for sickle cell anemia, even though his own family is plagued by heart disease. And do you know why?"

Lily shook her head.

"Because one of Fernanda's kids has it and he shares our pain about it. I mean, he doesn't actually know her, but somehow he knows what it feels like to be Jamaican and helpless to heal a child."

"Do all of your hosts know one another?"

"No. I mean, some of them feel my presence more strongly than others. Jack, the chef, used to hate seafood, but you know how much I love shrimp and lobster! I convinced him to rethink his views. He used to talk to me sometimes when he was sure we were alone. And Barney, who is the youngest host, absorbs everything he can from all the others. His doctors can't explain it, but they've come to recognize that he's a genius. He possesses the math and science skills of professors, the musical genius of a maestro, and yet he loves baseball and cooking. And not a single wicked thought enters his head. He's just good, and if he lives, he's going to grow into an amazing adult. Who knows what he'll be able to accomplish?"

"If he lives?" Lily echoed.

"He's doing better since he got my bowel, but most people who have bowel transplants don't live long lives. I'm hoping he'll be able to live long enough to change that, but he wouldn't be the first of my hosts to cross over."

"Someone died?"

"Yeah, Jack didn't make it," Dylan said. "He could see me you know, just before he crossed over into the light. He recognized me. He smiled. It was wonderful. I'll find him when we cross over."

"You've gone through so much – changed so much – do you ever... I mean, can you remember when you were my son?" Lily asked.

"Heck, yeah, Mom! Some of my most favorite memories are of you – like when you spent a week teaching me how to tie knots for my Cub Scout project. And I always knew that if I looked into the stands, you would be there, cheering for me at every single baseball game. I remember sitting between you and Grammy, toasting marshmallows in her living room fireplace. Tons of stuff like that. I remember everything."

Lily sighed. "Margaret was right. She said you would remember..."

A warning buzzer distracted Lily and she looked down once more. The old woman in the bed below had stopped breathing. A nurse turned off the alarms, while a doctor checked the clock and scribbled something on a chart.

"I helped Dad cross onto the lighted path when he left you last year," Dylan said. "He promised to wait for us on the other side. Let's go find him, okay, Mom?"

He held his hand out to her. When she extended her own hand to take his, she realized it was no longer old and her forearms were no longer scarred. She pushed her long, wavy auburn hair over her shoulder and floated with him, looking exactly as she had when she was the young mother of a thirteen year old boy.

A woman was waiting for them near the entrance to the lighted path.

"Hello, Margaret. It's so good to see you," Lily said.

Margaret smiled at her and then at Dylan. "I'm glad to see you found one another with no trouble. I overheard what you told that girl in your last moments of life. I was pleased to hear that you created so many ripples in your lifetime."

Lily shrugged. "I just followed the teachings of a great mentor." She glanced at the warm, inviting light, feeling its pull. "I suppose this is our last visit for a while, huh, Margaret?"

Margaret nodded, wiping a tear from her eye. "I'll miss you. Please make sure to find Bobbi and tell her that she is missed also. And please remember the most important thing I taught you."

"I won't forget," said Lily, "No matter what happens, it is never as important as what happens next."

"That's right," Margaret nodded, her eyes still glistening with bittersweet tears. "Have a wonderful journey."

A wolf-whistle caught the trio by surprise. "Now you look the way I always knew you could," Clay said, materializing next to Margaret.

"Hello, Clay," Lily said. "It's wonderful to see you again."

"You didn't think I'd forget to come and say goodbye now, did you, gorgeous?" He turned to Dylan. "Not everybody has such a good-lookin' mama, you know. You best stay close to her to keep scoundrels like me at bay."

As their laughter died down, Lily turned to the light once more. Its pull was becoming irresistible.

"Go on darlin'" Margaret said. "It's time."

"Yeah. And listen, if you see my witch, please give her my regards, okay?" Clay asked.

"You bet!" Still smiling, she took Dylan's hand. "Let's go find Dad, shall we?"

Hand in hand, mother and son floated into the light. Margaret and Clay watched until the lighted path faded to a glimmer and finally disappeared altogether.

"Are you considering following after Bobbi soon?" Margaret asked.

"Not yet, but lately I do seem to spend a good deal of time wondering what would have become of my life, if I hadn't stumbled onto Bobbi's wrecked truck that day."

He sighed and then winked at Margaret. "You know, just before I came to say goodbye to Lily, I spotted a young woman checking into the hotel and her eyes were all red from crying. You think we should pop over and give the situation a gander?"

Margaret smiled. "Yes, I suppose we better."

Clay offered her his arm and together, they vanished.

The End

About the Author

BonSue Brandvik lives with her loving husband in Belleair, FL, near the site of the Belleview Biltmore Resort – the inspiration and setting for her novels. She believes historic buildings embody irreplaceable echoes of the past and regrets future generations won't be able to experience this magnificent structure for themselves.

BonSue believes her role in the hotel's preservation is to record its history in her "Spirits of the Belleview Biltmore" novel series. By capturing and preserving the essence of historic Belleview Biltmore Resort, she hopes memories of the grand hotel, nicknamed the "White Queen of the Gulf," will live on.

The Belleview Biltmore Hotel 1897-2015

The setting for the "Spirits of the Belleview Biltmore" novel series is the historic Belleview Biltmore Resort, located in Belleair, FL. The Hotel Belleview, along with the town of Belleair that surrounds it, was built by one of Florida's founding fathers, Henry B. Plant, in

1895. Opened as a luxury winter resort on January 15, 1897, this amazing hotel continued to welcome people from around the world, including numerous famous (and infamous) guests, for almost 120 years.

In 1904, an addition on the East end of the Belleview Hotel almost doubled its size and, after the hotel was sold to the Biltmore Hotel chain in 1920, a South Wing was added. Over time, other additions increased the size of the hotel to a whopping 820,000 square feet – arguably the largest occupied wooden structure in the world.

The Belleview Biltmore closed on the last day of May in 2009 for a total renovation, but due to the collapse of the real estate market and subsequent financial crisis in the USA, the owners lost their funding and the renovation fell apart. Preservationists fought to save this wonderful hotel from demolition, but unfortunately, despite valiant efforts, the battle was lost in the summer of 2015. The development company that is currently in the process of demolishing this one-of-a-kind icon has promised to save approximately 5% of the original structure to incorporate into a small, 33-room inn on the property.

Hopefully, this token of preservation, along with the "Spirits of the Belleview Biltmore" novels, will help preserve the glory of the Belleview Biltmore Resort, recognize its enormous influence on the surrounding community, and honor the millions of precious memories people have made there over the years.

Interestingly, the tiny section of the Belleview Biltmore the developer plans to preserve is the exact location that Margaret Plant is said to haunt – the old lobby. The author doesn't know what will happen to the rest of the spirits that haunt the hotel, but it comforts her to know that Margaret will be able to stay at the Belleview for as long as she wants to!

For more information about the historic Belleview Biltmore Resort and to view photos, please visit the author's website at: www.BonSueBrandvik.com.

www.ingramcontent.com/pod-product-compliance
Lightning Source LLC
Chambersburg PA
CBHW032255020726
47495CB00001B/114